DEAD GROUND

Dearest Coz...

...another one for your groaning
shelves, you lucky chap...

Huge lax

XXXX

Exmouth
July, 2024

ALSO BY GRAHAM HURLEY

The Spoils of War

Finisterre
Aurore
Estocada
Raid 42
Last Flight to Stalingrad
Kyiv
Katastrophe
The Blood of Others

DI Joe Faraday Investigations

Turnstone
The Take
Angels Passing
Deadlight
Cut to Black
Blood and Honey
One Under
The Price of Darkness
No Lovelier Death
Beyond Reach
Borrowed Light
Happy Days

DS Jimmy Suttle Investigations

Western Approaches
Touching Distance
Sins of the Father
The Order of Things

Enora Andressen

Curtain Call
Sight Unseen
Off Script
Limelight
Intermission
Lights Down

Fiction

Rules of Engagement
Reaper
The Devil's Breath
Thunder in the Blood
Sabbathman
The Perfect Soldier
Heaven's Light
Nocturne
Permissible Limits
The Chop
The Ghosts of 2012
Strictly No Flowers
Acts of Separation

Non-fiction

Lucky Break
Airshow
Estuary
Backstory

DEAD GROUND

GRAHAM HURLEY

An Aries Book

First published in the UK in 2024 by Head of Zeus,
part of Bloomsbury Publishing Plc

9 7 5 3 1 2 4 6 8

A catalogue record for this book is available from the British Library.

ISBN (HB): 9781801108522
ISBN (E): 9781801108553

Cover design: Simon Michele | Head of Zeus

Printed and bound in Great Britain by
CPI Group (UK) Ltd, Croydon CR0 4YY

Head of Zeus Ltd
First Floor East
5–8 Hardwick Street
London EC1R 4RG

WWW.HEADOFZEUS.COM

For Erik Jeffery
with love

'History ages very quickly.'

– Honoré de Balzac

'Dead ground.'

An area hidden from direct fire

Book One

1

STUTTGART, GERMANY, OCTOBER 1936

He was thinking of Hitler again when the Mercedes finally rolled to a stop. He'd paid the Chancellery a visit only three days ago. The vast office. The damp handshake. And that sudden awkward brace of the shoulders he'd first put down to some intestinal episode.

Might these and other symptoms indicate a body at war with itself? Or was there something simpler gnawing at the heart of the Reich? People he trusted spoke of the ravages of the *Führer* diet. Mashed potato and poached eggs every day, one of them had pointed out, would put a cork up anyone's arse. Crude, he thought, but probably true.

'Señor Guillermo?' An unseen hand had opened the car's rear door.

'*Sí.*'

'*El avión esta esperando. Ya llegamos tarde.*' The aircraft's waiting. We're already late.

Guillermo reached for his bag and struggled out of the car. Early autumn, out here on an airstrip south of Stuttgart, smelled of burned kerosene. Clouds were massing in the west and the roar of the *Tante-Ju*'s three engines put paid to any serious conversation. Nonetheless he was curious about this man still holding the door. He was wearing flying overalls in

3

a shade of blue he'd never seen before. His accent suggested Madrid but the boyish nut-brown face spoke of somewhere much further south.

'*Espagñol?*' Guillermo shouted.

'*Sí.*' A brief military salute. 'Mañuel Ruiz, *señor.*'

'*De donde?*'

'Sevilla,' Ruiz grinned, then nodded at the aircraft. '*Vamos?*'

It was unusual to see a Ju-52 without markings, not a trace of the swastika on the big tailplane, and another surprise appeared at the top of the metal ladder propped against the fuselage: the towering, bulky figure of the *Luftwaffe's Generalmajor* Hugo Sperrle. He, too, was out of uniform but it made little difference. He still carried the weight of the new regime on the broadness of his shoulders, in the set of his jaw, in his nerveless assumption of command.

'Señor Guillermo?' Sperrle was peering down at the diminutive figure wrapped in a fur-trimmed greatcoat. 'You have gloves? Perhaps two pairs? There are blankets, I think, but I can only find one. Our Spanish friend needs us to be in the air. If he asks nicely, I'll let him handle the take-off and the climb-out. Flying at seven thousand metres will take us to Salamanca. If you die of cold, *señor*, I promise we'll fly you back for a decent funeral. If you can think of nothing better to do, you might consider a choice of hymns. Here—' he bent quickly, extending an arm as he leaned out of the cabin, '—time and *El Jefe* wait for no man.'

El Jefe was *Generalissimo* Francisco Franco, currently occupying the Bishop's Palace in Salamanca. Three bloody months had won him vast tracts of Republican Spain, and the time had come for the Germans to spell out the price of the help he was seeking to hurry the civil war to its end. Those negotiations fell, in the first place, to *Generalmajor* Sperrle, and now Guillermo felt the huge hand close around his as he clambered awkwardly up the ladder.

Sperrle, as he knew only too well, was relishing this little pantomime moment. Every seat had been stripped from the cabin except one, and the noise of the engines was deafening. Steadying himself against the backwards tilt of the aircraft, he counted the steel drums of kerosene lashed to anchor points on the cabin floor. There were five.

'Enough to get us home, *señor*.' Sperrle again. 'Your Spanish friends are short of everything but I'm guessing you probably know that already.'

Ruiz, the young Spanish co-pilot, had appeared. He stepped into the cabin and hauled in the ladder before shutting the door and making his way forward to the cockpit. Sperrle watched him for a moment, checked the lock twice, secured the ladder, then bent his big face to Guillermo's ear. The *Generalmajor* rarely smiled but this morning was clearly an exception.

'They say that about you, *señor*.'

'Say what?'

'That you can fool anyone. Even young Ruiz. He thinks you're a Spanish businessman. In fact, he *knows* you're a Spanish businessman because he told me himself. Six languages, multiple contacts on three continents and doubtless lots of money in the bank. As slippery as an eel, he wants to tell me, and as clever as a Jew. Might this be a compliment, *señor*? Or should we simple German folk be a little more wary?'

Guillermo could feel the warmth of Sperrle's breath on his face. He held Sperrle's gaze for a long moment, raised an eyebrow, feigning indifference as the cackle of the engines changed pitch and the aircraft began to move. Then came a playful squeeze on his upper arm, and the *Generalmajor* was fighting his way forward towards the open cockpit door.

'Heil Hitler, Herr Guillermo, *ja?*' There was a hint of derision in the briefly raised arm as he turned to offer a salute. Then the door closed, and he was gone.

Herr Guillermo? As the aircraft bumped away across the turf, Sperrle's passenger at last found a single grey blanket, and the frayed end of the leather seat belt that would secure him among the nest of fuel drums. The adjacent window gave him a perfect view as the long shadow of the wings pursued the Ju-52 towards the end of the marked runway. Then came a sudden jolt when Ruiz dabbed at the brakes and hauled the big tri-motor around before gunning the engines and starting his take-off run. With no seats and only three bodies aboard, the tail came up in seconds and Guillermo heard a creaking from the tethered drums as Sperrle's apprentice lifted the *Tante-Ju* into the air. Moments later Ruiz dipped a wing and banked away from the sun, steadying the aircraft as he climbed towards the south-west.

As ever, Guillermo had a plan. He'd flown at altitude before in an unheated plane but never for a journey as long as this. He knew and understood the trade-offs available to the pilot – lower fuel consumption and higher speed in thinner air – but cocooned in the warmth of the cockpit neither Ruiz nor Sperrle would waste a moment worrying about the icy tomb that lay behind them in the belly of the aircraft.

Guillermo had mistrusted hyperbole all his adult life but only last year, in an air force mess north of Milan, he'd listened to an Italian pilot describing a medical evacuation flight that had crossed the Alps with five badly injured soldiers, the victims of a particularly challenging exercise. Four of them had survived, but the fifth had succumbed to hypothermia and suspected lack of oxygen. His last action had been to pull the hood of his combat jacket down over his face for just a little extra warmth, and by the time the aircraft was back on the ground the muscles of his pale face were beginning to stiffen with the onset of rigor mortis. Mindful of a similar fate, Guillermo had therefore been in bed and asleep hours earlier than normal the previous night, determined to stay awake and fight the cold en route to Spain.

It didn't work. Ruiz climbed through layer after layer of cloud and as the temperature sank Guillermo pulled the blanket closer and huddled deeper into his greatcoat. Lately, he'd been aware of an occasional flutter in his chest, like a tiny bird testing its wings. So far he'd thought nothing of it. Nearly fifty busy years, constantly on the move, forever squeezing an extra hour from the working day, had left a number of other scars, some of them deeply personal, but as the aircraft finally broke cover and emerged into bright sunshine, Guillermo felt a sharper pain in the very middle of his chest.

He inserted a gloved hand between the folds of his greatcoat, as if the gesture might still his beating heart, then withdrew it again, turning his face to gaze at the eiderdown of grey cloud below, trying to plot how far they might have come. The direct route to Salamanca would take them into Swiss airspace. Ruiz was still climbing and, as Guillermo watched, the clouds parted to reveal the dazzle of early snow on a rich tumble of Alpine peaks. Some of them seemed close enough to touch and Guillermo stared down, transfixed by the implacable majesty of the Swiss Alps.

Half a lifetime ago, in another continent, he'd confronted a landscape like this, partly on foot and partly on horseback. Swamped by the memories, he edged the curtain a little wider. The icy bite of the wind deep in my lungs, he thought. The incessant struggle to keep exhaustion at bay. The bloody horse saving my life not once but twice, refusing to take paths that would have plunged us both into oblivion. No wonder I'd stored up so much trouble in that skinny chest of mine.

Guillermo yawned, hunched a little deeper beneath the blanket, and at last permitted himself a rueful smile. If he had one hero, one wise man, one pole star in his busy, busy life then it would be Edmond Locard, the French father of forensic science. Every contact leaves a trace, the sage had announced after a busy day at his laboratory bench. And he hadn't been wrong.

Guillermo awoke nearly two hours later to a stir of movement beside his seat. He jerked awake, conscious of the stillness in his chest, and his own breath clouding in the freezing air. Alive, he thought, turning his head away from the window, aware of a tiny hot jolt of gratitude.

'My apologies, Canaris.' It was Sperrle. He'd settled himself on a wooden crate he'd found from somewhere. A long, quilted aviator's coat thickened his bulk, and he was now preparing two large cigars.

'Guillermo, Herr *Generalmajor*. The name's Guillermo.'

'Relax, Wilhelm. The cockpit door is shut. Three engines? Plus a repertoire of love songs you wouldn't believe? Ruiz thinks he has a voice but he's wrong. I gather she's called Francesca and he tells me the best songs are the rudest.' He offered one of the cigars. 'Here, take it, enjoy it, call it a prize for surviving this pantomime. Guillermo is pretty enough but you owe yourself a proper name. Shall we go back to Canaris? Do I sense a nod of agreement?'

Canaris was staring at the proffered cigar. It was huge, probably one of the Cuban Havanas of which Sperrle was rumoured to have a limitless supply.

'Is this wise?' His gaze had found the nearest fuel drum.

'We have a choice, Wilhelm. We can warm ourselves with good conversation and the best tobacco in the world. Or we can tiptoe towards an icy death and perish miserably.' With a grunt he produced a small, flat tin and balanced it on Canaris' knees. 'Tap the hot ash in there. At least one bit of you might get a little warmer.'

'You're not worried?' Canaris was looking at the fuel drum again.

'Not in the least. In my job we make friends with risk, otherwise flying would never have happened. You, too, I imagine. To be honest, *Admiral* Canaris, the world of intelligence has always been a snake pit. In my trade you learn to trust others because that is often the price of staying alive. Not something, I imagine, that appeals to your average spy.'

'Staying alive?'

'Trusting others. Trusting *anyone*. Hand on heart, Wilhelm, how well do you sleep at night?'

Canaris smiled at the phrasing of the question. *Hand on heart*, he thought.

'I sleep very well.'

'I hear you have a camp bed in that office of yours in the Bendlerstrasse. Is that true?'

'Yes.'

'And you spend entire nights there?'

'Yes.'

'Alone?'

'Always.'

'And your wife?'

'Erika looks after the children.'

'Your choice?'

'Ours,' Canaris accepted the proffered match and sucked at the big cigar. 'These things can be easily misinterpreted.'

'On the contrary,' Sperrle pinched the dying flame between his finger and thumb and dropped it carefully into the waiting tin. 'Where I come from, that makes you a campaigner. In the desert you'd sleep beside the campfire. In Berlin, you lock the door and snatch whatever rest you can. Attention to detail, Wilhelm, and an eye for the unexpected. Hold your friends close and your enemies closer. But you don't need me to tell you that.'

For the first time Canaris allowed himself to smile. He'd headed the *Abwehr*, the Reich's biggest intelligence organisation, for nearly two years now. He knew Sperrle barely at all, more by reputation than anything else, but it was comforting to know that word of his own spartan ways had somehow seeped out of the *Abwehr*.

'Two more questions, Wilhelm. You trust an old airman?'

'I trust nobody. Your words, not mine.'

'Agreed,' Sperrle conceded the point with a nod and then threw back his head and expelled a long plume of thinning blue smoke. 'I didn't lie about young Ruiz. He really does think you're Spanish.'

'That was the point. Guillermo's a cover. Crude, maybe, but effective. In my business we rely an awful lot on conjuring tricks. You aren't what you seem to be. Which is where language comes in.'

'Are you ashamed to be German?'

'Of the right kind? Never.'

'The right kind?' Canaris held his gaze, refusing the implicit invitation to elaborate a little. Sperrle dismissed his reticence with a shrug, then changed the subject. 'And Franco?'

'Franco knows of me already. But I need to have left no trace en route.'

'He'd expect that?'

'Certainly. The man's a *Gallego*. He gives nothing away, ever.'

'*Gallego?*'

'From Galicia. It's a special part of the country, very green, very wet, very remote. You know how to recognise a *Gallego*? You meet him on a staircase. You have no idea whether he's going up or down. And you know what? He'll never tell you. No clues. Nothing given away. Juan Guillermo? A Spanish entrepreneur about his lawful business? It'll be the least he expects.'

'And when it comes to the real business? In Salamanca?'

'I'm the Head of the *Abwehr*. And he knows I have the ear of the *Führer.*'

'Seventeen visits to the Chancellery in a handful of months? Seventeen opportunities to get to know the man? Do I have that right? Or is it just Wilhelmstrasse tittle-tattle?'

'It's my job. I'm the messenger. I carry news he won't have heard from anyone else.'

'Good news?'

'Sometimes. Sometimes not. In either case it pays to be honest. Our Leader has a nose for a lie.'

'Ironic, my friend,' Sperrle slapped his thigh and roared with laughter. 'You know the little dwarf, too?'

'You mean Goebbels?'

'Of course. Dr Josef. Clever? No one doubts it. A man with untold talents? A man to rouse the nation from its stupor? Granted. But a man without a conscience? Without an honest bone in his body? On both counts, yes. Talk of lies, and we talk of the little dwarf. Our Leader must be a happy man with you at his door. Someone he can trust.'

'I like to think so. Some days he listens. Mostly, he talks.'

'That's what Goering says.'

'Goering's right. He learned to survive in dogfights over the trenches. Stay close. Keep the sun behind you. Then get closer still. That way no man sees you coming.'

'Even Hitler?'

'Especially Hitler. The Reich owes that man everything. And that's maybe where our problems start.'

'Because?'

'Because our Leader has Goering's appetite, in addition to the darker parts of Goebbels' soul. In the Rhineland he played a poor hand with brilliance. Germans rarely take that kind of risk.'

Canaris nodded, for once emphatic, driving the point home. Hitler had reoccupied the east bank of the Rhine back in the early spring with barely a handful of troops, daring the French to intervene. Neither Paris nor London had raised more than a murmur of protest.

'You think they were acts of cowardice?' Sperrle wanted to explore the implications.

'On the contrary. In London it passed as diplomacy. In Paris there was no appetite for another war.'

'And Hitler knew that?'

'Of course he did.'

'How?'

'I told him. I guaranteed that neither the French nor the British would march and he was very, very grateful. This is a man at home in Germany. Abroad bewilders him.' Canaris was gazing at the glowing end of his cigar. Then he glanced again at Sperrle. 'Tell me, Herr *General*, why are you being so ...' Canaris frowned, '... candid?'

'You mean reckless?'

'I mean candid. You know very little about me, yet you hand me bullets for my gun. We're beset by enemies, all of us. That's why we're wise to guard our tongues. Spies have long memories. Why are you trusting me like this?'

'Seriously?'

'Seriously.'

Sperrle's big face was briefly clouded by a frown. Then he looked up, and something in the view from the window caught his attention.

'There—' he grunted.

'Where?'

'Down in those mountains. We're crossing the Pyrenees. You want to take a look?'

Canaris did his bidding. More peaks. More valleys. More snow. But Sperrle hadn't finished.

'So is it true?' he asked. 'About the Andes? That you escaped internment after that ship of yours went down? Took to your heels? Fled Chile on foot, crossed the mountains and ended up at the door of our embassy in Buenos Aires?'

'That was a very long time ago.'

'I know. But did it happen?'

'It did, yes, but there was a horse, too, so I wasn't entirely alone.'

'But you did it?'

'We did, yes. The horse understood only Spanish but by then I was already fluent. I like to think we ended up good friends.'

'Who?'

'Me and the horse. I gave him a name, Pedro. I'm not sure he liked it but horses can be funny that way.'

Sperrle studied him for a long moment.

'And afterwards, you jumped ship and went to Europe. Yes?'

'Yes.'

'Another false name?'

'Yes. I'd acquired a Chilean passport in the name of Reed Rosas. I was a widower, very sad, very alone, but I had prospects in Amsterdam.'

'A job? Contacts?'

'A legacy. My mother-in-law was English. An enchanting woman, and very generous.'

'But false? She didn't exist?'

'Of course not. I was back in Hamburg by the end of September that year. If you want the full story, it was pouring with rain.'

'Rain?'

'Rain.'

Sperrle shook his head, seemingly bemused. Then he struggled to his feet, stamped the chill from his boots, tapped cigar ash into the tin, and extended a hand.

'They told me you were someone very different,' he grunted. 'And they were right.'

It was early afternoon by the time Ruiz wrestled the aircraft into a bumpy landing at Salamanca. The airfield was nearly deserted, just a thin scatter of ancient biplanes parked in an untidy line, sniffing the wind. The wind blew from the south and Canaris, shedding his greatcoat at last, was glad of the sudden warmth. He loved this country: the potholed roads, the windowless churches, the distant, bent figures of peasants working the patchwork of worn fields beyond the airfield perimeter, and most of all the respect that such folk had retained for each other. The simplicities of a country that still felt mediaeval was a world away from the murderous chill of Berlin, and Canaris knew at once that he was happy to be back.

'Are they sending a car, or do we walk?'

It was Sperrle. Ruiz's landing had done nothing for his temper and now he was keen to move on.

The car arrived within minutes, a dented Hispano-Suiza raising a trail of dust across the airfield. Canaris joined Sperrle on the leather of the backseat and passed on a series of courtly apologies from the driver. The hint of friendship, even complicity, had gone. Sperrle was in charge again, and it showed.

'Franco,' he grunted. 'We're really sure he's the man we should be talking to?'

It was a perceptive question. Francisco Franco had been a major presence in Spain for a number of years, making his name in North Africa, earning a reputation for ruthlessness and courage at the head of his Moorish army. But there were other generals claiming to be first among equals and Canaris went briefly through them, one by one, while Sperrle monitored the driver's efforts to pass yet another horse and cart.

'So why Franco?' Sperrle repeated.

'He's come back from exile in the Canarias. He's won a series of victories. He's made the most of his foreign connections. Three weeks ago, the first of the month, there was an investiture, a kind of coronation if you like, in Burgos. He's now *El Jefe*, the official Head of State. There's still plenty of war left to fight but it might help to be thinking *Führer*, or maybe Il Duce. Either way, the message is clear: *Una Patria, Un Estado, Un Caudillo.*'

'*Caudillo?*'

'The warrior-king. The best tunes in this country are always the oldest.'

Sperrle barked with laughter. 'So why hasn't he taken Madrid? Why do we have to fly hundreds of miles and freeze our arses off to point out the obvious?'

'Because he's cautious,' Canaris permitted himself a wan smile. 'And clever.'

'Explain.'

'Republicans in many of the cities are giving the rebels a harder time than they expected. In Toledo, they had to retreat to the Alcázar. That's a fortress of sorts. It dominates the city. In the end the Republicans would have starved them out, but Franco saw his chance. En route to Madrid he paused the advance and raised the siege. That kind of liberation comes at a price but Franco's Army of Africa was happy to present the bill. These people have no manners. They slaughtered the men and raped the women and tossed grenades among the wounded in the hospital. That sends a message to every other city in Spain, especially Madrid. Franco gets his way and the Spanish like that.'

'So why isn't he there? Why hasn't he taken Madrid and brought this filthy war to an end?'

'Because the Russians have arrived. Tanks? Armoured cars? Artillery? Their latest fighter? You know all this. That's why Franco needs us, but I'm sure you and I agree that we have to establish our rules of engagement. When Franco first knocked on our door back in March, Hitler was more generous than even you must have expected. Twenty Ju-52s instead of ten? All that airlift doubled with a lift of the *Führer*'s eyebrow? That got Franco's army to the mainland. Now he has to use it properly. Franco is a *Gallego*, as I mentioned. *Gallegos* think far too hard before even crossing the road. This is a man who's building a court around himself, and it might be wise to remember that.'

Sperrle nodded and Canaris began to wonder exactly how much attention he'd paid to the brief he'd recently despatched to *Luftwaffe* headquarters.

'How do you know all this?' he asked at last.

'I have agents in place, Herr *Generalmajor*, people I trust. First I get the lie of the land. Then we plot the sanest direction of travel.'

'Madrid, my friend.' Sperrle smashed his ungloved fist into the palm of his other hand. 'It should have fallen weeks ago.'

*

16

The Bishop's Palace in Salamanca lay within sight of the Cathedral. It was a handsome, three-storey building and made a visible impact on Sperrle. Navigating the tangle of nearby streets and plazas, it had been impossible to ignore the many representations of Franco. The *Caudillo*'s face was everywhere, on the walls of shops, offices and even schools, prompting what Canaris took to be a nod of approval from Sperrle. The Reich had been living with a personality cult for three years, but this flood of images was newly hatched: the domed forehead, the thinning hair, the pencil moustache, the strangely liquid eyes that seemed to know a great deal more than you did. Sperrle, still taking in the sheer scale of Franco's current headquarters, was impressed.

'This is why you insisted on morning suits?' He'd turned to Canaris.

'Not me, Herr *Generalmajor*. Franco's staff.'

The driver hurried them into the building. There were guards everywhere, Moorish soldiers in resplendent uniforms, immovable statues pledged to keep the peace amid the echoing footfalls on the polished marble floors. At the far end of the entry hall, Canaris caught a murmur of German from a knot of men studying some kind of plan. When he enquired further, the driver was only too willing to help.

'Engineers,' he said. 'From Duisburg. They're here to build us an air raid shelter under the basement. Are we grateful for your help? We are indeed.'

Canaris did his best to mask his surprise, and as they mounted the grandest of the two staircases he paused to admire a head and shoulders bust of the *Generalissimo*. Those same hooded eyes, that same air of gravity conferred on the guardian of Spain's traditional values. The bust was cast in bronze and was a tribute to how quickly Franco had installed himself as the unchallenged head of the Nationalist cause. It might take a while to bring Madrid to heel but there was no doubt who was now in charge.

Lunch was served in an airy first-floor dining room overlooking the huge courtyard. One end of the long table was occupied by Franco himself, his brother Nicolas, and a senior general introduced as Luis Orgaz. This was the first time that Canaris had been able to take a proper look at Spain's new *Caudillo* and he sensed at once that this wasn't the man on a thousand posters. Long hours at a series of desks had begun to thicken his features. There were hints of a belly when he stood to greet his guests. And most telling of all was his voice, high-pitched, soft, almost piping. Canaris, small himself, was aware that in certain quarters *El Jefe* was known as '*Franquito*', 'little Franco', and now he knew why.

The meal got underway, Sperrle stabbing at his tournedos Rossini while Canaris was content to pick at his meal and act as interpreter. From the start, anticipating awkward questions about the rebel army faltering on the edges of Madrid, Franco did his best to sketch the inevitable Nationalist triumph. How the capital city had been swamped with refugees from the surrounding villages, along with their sheep and cattle. How there were major problems with the distribution of food and water. And how most *Madrileños* went to sleep at night, deep underground in basement shelters or perhaps the Metro, praying for the rebel shelling and bombing to stop. General Varela, he said, had twenty-five thousand Nationalist troops at his command and the outcome of the final battle for Madrid was simply a matter of time.

'How long?'

Canaris sought to soften Sperrle's abrupt challenge but failed. Franco, unruffled, raised his pale hands in a gesture that could have meant anything, and then left it to Orgaz to tally once again the huge rebel advantage in men and equipment. Victory, he implied, would be a mere formality. God, limitless ammunition and the rightness of the rebel cause would bring the Republicans to their knees.

Sperrle dismissed the promise with a backward sweep of his hand, much as you might get rid of a persistent fly. He wanted to know about the lack of co-ordination between the troops on the ground and Franco's air assets. He demanded an explanation for the growing mountain of Soviet munitions. And, above all, he wanted a cast-iron guarantee that the final attack, when it came, would be properly planned.

'Berlin is prepared to help,' he promised. 'But only under certain conditions.'

Over the rest of the meal he spelled out those conditions. In essence, as Canaris knew only too well, a force of bombers and screening fighters would be despatched at once. It would be called the Condor Legion. It would have its own engineering support, its own aircrew, and would need its own airfields. This battle group would be under the command of Sperrle himself, who would report only to General Franco. That way, he insisted, Franco could appear to be in charge of Spain's new allies though real authority would remain in German hands.

At this point, Canaris was studying Franco with some interest. Everything he knew about the man suggested an arrangement like this would be an affront to national pride and therefore inconceivable. No Spaniard, *Gallego* or otherwise, would willingly surrender that degree of control. This was, after all, a *civil* war, a spilling of much Spanish blood. Key decisions must therefore remain for a Spaniard to take, not over-blunt intruders from the chilly north.

Yet Franco said none of this. On the contrary, he nodded, confirmed he understood and slowly pushed his plate away, ignoring Sperrle's renewed demands for a date for the final assault on Madrid. Then he smiled at Canaris, dabbed at his mouth with a napkin, and suggested they take coffee in an adjoining room.

'All of us?'

'You and me, Herr Canaris. I dare say we have much to learn about each other.'

The coffee, when it arrived, was delicious. Franco and Canaris settled in adjoining armchairs separated by a low table. Sunshine flooded in through the open window, and from the courtyard Canaris could hear the voices of excited young kids on some excursion or other.

For a while, he let Franco have his head. Still buoyed by putting the Republicans to the sword at Toledo, the *Generalissimo* talked as well about another rebel triumph in the north, at Oviedo, which happened to be his wife's hometown. It was victories like these, he insisted, that would pave the way to a lasting peace. What the people had at last understood was that this was a crusade rather than a war. The burning of churches and the butchering of priests would come to an end. Kilometre by kilometre, hectare by hectare, town by town, Spain, Red Spain, the Spain of the Republicans, and the Unionists, and the Anarchists, would be *cleansed*. Thus would he, the true *Caudillo*, discharge his sacred duty: to clean up Spain and return it to – yes – its rightful owners.

'The army?'

'Of course.'

'The Church?'

'Yes.'

'The businessmen?'

'*Absolutamente*. Without working, without earning, without money, without *enterprise*, we shall all perish.'

'And the King?'

Franco, barely even acknowledging the question, didn't respond, and Canaris at once understood this man's longer game. He'd been bold. He'd seized absolute power before anyone else could get their hands on it. Why on earth, after months of careful manoeuvring, would he want to give any of it away?

Canaris accepted a little more coffee and then set about what he called the realities of this messy war. Calm, understated, without a trace of Sperrle's bombast, he tallied the eight Soviet supply ships that had passed through the Dardanelles in the last month, and in two cases he'd even memorised the cargo manifests. A freighter called the *Kulak*, he said, had just offloaded forty trucks, twelve armoured cars, six artillery pieces, four aircraft, seven hundred tons of ammunition and 1,500 tons of food at the port of Barcelona. A second vessel, the *Komsomol*, was about to deliver tanks, medical supplies and yet more ammunition. All of this would be trucked down the coast and then inland to Madrid.

'On top of that, as I'm sure you know, the Republican cause has attracted fifty thousand volunteers, all of them from abroad. Many of them will also end up in Madrid. What will your General Varela have to say about that?'

'These are the International Brigades?'

'Yes.'

'Foreign mercenaries, Herr Canaris, none of them trained. With your help, we can kill them on the battlefield and send them home in coffins, but whatever happens we shall fight this wretched war our own way. If I make haste, I shall be a bad Spaniard. If I make haste, I shall be behaving like a foreigner. Give me aircraft, give me artillery, give me tanks and ammunition, and I shall fight the Reds on your behalf. But do not require me to hurry. Do not force me to win at any cost because that will mean a lot of my countrymen killed. I will occupy Spain the way I choose. It may win me less glory, but there will be a greater peace at the end.' He smiled. 'If that sounds like a speech, Herr Canaris, I'm afraid that's exactly what it is. I've said something very similar a thousand times, to much bigger audiences.'

Canaris nodded. This was, he thought, a bravura performance, proud, measured, and – for all his *Gallego* reserve – passionate. Later, perhaps tomorrow, he and Sperrle would hammer out an agreement that would despatch the Condor Legion within days. Freighters would arrive at Cádiz, already in rebel hands. Bombers and a handful of the new Messerschmidt Bf-109 fighters would fly south. A grateful Franco would welcome German U-boats to rebel-held ports on the Atlantic coast in readiness for the wider war that was doubtless on Hitler's mind. There might even be a meeting of minds over the Rock of Gibraltar, long an affront to Spanish pride.

In the meantime, having at last taken the measure of Franco, Canaris knew a relationship was on offer, something covert, something that might – in the longer term – offer comfort and advantage to both sides. For all his many talents, Franco was an innocent in a dangerous world. Clever? Yes. Brave? Undoubtedly. Ruthless? Of course. But in essence an ingénue, a beggar at a much bigger feast, with a great deal of ground to make up. And in that regard, to his own quiet satisfaction, Canaris was perfectly placed.

'One question, do you mind?'

Franco said nothing, spreading his hands wide. Go ahead.

'I'm a stranger to this city. Tonight I have to buy an important contact a meal he'll remember. Where might you suggest?'

Franco studied him for a moment or two. He might have been smiling but Canaris wasn't sure.

'Talk to that driver of yours,' he murmured at last. 'He knows everything about everything.'

El Placer de la Carne turned out to be a five-minute walk from Canaris' hotel. Awaiting a telephone call from Berlin had delayed the *Abwehr*'s Chief, and by the time he descended the stone steps into the basement he was fifteen minutes late.

Somehow expecting a restaurant on a far bigger scale, and perhaps a little more formal, Canaris was surprised to find an intimate space that reminded him of a church crypt. Every nook, every alcove, was occupied by a table and a loud buzz of conversation. The driver who'd brought them in from the airstrip had warned him that the place was popular, but he promised sensational food, albeit at a dizzy price, plus a particular Rioja that he insisted Canaris write down. Imperial Gran Reserva, he said. Once tasted, never forgotten.

Josef Veltiens occupied a table in a far corner of the restaurant. Now in his early forties, the passage of time had done nothing to lessen his obvious attractions. With his movie star looks and beautifully cut suit he could turn heads in any company, and as Canaris carefully picked his way between the clutter of tables, he was amused by the sight of a nearby woman quietly adjusting her seat for a better angle on this irresistible lone diner.

Veltiens had been a fighter pilot during the Great War, emerging with thirty-one kills and the award of the Blue Max, a triumph that had put his face on the cover of countless German magazines. He'd once told Canaris that the key to any victory, in war or peace, was never to lose your nerve. You waited, you arranged the odds in your favour, and you never betrayed a scintilla of doubt about the outcome. This belief in sangfroid tallied exactly with Canaris' own experience, and the two men quickly became friends. Only a handful of Veltiens' intimates ever used his nickname.

'Seppl.'

Veltiens was already on his feet, extending a hand. The basket of bread rolls on the table was untouched but Canaris was gladdened by the sight of the waiting bottle. Imperial Gran Reserva. The Rioja of the Gods.

'Your choice?' Canaris eased into his seat.

'It was here already, uncorked. Tempting, I know, but it seemed churlish not to wait.'

Canaris smiled. The driver, he thought. He must have asked for the wine to be readied when he booked the table.

'You've been here before?'

'Never. So many people. Doesn't anyone know there's a war on?'

Canaris could only agree. Privacy had lost out to the reputation of the place, and the sheer press of diners carving their way through choice cuts of carefully aged beef was slightly disconcerting. The nearest table was within touching distance, occupied by a middle-aged couple bent over a pad, and Canaris watched the man scribble himself a brief note in green ink before lifting his head and putting another question. Some kind of journalist? Or maybe a lawyer? He'd no idea.

Veltiens was half-Dutch, half-German. Like Canaris, he was a bird of passage and was at home in half a dozen languages.

Canaris poured the wine while Veltiens held the gaze of the woman at the next table. It was all too obvious that eating under these circumstances wouldn't be easy, least of all if you'd anticipated any kind of conversation.

'We speak Spanish, Seppl. All right with you?'

'Of course. Any reason?'

'Courtesy, my friend. We doff our caps to our hosts.' He raised a glass. '*Salud*. A pleasure to see you as interested as ever.'

'In?'

Canaris offered a tiny nod of appreciation in the direction of the nearby table. The woman might be a pound or two overweight, but her décolletage left very little to the imagination.

'Trade, Seppl? Business?'

'Never better. The Nationalists are hungry for anything I can get my hands on. Just now what I need most are ships. Last month I bought two freighters. Tomorrow, I hope to acquire a third. Ten million rounds of ammunition? Explosives by the truckload? Relying on others for delivery is hopeless. Either you do it yourself or Franco shops elsewhere.'

Canaris nodded. At a loose end after the last war, Veltiens had drifted into arms dealing. Using his own sailing ship, a sturdy if ugly duckling called the *Mekur*, he'd helped his beaten country to get up off its knees. Canaris had first met him in Hamburg, where he'd just delivered a consignment of arms acquired from London through an impenetrable tangle of middlemen. Since then, he'd criss-crossed the globe, acquiring clients from Istanbul to Nationalist China, and made himself a very rich man.

'Moscow, Seppl.'

'Where?'

'Moscow,' Canaris raised his voice. 'The Soviets. The nomenklatura. A gentleman called Ospivsky.'

'You know him?'

'I do. Not personally but by reputation. One of his jobs is to buy up weapons for the Republicans. You're looking surprised, Seppl, but that's because you're trying to fool me.'

'Never.'

'Good. We understand each other. Last week you were in Prague, the week before in Belgrade. That's where we sent all the waste matériel after the war, rifles, carbines, grenades, ammunition, all bought up by those thieving Czechs and Serbs.'

'This is a history lesson, Wilhelm?'

'Foreplay, Seppl. We have a proposition in mind.'

'We?'

'Me. On behalf of my elders and betters in Berlin.'

'And?'

'You talk again to your Czech friends, and maybe the Serbs as well. You buy in bulk. You buy enough for the Republicans to defend Madrid, to keep Franco out of Catalonia, to take on the rebels whenever and wherever they make their next move. Those weapons go to German armourers awaiting your call. They file down the striking pins, doctor the ammunition and attend to the grenades.'

'Attend to?'

'Either they reduce the explosive charge, or, better still, they insert instantaneous fuses. That way, our Republican friends are in for a very big surprise. We're talking *Stielhandgranaten*.'

'Potato mashers.'

'Exactly. Every time the string gets pulled ...' Canaris leaned forward, '... boom!'

Veltiens nodded, reaching for his wine glass.

'And then?'

'Then you flush all those doctored weapons back into the system. Warsaw? Helsinki? Amsterdam? Who cares. Just as long as they end up with our Mr Ospivsky. Keep them cheap. The Soviets love a good deal, as you probably know, and feeding the Republicans is proving more expensive than they anticipated, despite all the gold our friends here sent to Odessa.'

Veltiens smiled, raising his glass in a toast.

'Do that grenade thing again,' he said. 'This place can't get enough of it.'

Later that evening, a full transcript of this conversation was delivered to the Bishop's Palace. Franco was still engaged in a series of meetings and didn't study it until the following morning. He followed the green ink line by line and scribbled an instruction at the foot of the final page.

Sperrle and Canaris appeared at the Palace to resume negotiations over the Condor Legion in mid-morning, and Sperrle was puzzled by Franco's readiness to agree Berlin's stipulations for the supply of men and equipment. No quibbling about the need for Spanish supervision. Every assistance extended for Sperrle's legionnaires. Sperrle himself had anticipated a return to Berlin by the weekend at the earliest but the Ju-52 was readied for take-off immediately after lunch.

Canaris, who still had business to transact in Spain, said his farewells beside the Mercedes in the warm late autumn sunshine. Both men knew that German bombers would be appearing over Madrid within days.

'Remarkable,' Sperrle grunted. 'What on earth happened in that little man's head?'

Canaris smiled, said nothing.

2

VILLA PAZ, SPAIN, FEBRUARY 1937

Another belly-case.

Annie Wrenne had arrived only this morning, happy to accept a lift from a taciturn young driver she'd met at International Brigades HQ in Albacete. He'd never offered a name but he had an American accent, and beneath the mud and the dust on his new-looking ambulance she'd noticed a donation acknowledgement to the students, faculty and employees of Harvard University. The winding road to the makeshift field hospital at the Villa Paz was littered with huge potholes, often slowing the vehicle to walking pace.

'They bring the wounded this way?' she'd asked.

'Sure. Belly-cases are the worst. Eight miles an hour max. Any faster and you'll end up driving a hearse.'

'Belly-cases?'

'Shrapnel mostly. Sometimes a machine gun.' The driver's hand fluttered briefly over the lower half of his shirt. 'Either way you have to unzip and take a look.'

Now she understood. The Villa Paz stood on an abandoned royal estate south of Madrid, a handsome construction in grey stone that rose above the surrounding hills, and the wash of armies fighting this civil war. The biggest of the two operating rooms was on the ground floor, the walls and ceiling hung with bed sheets. When Annie asked why, one of the two nurses present explained that the sheets were fixed to catch dust and debris should the villa be bombed during an operation.

'This happens often?'

'Not so far. But once would be enough if you happened to be open on the table.'

Open.

The nurse, who was black, had an American accent and was busy helping to prepare the first of the latest consignment of wounded just arrived from the fighting at Jarama, south of Madrid. Annie, it seemed, would be part of the clear-up team assisting a surgeon she knew only as Dr Barsky. Her specific job, when she enquired further, was disposal.

'You're cleaning up, honey,' this from the same nurse. 'Bucket in the corner. It won't happen with this first guy but if we take an entire leg off a later case you may need something bigger. Swabs go in, too, plus all the other rubbish. You ready for this?'

Annie nodded. Barsky was standing beside the operating table, gazing down at the first casualty. The surgeon was a thin, intense-looking American with a neatly trimmed moustache, cocking his head this way and that before making the first incision. His forearms were yellowed from the iodine scrub and he had a nervous habit of stabbing at the bridge of his glasses with a gloved forefinger.

The naked figure on the operating table was already unconscious, his next half-hour or so consigned to the hands of the anaesthetist perched on a kitchen stool at his head. Annie judged the patient to be in his late twenties and, like everyone else in this pitiless war, he could do with a decent meal. His bony torso rose and fell under the ether. He had a lovely face, a week's growth of beard, even features still grimy from the battlefield, plus a mop of reddish-blond curls, and Annie found herself wondering whether he had any clue as to what might happen next. The only evidence of damage were two small entry wounds inches below his belly button, the whiteness of the flesh coloured where someone had shaved off the body hair and applied peroxide. A thin, pinkish liquid was seeping from both wounds.

'You ever seen any laparotomies done before?' Barsky's question was directed at Annie.

'A couple.'

'Where?'

'In Madrid.' She named the biggest of the city's hospitals.

'The guys survive?'

'Most of them, yes. One of them was a civilian, an older man, Spanish. He got caught in the open by a shell. His wife brought him to hospital and I helped look after him afterwards. His wife prayed over him every night, along with a couple of nuns.'

'And?'

'He died.'

Barsky nodded, said nothing. Then he inserted the scalpel beneath the breastbone and scored a clean, straight line through the layer of fat until he was inches from the navel. Annie watched, transfixed. All she could hear was the rustle and sigh of the diaphragm controlling the supply of ether and a muted grunt of satisfaction from the anaesthetist when he used his thumbs to once again check the dilation of the young warrior's pupils.

'Still good to go?' Barsky threw him a glance.

'Yep.'

The black nurse handed the surgeon a couple of retractors and waited for a moment or two while Barsky opened the abdominal cavity. Then came a handful of yellow sponges gently applied to the dark cave of viscera before Barsky asked for extra light and plunged his gloved hands among the waiting loops of intestine, trying to track the damage done on the battlefield just hours before.

By now, thanks to the iron laws of supply and demand in a city under bombardment, Annie had lurked at the edges of a number of operations, trying to help as best she could, always astonished by the sheer depth of the colours on offer. The last few years, before the war had started, had taken her to art collections the length of Spain, but nothing on a gallery wall had prepared her for the rich palette of the opened body, for the soup of glistening entrails, for organs the colour of turmeric, for the lighter yellow creaminess of body fat. This had to be the work of an artist of genius, the butcher's slab come alive, the entire canvas pulsing gently under the lights of the operating theatre. Hang an image like this on the walls of the Prado, she thought, capture its mystery and its essence, and you might rewrite the history of art.

Barsky was at work now, as busily methodical as the other surgeons she'd watched, lifting out organ after organ, holding arm's lengths of intestine up to the light before shaking his head and stuffing the viscera back where it belonged. At length, to his visible satisfaction, he found a small tear in a loop of bleeding tissue close to the entry wound, extending a hand for forceps and a needle to thread a line of small, swiftly knotted sutures before mopping his face and taking a tiny step backwards to assess his work.

Moments later, probing deeper behind the sutured wound, he found more damage in adjoining organs. The black nurse was already threading cat gut through the hooked needle when Barsky's bloodied forceps emerged with a splinter of shrapnel, and then another object which turned out to be a tiny square of sodden wool. The goddam fragment of shell, he grunted, had helped itself to bits of uniform in its haste to kill this gentleman. Further exploration revealed more lesions, all of them sealed with cat gut, and minutes later, after a nod to the anaesthetist, Barsky was tidying up inside and then closing the length of the initial incision, bigger, broader stitches, much like a housewife might tie a roast.

'He'll be OK?' Annie was looking at the surgeon.

'He's still young. Soup and milk to begin with, then an egg a day and lots of conversation.' He peeled off a glove and checked his watch. 'Think you can manage that?'

Annie nodded. Her gaze had returned to the body on the operating table, still unconscious.

'I'll do my best,' she murmured.

At the far end of winter, up here in the hills, the temperature was plunging in the shadowed spaces of the operating room. Cases came and went, a cough or two from the approaching ambulance, a traffic jam of casualties in the triage anteroom, and then a procession of broken bodies hoisted onto the table for Barsky's inspection, some of them not so young. One middle-aged Canadian had taken two bullets through his left leg in an abortive attempt to rush the Nationalist trenches. The muscle had begun to waste, a sure sign of malnutrition, and the force of the impact had shattered his femur, leaving jagged stumps of white bone protruding through the bloodied wreckage of his thigh.

According to the ambulance driver, he'd been given a great deal of morphine and seemed unaware of Barsky's forceps exploring the gaping wound, but when one of the nurses tried to take his glasses he shook his head. He had the glasses, much repaired with dirty white tape, clutched tight in his right hand.

They were, he muttered, all he had left after the worst ten days of his life.

There followed the beginnings of a negotiation, cut short by Barsky who'd decided to take off the leg. Every kind of shit imaginable, he grunted, had already infected the wound and the guy on the table would be doing a lot of reading from now on. The Canadian stared up at him, befuddled by the morphine, unable to follow this sequence of events, and Annie watched the anaesthetist reaching for the rubber mask. The Canadian fought the ether for a couple of seconds but Annie saved his glasses as his eyes closed and his grip slackened. Without thinking, she began to wipe a day's grime from the lenses, a gesture that brought the ghost of a smile to Barsky's face.

'It might be kinder to leave this guy's world out of focus for a while.' He was shedding his surgical gown to put on a thick sweater underneath. 'We agree?'

The amputation was the work of minutes. Annie had been spared this operation in the Madrid hospital but the busy rasp of the saw made her shudder. The sight of Barsky sweating like a logger over the cleanness of the cut would stay with her for years to come, and when the exhausted surgeon mopped the blood from the severed limb and handed it to Annie, the black nurse told her to take it outside to the courtyard. In the shadows in the far corner, she told her, was an empty wine barrel. Tomorrow, this and doubtless other limbs would be either buried or burned.

The cut was high, up towards the Canadian's groin, and Annie carried the dripping leg down the corridor towards the courtyard door. The sheer weight came as a surprise but what she hadn't expected was the warmth of flesh and blood. It was, in a way, still alive, and when she paused beneath the light at the end of the corridor she noticed a single silver ring on one of the

Canadian's toes. It was thin and cheap, a child's trinket from a market stall, but it might still be precious to the man. Should she try and remove it? Wrestle it over the knobbly bones of the toe? Return it tomorrow as some kind of consolatory present? Or should she stick to the rough essence of this hideous script and simply do what she'd been told? The answer came from the still-open door of the operating room. Barsky was through with the Canadian. After getting rid of the leg, it was now Annie's job to summon the next case from the triage nurses.

It was gone midnight when the last of the casualties from Jarama was eased off the table and carried upstairs to the smallest of the wards. He was young and thin and very long, and his bare feet hung over the end of the stretcher. Two orderlies wrestled his dead weight out of the room while Barsky lit a cigarette and stood in the open doorway watching the nurses scrubbing every surface with carbolic soap in preparation for tomorrow's caseload. Minutes later came a series of heavy thumps, followed by the rattle of falling plaster. The nurses paused, exchanging glances. The Nationalists were never supposed to bomb after dark.

Barsky, as imperturbable as ever, took a final lungful of Lucky Strike and then gestured vaguely towards the ceiling.

'The guys have been knocking the corners off the walls on the staircase,' he said. 'Makes getting the stretchers up so much easier. This goddam war is the mother of invention. All you need when it really matters is a lump hammer.'

The night's work was over. Annie had been assigned a mattress on the floor of a stable block. She was vague about where this might be but, stepping once again into the chill darkness of the courtyard and gazing up at the cloudless vault of the sky, she suddenly realised how hungry she was. A snatched breakfast back in Albacete had comprised two slices of pale bread washed down with a tinful of lukewarm *café con leche* that had tasted of chicory and the overwhelming sweetness of condensed milk. Since then, nothing.

'Any idea where I might find food?'

The black nurse, like Barsky, was a heavy smoker. Annie had spotted her cigarette in the darkness, just yards from the empty barrel where she'd left the Canadian's leg.

'Salaria,' she extended her other hand. 'I guess we owe each other a name.'

'Annie.'

'Hi, Annie. You want chow?'

'Need would be closer. Just tell me where. A clue is all I'm after. Something to eat and where to find the stable block. Sorry to be so pathetic.'

Salaria laughed softly, and then led the way back inside the main building. Stepping out of the starlight, it was suddenly pitch black, but Salaria took her elbow and led her down a series of corridors.

'The generator's out again. Happens a lot. I guess we should be used to it by now, but we cuss it every time it happens.'

She cautioned a turn to the left, and through an open door Annie was suddenly peering into a biggish space lit by two candles. In the light of one of them, a seated figure at a table was cleaning what looked like a revolver. Behind him, where more tables receded into the darkness, a single couple were bumping listlessly together in some kind of dance.

'It was a rumba when the power went out,' the figure with the gun gestured at the disc on the non-revolving turntable, 'but I guess they're making it up now. Kinda intimate, don't you think? Their own little secret?'

Salaria ignored him, collecting the second candle and leading Annie to a big pantry at the back of the room.

'These here are *garbanzos*. You're familiar with *garbanzos*?'

'Of course.' *Garbanzos* were chickpeas. Wake up anywhere in Spain, thought Annie, and chickpeas would have got there first.

'And here's a couple of boiled mule's ribs,' Salaria hadn't finished. 'These potatoes look nothing at all but don't be fooled. You know the trick that never fails? This little fella.'

She'd reached for a jar of something thick and red. Annie took a sniff. Tomato paste.

'And here. Take this.' From God knows where, Salaria had produced a plate. 'Spoil yourself, Annie. No one's watching.'

Annie took one of the ribs and circled it with a necklace of the tiny Castilian potatoes while Salaria spooned a hillock of tomato paste onto the side of the plate. A sprinkle of *garbanzos* completed the dish. Salaria steered her back towards the door.

'You want that we eat inside? Or you wanna go back to the view? I know a neat little place we can earn ourselves some privacy.'

'We?'

'Me and thee. This time of night I could use a conversation. Twelve hours flat out's supposed to put you in bed but it never works that way with me. The body's given in but the brain hasn't. Tell me about yourself, honey. And for pity's sake, *eat*.'

She led Annie back to the courtyard. This time their destination lay outside the main building. A sizeable rock with a flattish top wedged against the exterior wall appeared to serve as a bench. At Salaria's insistence, Annie started on the mule rib, tearing the tough meat off the bone with jerky movements of her head, exactly the way she'd once watched a lion demolish the leg of an antelope on a newsreel in a Dieppe cinema. The experience was truly carnal, an abject surrender to hunger, and she caught the curl of a smile on Salaria's lips as she finally pushed the meatless rib to one side, demolished the potatoes and chickpeas, and then leaned back against the rough stone wall. The stones were cold at this time of night but she could feel the bones of the building pressing against her flesh.

'Well?' This from Salaria. 'You gonna tell me why and how, or do I have to guess?'

'You first,' Annie was wiping her mouth. Contentment, she thought, tasted of dead mule.

'Me? I'm a Georgia girl, born and bred. You ever meet the peasant folk hereabouts? Poverty? Eating whatever you can grow? Nothing to rely on? Everything owned by someone else? Spain reminds me of the Deep South except we never had no truck with bishops. I feel real at home here. You're getting the picture?'

'I am. Tell me about Dr Barsky.'

'The guy's a legend. He was a legend in New York and he's a legend here. Don't get me wrong. This isn't big-city medicine. We're missing all kinds of the fancier stuff but Barsky's out here making things happen and we're very happy to join the party. The guy's got two major talents. He knows how to raise money, and he's very good at mending folks in bad shape. Now then ...' she gently removed Annie's plate and put it to one side, '... tell me about you.'

Very good at mending folks in bad shape. Annie was back in the operating room, back beside the first of the afternoon's casualties.

'That young lad who needed the laparotomy...' she said quietly.

'What's he got to do with any of this? You're telling me he's some kind of friend?'

'Not at all.'

'You didn't know he was English?'

'How could I tell?'

'Good question. His name's Giles. Giles Roper. XV IB. Unlucky to be in the wrong place at the wrong time. Lucky as hell to be in the hands of our Mr B.'

Annie nodded. She was becoming fluent in the strange argot of this conflict, everything reduced to the terseness of countless acronyms, all of them marching in lockstep as the civil war gathered momentum, and she knew that XV IB was the Fifteenth International Brigade, a bunch of fervent volunteers from every corner of Western Europe and North America. Giles Roper, she thought. Early spring sunshine had already weathered his face and neck on the operating table but it was impossible not to remember Barsky's scalpel slicing through the whiteness of the rest of him.

'Well, honey? You're telling me you volunteered with the Fifteenth?'

'Not at all. To be honest, I'm not the volunteering kind. I'm afraid I came a different route. Shameful, I know, but there it is.'

For the next half hour or so, Annie found herself describing the journey that had brought her to the Villa Paz. How she'd first come to Spain a couple of years ago, armed with a degree in modern languages. Her university course, much to her surprise, had seeded a passion for the giants of Spanish painting, Goya in particular, and a couple of years after graduation she'd come to Spain and worked as a translator in Madrid while trekking from gallery to gallery, using canvas after canvas to try and get under the skin of a country that had begun to fascinate her.

'You speak the language, honey?'

'I do, yes.'

'And I'm guessing you paint, as well. Am I right?'

'Sadly not, but I'm at home in front of a painting. I can see the clues that matter. Look hard enough, Goya especially, and Spain begins to explain itself.'

'But these are old guys, surely.'

'You're right, but that's the other thing you get to realise.'

'That they painted the truth?'

'That nothing's changed. The place is still poor. Most Spaniards get a rough deal. You said so yourself. The country belongs to the army, the Church, all those big landowners. After that …' Annie gestured at the darkness at the foot of the hill, '… there's not much left to go round.'

'And that's why you're here? Fighting the Fascists? The priests? The guys with all the money?'

'I'm here to understand Goya a little better. And just now I'm starting to think it might be the same thing.'

Salaria nodded, and lit another cigarette while Annie fought the urge to shiver. Spain in late February could be unforgiving.

'I joined the Communist Party a coupla years back,' Salaria tipped back her head and expelled a long plume of blue smoke that drifted away on the night wind, before wetting two fingertips and returning the cigarette to the packet on her lap. Annie had been aware of her hands since they'd first met: long fingers, perfectly shaped, sensibly clipped nails, no rings. In a way, thought Annie, those hands spoke for the rest of her. She wasn't tall, she wasn't overly handsome, but she had a warmth and a confidence that could fill any room.

'This was back home? In America?' Annie asked.

'Sure. I was working in New York, Harlem Hospital. In my country, it doesn't pay to be coloured, nor to be a Commie. The boat sailed last month. Here, believe it or not, life is much simpler.'

'So you've been here how long? Days? Weeks?' Annie was astonished.

'Just ten days, but already it feels like a lifetime. One of the older guys on the boat told me that wars have no respect for time nor place. He'd fought over here before against the Germans, some place in France, so I'm guessing he'd know. One last question, my child. Do you mind?'

'Not at all.'

'I had a peek at the passport you left with Dr Barsky. Are you really twenty-seven?'

'I am, yes. Is that some kind of compliment?'

'Sure,' Annie caught a flash of white teeth. 'I had a lovely friend one time, back in Georgia, and she looked a lot like you. She was a white girl and she had the face of an angel and hair cut short the way you wear yours, which I guess was one of God's little jokes because she was wicked as hell. Men loved her, of course, couldn't get enough of that wonderful innocence.'

'And?'

'She died a while back in Atlanta, just turned twenty. She met one guy too many and he killed her for saying no. Guy went to the chair for it in no time at all. Good riddance, says I.' She got to her feet and smoothed the creases from her woollen coat, then glanced down and extended a hand. 'I'm told your Mr Roper's doing well, by the way, even took a little condensed milk this evening. Number three ward, top floor. Last bed on the left, honey. The one by the window.'

3

Asleep in seconds, still fully clothed, Annie dreamed of the afternoon she signed up to be a nurse. She was in Madrid. Political chaos had triggered an attempted right-wing coup in the city but Republican militias had massacred the rebel troops, aware of developments elsewhere in Spain. Franco's Army of Africa was sweeping north, piling victory on victory, seeding vile stories about exactly what Spain's capital could expect from the rapacious Moors in revenge for all that spilled Fascist blood. By October, mercifully, the marching Nationalist boots had paused on the other side of the river.

Outnumbered by the Republican defenders of the city, General Mola became a hate figure on the Gran Via but his army gathered itself for a push across the water and dug in among the buildings of the university. There they stayed, calling for German bombers from the Condor Legion to give *Madrileños* a taste of the months and maybe even years to come.

Annie had never been under fire before. At first, like everyone else, she was cowed by the bark of rebel artillery, and the sudden explosions, far too close, that filled the street with dust and rubble and seemed to suck the air from her lungs. That was bad enough but like every other novice in this deadly new game, she was abruptly aware of the damage that high explosive and hot shards of metal could wreak on mere flesh and blood: a headless corpse in the gutter, a little girl face down on the pavement, totally lifeless, a doll abandoned and tossed aside by the sudden eruption of violence.

On one occasion, according to people she knew, a big artillery shell had exploded among women queueing outside a bakery. Bodies had been torn apart by the blast, many of them unrecognisable, the tally of dead impossible to count until a priest took charge, counted the arms and divided by two. By now, German bombers were droning over the city as if they already owned it. Annie quickly decided that Metro stations were the safest refuge when the whistles blew ahead of yet another raid, and it was there, among the bombed-out families living on the underground platforms, that her shock turned to anger and she decided to enlist.

It took the best part of a day to find out where to go. Finally, on her fifth attempt to beg for a role in a war that wasn't strictly hers, she found a small, chaotic first-floor office in a side street beyond the Atocha station. A youngish Spaniard in what might have been a uniform was perched on a desk littered with forms. The flappy sole of one of his boots badly needed the attentions of a cobbler. He had a telephone in one hand, and a pencil in the other, and he was shouting down the phone the way you might address someone on the other side of the street.

Sitting on the floor with their backs against the wall were a number of older men. One of them was asleep but the others were monitoring the conversation with some interest. Something called an *auto-chir* had apparently gone missing. The man on the desk was apoplectic. Had it been stolen? Borrowed? Blown up? Did anyone in this *puta* of a city have any idea what these things were *worth*?

The conversation continued. People came and went. One of them brought two cabbages, each wrapped in a soiled page of the hated *Arriba*, the city's leading right-wing newspaper. Another struggled into the office with a caged songbird and a basket of towels torn into strips, leaving them both on the desk. The bird was small and brown and – according to its owner – only performed at dawn. The bird turned its back on the room and shuffled uncomfortably on the taped-up bar while one of the men whistled softly in its direction.

The conversation at last came to an end. All eyes were on Annie.

'*Auto-chir?*' she asked.

'Special truck. Operating theatre on wheels. American money. You're telling me you know where it is?' This from the man still sitting on the desk.

Annie shook her head. She'd come here looking for a job. She wanted to help. She wanted to be a nurse, a driver, a cook, anything.

'Nurse? You know about nursing?' Already his hand was reaching for a scrap of paper.

Annie nodded. It was a lie but the man on the desk said nothing. Already she sensed the interview was over. She spelled her name and offered an address that would find her. One of the men hunched on the floor had been studying her bare legs. He was heavy-set and unshaven. His thick fingers were yellowed with nicotine, and his Spanish, heavily accented, was primitive.

'I have a fever,' he confected a stagey cough. 'You'll make me better if I come round?'

Annie stared down at him, trying to muster a reply, but then a gentle nudge on her shoulder broke the dream, and she found herself looking at a black face in the thin dawn light.

'Here,' steam was rising from Salaria's proffered tin mug, 'No sugar, I'm afraid.'

*

Giles Roper was still asleep by the time Annie made it up to the ward. Beds of every description had been jigsawed into the room and most were occupied. Heads turned as she picked her way down the narrow central aisle, recognising the Canadian she'd last seen on the operating table. A bundle of rolled-up clothes served as the man's pillow, and a single blanket was tented over the bandaged stump of what remained of his leg. When she asked how it was with him, he seemed to have difficulty with the question. When she asked again, offering to fetch boiled water from downstairs, he shook his head.

'Done,' he grunted, gesturing down at the blanket. 'Gone.'

Annie gazed at him for a moment, knowing that nothing she could say could possibly help on a morning like this. Maybe she should have retrieved the toe-ring, she thought, but then she dismissed the thought. She'd looked in the wine barrel that morning but the leg had disappeared, which was maybe just as well.

'I'm sorry,' she said.

'Sure,' the Canadian turned his head away, his eyes moist behind the glasses.

Roper, when Annie found him at the end of the ward, had overheard the conversation.

'Poor bastard,' he muttered, before his hand fluttered in the direction of the nearby window. 'Can you …?'

'It's freezing outside. Ice everywhere.'

'I know but …' His voice was weak, the delivery hesitant, but there was a little colour in his cheeks and his eyes never left her face.

'And everyone else?' Annie asked, nodding at the window he wanted her to open.

'We stink.' Wincing with pain, he moved sideways beneath the single blanket.

Annie ignored the invitation to sit down. She wanted to know how he was feeling.

'Never better.' He tried to muster a smile. 'That's a joke, by the way.'

'Are you hungry?'

'No.'

'You should eat.'

'What have you got?'

'I can find an egg. How would you like it done?'

The question seemed to intrigue him. He took his time to answer.

'Poached,' he said at last.

Annie nodded. She'd need to find clean water but she thought that might be possible.

'Anything else?'

'Toast. And marmalade.' His eyes closed. 'With fresh butter.'

Annie was gazing down at him, aware for the first time of the pad and newly sharpened pencil carefully tidied on the battered wooden stool that served as a bedside table. Barely hours ago she'd watched Barsky helping himself to loop after loop of this man's intestines. Now this.

'Tell me what hurts,' she said.

'Everything,' his voice was barely a whisper. 'But that never makes for conversation, does it?'

He tried for another smile, which might have been wry, then frowned as she reached for the blanket and pulled it gently away.

'What are you doing?'

'I need to look at the wound. It's what we nurses do.'

Annie drew back the blanket and the sheet beneath. The wound was slightly inflamed, a little red around the edges, and she'd have to get a second opinion from Salaria, but she could see no signs of discharge. She studied it a little longer, then folded the blanket lower.

'Did you pass water during the night?' she asked.

'I did. It's in the pot under the bed. Shit …'

'That hurts?' Annie had gently palpated the tightness of his lower abdomen.

'Yes.'

'How much?'

'A lot. A bit. God knows. Have we finished?'

'I'm afraid not. I'm here to wash you.'

'*All* of me?' He looked briefly alarmed.

'I'm afraid so. All part of the service.' Annie put the blanket back in place. 'You needn't be shy. I was in the operating room last night.'

'With me, you mean?'

'Yes.'

'So you saw the whole thing? The whole operation?'

'I did.'

'And?'

'You were in good hands. Dr Barsky did a fine job. It's our job now to get you better.'

'*Our* job?'

'My job. And whoever else passes by.'

Roper nodded, watching Annie at last ease the window open an inch or two. By the time she returned to the bed, the blanket was up to Roper's chin.

'Strange,' he muttered.

'Strange in what way?'

'You probably know more about me than I do myself.'

'Because I've had a peek inside?'

'Because you've caught me on a bad day. I'm normally a bit tougher than this, a bit less pathetic.'

'That sounds like an apology.'

'It is.' He was frowning now, his face filmed with sweat. 'You're serious about the wash?' he asked.

'I am, yes. Germs love dirt. You're happy for me to come back?'

Roper gazed up at her for a long moment, then closed his eyes. 'Very,' he murmured.

For the rest of the week, a succession of twelve-hour days, Annie was moved from job to job, a couple of shifts on one of the wards, back into the operating room to earn a gruff compliment or two from Barsky, and sometimes a posting to the triage anteroom under the supervision of Salaria. The latter experience, at first, was close to overwhelming. An incoming ambulance would rattle up the hill, squeeze in through the twin stone pillars that flanked the villa's entrance and come to a halt in the courtyard. The driver and his attendant escort would throw open the rear doors and stretcher the worst cases into the lesser chill of the villa itself.

Some of these men carrying head and other wounds would be barely conscious, a flicker or two of curiosity as Salaria and Annie removed their clothing. Annie's first instinct was to gently coax a shirt or a pair of trousers off the victim, but any kind of pressure risked grinding the broken end of shattered bones against unseen muscle, and so Salaria taught Annie how to use scissors to ready a man for inspection, thus avoiding yet more damage.

The men themselves, to Annie's surprise, were mostly stoic, as if already resigned to the numbing inevitability of serious injury. A handful, especially the French volunteers, wanted to know whether they were going to survive, and when Annie bent to reassure them that all would be well, they took comfort from her fluency.

'You're French?'

'Partly.'

'You'll see me through?' They tended to reach for her hand.

'*Bien sûr*.' Of course.

Roper, too, spoke a little halting French. After three days on a carefully liquid diet, Annie had managed to lay hands on a single egg which she'd carefully scrambled in condensed milk with a dressing of chopped herbs from the courtyard's kitchen garden.

'The water here is best avoided,' she was watching him fork the egg into his mouth. 'Poach the egg and you'd be dead in minutes.'

'Delicious,' he wiped his mouth, a man reborn. 'Maybe a little more salt next time?'

'You're hallucinating,' she lifted the tray from his lap. 'And something tells me you need the toilet.'

She helped him out of bed. The single lavatory was at the end of the corridor outside, and she was aware of the gaze of other patients as she walked him slowly towards the open door. When they got to the toilet, he asked her to wait outside.

'*Ça va?*' That's OK?

'*Bien sûr*.' She smiled at his accent.

He half turned in the narrowness of the toilet and gave her a wink. Then he shut the door and Annie heard him settling noisily on the seat before wanting to know whether the blokes on the ward were right.

'About what?'

'About you being French.'

'Half-French,' she said. 'Probably the best bits.'

'And the rest?'

'English. I grew up in a little village in Normandy. We loved it.'

'We?'

'Me and my mum. My father was a diplomat which meant he kept his distance most of the time. He was in the Middle East a lot. Then India. How's it going in there?'

'Slowly. Everything comes to those who wait.'

'For God's sake don't strain, else you'll be back on the table.'

'You're telling me you fancy another look?'

'I'm telling you the egg is supposed to have done you good. Did I hear you pass wind just now?'

'You did.'

'Excellent. I'll tell Dr Barsky. He'll be thrilled.'

'I get the feeling you're enjoying this.'

'Wrong, I'm afraid. Keep trying but, like I say, not too hard. Patience can be a friend in this country.'

'You're not wrong.' He laughed softly. 'If you want a confession, it used to drive me mad.'

'Spain?'

'The Spanish. You have to try hard to wreck a country like this, but that's another conversation. There ...' A chuckle this time. 'Done.'

'Really?'

'Really. My arse has been a hero, and so have you, but the rest of me wants to go back to bed.'

Five days later, March by now, Annie stole half an hour from her busy schedule to walk Roper down three flights of stairs into the thin sunshine of early spring. Barsky had been impressed by his English patient's progress and was insisting on as much exercise as Roper could take.

By now, Annie had scouted the rock-strewn hillocks that buttressed the Villa Paz and had found a corner of a meadow on the south side of the building, brightened by gorse bushes in full flower. A rough semi-circle of grey rocks scabbed with lichen offered shelter from the northerly wind and she helped Roper fold his long body onto the softness of the grass. She'd raided the villa's supply of clothing that the late owners would no longer need, and the heavy woollen jacket with its lightly ripped lining fitted him rather well.

'Here. Call it a thank-you. How did you know about me and sunshine?' He'd broken off a sprig of gorse, sniffing the rich yellow flowers, and after he'd passed it to her he settled back against the rock, his face to the sun, and closed his eyes with a small, contented sigh.

'You know about gorse?' This is from Annie.

'I know about sunshine. I've never hated winter quite as much as here. Believe me, this is heaven.'

Annie smiled. Gorse flowers smelled of nothing.

'Back home in Normandy we girls were never allowed to kiss our loved ones when gorse was out of season.'

'You're making it up,' one eye had opened.

'I'm not. It's a sign of fertility. That's why you always add it to the bridal bouquet.'

'And it worked?'

'Always.'

'You're telling me you've got kids? A husband? Some patient Frenchman back at the ranch?'

Annie laughed, and then shook her head. No Frenchman she'd ever met had the patience to wait for anything.

'It's all folklore,' she said. 'In the *bled* people have nothing to do but make babies.'

'The *bled*?'

'The back of beyond. *La France profonde* is where the real gorse lives. Tell me about your war.'

Roper nodded and shifted slightly against the rock as if he'd been half expecting the question. Then he started fingering a button on the jacket, opening both eyes and staring into nowhere. He'd volunteered in the first place, he said, for a mess of reasons, none of which had survived his first days with the XV International Brigade.

'We were trucked to a dump of a village called Madrigueras for basic training. I knew that rifles and machine guns and all the rest of it were hard to come by, but I never expected football rattles.'

'Football rattles?' Annie was laughing again.

'Sure. I'm guessing they sound like a machine gun. They *do* sound like a machine gun. We used to do exercises in the afternoon. We were the attackers. We'd scramble around pretending to be fierce and then the defenders would give us a rattle or two and we'd all dive for cover and give answering fire with our brooms and our walking canes. The whole thing was a joke but in a way it set the tone. I'd never been in a war before, not a war like my Pa's war, all the trench stuff, the mud, the gas, all that, but the older guys in the Brigade were quite taken in the early days. No marching bands, no medals, no gold braid, none of that. There's still no saluting in the cities, and even less at the front, but then the enemy arrived, and the fighting, and everything changed. You learned bloody fast because otherwise you were dead. Have I told you about last week? Probably not.'

'Last week?'

'Yes,' he nodded, gesturing vaguely off to the right. 'The Moors were trying to cut the road between Madrid and the coast. We'd dug trenches in the Jarama Valley to stop them. You cut them in a zigzag pattern because you want to limit blast and shrapnel, and you dig them deep because you might be there a while. We'd got bloody good at it.' He paused a moment, the faintest smile on his face, then he frowned and shook his head. 'The rifles they gave us in the first place were rubbish, never worked properly, and the German stick grenades had a habit of blowing you to pieces, but we had machine guns by then and every time the Moors came at us, up the hill, we'd give them a good hosing. This went on for days. There were hundreds of bodies out there. Even in winter, they get to smell. Then came the afternoon they appeared again, broad daylight, line abreast. They were unarmed, no rifles, and they were singing the Internationale and every single one of them had their right hands above their heads, fists clenched. You know what that means?'

'It's the Popular Front salute. You see it everywhere in Madrid.'

'Exactly. But we thought they were surrendering. We thought they were seeing it our way, nice gesture, bit of respect. Then one of our blokes saw a French grenade in one of the clenched hands. They were really close by then and they pulled the pins, blowing themselves up and some of us, too. Me? I was OK. Thank God for that trench ...' He broke off, ducking his head, then looked up again. 'We still get deserters coming across, just a handful, blokes who've had enough, and you know what we make them do now? We make them clap their hands as they get close. Simple, isn't it? No grenades, no one blown up, just a round of applause. If this was a theatre, no kidding, I'd want my money back.'

'You've had enough?'

'For now, yes. It's not the wound, the getting injured, the way I am. Out in the trenches, fighting or no fighting, you get something the blokes call "dirt-fever". You've maybe signed up because a war like this, a decent war, a war for justice and all the other stuff, was on your list, like the Sistine Chapel or the Pyramids. Then, day and night, you find yourself fighting another war, against night coughs, and jaundice, and sores, and itching, and diarrhoea one whole day, maybe two, and then not taking a shit for a week. That's "dirt-fever". Then the Moors come and if you don't drop them first they'll either kill you or take you prisoner and get up to all kinds of playful little tricks, and after a day or two, believe me, you'll be praying for someone to put you out of your misery. That Canadian bloke ...'

'The one who lost his leg?'

'Yes. He used the word "gone" the other day. He was talking to you down the ward. I was listening. I heard him. He meant his leg, of course, but on the battlefield "gone" means something else. You can see it on a man's face, in the way he behaves, in the way he stops talking, in the way he no longer trusts language. It's what happens when he's marching up to the front line and some peasant at the roadside gives him a whistle and points at the sky just once too often. You go to ground, of course, try to make a scrape for yourself, try and find somewhere to hide, and then you cover your head with your hands, and pray that the Condor guys up there can't see you, but the truth is that you can't connect the dots any more. What are you doing here? Just meat on the griddle? What has any of this got to do with liberty, and equality, and honour, and all the rest of it? That's when your own death becomes nothing more than a matter of time. Tomorrow? The next day? Who's counting? You understand what I'm trying to say? Trying to tell you? That's when you've *gone*.'

When Annie reached for his hand, he withdrew it.

'I'm sorry,' she said, 'I'm trying to help.'

'You're helping lots.'

'How?'

'By finding this place, by bringing me out here, by *listening*. Here's a confession. I've been trying to write a book, some kind of personal account, but nothing, believe me, beats this. Do I need an audience? Yes. Why? Because someone has to tell me why all this stuff matters.'

Annie nodded. She thought she understood.

'You see that pile of rubble down there?' she said.

Roper shifted his weight again, shading his eyes against the sun, doing his best to follow her pointing finger.

'Among the trees, you mean?'

'Yes. Down by the brook. This whole estate belonged to the Infanta. Her name was Christina. This is royal blood, the monarchy, Old Spain the way it used to be. Everything you can see, miles and miles of it, all of it was hers. There were peasants on the land but they were her peasants and did her bidding and from time to time some of them would need a lesson or two and so she locked them up. Salaria showed me an old photo only yesterday. It was a lovely little building and you know what happened the minute the war started? The Republicans chased the Infanta away, and requisitioned the villa, and the peasants laid hands on some dynamite and blew the place up.'

Roper nodded, then turned to face her, an effort that made him wince in pain.

'And that's why we're fighting this war? For the pretty little house down there?'

'For the peasants,' she reached again for his hand. 'Though it may be the same thing.'

4

Five days later, Barsky posted a list of post-operative patients he deemed well enough to be transferred to the coast for the rest of their convalescence. The fighting in the Jarama Valley, though sporadic now, was still filling ambulances for the journey to the Villa Paz and he needed space for the newly wounded. One of the names on his list was Giles Roper.

By now, Annie thought she might be falling in love. The realisation had come to her the evening Salaria had offered a quiet word of advice. They were sitting in the once-grand first-floor quarters that had served as the Infanta's bedroom and personal retreat. The ornate mirrors on the wall were fogged and pitted with age and some of the wallpaper was beginning to come adrift but it was still possible to imagine this room in its former glory, at the very heart of a different Spain. The huge bed now slept three of the senior nurses, and one of them was Salaria.

'You've met big John, honey? John O'Reilly?'

'I have, yes.' O'Reilly was an Irishman from Tipperary, a looming presence who dwarfed Salaria. Heavily armed, he rode on the ambulances, sitting beside the *chofers*. It was his job to anticipate trouble on the road and at the front, and it was said that he probably knew more about this strange war than any other volunteer. What was also common knowledge was his passion for Salaria Kea.

'John's on the roster for tomorrow, honey. Early start for the Pasionaria Hospital at Murcia. My guess is that your Giles will be one of the lucky guys in the back.'

'*My* Giles?'

'Sure. Wars have no time for secrets. Living the way we have to, people watch, listen, compare notes. We're not talking blame here. Conditions like these, we all make mistakes.'

'That's a big word. What are you telling me?'

'The man's got under your skin. It's plain to see. You're up there at his bedside more than you need be. You took him out again yesterday and a couple of days before that. I'm sure it all helps, honey. I'm sure you're making him better. Question is, where does it stop?'

'And is that any of your business?'

'No, honey, but it might be John's.'

'How come?'

'You need to talk to him. You need to listen good. He's wise, no bullshit, and he knows how to read a man.'

'You want to tell me more?'

'Not me, honey, John. Talk to him, give him a little time, a little space. Think hard about what he's really saying, and then make up your own mind.'

What he's really saying? That night, the handful of English nurses at the Villa Paz decided to throw a farewell party for the convalescents heading for the coast. Their quarters, which included a dormitory which Annie was sharing with faces that always seemed to change, lay in the deep recesses of the villa, and only last week some of the nurses had done their best to turn a bare room used for storage into a kind of companiable den: a splash of whitewash on the walls, chairs with at least three legs scavenged from elsewhere in the building, a moth-eaten carpet curling at the edges and smelling of damp, artful lighting when the power was on, a deep-toned radio permanently tuned to Radio Toulouse, dusty bottles of vermouth tasting of quinine, and a chipped bowl of water for the Infanta's ancient dog, whom they'd christened Reggie. Invitations scribbled on the backs of autopsy forms were distributed to any patient judged capable of movement and conversation. Roper's said, 'Come and join us and dance for as long as you like. We're here to make you better.'

But Giles Roper didn't want to dance. Annie waited for him to appear as, one by one, the room began to fill with convalescents. Most of them arrived on the steadying arm of a nurse, either English or American. Many were recovering from limb fractures and Annie watched them pausing at the open door, their faces suddenly alive at the sound of the music pumping out from Radio Toulouse. Each new offering was busily introduced by the evening's studio host, who evidently specialised in crudely sexual double entendres, but very few people in the room spoke French, and so Annie – as translator – found herself trying to juggle the endless references to body parts and sexual preferences.

'He's trying to cheer us all up,' she confided airily to a slightly thin-lipped Matron, a born-again Baptist from Nottingham who consulted her bible most evenings. 'I think it may be a joke but with this man you never know. But it's the music that matters so I suspect we should be grateful.'

The nurses cleared a space in the middle of the room and after the bottles of vermouth had passed from hand to hand, the floor quickly filled with convalescents making their cautious return to moves some of them barely remembered. Most of them were back in their ragged uniforms, with collarless shirts, rumpled trousers, disintegrating boots and the occasional holstered revolver. They danced awkwardly like marionettes, mending arms held high in wire splints, their eyes already moist from the vermouth.

The nurses stepped carefully between them, picking up the beat of the music, parrying clumsy advances with a smile or a playfully wagging finger, and then the music changed after an especially gross joke about birth control, and the dancers paused, wondering how to take most advantage of Jeanette MacDonald singing 'Isn't It Romantic?'.

This was an open invitation to something more intimate than ragtime, difficult to turn down, and in the spirit of convalescence Annie joined the dancers, moving like all the other nurses from partner to partner in a canny bid to sidestep too much smooch. Her second partner, a young American barely out of college, said he'd been ogling her since the moment he'd arrived. At first, Annie thought he meant here and now, joining the party, but it quickly turned out that he meant nearly a fortnight ago, hauled out of an ambulance on a stretcher after a nasty encounter with a Nationalist airburst.

'Those goddamn scissors,' he grinned. 'Fully clothed to stark naked in the time it takes to tell the joke about the two elephants in the fridge. You never heard that joke? You want me to tell you?' Annie nodded, trying to keep him at arm's length. 'Simple. Silly, too. You ready for this?' Annie nodded a second time. 'How do you know there are two elephants in the refrigerator?'

'Pass.'

'They giggle when the light goes off.' The grin was even wider. 'You get it? Elephants in the fridge? Giggling in the dark? C'm here. Closer. I love this bit.' He tossed his head back, mouthing the lyrics. '*Merely to be young, on such a night as this.* Isn't that great? How old are you? We've all been trying to figure it out.'

'And?'

'You want my guess?'

'I do.'

'I think you're my age.'

'You're very kind.'

'And wrong?'

'I'm afraid so.'

'Even younger? Jeez. One guy thinks you're still in your teens. He's a little crazy.' The American tapped his head. 'Probably blast damage. He's over there. You mind if I give you a kiss?'

Annie was about to feint to her left as the young American made a clumsy lunge but she was saved by the sudden bulk of a much older man.

'You're next on my dance card, young lady. May I?' Soft Tipperary accent.

With a parting smile for her eager suitor, Annie stepped aside. John O'Reilly, like many big men, was surprisingly light on his feet and he drew her into an easy waltz, steering a faultless course among the wreckage on the dance floor.

'You'll not be taking any of these eejits seriously,' he smiled down at her.

'Never. It's all part of the service. But thank you.'

'My pleasure. You've talked to Salaria?'

'About Giles? I have.'

'Good. None of my business, of course. Goes without saying. You're a wonderful dancer, by the way. Good feet.'

'I'm flattered.'

'Don't be. When God invented rhythm he had women in mind.'

'And men?'

'Most of us should count ourselves lucky. We're beggars at the feast, undernourished one moment, greedy the next.' He beamed down at her. 'Be careful, Annie, that's all I really want to say.'

'We're back with Giles?'

'We are.'

'And?'

'I've known the boy a while. I came across him first at Madrigueras. He appeared with the latest training intake. He always wanted to be different, you could see that at once, never bothered to hide it.'

'Different how?'

'Different background. Different motivation. Even in a war like this, two sides of the family falling out, you play for the team. Honest to God, I'm not sure he knows what the word means.'

'Family?'

'Team. The Brigade. Those mates of yours, those buddies. The man's a loner. He's also mad for the ladies. I'm talking plural, Annie. We Irish exaggerate, always, it's part of our charm, but in this case there's no need because the boy Roper does our work for us. In Madrigueras he had money. Money buys *chicas*. He also has charm when he can be bothered, and just a dab or two of mystery. He's told you about the book?'

'He has.'

'Never fails. The man's a thinker. The man ponders. The man's forever teasing out those bigger questions the rest of us are too dim to understand. That can be catnip to certain kinds of women.'

Annie nodded, remembering her first glimpse of Giles's precious pad beside his bed. It had intrigued her then, and everything they'd shared since had simply added to her curiosity.

'You're telling me he's a phoney? That he's some kind of actor?'

'Kind of. Whatever works might be closer.'

'Works how?'

'Gets him what he wants. Maybe needs.'

'Which is?'

'Control. Undivided attention. The whole of you, Annie. Down in one.'

'I'm some kind of meal?' she said lightly. 'Or maybe drink?'

'Exactly.'

She gazed at him, expecting laughter, but it dawned on her that this big generous Irishman of Salaria's was serious.

'And fighting?' she asked. 'Was he any good at that?'

'Exceptionally good, according to fellas I've talked to. Keen, brave, but ...' he shrugged, '... crazy, too.'

'Crazy how?'

'Crazy because he always wants applause, attention. Guy like that, you get the sense there's only one thing he really fears.'

'Which is?'

'Being ordinary.'

'And that's a bad thing?'

'Not at all.'

'Then why are you telling me all this?'

'Because the fella may not be what he seems.'

May not be what he seems. The dance over, O'Reilly gave her a hug and disappeared in the direction of Salaria, who had discovered a fresh supply of vermouth. A little drunk by now, Annie fended off the attentions of yet another of the Villa Paz walking wounded and made her way back through the semi-darkness of the old building to the staircase that led up to the wards. She liked John O'Reilly. She liked his bulk, the easy way he had with language, and she trusted him. Yet something in the conversation they'd just shared had angered her.

She was twenty-seven, for God's sake. She'd known plenty of men, certainly made a mistake or two, but felt confident about her own judgement. She told herself that she could spot a phoney at a thousand yards. She told herself that tuning into another human being, male or female, was a pleasure as well as an art.

And she told herself that she hadn't got Giles Roper wrong. Of course he was bloody different. That was the whole point.

No one stole into her thoughts, waking or otherwise, without having something new, something unusual, something beguiling to say. They'd talked now on a number of occasions, three times alone and at length, and on each occasion he'd never let her down. That he was physically damaged was a matter of record. She herself had peered into the very middle of him, had watched Barsky save him for another day, another wound, but she sensed that the damage didn't stop there, that he'd somehow bought a ticket for a journey he'd never anticipated, and that a listening ear was the very least he deserved.

On the third floor, when Annie opened the door, Giles's ward was in darkness. The spill of light from the corridor revealed a handful of hunched shapes, patients still too damaged to make it downstairs. Very quietly, trying to steer a straightish course, Annie made her way towards the window. Expecting to see Giles in bed, probably asleep, she found the single blanket carefully turned down, the ghostly white of his notepad still on the bedside stool. She paused a moment, rubbing her eyes, trying to make sense of the shape lying on the pillow. Then she reached for it, picked it up, sniffed it. A gorse flower. Scentless.

She found Giles out in the freezing darkness, his long body wrapped in a greatcoat, propped against the rock they'd made their own. A stir of movement nearby and the faintest mewing also told her that his cat was here, too. The cat was a skinny semi-feral tabby he called Bones, who stalked the courtyard. There was plenty of offal from the operating rooms around if you knew where to find it, and Annie suspected that Giles might oblige with the odd tit-bit when the animal got really desperate.

'You sent me a message,' she settled beside him.

'Of course I did. Is that my blanket?'

'Yes. Even in the ward it was freezing. This was the best I could do.'

'You're very welcome,' he paused. 'And you're very drunk.'

'Right again, Mr Roper. It's what happens at parties. Even here. Maybe especially here.'

'So what did I miss?' He was reaching for the cat, but Bones had disappeared.

'Not much. To be honest, it was a bit of a peep show. Never mix vermouth and music with plaster casts.' She told him about the dancing.

'Awkward,' he grunted. 'I imagine.'

'You imagine right.'

He gazed at her a moment, and then asked what she knew about Murcia.

'*Nada*. Nothing.' She tried to muffle a hiccough. 'It's on the coast. Salaria says the Pasionaria Hospital is supposed to be good. It'll be warmer, too, warmer than here. Think positive.'

'Positive?' He shook his head, and then rested it back against the rock, his eyes closed. 'Is that a serious proposition?'

'I'm afraid it is. Listen.'

'To what?' He was frowning now.

'Down there. In the valley. Can't you hear them?'

The frown deepened. Then, after a while, he smiled.

'Trucks,' he said. 'No lights.'

'Exactly. The road's still open. Madrid to the coast. And you know what that means? It means that battle of yours was worth it. You're cold, aren't you?' Annie studied him a moment, and then opened her blanket. 'Come here. Come in with me.'

'That's too easy.'

'Good. Then just do it. Don't think too hard. Don't worry it to death. I admit it, I've drunk too much of that poisonous vermouth, but this is the real me, Mr Roper. Just do it.'

For a long moment, he didn't move. Then came what sounded like a sigh and he shuffled sideways until she could enfold him in the blanket. When she found his hand, she gave it a squeeze.

'Nice,' he murmured.

'Nice how?'

'Just nice. People think I'm a loner, and they're right, but being alone has its consolations.'

'Like?'

'Maybe this. Maybe finding someone similar.'

'Similar?'

'Like-minded.'

'You think I'm alone? Some kind of solitary? No one for company? Starvation rations?' Annie giggled. 'Nothing to drink?'

'I think you know how to listen, how to understand, and, believe me, that's rare.' He paused, bit his lip, tipped his head up, staring at the canopy of stars. 'I had the dream again last night. It happens more often than it should.'

'What dream? Tell me.'

'I shouldn't. It doesn't matter. You've had a great evening. You don't need this.'

'I do. I'm here. You said you trusted me. It won't hurt,' she squeezed his hand again. 'Promise.'

He nodded, his face suddenly very close. Then he shut his eyes and shook his head.

'I can't,' he muttered.

'You can. You must. Just do it.'

'Really? That simple?'

'Yes. And afterwards you'll feel so much better.'

'Sweet.' The chuckle was barely audible.

'It's what a girl does, Mr R. Drunk or otherwise. So ...? You're going to tell me ...?'

At last he shrugged. It was a long time ago, he said, a place called Felixstowe. This was home, a lovely seaside town in Suffolk. He had a best friend at school. His name was Edward, Eddie for short. They both had bikes and they were both mad about Thames barges.

'Thames what?'

'Barges. Big old boats with flat bottoms and huge sails the colour of rust.' He used his hands to sketch the sails in the darkness. 'They carried malt down to the breweries in London. There were dozens of these barges at a place called Pin Mill on the river and if you asked nicely you could get aboard.'

'And go to London?'

'Not me. Eddie. But this was much later. He'd palled up with one of the skippers, learned how to sail the thing properly, how to work the ropes, the tides, everything. We'd moved apart by then, gone our separate ways, but those early days together were really special, the mad things we got up to, where it might lead, how we felt about the world, each other, all that.'

'Each other?'

'Yes.'

'Meaning?'

'We were young. We were kids. You try everything. That's what kids are for.'

'And?'

'Someone came to the door, a policeman. This was years later. I was off to college, close to leaving home.'

'So what happened?'

'The policeman asked me who I was. I had to prove it. Then he gave me a note to read.'

'From who?'

'Eddie. It was written to me.' He shook his head, turned away. 'Before he hanged himself.'

The phrase lingered in the chill of the night air. No wonder, Annie thought. No wonder this man of mine is so complex, so difficult to reach, so walled-off, so *inward*. As gently as she could she tried to coax a little more about Eddie, about why he'd done it, and about how you'd ever cope over the months that followed, but Giles had gone again, shut the door on his hauntings with a mumbled apology for spoiling her evening. It was over, done. Eddie had gone. End of story.

She didn't believe him, and she was tempted to tell him so, but in the end she just held his thin body, rocking to and fro the way you might comfort a child. After a while, she stirred and held him at arm's length.

'One question. Do you mind?' He shook his head, said nothing. 'Will you miss this place? Yes or no will be fine.'

'No.'

'And me? Us? This?'

For the first time he smiled, then reached up from the blanket and softly cupped her face.

'Yes,' he said.

5

It took Annie several days to properly register the hole in the very middle of her life at the Villa Paz. No Giles, she thought. No carefully confected excuses to visit his ward. No solitary egg scrambled in whatever safe lay to hand. No wondering exactly what he'd just scribbled on yet another sheaf of paper. Not even the chance to say a proper goodbye.

Giles's bed was now occupied by a much older man, a Russian with heavy Slavic features and the raspy breath of a chain smoker. He'd lost a foot and half his lower leg to a land mine, and no matter how wide the window the consequences of the amputation hung in the air. Barsky, who checked him daily, acknowledged that the rest of the leg would probably have to come off if he was to survive.

Salaria, whose diagnostic skills extended way beyond triage and the operating room, knew at once what was troubling Annie.

'Forget him, honey. He's in a better place.'

'You're telling me he's died? Giles?'

'I think he's out of your life. Maybe your better place is here. You want extra shifts? Something to occupy that busy mind of yours? No problem.'

It didn't work. The battle of Jarama was over and done, the failed rebel offensive leaving the road from Madrid to the coast still open, but the tides of violence were lapping elsewhere, taking yet more lives, and the daily tally of incoming ambulances, each laden with more wounded, never seemed to diminish. A handful of these men were British. Most of them were young, and frightened, and only too happy to share their bewilderment and their pain with a listening ear.

The act of volunteering had seemed, all those months ago, to have been so simple: a pledge to defend the cause of freedom regardless of the cost. How to measure that cost had remained a mystery, something to be pondered and discussed, but nothing had prepared them for the realities of the battlefield. Out there, they murmured, were a bunch of strangers – tough, experienced, terrifyingly merciless – and they knew a thousand ways to kill a man. Crouch in a shallow trench, draw a bead on the oncoming line of Moors, and pray to God your rifle worked. Either way, yours or theirs, lives were on the line. Would this be the moment your candle guttered and died? Or would you be spared for an extra day or two?

To confessions like this, Annie was very willing to lend an ear, partly because she was sorry for them, for their innocence and their angst, but mainly because there'd come a moment when she could ask a question of her own. Had they ever come across a Giles Roper? Did the name mean anything to them?

In most cases, the answer was no, and after nearly a week of shaken heads Annie was beginning to wonder whether Giles, her Giles, had made the whole thing up. But then a slightly older Brit appeared. He had a bullet hole in his calf that was already infected. Whether or not to amputate below the knee was the finest of judgements but, after cleaning out the wound, Barsky decided to put his faith in the villa's tiny store of penicillin, instructing Annie to make twice daily inspections.

The volunteer's name was Frank. He came from a mining family in Yorkshire and he definitely knew Giles Roper.

'Mad bastard,' he said. 'Know him, do you?'

'A little.'

'He's been through here?'

'He has.'

'And he's still alive?'

'As far as I know.'

'Good.'

'Why good?'

'Had something about him, that lad. You probably saw it. We need more Ropers. He cheered the place up.'

He cheered the place up. That same afternoon, Annie cornered Salaria having a cigarette in the sunshine. Annie wanted to know whether she might be released for a couple of days.

'You'd have to get yourself there,' she said at once.

'Where?'

'Murcia. The Pasionaria.'

'Is it that obvious?'

'Afraid so, honey. Ain't no fooling anyone in a place like this.'

Annie nodded. To the best of her knowledge, Murcia was three hours away by road.

'Ambulances go there,' she said carefully.

'Sure, and most of them are full.'

'No space at all?'

Salaria gazed at her for a long moment, and then tapped ash onto the flagstones.

'You'll be coming back?'

'Of course.'

'Then leave it with me.'

Annie was on the road east by dawn next morning. The field ambulance, a gift from Hollywood, California, had offloaded yet more wounded, this time from the battle of Guadalajara, and was now heading for Murcia with half a dozen recovering convalescents for the Pasionaria Hospital. To Annie's relief, John O'Reilly wasn't on board but Salaria had made her promise that she'd be back within a couple of days. Two nurses were showing symptoms of typhus while a third had broken her wrist in a fall.

Driving into the rising sun, Annie closed her eyes and spent most of the journey sleeping fitfully from bend to bend, lulled by the incessant gear changes and the roar of the engine on the steeper hills. Once she felt a hand from the back of the ambulance settle briefly on her shoulder while a throaty voice begged for a cigarette but she ignored it. The outskirts of Murcia, hours later, were choked with horses and carts and makeshift stalls set up beneath the spindly trees on the side of the roads. The stalls were piled high with produce, short, squat women in black haggling over armfuls of tiny potatoes, and in late spring the hot wind that gusted in through the open window already tasted of high summer.

'Gypsies,' the ambulance driver was American, a tiny man who rarely smiled. 'They thieve from the fields and try and pass themselves off as peasants.'

Annie nodded, saying nothing. Her busy weeks at the Villa Paz had been a world away from the teeming streets of urban Spain, but even Madrid hadn't been quite as chaotic as this. The ambulance had come to a halt behind a long, untidy line of traffic.

'What's going on?' She was looking at a gaggle of women moving slowly from vehicle to vehicle, their palms outstretched. Some were carrying babies. Most had children in tow, thin, listless kids barefoot in the dust.

'Refugees,' the driver was rolling himself a cigarette. 'Franco's lot chased them out of Málaga and up the coast towards Almería, and then here. Bastards bombed them every which way. This city was never big to begin with. Now, you can barely move.'

'How many?'

'Tens of thousands. Maybe more. Thank God it's not winter.'

'And the bombers?' Annie gestured upwards.

'Not so far, not here. Different story in Cartagena, out on the coast. They get raids most days. The Germans go for the freighters in from Russia. These days most of the city lives underground.'

'You've been there? Seen it for yourself?'

'Once. Never again.' His eyes strayed to the rear-view mirror. 'Guy in the back with a plaster cast. See what you can do.'

Annie struggled into the rear of the ambulance. She knew this man, a Canadian from upstate Ontario recovering from a rebel bullet that had shattered his femur. He gestured at his groin. He badly wanted to pass water but knew there was no way he was getting out of the vehicle.

'Bucket in the back.' The driver again.

Annie found the bucket and did what she could in the way of aim. She wasn't entirely successful but the Canadian was beaming with relief.

'Lucky guy,' he was making himself decent again.

'Who?'

'That Roper of yours.'

The Pasionaria Hospital lay in the middle of the city within sight of the river. At the front of the building, dozens of convalescing patients sat in the sunshine, sharing cigarettes, taking it in turns to peer at a newspaper, or simply enjoying the mid-morning heat. Inside the building, Annie found a robed nun sitting behind the wooden table that evidently served as a meeting point and helped the driver translate the words he needed to off-load his charges from the ambulance. The nun summoned two male nurses, and then turned back to Annie.

'You're from ...?'

'The Villa Paz. Giles Roper? You know the name?' She knew at once the question was too abrupt, too direct, too clumsy.

'Señor Roper?' The nun looked her up and down and permitted herself the ghost of a smile. 'A friend, perhaps?'

'Yes. You know him?'

'I do,' she nodded. 'First floor. Turn right at the top of the stairs, my child, and follow the corridor to the end.'

My child. Annie watched the first of the convalescents from the ambulance stumbling awkwardly in from the brightness of the sunshine, a male nurse on each arm, and then made for the stairs, heading upwards. The hospital had the feel of a busy railway station, passengers everywhere, but these people – overwhelmingly men – negotiated the stairs with great caution. This was a world, she thought, of wooden crutches, black woollen berets, shag tobacco roll-ups lodged behind one ear, and loose cotton trousers, both legs often knotted below the knee.

At the head of the stairs she stood aside for a passing stretcher, then hugged one wall of the long corridor as she made her way towards the ward at the end. The ward was enormous, high ceilings, tiled walls with floral motifs and dozens of beds, most of them occupied.

She lurked beside the entrance, looking for Giles, not finding him. Then a figure appeared beside her. Naked from the waist up, he was an older man, Spanish-looking, Andalus-brown, shuffling patiently on his knees towards some distant bed. Annie's instinct was to help him and he came to a halt and turned towards her, as if he understood.

'*Sí?*' One eye was cloudy, the other bright. 'You're new? You've come to make us better, *señora?*'

'I've come to find someone. Giles? Giles Roper?'

'*Sí. El Inglés.*'

'You know him?'

'*Sí.*' He gestured vaguely towards the window. 'All week he goes to the plaza for *café con leche*. All the time ...' he made a loose gesture with his left hand.

'Writing?'

'*Sí.*' He tapped his head. 'Up here, very wise. You know the plaza? Outside the cathedral? Five minutes, *señora*.' He reached up for her hand and kissed it. 'You get lost, ask anyone.'

Annie didn't have to. The bulk of the cathedral loomed over the clutter of neighbouring buildings, and after she'd said her goodbyes to the ambulance driver she left the hospital and took the path beside the river, pausing to watch a small island of matted green weed drifting slowly past on the current. The water was brown and turbid and seemed to speak of some disturbance upstream, a country and a season out of step with the rhythms of peace, and for the first time she wondered exactly what she was going to say to this man who'd slipped through her normal defences and made himself so inexplicably at home.

Was he expecting a visit like this? Had he missed their times together? The conversations they'd shared, those quiet moments of complicity that are impossible to fake? Had he awoken in the smallest hours with the taste of regret on his lips? Regret that they hadn't taken this sudden rapport a little further? That they hadn't followed the implacable logic of a war that could so easily, in the space of a single breath, eat you alive? In short, was it madness that they hadn't, just once, made love?

The thought put a smile on her face, a reaction she didn't altogether understand, and she decided that thoughts like these served no purpose. She'd come to find out how he was getting on. The opportunity had presented itself and she'd been happy to accept it. In a couple of days she'd be back at the Villa Paz, back with Salaria and Dr Barsky, back in the world of twelve-hour days and a midnight plate of cold chickpea stew. And as for Giles Roper, he'd doubtless be making his own return to the war that had delivered him to the operating table barely a month ago.

She found him, as promised, in the plaza in front of the cathedral. She spotted him at once, alone among the three empty tables outside the distant café, a jug of water at his elbow, his face shaded by a broad-brimmed hat he must have borrowed from somewhere. She knew exactly what this man had owned when he arrived at the Villa Paz, and the short answer was nothing. And now he had the hat, and a loose cotton shirt that looked equally foreign and a pair of shorts that belonged on a fatter man. From time to time he looked up, staring into space, and scratched his knee, before returning to the pad on the table. What was he writing? What was so impossibly important that it had to be done in heat like this?

Comfortable in the shadows across the plaza, thrown by a big three-storey building that looked as old as the cathedral itself, she became aware of a hunched figure seated in an alcove to her right, a mountain of a man, his back to the ribbed stonework. He was wearing a torn pair of trousers and a grubby shirt with buttons missing and a fading check print and he, too, had covered his head, in this case not with a hat but with untidy coils of once-red cloth that might, in other hands, have made him look Moorish.

Inert, unmoving, his head slumped on his chest, she wondered whether he might be asleep in the heat but then he stirred and shook himself like a dog and looked cautiously up, a movement that spoke of a deep reluctance, and the moment he turned towards her she understood why.

The last few months, first in Madrid and then at the Villa Paz, had hardened her to battlefield wounds, to the reach and impact of modern weapons, to the dark chemistry of high explosive, but this man's ruined face was something she'd never seen before. His features had become muddled, out of place, lost. His left eye, half-closed, had drooped, cushioned by the livid flesh of his pitted cheek, and the diagonal slash of his mouth seemed to lack a lower lip. A thin dribble of saliva pinked his chin and, most bizarre of all, a tuft of black hair had mysteriously appeared on the wreckage of his nose. If you ever needed a living poster to thin the queues of volunteers for this ghastly bloodbath, then here it was.

'What happened?' Her question, in Spanish, was involuntary.

'A church fell on my head.' The throaty growl emerged through a row of broken teeth.

'Here?'

'Madrid. You know Madrid?'

'Yes.'

'Then you know you have a choice when the bombers come. The Metro or the house of God. The Plaza de Infanta? Off the Gran Via? There. It could have been worse. The place was full of animals, donkeys, cows, and the bomb killed most of them. So maybe God spared me, or most of me, or just the bits that matter. A man can think too hard about these things.' He gestured round. 'Lovely day. Warm, too.'

Annie nodded. She'd noticed the scruffy tin beside the man's bare feet. Two five-centimo coins, barely enough for a box of matches. She dug into her purse, added a twenty-five-peseta coin. The man stared at the tin, then rubbed his good eye.

'You're Spanish?'

'French. With a bit of English.'

'Why?'

The question floored her. Why the mix? Why on earth not?
Then came a sharp bark of what might have been laughter and
one big hand began to uncoil the turban around his head.

'I meant why here,' he grunted.

'I'm a nurse. I'm working.'

'Good. D'you mind?' His head was bare now, the turban
carefully folded in his lap. His scalp, whiter than his face, was
latticed with crude suture wounds and some had reopened,
seeping thin viscous fluids. Another tuft of jet-black hair, absurd,
erect, ungovernable, had somehow survived the surrounding
carnage. Annie picked up the turban, sniffed the stains.

'Pus,' she said. 'You need treatment.'

'Pus? *Purulento?* Where did you learn Spanish like that?'

Annie ignored the question. She told him about the Pasionaria
Hospital, how close it was. They'd clean the wounds and maybe
give him something to stop the infection, but he shook his head.
He'd seen far too much of far too many hospitals and now he
was rather enjoying the sunshine and the company.

'You want to tell me more? You want me to make space
down here?'

Annie shook her head, then took one more look at his scalp,
closer this time, and then knelt quickly to the tin and retrieved
her twenty-five-peseta coin.

'I need to get some disinfectant,' she said. 'As long as you're
still here, you'll get the money back.'

'Make it fifty?' He'd summoned the grotesque makings of
a grin.

'Done.' She was eyeing the distant figure of Giles Roper, still
bent over the pad. 'It might take a while.'

*

Annie stepped into the sunshine, feeling immeasurably better. This war, thank God, never left you alone, and the questions she'd been asking herself about Giles seemed suddenly trite. A pair of surgical scissors to excise the odd rogue stitch, she told herself. A strong disinfectant. Something to probe the wounds and clean up afterwards. And maybe a light dusting of sulphonamide powder to fight the infection.

She approached the café table and then came to a halt. Only when she moved to throw her shadow over the racing pen did Roper look up. He shielded his eyes against the sudden brightness of the sunshine.

'Me,' she murmured. He didn't react, just stared up at the black silhouette. 'Nurse Wrenne,' she added. 'A voice from the past.'

At last he smiled, and struggled to his feet. The effort raised a twinge of pain, then another as his hands sought the comfort of the table's edge. She wanted to sit him down, to tell him to take it easy, but there was another instinct, much stronger. He was suddenly real again, overpoweringly so, and she wanted his arms around her. She wanted to feel his long body pressed to hers. She wanted to touch him, to smell him, and then to hold him at arm's length and take a proper look. On the other side of the plaza, she was half aware of the beggar watching this little cameo. So much for Nurse Wrenne, she thought.

Moments later, Giles was back in his chair. So far, he'd managed nothing in the way of conversation, save a gasp of surprise, or perhaps pleasure, for which she was deeply grateful.

'Nothing to say, Mr Roper?'

'Everything to say. Everything. Here—'

He was flicking back through the writing pad, and as she sat down he tore off a page, and then another, and passed them both across.

'For you,' he murmured. 'Your fault.'

'Fault? This is guilt I'm supposed to be feeling?'

'Just read it,' he put his hand over hers. 'Please.'

She did what she was told, feeling a deep sense of pleasure stealing over her. The poem was called 'Missing in Action' and made space on the page for an almost jazz-like series of riffs on the simplest of propositions: *Miss You*, it began, before plunging into a breathless series of excursions into the brevity of their shared journey. Miss You because we never quite had the right kind of time together, Miss You because of that last sentence we never quite had the time to finish, Miss You because this bolt of lightning never strikes twice.

'You're sure about that?' she said lightly, her finger on the last phrase.

'As sure as I can be about anything.'

'Nothing before? Nothing afterwards?'

'Before was a desert. No you. Afterwards is just us. Think oasis. Think water. Think *life*.'

'You're on medication?'

'Of course. You're thinking side effects?'

'I'm thinking you need a good lie-down. Somewhere dark and not quite as hot.'

'Until the fever passes?'

'I hope not.'

'Sweet.'

'Me?'

'Us.' He squeezed her hand. 'How long have we got?'

'Big question, Mr Roper. I have to be back in harness two days from now.'

'Who says?'

'Me. And Salaria. But mainly me.'

'Should I take that personally?'

'Not at all. A girl's got a war to fight, and I expect you have, too. That's what started this little affair so think unfinished business.'

'And afterwards?'

'Afterwards will be history someday.' She nodded down at the open pad. 'As I'm sure you've anticipated.'

She explained briefly about the beggar across the square. They needed to get back to the Pasionaria and pick up certain items to keep her conscience in good order, an errand that would benefit from Giles's presence. He nodded absently, barely sparing the shadowed alcove across the plaza a second glance, but when Annie enquired where she might stay a couple of nights he beckoned her closer, as if sharing a secret.

'There's a little hotel some of the nurses from the hospital use. It's very close, pretty basic, cheap, too. Hostel de las Cuáqueras?'

'The Quaker Hotel.'

'That's it. This town's full of do-gooders. You know about the refugees? The caravan of death? All that?'

'I know about Málaga, if that's your question. The caravan of death sounds horrible.'

'That's because it was. Thousands of them have ended up in a block of flats way out of town. They call it the Pablo Iglesias. I gather the conditions are dreadful. Kids running amok. Old folk with nothing to eat. Total slum.'

'And that's where the Quakers come in?'

'Yes.' He briefly checked his watch. 'Perfect.'

'What is?'

'Nearly one o'clock. They rent the rooms from early afternoon.'

They returned to the Pasionaria, Giles hanging on Annie's arm. Walking was evidently still an effort but he refused her invitation to take a rest from time to time. At the hospital, he sat beside her and scribbled a list of everything she needed for the beggar back in the plaza. When she offered to spare him the stairs he said it wouldn't be a problem. One of the older nuns held court in a complex of rooms on the ground floor that served as the hospital pharmacy. Giles double-checked the list and then limped away through the mill of patients and relatives that never seemed to leave the hospital alone.

Minutes later, they were out in the sunshine again, Annie carrying a box of medical supplies. Giles suggested a detour via the hotel to check whether a room might be available, which seemed, to Annie, altogether sensible. When she gently suggested he could do with a rest, he shook his head, but he was sweating in the heat and glad of the cool of the hotel's tiny reception area when they stepped in from the street.

'I should be doing this,' Annie said when he headed for the counter. 'After all, it's my room.'

'And a guest?'

'More than welcome.'

A woman appeared and consulted a list of rooms. Annie asked for one on the ground floor, paid for two nights, and consigned the key to Giles once the woman had disappeared.

'Number 7,' she murmured. 'Leave the door on the latch.'

Back in the plaza, the beggar appeared not to have moved. Neither were there any more coins in his tin. Annie unpacked the box and knelt beside him, using squares of linen soaked in disinfectant to swab the suture wounds before tidying the wisps of black cat gut with scissors. At the bottom of the box she found a tube of sulphonamide ointment and a selection of plasters and, once she knew she'd checked the seepage, she said that she was done.

'That's it?'

'Until tomorrow, yes.'

'You're coming back?'

'Of course.' She'd found two twenty-five-peseta coins. 'Same time, same place.'

'And this?' he gestured at the filthy turban.

'I'll get rid of it, find something more suitable. Those wounds of yours need to heal in the open air. Spend the money on food, by the way, not drink.'

'You're a Quaker?'

'Certainly not.' She got to her feet and shook the dust before peering down at him. 'My name's Annie, by the way. And you?'

'People call me *El Diablo*, the kids especially.'

'The Devil?'

'*Sí.*' He nodded towards the nearby cathedral. 'Find a stonemason with a sense of humour and I'd be up there with the rest of the gargoyles.'

El Diablo. The name settled deep in Annie's brain as she made her way back to the Hostel de las Cuáqueras. How would anyone ever cope with a set of injuries like that? And if the visible damage was so catastrophic, what must the rest of him be like? She shook her head, robbed of an answer, and then another name ghosted into her head. Goya, she thought, and the dark vision of an earlier Spain he'd made his own.

Giles was lying naked on the single bed when she let herself into the hotel room.

'No secrets,' he smiled up at her. 'This is how the story started.'

'You, me and a cast of extras? You were halfway to fairyland, as I recall, which was doubtless just as well. You're a handsome man, Mr Roper. I even thought so then.'

'And now?'

'Now you need to eat a little more.' She settled on the bed beside him, eyeing the long scar where Dr Barsky had zipped him back together again. 'Nice job,' she smiled. 'Fabulous blood supply.'

'Does that surprise you?' He was beginning to stir. 'Or can we find another verb?'

'Gladden will do.'

She stripped quickly, leaving her clothes in a pile beside the bed. He stared up at her, the face of someone suddenly much younger, and then extended a hand. She took it for a moment, feeling the knuckles one by one, then ducked her head and kissed the tips of his fingers.

'This is the full examination? I get the results now, or do I have to wait?' He lay back, closing his eyes, and a tiny sigh announced the moment when she abandoned his hand and began to plant a line of kisses the length of his scar. When the ridge of hardened tissue ran out, she nuzzled the regrowth of pubic hair.

'Impressive,' she murmured.

'You're very kind.'

'I meant the way you've recuperated. Were you born hairy?'

'I was born lucky. Hair never came into it. Jesus ...'

She was using her tongue now, tiny playful little flicks where he least expected them.

'You've done this before,' he murmured.

'You think so?'

'I know so. Gorse will never smell the same, believe me.'

'But gorse has no smell.'

'Wrong. Gorse smells of this.'

'But we've barely started.'

'Exactly. Tell me something.'

'Of course.'

'Does every woman want to be a whore in bed?'

'Every woman wants to be surprised. This one especially.'

'Surprised how? By me? By something I've done?'

'By me. By something you've been clever enough to set free. So far, Mr Roper, you've managed it at arm's length and that, believe me, isn't easy. Do it again, do it properly, do it now, and we're both in deep trouble.' She smiled down at him. 'We agree? Just nod.'

They made love all afternoon. Giles had an urgency that sat awkwardly with the aftermath of his operation, but Annie assured him there were no prizes for wrecking his convalescence and after that he consented to being pleasured in a number of ways that satisfied them both. Finally exhausted, Annie lay beside him, her mouth inches from his ear. She wanted to know when he was due back at the hospital.

'It doesn't really matter.'

'I don't believe you, Mr R. Nurses can be unforgiving, especially nuns.'

'It's not the nuns you have to worry about. There are commissars attached to every hospital. They need us back in the line, back for another pop or two, and they make sure we never run away.'

'So what's the worst they can do?'

'They can put me in front of a firing squad. It's neat and it's brutal and it means that way every soldier has a choice. A bullet from our side for desertion or a bullet from theirs for doing the right thing.'

'Horrible.'

'This comes as some kind of surprise?'

'Not at all. Goya knew that. You know about Goya?'

'Tell me.'

'Different war, same rules. Some people say he painted like an angel but that wasn't strictly true. What he did was watch, and learn, and make notes when it mattered. He was a reporter. He drew on real life and Spain obliged with every kind of madness and violence you can imagine. He went deaf in the end, which was a blessing of sorts, but what survives is truly remarkable. One day I'm going to take you to the Prado in Madrid. His *Pinturas negras* will change your life.'

She walked her fingertips across the flatness of Giles's belly, smiling to herself.

'*Pinturas* what?' He caught her hand, gave it a squeeze.

'The Black Paintings. They date from the end of his life. From where that poor man was standing, there was no turning back. Odd, really.'

'Odd how?'

'The beggar I met today'. She propped herself up on one elbow, looking down at him. 'You never saw his face. He belonged in those paintings, in Goya's *Pinturas negras*. Saturn eating his son. Old crones practising to be witches. Men beating each other to death. Hideous.'

'And you like this stuff?' Giles was stirring again.

'The violence? Never. The vision? Of course.'

'How come?'

'Because, in the end, we're nothing but maddened animals.' Her hand had slipped between his thighs. 'And Goya caught that perfectly.'

Giles finally left in mid-evening. Annie offered to walk back to the hospital with him but he shook his head. He said he loved her. And when he lingered at the open door, promising to return next day, she knew he meant it.

'Me, too,' she said simply. 'So let's pick up with Goya tomorrow and see what happens next.'

For once, she slept without dreaming, drained by the early start, the unseasonal heat, the chaos on the busy streets, and by everything that had happened thereafter. She had absolutely every intention of returning to the Villa Paz but sensed as well that her real interests lay here. When she asked Giles when he might have to return to the front line he'd simply shrugged, told her he didn't know. Decisions like that were, he said, in the hands of the doctors and perhaps the resident commissar. When the war called, he'd have to do its bidding, but until that moment came there was plenty left to find out about each other.

Annie could only agree. Next morning, she made enquiries of the woman who manned the reception desk. She was a qualified nurse. She knew the city faced the challenge of feeding and housing tens of thousands of refugees. She'd heard talk of some kind of refuge called the Pablo Iglesias. Was there anyone who might tell her a little more?

The woman, impressed by her Spanish, lifted the ancient telephone and placed a call. Minutes later, on a scratchy line, Annie found herself talking to an English voice with hints of a northern accent. She said her name was Francesca Wilson and, yes, she had a great deal to do with settling the refugees down. It was an arresting phrase, patronising on one level, heartfelt on another, and when Annie briefly tallied her experience in Madrid, and latterly at the Villa Paz, she began to warm to the conversation.

'You want to help out? Is that my understanding?'

'Yes.'

'You're aware we have no money? Very little of anything, to be precise?'

'Yes.'

'And none of that makes any difference?'

'Not at all. If you can feed me, that would be wonderful. The rest I can take care of.'

'Excellent. You have a position on condensed milk? On powdered eggs when we can get them?'

'I live on nothing else.'

'Music to my ears, Miss Wrenne. The Villa Paz, you say?'

'That's right.'

'That remarkable Dr Barsky?'

'The very same.'

'Better and better. Leave your details at the hotel. I'll be in touch.'

The conversation buoyed Annie through the rest of the morning. She returned, as promised, to find *El Diablo* in his usual spot. She attended once again to his ruined scalp and presented him with a straw hat he might wear in place of the turban. The airflow, she said, would do nothing but good for the suture scars as they began to heal, and if he thought an all-over wash might brighten his day, she'd be happy to make the appropriate arrangements.

To her surprise, her new patient wouldn't hear of it. If she thought he slept rough, she'd be wrong. He had modest lodgings he could call his own and even the rich smelled bad in this city. In short, he was grateful for her help, viewed the straw hat as a mixed blessing, and looked meaningfully at the emptiness of his tin as she prepared to leave. Another fifty pesetas put a crooked smile on his face and she was about to turn away when he waved a big hand at the empty tables on the other side of the plaza.

'That friend of yours,' he said. 'The one with the limp.'

'Yes?'

'He's here every morning. Have you frightened him off?'

'On the contrary,' she returned the smile. 'I've been keeping him very busy.'

Giles was back in her hotel room by early afternoon. Naked under the single sheet, Annie was reading *Madame Bovary*, a copy of which she had found in the bookcase in the tiny room that served as the hotel's lounge, and the moment she looked up to see his face at the open door she knew that something had changed.

'John O'Reilly?' he said. 'Big guy? Irish?'

'Yes?'

'He was on this morning's ambulance. He gave me this.'

He produced a single sheet of paper, folded twice.

'You've read it?'

'Yes.'

'What does it say?'

'It says that Barsky wants you back. Needs is probably closer. The place is full to bursting. They can't cope.'

'And what did you say?'

'I said I'd pass the message.'

'In person?'

'Of course. Is that a problem?'

Is that a problem? She made room for him on the bed.

'John wants to take me back?' she asked.

'Yes.'

'When?'

'This afternoon.'

'This afternoon when?'

'He didn't say.' Giles paused, reaching for her hand. 'What's the matter? There's lots of war. There'll be plenty left.'

'It's not the war I worry about.' Annie was frowning now. 'It's us. Or, more to the point, John O'Reilly. I don't know what you've done to upset him but now's the time to tell me.'

'Tell you what?'

'He thinks you cheat. He thinks you might be bad for me. He's appointed himself my guardian bloody angel, which is rather quaint on his part, but after last night I need to know that I'm not deranged.'

'Meaning?'

'Meaning he's wrong. Meaning he should mind his own business and leave us alone.'

'And you? What do you think?'

'About last night?'

'About us. What's happened. What it means. Where it goes next.'

'It stays here,' Annie reached for his hand. 'With you and me.'

'But you're going back to Paz. Or that's what you told me last night. I put it down to conscience, which is another reason I love you.'

Annie held his gaze. When he sank onto the bed beside her, she told him she wanted to make love again.

'We can do that small thing?' she asked.

'Of course.'

'And John?'

Giles said nothing for a moment. Then he slipped his clothes off and straddled her chest.

'Fuck John,' he reached blindly behind him, finding her wet already. 'The war can wait.'

6

In two brief summer days, life at the Villa Paz seemed to have changed beyond recognition. On the journey back from Murcia, alone with Annie in the empty ambulance, John O'Reilly never once mentioned Giles Roper. Instead, he warned her of the sudden torrent of wounded men hauled in from the battlefields around Madrid.

This was bad enough, he said, but what made it worse was the occasional appearance of German aircraft overhead. None had yet to drop a bomb but they had an insolence, he said grimly, that put your nerves on edge, especially if you happened to have witnessed what they could do in Madrid. And so security at the villa had been tightened.

All vehicles, including ambulances, had to be parked at least three hundred metres away from the main building, heavily camouflaged by bushes and spare blankets. The laundresses had been henceforth forbidden to lay anything white outside to dry in the summer heat. There were to be no exterior lights whatsoever after dark, all doors and windows to be shut, the cracks stuffed with rags.

'The heat inside is something fierce,' he said grimly. 'And then there's the smell.'

He was right. It was dark when they arrived, winding up the long road towards the black mass at the top of the hill. The countless villages en route had also been blacked out because no one could afford kerosene for the lanterns, but there was something sinister about the Villa Paz abandoned to the long night of this filthy war.

It got worse. Next morning's operations started shortly after dawn with the arrival of two ambulances from God knows where. Two days with Giles seemed to have rinsed Annie's memories of what had to happen next, but within minutes she was back in the fog of ether, in the rush of many feet, of soft groans coming from unseen stretchers, of the tiled floor slippery with spilled blood. Both operating tables were going full blast and, summoned by Dr Barsky, she found herself stepping into a nightmare tableau of silent figures dressed in white bent over yet another body, of naked flesh and busy hands plunged deep inside an open chest, of abandoned rags floating in slop jars of reddish liquid.

Despatched with a bucket of dismembered limbs, Annie found herself in the courtyard shed reserved for the dead. Even this early, the smell and the buzz of the flies made her stomach heave and she lingered just long enough to register the bodies laid side by side like newly sawn cordwood. The wan clay complexion of death is the only present that war will ever leave you, she thought, and a phrase of Giles came back to briefly haunt her. This war brooks no argument, he'd told her barely hours ago. Whatever your feelings about your fellow man, about life and love and liberty, all you can do, all it expects of you, is to go out and make more dead. Look for a rationale, look for a reason to salute yet another perfect morning, and there it is. A rifle in your arms and murder in your heart. The road to pacifism, he said bitterly, is guarded by a million bodies.

The thought of Giles, of his touch, of his smell, of his moments of sudden anger softened by tenderness, wouldn't leave her alone. He had the innocence of a child and the angst of someone much older. Single-handedly, without the comfort of others, he seemed to have understood the essence of the battlefield and brought it home to her. This act of trust, as she saw it, had given their couplings an edge of desperation, and afterwards she let him even deeper inside another part of her.

This was where she kept her hopes and dreams, the world she really wanted for herself, the life this horrible war might yet make possible. Pressed by Giles, she'd shared moments from her childhood and adolescence, moments when the world had suddenly come into the sharpest focus. These memories had a raw intimacy she could only ever share with someone like Giles, someone who'd understood the urgent tug of a past she treasured, and before they'd left the Hostel de las Cuáqueras for that last time, she'd told him about a canvas by Bartolomé Murillo.

'Santa Tomas de Villanueva giving alms,' she'd told him. 'One day I'll take you to see it and when I do you'll have to look in the lower left-hand corner. That's where she is, the mother and the child. The mother is sitting down, half holding the child, and the child is looking up at her. It's beautiful. Truly beautiful.'

'But why?' Giles had been very close, his head on her breasts.

'Why what?'

'Why is it so important?'

'Because it's about trust, as well as beauty,' she'd kissed him. 'And because the mother could be me.'

Two days later, she knew she had to leave the Villa Paz. The temptation was to lean on Salaria again, to take advantage of her better nature, to plead exhaustion and despair and all the other blessings that a war like this could confer, but she knew that would be an act of cowardice and so she left it very late in the evening, the cleaners still busy with the mops and the bleach in the operating rooms. Dr Barsky was out in the courtyard, the big door firmly closed behind him, the tiny forbidden glow of his cigarette between his bony fingers, his head turned up towards the stars.

'You've had enough,' he grunted. No need – nor time – for an explanation. 'I'm driving to Murcia for meetings tomorrow. You're welcome to ride along.'

They left very early next morning, in the last of the pre-dawn darkness, Barsky smoking one cigarette after another as they descended towards Murcia and the coast. Annie tried to stir a flicker or two of conversation from the embers of her weeks at the Villa Paz but quickly sensed that Barsky wasn't interested. This man must have a million things on his mind, she told herself. Why on earth would he want to listen to a feeble volunteer would-be nurse who hadn't managed to stay the course?

He dropped her at the Pasionaria Hospital without bothering with a proper goodbye. The last she saw of him was a squeal of brakes as he scattered the traffic on the road that ran beside the river. He drove the way he mended broken bodies, she thought. With minimal patience and a blind faith in whichever God suited these demented times.

It was still early, barely eight o'clock. Giles, with luck, would still be in bed up in the big ward she'd visited barely days ago. She made her way to the first floor and stood in the open doorway before venturing in. Every bed was occupied, face after face on the single pillows, some still asleep, others not. None of them looked like Giles but she had to be sure and so she ghosted her way towards the spill of sunshine at the far end, aware of heads turning here and there. No Giles.

Then came a low voice from the bed next to the window. It was the older man she'd met the first time she'd been here, no legs below the knee, his face deeply seamed and Andalus-brown.

'*El Inglés?*' he asked.

'Yes.'

'Too late.'

'Too *late*?'

'He's gone to Benicàssim.'

Annie shook her head. The old man doubtless meant well but she had no idea what he was talking about. Benicàssim?

'It's down on the coast. Everyone goes there, as long as you're lucky.'

'Why? Why do they go?'

'To get better. And then more better. And then better still. You have a cigarette, *señora*?'

Annie shook her head, and then fled. Only when she was back on the ground floor, among the gathering crowd of visitors, did she manage to steady her pulse. Some kind of convalescent facility, she told herself, yet another step on the journey back to the trenches. She was right.

'Benicàssim is two hours away,' this from the nun who presided over the pharmacy. 'Beaches. Swimming. Good food. You've never heard of it?'

'Never. How do I get there?'

'We have transport every day. You have someone in mind? Someone you need to see?'

'Giles Roper.'

The nun studied her for a moment, saying nothing. Unnerved by the sudden silence, Annie asked whether he might have left her a note.

'My name's Annie,' she said. 'Annie Wrenne.'

'You're not Spanish?'

'No.'

'You speak like one of us.'

'Thank you,' Annie forced a smile. 'No note?'

The first of the day's transports for Benicàssim left mid-morning, barging through the normal clutter of horses and carts that plagued the city's centre. Half an hour later, the open road coiled through the mountains and down towards the coast. It was already hot and Annie was glad of the wind sluicing through the open window. Giles had tried to get in touch with the Villa Paz and failed, she told herself. Or they'd got the message and neglected to pass it on. She tried to relax on the hardness of the wooden seat, a smile on her face. Anticipation smelled of thyme with notes of wild garlic from the stony untilled fields beside the potholed tarmac.

Benicàssim, when they finally reached it, was full of young men in uniforms, and only the occasional limp betrayed the resort's real function. Annie prowled among the gaggles of convalescing heroes along the promenade, marvelling at the rich soup of languages, English one moment, French the next, then a volley of compliments from a couple of admiring Russians as she walked past.

These were men who'd already tasted combat, she told herself. They'd already paid their dues to the gods of war yet seemed strangely cheerful at the prospect of another chance to risk their young lives. Had she got it wrong about the International Brigades? Had Giles misled her, with his writerly pessimism, with his darker thoughts? In her heart she knew the answer was no, but just now she had to find him and in truth she had no idea where to start. These people had to be living somewhere, she told herself, and an address might be nice.

A crowd of tanned young men outside a biggish hotel at the end of the promenade was a clue. She mingled among the watching faces until she found someone who might know. He was English. He was carrying a punctured football, the laces frayed, and told her she reminded him of his kid sister.

'Is that some kind of compliment?'

'Certainly is. She's a corker.'

Annie asked about Giles. Tallish. Blond curls. XV Brigade.

'Been here a while?'

'I doubt it. I think he probably arrived yesterday.'

'Then you should go to the school. They try and get newcomers to talk to the kids, us English in particular. Everyone wants to learn the lingo.' He gave her directions and wished her luck. 'We're all on the beach down there later.' He showed her the football. 'Bring him along.'

The school was in a dusty street two blocks away from the beach. A long table had been set up in the sunshine in the school's front yard and a couple of dozen children were perched on the wooden benches, desperate for their turn to chant the careful lines of English chalked on the blackboard. A setting like this, Annie knew, would offer a perfect role for Giles. It would appeal to what he'd once told her was his calling, to his reverence for language, spoken or otherwise. On occasions he could be a child himself, something that had taken her by surprise, but his face wasn't to be seen among the convalescent young warriors talking to the kids.

Curious, she made her way around the side of the building, hugging the shadows, not quite sure whether she was trespassing or not. The school was physically small, no more than a handful of empty classrooms brightened by displays of children's drawings. Only at the back of the building was there any evidence of occupation.

Two figures, both adults, were standing in front of a blackboard, surrounded by a scatter of tiny desks. They had their backs to the window. One of them was a woman, motionless, staring at the shapes on the blackboard. She was wearing a twist of scarlet ribbon in the fall of black hair, and her legs were bare and brown beneath the patterned cotton dress. The other, Annie knew at once, was Giles. The tumble of reddish curls over the collar of his shirt. That special body language when he was telling a story, tiny movements with his hands, slightly stagey pauses for the sake of effect, a repertoire of tricks to compel attention. Just now he was adding a line or two with a stub of chalk to shapes he'd drawn on the blackboard. Annie recognised the bulge of East Anglia on the shape of the British Isles, and as she watched he added an extravagant cross. Felixstowe, she thought. The town on the coast where he'd grown up.

The woman was nodding, asking some question or other, wanting more of this story of his, and Giles obliged with a flourish of chalked lines that resolved themselves into what was unmistakably a boat. Giles's precious Thames barge, she thought. The huge mast. The big jigsaw of sails. The long line of the hull. The outings with Eddie on their bikes to Pin Mill. And maybe the moment, much later, when he got news of his best friend's suicide.

Annie's mouth was dry. Despite the heat, she felt an iciness where her heart should have been. This was bad enough, this man of hers sharing an intimacy he swore he'd guarded all his life, a tale she'd struggled to drag out of him back at the Villa Paz, but now she watched the woman's hand finding his, giving it a squeeze, and then she turned her head, gazing up at him, her eyes doubtless moist, exactly the effect he was after. She was young, and pretty, and entirely helpless in the hands of this stranger who'd stepped into her life. Now he'll turn away, she told herself. Now he'll shake his head, and frown that special frown, and play the hapless victim of fate before submitting to a hug and doubtless other consolations. And he did.

*

She left Benicàssim that same afternoon, riding in the back of an open truck in the company of dozens of uniformed young volunteers, newly mended for whatever the civil war had next in mind for them. She was mute among the crush of bodies, deaf to game attempts to spark a conversation, blind to the open curiosity of those closest. All that mattered was the lift to Murcia, and the knowledge that this brief episode in her life was over.

She was certain that neither of them had seen her lurking outside the classroom. With luck, he might not survive his return to the battlefield. How come she'd got this man so badly wrong? How come she'd never had the wit to listen properly to Salaria and John O'Reilly? How come she'd unlocked her door to Giles Roper, and invited him in, never suspecting for a moment that he'd take a look around and help himself to whatever took his fancy before moving on to the next dupe, and the one after that?

Dupe, she thought. Fool. Ingénue. Lamb to the slaughter. Just another victim of this implacable war.

These were the sticks she used to beat herself as the big old truck rumbled on, and by the time it was slowing in the outskirts of Murcia, her numbness had turned to anger and she felt a whole lot better. She passed the word for the driver to drop her off beside the river in sight of the cathedral, and she raised a brief smile as the men blew her kisses and the truck set off again.

The woman at the Hostel de las Cuáqueras recognised her at once, lifting the phone and dialling a number when she enquired about Mrs Wilson.

'Annie Wrenne?' The voice at the other end was strangely comforting. 'Am I right?'

'You are.'

'And might you be joining us?'

'Yes.'

The arrangements were pleasingly simple. Annie was to book herself in for a single night at the hostel. Thereafter, cheaper lodgings would be available. She'd probably have to share with one of the other nurse-volunteers but sharing came naturally in a war like this. Tomorrow morning, around eight, someone would pick her up from the hostel and bring her here, to the Pablo Iglesias.

'Get a good night's sleep, my dear. I'm afraid you're going to need it.'

Afraid? Back out in the sunshine, her room booked, Annie made her way back to the plaza beside the cathedral. The thought of thousands of homeless refugees weathering the current storm in a half-built block of apartments filled her with something close to glee. With luck, the mothers would be impossibly needy. The kids, unloved, half-starved, would be running amok. The plumbing would have failed months ago and the smell would be unbearable. Somewhere in the building would be a huge cauldron of yesterday's chickpeas or maybe cold porridge, and if her job was to spoon this gloop into a thousand waiting mouths then so be it. Given the trap she'd just escaped, she could think of nothing more welcome. She'd become a human being again. She'd be of some bloody *use*.

The beggar, *El Diablo*, was occupying his usual alcove. To her surprise, his tin was brimming with coins.

'How come?' She settled beside him.

'You think I've had a good day?' he asked.

'I know you've had a good day.'

'Wrong. I changed your twenty-fives into centimos.' He nodded at the tin. 'I thought that would turn me into a good cause. One woman stops to drop a coin? Others will do the same.'

'And?'

'I was wrong. It didn't work.'

'Nothing?'

'Nothing.' The thought seemed to amuse him. Then he nodded at the still-empty tables across the plaza. 'And that friend of yours?'

Annie said nothing for a moment, then she lay back, feeling the warmth of the old stones through her dress.

'Gone,' she said.

'Dead?'

'Good as.'

The beggar nodded. Then he extended a big hand. Annie stared down at it, surprised by how clean it was.

'Carlos,' he grunted. 'Carlos Ortega. You mind me saying something? About that friend of yours?'

Annie ignored the proffered hand and shrugged. Go ahead. Nothing could surprise her any more.

'He never wanted for company,' he said.

'Women?'

'Of course. You were the last.'

Annie nodded. Then her gaze settled on the straw hat.

'And up there? Your poor scalp?'

'Better,' he grunted.

Book Two

Book Two

7

BERLIN, FRIDAY 10 FEBRUARY 1939

Hans Otto Zimmermann.

Canaris had summoned him to his office for the early evening of this chill grey winter day, anticipating the need to share Hitler's latest thoughts on what the Thousand Year Reich might expect in the months to come. Hours ago, along with a sizeable gathering of senior commanders, German's Head of Military Intelligence had settled in one of the front seats at the Kroll Opera House, a notepad on his knee, to await the *Führer*'s arrival, and now – stamping the snow from his boots – he mounted ten flights of stairs in the Bendlerstrasse to find Zimmermann occupying a battered leather armchair in the *Abwehr Direktor*'s outer office.

Zimmermann. A handful of senior *Abwehr* officers knew him as 'HOZ', though his codeword, rarely used, was 'Erasmus'. He'd come to military intelligence as part of Canaris' early determination to expand the agency, and his current rank of *Oberst*, conferred before he was even thirty, was a tribute to the many talents Canaris had sensed from the moment they'd met.

For one thing, with his lean good looks and his faultless dress sense, he was quietly impressive. For another, so unlike most of the figures that haunted the upper reaches of the Reich dung heap, he was totally at ease in the larger world beyond the current German frontiers. He was fluent in almost as many languages as Canaris himself. A visit to a theatre or an art gallery was a pleasure he both sought and enjoyed. And – most important of all – he understood the overwhelming need to keep his own counsel.

Regardless of how many times they might meet, how many conversations they might share, no one in the Bendlerstrasse really knew where Zimmermann truly stood on any issue, including his sexuality. Even Canaris himself, who'd long ago made the judgement that Zimmermann's patriotism – his loyalty to an older, half-forgotten Germany – was sound, knew better than to venture beyond a certain point when it came to the many ways his rising star chose to organise his private life. Except that now was different.

'*Komm.*'

Canaris unbuttoned his overcoat and led the way into his office. The sight of the *Direktor*'s camp bed, and the blanket-shrouded basket that still seemed to smell of wet dog, drew the faintest nod of what might have been approval from Zimmermann. The dog had been banished to a draughty kennel in Canaris' back garden after disgracing itself at a parade to mark the *Führer*'s birthday, but the *Direktor*, unusually, had never mustered the energy to get rid of the basket. Zimmermann wasn't alone in speculating about the real thrust of the basket's survival. Was Canaris turning his back on the showy baubles that decorated so many of the senior lairs along the Wilhelmstrasse? Was this little *gemütlich* gesture a way of keeping his distance from the other tribal chiefs?

'So how was our Leader?' Zimmermann asked.

'Our Leader?' Canaris settled himself behind his desk, musing on Zimmermann's question. 'Madness,' he murmured at last. 'The man is utterly grotesque.'

'*Lebensraum?*'

'Of course. And lots of it. The German problem of space, as he likes to call it these days, kept us enthralled for more than two hours. I don't doubt he's serious, far from it, but when Goebbels tells me our *Führer* has something of Napoleon about him, I dare say he should go back to his history books. A masterful overture, Zimmermann, but a final movement you'd be wise to avoid.'

Zimmermann nodded, said nothing. These last few weeks since Christmas, Canaris had drawn him into a series of confidences about last year's plot to head off Hitler's determination to tear Czechoslovakia apart. Across Berlin, thanks to quiet conversations behind locked doors, senior figures had agreed that the real interests of Germany would be best served by a change of leadership. A detailed plan to seize the *Führer* and stage a military coup in Berlin had won covert support from a number of key generals, as well as figures from within the *Abwehr*, and would – in Canaris' estimation – have ended the *Führer*-madness.

Alas, the British and the French had bent the knee in the face of Hitler's many threats and given their support to what Hitler described as a cast-iron set of undertakings. The scrap of paper signed at Munich, as Canaris had said at the time, would prove a death sentence for the Czechs, and later for both the French and the British.

'These people are for the pot, Zimmermann. First he'll skin them, then he'll boil them, and then he'll eat them. They'll all get the treatment. They'll all end up in the Greater Reich, along with a number of other ghost countries who should be paying greater attention. There are two mysteries about our Leader, first that he spells it all out, exactly what he plans to do, and second that no one ever listens.'

'Or believes?'

'Precisely. This afternoon he couldn't have been plainer. What he has in mind are extreme measures, and I don't doubt for a moment that he means it. Extreme in ambition, and extreme in execution. The last time we met, he wanted word on what he might expect from the Czechs in Prague. I warned him about their armaments industry, just the way I briefed him about their fortifications on the western border back last year. Tanks, I told him. Emplaced artillery. Minefields sewn with a touch of that Bohemian magic. But he dismisses it all. He believes small print is for small people. We're back in the Opera House, Zimmermann. The larger the gestures on stage, the more often he can bring us to our feet.'

Zimmermann nodded. He couldn't fault a single element in this analysis, neither did he want to, but he knew the darkness around Canaris was thickened by enemies far closer to home.

'And *Onkel Heine*?'

'*Onkel Heine* assumes history is on his side. War awaits us everywhere, Zimmermann, and the deepest wounds will be self-inflicted, here in Berlin.'

Onkel Heine was Heinrich Himmler, head of the *Schutzstaffel*, or SS, an organisation that started life as Hitler's Praetorian Guard and whose territorial ambitions knew no bounds. Their intelligence arm, the *Sicherheitsdienst*, was already gobbling up *Abwehr* turf, a feast Canaris was determined to bring to an end.

'Himmler,' he said wearily, 'will do his master's bidding, which is another reason for reading that wretched book. On paper, the fate of the Jews and the Slavs and anyone else unlucky enough not to be German reads like the ravings of a lunatic. *Onkel Heine*, alas, is a masterful organiser and has no sense of the grotesque. Neither will he think twice about putting the Israels and Saras of this world out of their misery. All he needs is opportunity and in that sense he and our *Führer* speak the same language. Unduly harsh, do you think? Or the simplest and most savage of truths? This afternoon, I fear, was merely a pause in the journey. The real question, as ever, is where it will take us all.'

Zimmermann nodded. Like other senior officers in the *Abwehr*, he had no time for either *Mein Kampf* or any of Himmler's wilder Aryan fantasies but it was wise to have a healthy regard for some of the SD's intelligence officers, and for the sheer weight of Himmler's presence at the *Führer*'s elbow. Both he and Canaris understood only too well that survival in Hitler's Reich depended on never kidding yourself. You had to be ahead of the game. You had to be imagining what might happen next year, and the year after that. And you had, above all, to be right.

'So?'

Canaris at last permitted himself a smile. The question, that single word, expressed the essence of Zimmermann. We understand the odds we face. The question now is what we do about them.

'Spain,' Canaris murmured. 'Franco. Spring will bring him victory. The battles on the Ebro have put paid to the Republicans. London and Paris will recognise his regime next week or perhaps the week after. Madrid will fall before Easter if not earlier, and after that their wretched civil war will be over. On this, I take it, we both agree.'

'Of course.'

'Good. Which takes us back to our little *Franquito*. Your thoughts on what the man might do next?'

'He'll be knocking at our door again. I guarantee it,' Zimmermann said.

'Asking for what?'

'He needs arms, food, fuel. He has a country to run and his enemies haven't gone away. Above all, he wants a seat at our table. *Der Führer? Il Duce? El Caudillo?* The man can't help himself. He's dreamed of medals, of preferment, of total control all his life and nothing has changed. You're right. He's within weeks of winning but victory won't be enough.'

'But he has nothing to trade, Zimmermann, nothing to bring to the table. Spain is half-dead. He's knocked it to pieces. It's exhausted. On the face of it there's so very little left but in our game mere impressions will never be our friend.'

Zimmermann held the older man's gaze. He understood the way Canaris conducted his affairs, approaching every problem, every challenge, every situation the way a wise predator circles his prey, looking for the unexpected angle, the neglected opportunity. His years of working for this man had taught him a great deal, not least because Canaris' temperament so closely resembled Zimmermann's own mistrust of the obvious.

'Go on, Herr *Direktor*,' he murmured.

Canaris produced a bottle of schnapps from his desk drawer, a gesture so unusual that Zimmermann raised an eyebrow in surprise. Unbidden, he fetched two glasses from the mantelpiece over the unused fireplace. After a toast to sanity, Canaris returned to the aftermath of his afternoon at the Kroll Opera House.

'That fool Ribbentrop turned up after Hitler left,' he said. 'Luckily, he was drunk. As you well know, he's never liked us, largely I imagine because we've never bought the lies he's fed his lord and master. When it comes to abroad, Hitler can be putty in his hands. The man speaks English. The man's well connected in London and Paris. But what Hitler has never properly fathomed are the enemies he's made. The English think he's boorish, and stupid, and clumsy, and far too loud, and they're right. As it happens, that didn't stop Hitler making him Foreign Minister and now the oaf wants to teach us a lesson. Largely by turning conversation into one long boast.'

'This afternoon?'

'Indeed.'

'Boasting about what?'

'The year to come. Happily we were alone, which made things a great deal easier. Even sober, Ribbentrop has no sense when someone might be taking advantage. Drunk, he's virtually defenceless. Press the right buttons, murmur softly in his ear, and he'll tell you everything.'

Canaris took a playful sip of schnapps, evidently enjoying the memory. Ribbentrop, he said, had offered a tally of *Führer*-triumphs to come. Hints of a deal with Moscow. The nonsense about Poland to be settled at the latest by September. Next year's campaign season to open with a descent on Norway, Denmark, and then – most important of all – Belgium and France. By then, the British would be suing for peace, negotiations which Ribbentrop would be pleased to handle personally.

None of this, of course, had come as a surprise to Canaris. On the contrary, the *Abwehr* had already assembled most parts of the *Führer*-jigsaw, largely on the basis of demands for specific intelligence, but as Ribbentrop was draining the bottle, Canaris had played dumb and asked what might happen if the British refused to surrender.

'And?'

'He thought that highly unlikely.'

'But if it happened?'

'Then pressure might be applied elsewhere.'

'Like?'

'Gibraltar,' Canaris reached for his glass again. 'A thought, may I say it, that has also occurred to me.'

'Franco kicks the British into the sea?'

'We kick the British into the sea. Does that require Franco's help? Of course it does. The Pyrenees are his front door. We need the key, and after that we make our way south and attend to the business in hand. With the British gone, we can close the Mediterranean to their shipping. A promise like that will put a very big smile on faces in the Chancellery, as Ribbentrop knows only too well.'

'He's shared this already?'

'So he tells me. He foresees yet another meeting between us and them. That means Hitler and Franco. Hitler will summon him to Berlin, or perhaps the Berghof. Franco will prefer to meet on Spanish soil, or perhaps the French border. As ever, it will be a question of face.'

'Soon?'

'I doubt it. Much has to happen first. But that's hardly the point, Zimmermann. You're in a room with the fool Ribbentrop. He wants to show off. He wants to humiliate us. He wants to stamp on our ugly faces and grind the *Abwehr* into the dirt. So how does he do that?'

'*Onkel Heinrich*,' Zimmermann said softly.

'Indeed. The clue is in the rank. SS *Gruppenführer* Joachim von Ribbentrop. This is a man who can't resist a new uniform. Dress him in black, put the death's head on his cap, and *Onkel Heine* has the man in his pocket.' Canaris paused, then smiled. 'Opportunities again, Zimmermann. Thanks to Gibraltar, Spain will become the honeypot. No one in this city will be able to afford to ignore it. That's where reputations will be made. First Ribbentrop. And then *Onkel Heine*. They'll need to be there. They'll need to be visible. Ribbentrop we can discount. *Onkel Heine* we can't. Unless we stop his nonsense, we may regret the consequences.'

'Meaning?'

'Meaning we need to be thinking ahead, Zimmermann. We need to be devious and nimble and alert for every possibility. We need to decapitate the SS, to bring it to its knees, and for this reason *Onkel Heine* deserves a bullet in his fat head. Organising an operation like that on home soil, no fingerprints, is near impossible, which is why the wretched man so rarely leaves the Reich. Thanks to his own private army he feels secure here but if ambition takes him abroad, and he has to lower his guard, the situation might be very different. The key to that delightful prospect? Just a single word?'

Zimmermann reached for his glass, studied it for a moment, then smiled.

'Spain,' he murmured. 'You're right.'

8

Exactly a week later, on Friday 17 February, Zimmermann flew to Munich, where he had supper with a close friend at an address near the *Englischergarten*. He stayed overnight in the apartment, and the following morning that same friend drove him to the Alpine village of Oberstdorf in the Allegau, which Zimmermann happened to know rather better than he let on. Canaris, whose preparatory work in situations like these was never less than faultless, had instructed him to be in the restaurant of the Hotel Trettach by noon. A table had been reserved in the name of Constanz and he should expect a guest, a British MI5 agent called Tam Moncrieff.

Although he'd never met him, Zimmermann knew of Tam Moncrieff. He came from a military background of some kind and now he had a desk at the St James's Street headquarters of the British Security Service, plus a working relationship with an *Abwehr* agent called Wilhelm Schultz. It was Schultz, following a brief discussion with Canaris, who'd made contact through a cut-out in Stockholm. Schultz and Moncrieff, it seemed, went back to an episode on the edges of last year's plot to mount the coup against Hitler.

Moncrieff, said Canaris, spoke perfect German and – more to the point – carried the scars of a brutal interrogation in the basement of the Gestapo's Berlin headquarters in Prinz-Albrecht-Strasse. While he was no friend of *Onkel Heine*, he had a great deal of respect for Willi Schultz, one of the old *Sturmabteilung* streetfighters who'd swapped his brown shirt and his scuffed boots for a desk in the Bendlerstrasse. In Canaris' dry phrase, Moncrieff might be open to the prospect of a little mischief-making in the growing chasm between Berlin's rival intelligence agencies. Not least when it came to the necessary business of laying a false trail or two.

'You want Moncrieff to shoot *Onkel Heine*?' The prospect appeared to amuse Zimmermann.

'God, no.' Canaris had looked briefly pained. 'British fingerprints are all we need. Money might be perfect. Enough to hire a marksman we can trust to deliver.'

'Spanish?'

'Of course. The best of these people are always up for hire.'

So far, so good. The journey from Munich took nearly three hours, thanks to military traffic, and the Hotel Trettach lay in the centre of town. Getting out of his friend's car, Zimmermann could hear the bubbling of water from the nearby river, and when he turned to check the Nebelhornbahn, he caught the glint of sunshine as one of the cable cars surged up towards the crescent of Alpine peaks. Oberstdorf, he knew, was the most southern of the Reich's townships. Head any further into the mountains and you'd have to abandon your car and trust one of the footpaths that snaked up towards the Swiss border.

'Is everything ready?' His friend was an older man, Walther. His legs were never made for lederhosen, but Zimmermann liked that he didn't care. Winter in the Allegau expects bare knees, he'd told Zimmermann in the car, and a wise man does its bidding.

'Everything's fine,' Zimmermann said. 'Except you promised me snow.'

There was no snow, not down here among the scatter of pretty chalets, though the mountains gleamed white against the blueness of the sky. Zimmermann had been here in this same town a month before Christmas, feeling the pulse of the place before he made a decision whether to go ahead or not, and he thoroughly approved of what he'd found.

On the bleaker days behind his *Abwehr* desk, Zimmermann had begun to suspect there wasn't a square metre of the Reich in which Nazism hadn't taken root but Oberstdorf had proved him wrong. Thanks to tourists, it had spirit and money and a bottomless sense of self-respect. It had a paid-up Nazi mayor who was happy to shield the town's Jews. It thrived on generations of foresters, farmers, innkeepers, nuns and mountaineers, and Zimmermann knew that these folk had no love for the paunchy zealots from the Munich bierkellers. Layabouts, leeches and profiteers, the town's butcher had muttered in front of a nodding queue of local women. Those *Untermenschen* don't belong here.

The restaurant was already full. Zimmermann, casually dressed for the weekend, scanned the tables. The only one with a single diner lay beside the big picture window, in the full glare of the winter sun. His back to the window, the diner was no more than a silhouette. Tall, Zimmermann thought. Big hands cupping the spread of the menu, and a hint of a back problem in the way he sat.

Zimmermann signalled a nearby waiter and enquired about a Herr Constanz. When the waiter indicated the lone figure beside the window, Zimmermann asked for the thin gauze of the curtain to be pulled to shield the worst of the glare before he settled at the table.

'You're Herr Zimmermann?' Moncrieff was already looking up, the menu abandoned.

'I am. I also answer to Hans.'

Moncrieff nodded. While the waiter attended to the curtain, he gestured slightly awkwardly at the spare seat. Zimmermann was right about the back problem. The specialists the Gestapo used in the Prinz-Albrecht-Strasse basement certainly knew their trade.

'Beyond the bottom of the stairs, the place stinks of bleach and loose bowels,' Zimmermann was making himself comfortable. 'The first time I got the tour, the smell disgusted me which I gather was rather the point. Himmler's people live in caves, always have done. Sunshine ...' he gestured at the window, '... makes them nervous.'

'You know about what happened?' Moncrieff beckoned him closer.

'Of course. It's a matter of record. The Gestapo assume we never check, that we lack the means, and in both cases they're wrong. As a matter of interest I also know the club Herr Kriesky took you to. A little fuck-palace called the Kasbah out beyond Bergmannkiez? Masks for the clientele and boys to do your bidding? Am I right?'

'You are. I'm impressed. It's Tam, by the way ...' Moncrieff offered a handshake across the table, '... and you were right about the bleach, too.'

'Kriesky was an American banker.'

'He was.'

'So why did you kill him?'

'Because he was greedy. Because he had a hand in the murder of good friends of mine. And because he chose the wrong time, the wrong place and the wrong person to make it all come right again.'

'You said no? You turned him down?'

'I broke his neck. Do it right and it takes a second. The Gestapo make it last much longer, as you doubtless know.'

Zimmermann at last released Moncrieff's big hand and smiled. 'My apologies,' he said.

'For what?'

'For everything. For Kriesky. For those urchins in the Kasbah. And most of all for our friends in the Prinz-Albrecht-Strasse. Your German is impeccable, by the way, and you deserve a proper conversation. *Komm.*' He nodded towards the door. 'I have a friend outside and he knows a much better place than this.'

Zimmermann escorted Moncrieff from the hotel restaurant, and out into the sunshine, keeping an eye open for whatever back-up Moncrieff may have brought along. When no one else emerged from the hotel, he took a long look around the parking space before opening the rear door of the Mercedes and gesturing for Moncrieff to get in. The Englishman, Schultz had told him, was in fact a Scot, a difference that seemed to matter. From the parking lot, no one appeared interested enough to follow them.

Zimmermann's friend and chauffeur engaged gear. After introductions, Walther nodded at Moncrieff in the rear-view mirror, a greeting of sorts, and then headed the big saloon towards the mountains. When the road ran out, he took an unsurfaced path to the left. Crusts of snow in the frosted grass crunched under the wheels. Next came a wooden bridge over a river that Walther appeared to know well. The planking looked far too ancient to bear the weight of the car but he aligned the wheels with a flick of his thin wrists and, seconds later, after an ominous rumbling, they were back on dry land.

'Am I still expecting lunch?' Moncrieff enquired.

They stopped barely minutes later in the lee of a huge rock veined with lichen and moss. It was at this point that the wideness of the path ran out. Walther nursed the big car into a seven-point turn until it was pointing back towards the river and the bridge. From the boot he produced two heavy blankets and a sizeable wicker basket, spreading the blankets in the sunshine and worrying over the absence of a corkscrew for two bottles of Riesling.

'Here.' Moncrieff offered a heavy-looking penknife. '... or do you want me to do it?'

Walther, delighted, handed Moncrieff both bottles and rummaged in the basket for glasses. The bottles uncorked, Moncrieff wanted to know where the path led next. Walther, busy in the basket again, ignored the question.

'Hans?' Moncrieff was looking at Zimmermann.

'It goes to Sonthafen. That's about six miles from here. *Ordensburgen*? You've heard of these places?'

'Adolf Hitler Schools? Finishing academies for the cream of the cream? You're telling me they actually *exist*?'

'Of course. Teenage boys. The fittest, the blondest, the most racially pure, hand-picked to steer the Reich to greater glory. You know what happens on Friday nights? *Onkel Heine*'s local helpers put the prettiest Oberstdorf girls on the bus and send them over to Sonthafen for folk dancing and whatever else. The delicate expression is intermingling but it boils down to a weekly exercise in eugenics. Does the name Heckmair mean anything to you?'

'He's a mountaineer,' Moncrieff said at once. 'He climbed the north face of the Eiger last year. Him and three others. Goebbels couldn't wait to make him famous.'

'You know about the mountains?'

'I live among the mountains. No one's ever heard of the Cairngorms because Scotland's off the map for the English, but that's where I grew up. Mountain people are different. Different blood pressure. Different view of the world. Show a mountain man an impossible climb and he'll prove you wrong.'

'You're right,' Zimmermann was quietly impressed. 'The Eiger has yielded to the irresistible force of German resolve. That's Goebbels again. The north face didn't fall to Heckmair, nor the other three, but to the miracle of German *will*. When the entire population believes this shit, Moncrieff, we're all in trouble. But you know who wouldn't buy it?'

'Tell me.'

'Heckmair himself. Hitler invited him to Nuremberg last year for the rally. I understand you were there.'

'I was. A little guy called Dieter Merz performed over the Zeppelinfeld in a Bf-109. Unforgettable flying. But tell me about Heckmair.'

'Hitler had him over to the Deutscher Hof where he always stays. Thanks to Goebbels, Heckmair was already a Nazi saint. They watched the torchlight procession together from Hitler's balcony. The word Heckmair used afterwards was "disturbing". This was a man of the mountains, a man you'd recognise, a man alone, a man who understands gravity. He told me later that there was no room for grandstanding or mass hysteria on a difficult traverse, and when Goebbels tried to recruit him after the rally, full-time stardom guaranteed, the man refused. He lives in Oberstdorf now. Still climbs. Probably always will.'

Walther had laid out a picnic on one of the rugs, a delicate selection of local meats, cheeses and pickles, and was now rocking back on his haunches, looking hard at Zimmermann.

'Tell him about that tailor of yours,' Walther nodded vaguely south. 'Tell him what happened.'

'Why?'

'Because you've made a new friend, Hans. And that doesn't happen often.'

Zimmermann was helping himself to a plate of assorted *Wurst*. When he glanced up, Moncrieff gestured for him to carry on.

'His name's Groenstein,' Zimmermann murmured. 'He was my tailor in Berlin.'

'Jewish?'

'Of course. Appearances are important in our business. Who else would I trust?'

Moncrieff smiled. Walther was right. There was an iciness about Zimmermann, a sense of a man with a wary eye for life's sharper edges, a martinet who didn't tolerate fools, but Moncrieff sensed warmth as well. Trust had no place in the world of intelligence but sharing dealings you'd had with your Jewish tailor, if true, would be rare as well as reckless, especially given Moncrieff's role in MI5.

'So what happened?'

'You really want to know?'

'I do.'

'Why?'

'Because you'll have a proposition afterwards,' Moncrieff murmured, 'and it might help to get to know you a little better.'

Zimmermann nodded, forked a disc of pickled cucumber into his mouth, then dabbed at his lips with a fold of handkerchief. His every movement, his every sentence, Moncrieff realised, carried a certain polish, nothing untidy, nothing left to chance. Just now, he was studying a perfect fan of thinly sliced *Blutwurst*.

'This was the back end of last year, the week after Kristallnacht. Groenstein had a wonderful business, and I got the impression he was prepared to sit things out, but his wife definitely wasn't.'

'Children?'

'Three. Two little girls and an older boy, all of them delightful. Lovely house, decent neighbours, but the wrong name. In the end he phoned me and asked for a meeting.'

'Asked?'

'Begged. This isn't a word I'd ever associate with Groenstein. It obviously meant things were serious.'

Moncrieff nodded. News of Kristallnacht had arrived in London the day after Nazi mobs had run riot in towns and cities across Germany, smashing the windows of Jewish businesses, torching synagogues and beating up anyone luckless enough to be wearing a yellow star. Colleagues at MI5 headquarters in St James's Street had difficulty believing some of the reports, but after his encounter with Gestapo interrogators Moncrieff shuddered as the first photographs came through. Pavements littered with broken glass. Jews sprawled and bleeding in the gutter. Moncrieff had looked this regime in the eye, and he knew it was capable of anything.

'So what did you do?' he asked Zimmermann.

'I told him they had to get out, all of them, and quickly. They had money, of course, but that could never leave the country. Neither would most of what they owned. A bag each, I told him. No more.'

'You *organised* this?'

'I did. I liked the man. The suits he made me even smelled right, perfect stitching, never a corner cut. I laid false trails, of course. You'd understand that. I told him Hamburg or perhaps Bremerhaven for the crossing to New York. I even laid hands on some paperwork that might suggest an American sponsor. In a way, Moncrieff, it was a page out of his own book, everything perfectly prepared, perfectly scissored.'

He fell silent for a moment, helping himself to another curl of wurst, and as he did so Moncrieff caught the rapt attention in Walther's face. This man loves him, he thought. For this and maybe a thousand other reasons, Zimmermann knows how to touch a special nerve.

'You brought him here?' Moncrieff asked. 'To Oberstdorf?'

'I did, all of them, the whole brood. I'd heard of the place. Most of these people pay lip service to the regime. In many ways it was perfect. It had the feel of the old Germany.'

'And?'

'I drove them down from Berlin myself. I'd paid for two men to take them on to the Swiss border. They moved at night, sleeping in barns during the day. I have contacts in Bern, as you might imagine. They were met on the border and to the best of my knowledge they're now living in Zurich.'

Moncrieff nodded. He'd never anticipated a story like this. A man so disciplined, so watchful, so tightly buttoned, and yet so reckless.

'Remarkable,' he said.

'It happens, Moncrieff,' Zimmermann shrugged. 'Under certain circumstances the Swiss can be more than accommodating.'

'I meant the escape itself, the journey out.'

'They were tough people, even the wife, even the young ones.'

'I meant your own role.'

'My own role?' The softest laugh. 'Sometimes this bunch of thugs leave you no choice. We live in a world of mirrors, Moncrieff. You can hide from the truth for only so long.'

'So no regrets?'

'None. Except it's now impossible to find a decent tailor.'

They finished the picnic. The wind had begun to stir, bringing tiny flakes of snow from a nearby drift, and any warmth in the sun had gone. A glance from Zimmermann prompted Walther to start tidying up the remains of the food, but when Moncrieff stirred and offered to help, Zimmermann asked him to sit down again.

'Tell me about Schultz,' he said.

'You know the man. What is there to tell?'

'I mean your own impressions. Perhaps your own relationship.'

Moncrieff studied him for a long moment, trying to anticipate where this conversation was going.

'I'd give him a job tomorrow,' Moncrieff said at last. 'I think he's honest. I know he's effective. Talented brawlers often make for lousy spies but that doesn't seem to be the case with Schultz.'

'He says you have jurisdiction in Gibraltar. Might that be right?'

'Yes. MI5 doesn't regard it as abroad, never has. It's a bit of England attached to the bottom of Spain. Why do you ask?'

Zimmermann refused to answer the question. Instead he raised the issue of Moncrieff's sister service, MI6.

'We watch these people,' he said carefully. 'Occasionally they're good, but not often. Schultz isn't surprised you found a home in MI5.'

'Tell him I'm flattered. MI5 found me, incidentally. But that's often the way it works.'

'And your brothers in MI6? Do you have a view?'

'They're bred from a different blood line, often literally. Turf matters in our world, probably in yours, too, from what we hear.'

'This is Schultz talking?'

'Schultz and others. Himmler has a talent for making enemies. He also has friends at court, powerful friends in the highest places. In your shoes, Hans, I might be looking for something else to do with my life.'

'Really?' There was no warmth in Zimmermann's smile. 'You think I might become a tailor?'

'I think you might be taking precautions, baiting traps for the men in black. Otherwise you'll wake up one morning and find Waffen-SS tanks on the Bendlerstrasse.'

'As bad as that?'

'Probably worse. At the Prinz-Albrecht-Strasse they drown you in slow motion. I've heard people I respect thinking that might be the best of deaths. Believe me, it isn't.'

'But you survived.'

'In part, yes.' Moncrieff was frowning now. 'What do you want, Hans? What can we do for you? The picnic was more than welcome. It's been a pleasure meeting you and your friend. I have a false passport in my pocket because the Gestapo have banned me from ever coming here again, but I have the warmest memories of the way it used to be for us all. Getting back to those days would be a real pleasure. Just tell me how we could help.' He paused for a moment, then reached for his coat. 'You can do that? Before we all freeze to death?'

9

A little over a month later, towards the end of March, Annie Wrenne found herself on the dockside at Alicante, tugged backwards and forwards among a vast mass of refugees, utterly helpless to control which direction she might take next. It had been this way all morning, the crowd growing thicker and thicker as more women and children somehow threaded themselves onto the warm concrete, hunting for the tiniest space for their children and their pathetic assortment of bags.

The tallest among them had eyes only for the English boat that had arrived a couple of days ago. Some people said it had been carrying a cargo of coal. Others hinted at a darker manifest. But either way the only thing that mattered was where it might be going next. France? North Africa? Mexico? The rumours had spread all day, more tinder to the conflagration that was the climax to this terrible war, but everyone knew that the destination was irrelevant. The boat was now said to be empty and the only thing that mattered was getting away from the twin jaws of the rebel advance before Franco's savages massacred them all.

Annie had come here, yet again, as a volunteer. She knew many of the faces on this quayside, mothers from the towering slum that was the Pablo Iglesias. She'd worked there day and night for most of the last two years, occasionally fed snippets of news from foreign contacts in Murcia, and she knew that this scene of utter chaos on a warm afternoon on a once-pleasant stretch of coast was the sum of countless international failures. The British and the French had clung grimly to the fig leaf of non-intervention while the Germans and the Italians had reduced city after city to smoking ruins.

The callousness and cynicism of two countries she counted as her own had often reduced her to despair. And now, literally fighting for room to breathe, she recognised how helpless she'd become. If the crowd swayed to the left, she went with it. If a ripple of movement took her towards the heavily guarded gangplank, then she too felt a tiny tremor of anticipation. Once aboard this boat, once they were at sea, there would be hundreds of women who'd once again need her help. Which, in a way, was all she had left to offer.

By the end of the afternoon, she became aware of the smell. That, too, took her back to the Pablo Iglesias. It was the stench of latrines without doors, of babies without nappies, of the ravages of a brutal diet and little sleep. Half close her eyes, surrender to the press of thousands of bodies, and she returned without a moment's effort to the ceaseless battle to get through to the end of yet another exhausting day. Refugees in this war were like an army of extras in a movie she never wanted to see again. Disease, malnutrition, even family quarrels that turned ugly, took many of them away, yet there were always new faces at the unguarded door to the street, fresh demands on the fast-depleting stock of Quaker resources, and Quaker goodwill.

Where these people came from had remained largely a mystery. War, Annie had concluded, was the mother of a million orphans and there never seemed enough time to dignify each swollen belly with a story of its own. No one had thought to provide helpful details, the way you might label a suitcase, and as a direct result her life in Murcia had become one long blur, repetitive, exhausting, slightly out of focus, until it ended here, in the war's final paragraph, with a crush of abandoned souls fighting for the blessings of yet more misery.

The smell, she thought again. Something new, something she'd never quite recognised before, a sour sweetness that hung like a miasma above these thousands of heads. In an act close to surrender, she let her mind roam free, hunting for that one word that would tell her what was happening. Then came a collective sigh that quickly thickened into something far more urgent as a rumour swept through the crowd. People were shouting. Women were screaming. The guards had stepped away from the gangplank. Either people were starting to board or the boat was sailing away. Annie sought an answer from the woman beside her, but however she phrased the question the woman could do nothing but shrug and hold her tiny baby a little closer. Then Annie got a proper look at her face, hollowed by hunger, and at the expression in her eyes and that single word was suddenly all too obvious. It was fear.

'*Señora?*'

At first Annie hadn't noticed the lightest touch on her shoulder. Hours of jostling as the crowd got thicker left no space for delicate gestures like this. Then the question came again, a voice in her ear, the warmth of a stranger's breath on her cheek, and she struggled round to find herself looking up at a face that had always been unforgettable. The half-closed eye, the droop of his mouth, the trickle of saliva caught in the rough tangle of beard, the tuft of black hair erupting from his crooked nose. The last time she'd seen this man he'd been begging for a coin or two from passing strangers in the plaza outside the cathedral back in Murcia. She'd attended to the ruins of his scalp. They'd shared the beginnings of a conversation. He'd even told her his real name but that had long gone and all she could remember was the word the street kids shouted.

'*El Diablo?*' She was trying to back away.

'Carlos Ortega.'

She nodded, lost for words, aware only of his hand closing on her arm as he began to force a passage through the crowd.

'What are you doing? What's going on?'

'Trust me.'

'Why? Let go of me.'

'This is for the best. Believe me.'

'You're not getting on the boat?'

'No one's getting on the boat.'

'How do you know?'

'Trust me. By nightfall, most of these people will be dead.'

Heads turned in alarm. Nothing was private. Annie was staring at him. The last two years had taught her a great deal and one of the harder lessons was that literally anything could happen in a war like this. The comfortable assumptions of her former life had melted under fire. Unseen aircraft could kill dozens in seconds, and did. Rampaging rebels locked hundreds of prisoners in bull rings and slaughtered every last man. City gutters ran with blood for no discernible reason. There was no script to this mad carnival of violence, no logic, little explanation, just word of yet another atrocity, passing from mouth to mouth until disbelief turned to numbness, and you shrugged and did your best to stay alive and carry on. So why shouldn't this ruin of a man be right? He, above all, should understand the terrifying marriage of the wrong time and the wrong place.

'How do you *know*?' she asked again, but already she suspected the question was irrelevant. He just did.

'Trust me,' he grunted for the third time. 'This is a kind of thank-you.'

It took them nearly an hour to make it back through the press of bodies to the dock entrance, Annie reluctant at first, haunted by this act of desertion. She might have lost sight of the women and kids from the Pablo Iglesias but they'd still need her, still be counting on her help when it mattered. She could try and see to it that they got on board, that they were looked after. If the boat was English, then so was the crew. Her charges would need a translator as well as a guardian angel, they'd need support of every kind, but then the crowd began to thin and Annie caught sight of armed militia tumbling out of the back of a line of trucks and she quickened her pace beside the bulk of Ortega. Whatever other injuries he'd sustained in the ruins of the Madrid church didn't appear to bother him, and he moved with the purposeful lope of a big man in a hurry.

Ahead, Annie could see the bright stucco of the houses along the waterfront, shaded by a line of palm trees. There were shuttered cafés and yellow trams and the long white road she'd seen earlier that wound up the hillside towards the Castillo de Santa Barbara. Half close your eyes, she thought, and this could be peacetime, a sleepy spring afternoon with nothing to do but enjoy the sunshine and perhaps a stroll along the beach. But then she paused briefly to catch her breath and glanced over her shoulder. The dock was still black with refugees and the militia from the lorries were herding newcomers in through the open gates. Was this how you organised a massacre? With shouted oaths and the butt of your rifle? Who gave the order to fire? And how many men would it need to tidy up afterwards?

Ortega had reached the main road. Impatient, he gestured for her to join him. He had a car nearby. They needed to be away from this place.

'But why? Just tell me.'

Ortega looked down at her. She didn't know what to make of the smile, in fact she wasn't sure it was a smile at all, but there was no mistaking the big finger pointing at the sky.

'Planes?' she at last began to understand.

'Of course. The Germans are running out of places to bomb. First the port, and then the town.'

'And you *know* this?'

'I do, yes.'

He took her arm again, waiting for a horse and cart to pass, and then steered her into the maze of streets across the road. The car was an enormous limousine with a sleek body and gleaming black paintwork. The bonnet seemed to go on forever and the line of the wheel arch as it swept backwards and down to become the running board was, to Annie, a work of art. The unlikely presence of a vehicle like this was further brightened by a harassed Civil Guard shooing off a bunch of street kids. With a curt nod, Ortega folded a note into his hand before peering hard at the bodywork, wetting a finger, and removing some imagined blemish.

'Hispano-Suiza,' he grunted.

Annie got in. The name meant nothing but the car smelled of old leather and new money. Neither had any place in the Spain she'd come to know but when she asked Ortega for more details he told her it didn't matter. They were in the delivery business.

'So where are you taking it?'

'Back where it belongs,' he started the engine. 'Isn't that the sweetest sound you ever heard?'

Annie could hear barely anything, which appeared to be the point. They were purring out of the town, Annie keeping her leather bag close. She was wearing a money belt around her waist beneath her blouse. She'd hand-sewn it only days ago, knowing she'd have to leave Murcia. Just now it was damp with sweat but it had more than enough room for the handful of pesetas she'd managed to muster for the journey north.

'You came to find me,' she said at last. 'You weren't back there by accident.' Ortega nodded. Mopped his ruined face with the back of his hand. Said nothing. 'So how did you know where I'd be?'

'I asked around.'

'Asked who?'

'The woman in the Quaker hotel. She said you were living with other nurses from the Pablo in a shared house. When I asked nicely, she gave me the address.'

'She had no right to do that. You're telling me you went there?'

'Yes.'

'When?'

'Three days ago. The place was empty except for a Canadian woman. Glasses. Thin. She was packed and ready. I told her what a friend you'd been to me,' his thick fingers settled briefly on the suture scars that latticed his scalp. 'We talked about you a little. She knew the war was at an end and she said you'd all been making plans. Alicante, she told me. And then wherever next.'

Annie nodded. Béatrice was a *Québécoise* who also worked at the Pablo Iglesias. She'd helped Annie in all kinds of ways in the early days, and they'd stayed good friends.

'You thought I'd be following her?'

'I knew you would. I guessed you all would. I went back after she'd gone. I found a note under your pillow with an Alicante address.'

'That's where I stayed last night. That's horrible.'

'Finding the note?'

'Looking in the first place. Tracking me down. What am I to you? Why go to all this trouble?'

'You helped me when it mattered.' Ortega's thick fingers were drumming on the huge steering wheel, his body swaying back and forth to some imagined music. 'When a man's on the bones of his arse, believe me, that's rare.'

'And things got better after that?'

'Yes. Up here first …' His fingers stroked his scalp again, '… then everywhere else.'

'You were still begging?'

'Still watching,' he shot her a glance. 'Watching's what I do. It helps to be curious in the first place but that's in the early days. After a while it becomes a way of life, something you can never shake off, something you can never do without. If you're lucky, it can even give you a living.'

'You mean money?'

'Yes.'

'Enough for a Hispano-Suiza?'

Ortega shot her a look, ignoring the joke. 'Enough to fill your belly. Enough to let you sleep at night. Enough to make you hungry for tomorrow.'

'More money?'

'More looking. Wars, believe me, are full of opportunity, especially wars like this.'

Annie nodded. In a way she only half-understood, she'd allowed herself to be kidnapped, to be plucked out of the chaos of the dockside before embarking on the shared risks of a voyage into the unknown. It was, she supposed, an act of trust, or perhaps of helplessness, but either way she realised that this tormented country had just dealt her another surprise hand, and that her sole responsibility was to ride along.

Watching, she thought. Remembering. Then a gruff word of appreciation to the gods of war. *Los desastres de la guerra*? Give this man pens and ink, and he could be Goya.

'So where are we going?' she asked after a while.

'Madrid,' Ortega grunted. 'Where else?'

'But Madrid's about to fall.'

'Exactly. Which is why this car's going home.'

The first roadblock lay fifteen kilometres west. By now, the file of refugees still trudging towards the coast had thinned to a trickle. Two trucks were parked across the road, nose to nose, guarded by Nationalist troops in uniform. This was the first time that Annie had taken a good look at Franco's soldiers and the contrast with the Republican militias were obvious: newish-looking carbines, sharp salutes for the sudden appearance of an officer, and a hint of respect as the latter bent to the car's open window.

Ortega produced what looked like a typed letter. The officer scanned it at a single glance, stepped backwards to admire the vehicle, and then waved Ortega on his way.

'He knows you? That man?'

'He knows how to read a *laissez-passer*.'

'You work for these people? You're one of them?'

'I work for whoever pays me best. Always have done.'

'Then the answer has to be yes. The Republicans have no money. Only the Nationalists got fat in this war.'

Ortega's bark of laughter filled the car.

'You think you're riding with the enemy? Is that it? The war's nearly over and at least you're still standing.' He tapped the clock on the dashboard. 'The Germans are half an hour away. The Condor bombers will be in the air by now.'

'You know this?'

'Of course.'

'How? Why?'

'Because they trust me. By midnight, Alicante will still be on fire.'

Annie nodded, knowing she had no choice but to believe him. All she could think of were the faces and the smell of the women on the dockside, and of the nurses from the Pablo who were doubtless among them. Fear never lies, she thought, fighting the urge to imagine the carnage to come. More bodies. Fresh blood. The harbour full of the dead and nearly dead.

'And when we get to Madrid ...?'

'You'll have a room of your own in a nice house in a decent area. The bombers haven't touched it and no shell ever landed there. Why? Because one day we knew the time would come to resume business as usual, and that time is now.'

'We?'

'We.'

'That sounds like imprisonment on my part.'

'Not at all. Back in Murcia you told me about your contacts at the university. Just now they may want translators. You need to restart work on that Goya book of yours and maybe a thousand other projects. As far as Madrid is concerned, Franco will bandage up the wounds, and brush our hair, and clean our teeth, and make us look respectable, and then we might be friends again.'

'How do you know all this? About me? About the Goya book?' Annie was staring at him, wondering what else Béatrice might have told him, appalled by the depth of his knowledge, by this sudden intimacy with a virtual stranger.

'Nothing in life is a secret ...' Ortega's finger slipped across his pitted cheek and settled briefly under his good eye, '... if you know where to look.'

10

Canaris returned to Salamanca the following morning. Madrid had fallen to rebel armies, effectively bringing the civil war to an end, and Canaris carried a personal message of congratulation from the Chancellery over the *Führer*'s signature. Expecting to meet Franco at the Bishop's Palace, he was greeted by General Orgaz who regretted that he had bad news.

'I'm afraid the *Generalissimo*,' a vague gesture towards an upper floor, 'is not well. The pressure of events, *Admiral* Canaris, coupled with a chest infection. Just now the *Caudillo* sleeps.'

Canaris expressed his sympathies and presented the letter from the Reich Chancellery. Orgaz studied the embossed seal on the back of the envelope for a moment and then weighed it briefly in his hand as if it might contain something suspicious. Then he looked up at Canaris again.

'I dare say we all have much to discuss. Perhaps tomorrow? Or the day after? The doctors will be attending again this evening. The *Caudillo* is a strong man. Naturally we hope for better news.'

Canaris could only nod. The last forty-eight hours, according to reports that had landed on his Berlin desk, had seen the bloodless surrender of city after city. Franco's armies had made an appearance, shaken the tree, and Jaén, Cartagena, Cuenca and Guadalajara had fallen into the Nationalists' lap. Last night, according to this morning's pilot on the flight south, the port of Alicante had been heavily bombed in a final spasm of violence before the Republicans prepared to sue for peace.

'The *Generalissimo* will awake to a new Spain,' Canaris murmured. 'Under the circumstances, I can think of no better tonic.'

Orgaz, he could tell, was enjoying this little exchange, two military men indulging themselves in a delicate pas-de-deux which wouldn't have disgraced a brace of diplomats. Franco may or may not be indisposed but nothing must ruffle the stillness of the waters between Madrid and Berlin.

'The *Caudillo* is much exercised by the loss of so many brave men,' Orgaz was looking grave. 'Already he has plans for a national monument. Do you know the country north-west of Madrid, by any chance?'

'I'm afraid I don't.'

'It's wild, mountainous, truly spectacular. When the opportunity presents itself, the *Caudillo* sometimes hunts there. A particular location has caught his attention. Next month, when the dust has settled and the country has caught its breath, we plan a visit. The Valley of the Fallen, *Admiral*. Everything worthwhile always starts with a title.'

Canaris did his best to look impressed. Spain, he knew, was a country where gestures like this truly mattered. Whether or not the war's survivors would get through the imminent shortage of more or less everything was anyone's guess but Franco clearly understood the importance of looking after the dead.

'You'll stay until the *Caudillo* is receiving visitors, *Admiral*? We can help in the matter of accommodations?'

Canaris shook his head and offered his apologies. He was, as ever, on the shortest of leashes. His presence was required back in Berlin and his master, eager for word from Spain, had little patience.

Orgaz said he understood. 'The *Caudillo* sends your *Führer* fraternal greetings,' he flashed a brief smile. 'Your victories in Austria and Czechoslovakia have been a lesson for us all, especially where France and Britain are concerned. These are challenging times, *Admiral*, and nothing speaks louder than action.'

'I'm sure the feeling's mutual, General Orgaz,' Canaris nodded at the envelope. 'Madrid perhaps? Next time we meet?'

Josef Veltiens, the Dutch arms dealer, had already arrived when Canaris returned to the airfield.

'Seppl ... you're early.' Canaris pumped his hand.

'No choice, I'm afraid. My nice Italian friends have lent me one of these for a month and their pilot has a date with a lady in town.'

Canaris was looking at the nearby aircraft. It was a three-engined Savoia-Marchetti, doubtless a veteran of countless bombing raids over Republican Spain.

'This is all for you?' Canaris was impressed.

'It's a horse and cart, my friend. It has to earn its living, just like me. With one hand they offer the plane and a sweet boy called Giuseppe who claims to be a pilot. With the other comes a shopping list you wouldn't believe. How come the Italians are in love with heavy tanks?'

'You should be knocking on the Czechs' door, Seppl. Now we have the key, I'm sure they'll give you the keenest prices.'

Veltiens nodded. Only weeks earlier, Hitler had sent the *Wehrmacht* into what remained of Czechoslovakia, and now controlled the entire country. Another fifteen million souls had been folded into the Greater Reich but the real prize was the Skoda arms factories in Pilsen. Czech artillery and tanks were both famed and much-feared if you happened to be on the receiving end, and even their small arms, always reliable, had flooded international markets.

Veltiens led the way to the aircraft. Low cloud was tumbling in from the west, blown by a chill wind, and there was a hint of rain in the air. The cavernous fuselage smelled of spilled kerosene with a lingering hint of vomit, but the empty two-man cockpit offered a little privacy, as well as warmth.

'You're early, *mein Admiral*.' Veltiens had settled in the pilot's seat. '*Franquito* has nothing to say for himself?'

'*Franquito*'s not well. At least that's what they're telling me,' Canaris unbuttoned his coat. 'Everything happens very slowly in this country, Seppl, as you know. Winning may be a bigger shock than they ever imagined. News like that takes a little digesting.'

'So what happens next?'

'That's what I came to find out but most of it doesn't really need a conversation. Franco's got what he wants. The old owners are back in charge and the little people are on their knees. Franco can help himself to whatever he likes, probably for as long as he likes, and that will suit him very nicely. The biggest battles have come and gone but he has a country to feed and an army to keep on its toes and no visible means of paying for either. Franco's no accountant but the man is a peasant at heart, a born *Gallego*. He counts on his fingers, and people like that know the price of everything.'

'You Germans have money. The Reich has money.'

'That's true. And Franco knows it. We've been more than generous over the last three years, and so have the Italians, while the British and French have been minding their own business, which suited him just fine. So now Franco's settling his podgy arse at the top table. He's given himself grand titles and joined Hitler and Musso. Brothers-in-arms, Seppl. Franco's in the casino of his dreams, and he's won his war, and now he wants to cash in.'

'And you?' Veltiens was smiling. 'Your role at the gaming table?'

'I'm there to calculate the odds and to listen to my master and maybe to tender a little advice.'

'To Hitler?'

'To you, Seppl. This afternoon was supposed to be about negotiation, just the very first moves, feeling Franco out, gauging exactly what he wants. That hasn't happened but I'm here to tell you he has assets we'd like, raw materials, ports on the Atlantic seaboard, plus access to Gibraltar. All of that has a cash value and if you steal a look at Franco's shopping list, arms will be at the top.'

'Before bread?'

'Before everything. Seizing power is one thing. Keeping it, Seppl, quite another.'

'You're offering me some kind of deal here?'

'I'm offering you advice.'

Veltiens nodded, then reached automatically for the control yoke, a gesture that made Canaris smile.

'He lets you fly this thing?'

'He does. Young Giuseppe drinks far too much. I handled both the take-off and the landing today. I think the prospect of his lady friend makes him nervous.' The smile faded. 'How much?'

'How much what?'

'How much for this advice of yours? Let's call it access. Name me a figure, or better still we can agree a percentage on whatever contract sum the Spanish come up with. Berlin supplies the money. I supply the arms. You get a slice of their payment, net of course, after expenses.'

Canaris sat back in the leather seat, staring at the first fat drops of rain exploding on the windshield. He'd never taken a bribe in his life and he had no intention of starting now.

Except.

'You're familiar with the Mosin-Nagant 7.62mm rifle, Seppl?'

'They're everywhere. The Soviets have been using them forever.'

'This has to be the sniper version. Five shot internal magazine, 3.5 fixed-focus scope. Plus hollow-point ammunition.'

'Really?' He was eyeing Canaris with fresh interest. 'You have a specific target in mind?'

'I'm asking you a question.'

'No problem. But why don't you use your own kit? The Gewehr 98's a beauty in the right hands.'

'I'm sure you're right. But that's rather the point. The right hands want the Mosin-Nagant.'

'You're hiring someone? This is a freelance job?'

Canaris frowned, wouldn't answer. Veltiens gave him a long, appraising look.

'This is for exterior use? Or are we inside?'

'No idea. Yet. Why do you ask?'

'It makes a difference to the ammunition. Outside in weather like this your target will be wearing thick clothing, maybe even body armour. At any kind of range you need penetration guaranteed.' He paused, then grinned. 'Christ,' he said. 'You're shooting Franco? You're telling me you've had enough?'

'I'm telling you nothing of the sort. This is advance planning, strictly provisional. We may need it, we may not, I just have to be sure of two things. One that you can deliver, and two that you keep your mouth firmly closed. Just you and me, Seppl, and the small fortune that doubtless awaits you now this wretched war is over.' He began to button his coat. 'We have a deal?'

*

Moncrieff had never been to Gibraltar before. Peering out through the windows of the de Havilland Rapide, he watched the looming Rock dizzily rotate as the pilot dipped a wing and hauled the biplane into a final turn before sinking fast towards the chequerboard of sports fields and a racecourse that appeared to double as an airstrip. The aircraft touched, touched a second time, and then settled on the racing turf.

The youngish figure at the foot of the aircraft's steps was wearing the brown uniform of an Intelligence Corps lieutenant. Moncrieff had spoken to him only yesterday from London but it was good to put a face to the voice on the crackly international line.

'Martin Rees?'

'The same. Welcome to Gib.' He gestured at a line of marching sailors who seemed to have appeared from nowhere. 'We thought we'd lay on a proper welcome.'

For just a moment, Moncrieff was fooled. Then he caught the hint of a smile. The matelots, it seemed, were rehearsing for the reintroduction of the Women's Royal Naval Service. After a twenty-year stand-down, the WRNS would shortly be back in business.

'That's very gallant of you,' Moncrieff accepted a handshake, his gaze drifting up the Rock. Wherever you were, he thought, however hard you tried to ignore it, the huge outcrop of limestone, so dramatic, so unforgiving, dominated everything. Here on the landward side, topped with a scarf of wispy grey cloud, it seemed to fall sheer to the dusty wasteland below. A thousand feet? Higher? Moncrieff, to his shame, wasn't sure but that wasn't the point. Study it through enemy eyes, try and imagine a frontal assault, and you'd retire with a very big headache.

'Impressive?' Rees had noticed Moncrieff's interest.

'Unassailable. Beyond reach. Geology like that, we'll be here for a thousand years.'

'Alas, no, sir. Three cheers for the matelots, though. I've told them you were a major once upon a time so you might get a salute.'

A uniformed sub-lieutenant drove them to the Defence Security Office among the sprawl of government buildings on the west side of the promontory and Moncrieff once again took his time to take in the view from the tiny square of car park. From here he could see a handful of frigates and a depot ship tied up alongside while an aircraft carrier and its attendant destroyer were anchored out on the blue waters of the bay. A naval tender had just nudged the side of the destroyer and he caught the pipe of a bosun's whistle as a line of uniforms scaled a ladder and stepped onto the deck.

'And over there?' Moncrieff was pointing to a smudge of distant buildings across the bay.

'Algeciras. That's Spain, of course. On Fridays we drink with our friends from the *Abwehr* at the La Reina Christina Hotel.'

'You speak Spanish?'

'Yes. And most of the Germans do, too.'

'So what do you make of them?'

'Good company, by and large. They watch us like hawks, of course, and they have a presence everywhere. Algeciras. La Línea. Out in the Campo.'

'And the Spanish?'

'Money always talks and the Germans have deep pockets. We've always relied on local Spanish labour coming in from the mainland every day so my best guess ...' he shrugged, '... I expect you can work it out.'

'The enemy within? Spies in the camp?'

'Of course. The *Abwehr* boys are good. One imagines their files in perfect order. Can we do anything about that? Alas, no. But I suspect that's not why you're here. Maisie's been kind enough to lay on a spot of lunch.' He nodded towards the office. 'Shall we?'

Lunch was a plate of ham sandwiches enlivened with jars of assorted pickles. Rees uncorked a bottle of local red wine he described as reliable and enquired about Moncrieff's days in the Royal Marines.

'Why do you ask?' The sandwiches were dry and under-buttered.

'I'm curious, that's all. As you might imagine, we have lots of dealings with the Security Service but it's rare to come across someone with your background.'

'You wouldn't view it as a qualification?' Moncrieff enquired.

'Quite to the contrary. Nearly ten years in the Corps? Do I have that right?'

'You do. I'm impressed.'

'No regrets in leaving?'

'Plenty. I missed the blokes at first, and the physical challenge is something that gets under your skin, but they work you very hard day and night and bits of you start to protest. In my case I fell off a cliff face in Scotland and my back will never be the same again. It was a great life and bits of it were unforgettable, but your body has the final say. If you want the truth, MI5's timing was perfect.' Moncrieff abandoned his sandwich. 'So tell me about Gibraltar.'

Rees nodded, happy to change the subject. The Rock, he said, had been handed to the British a couple of centuries back, one of the prime cuts from the Treaty of Utrecht. Successive tenants had added touches of their own to a natural fortress, and if he might stretch the metaphor a little further it was maybe best to think of the place as a chunk of cheese, preferably Roquefort. The limestone yielded easily to tunnelling and over the years the Rock had been much nibbled and wormed by a fear of enemies and the sheer passage of time.

Nibbled and wormed. Moncrieff liked this young man a great deal.

'Trust to God and keep digging? Am I getting the right picture?'

'Trust to Allah in the early days but you're right. The Spanish are crazy about fortifications and we were, too. Go to any city on the mainland and you'll find a fortress, turrets, thick walls, plus a drawbridge and a huge door you can bolt three ways. Gibraltar is the biggest of them all, which makes some of our people very happy. We've been here for hundreds of years and no one's going to shift us.'

'I see,' Moncrieff nodded. It was impossible not to catch the note of reservation at the end of this sentence. 'But you think they're wrong?'

'I think they're optimistic. Boiling oil and chucking the odd rock is one thing. Warfare, alas, has moved on.'

Moncrieff reached for his wine. He wanted more of this, more of the raised eyebrow, but Rees was already corking the bottle and laying it aside for later. Now, he said, would be perfect for a brief tour of the estate, after which everything might make a great deal more sense.

'Brief?' Moncrieff tapped at his watch. 'I have all day.'

'But that's rather the point, sir. People make a lot of fuss about this little outpost, but in essence it's tiny.'

They were back in the car, Rees this time at the wheel. First he wanted to give Moncrieff just a taste of what Gibraltar could offer if you happened to be stepping ashore after weeks or even months at sea. Moncrieff nodded. His days in the Royal Marines had taken him to every UK naval port, and within minutes he knew he was looking at Portsmouth with palm trees.

Cluttered shops and scruffy market stalls in Grand Casement Square that wouldn't have been out of place in the bustle of Pompey's Commercial Road. Pubs to keep the spirits up on runs ashore: the Star, the Angry Friar, the All's Well. Cafés shaded against the sunshine, peddling fish and chips. A prim, white-washed Anglican church, the tiny square of garden tended by three elderly Spaniards.

Finally, Rees eased the Morris through the southerly gate in the city walls and parked at the kerbside beyond.

'This might be interesting, sir.' He suggested they take a look.

Moncrieff eased his long frame out of the car and stretched in the sunshine. Beneath the thick walls, shadowed by shrubs and palm trees, he was looking at a clutter of gravestones. This, murmured Rees, was the Trafalgar Cemetery.

'You mean they were all buried here? After the battle?'

'Alas, no. Nelson's body was shipped home, of course, but most of the dead were buried at sea. This little plot is mainly for yellow fever victims. Only two from the battle ended up here.'

'So why the Trafalgar Cemetery?'

'Sleight of hand, sir. We get lots of VIP visits. People with the right braid on their shoulders love paying their respects.'

The graveyard was a tiny triangle, even smaller than Moncrieff had first assumed. Rees led him to a grey weathered headstone and saved him the chore of bending to decipher the name.

'Captain Thomas Norman,' he said. 'A fellow Marine. He survived for a while but died in the naval hospital. We had a similar situation a couple of years ago when the *Deutschland* arrived.'

'The German pocket battleship?'

'Exactly. The Republicans had bombed her off Ibiza. Twenty-three dead, eighty wounded. Naturally we did what we could for the wounded and buried the dead but the Germans came back later to collect the bodies so we had to get the spades out again. Not a pretty sight.' He broke off to gaze at the rows of headstones that lined the gravel paths, and Moncrieff began to glimpse the role that outposts like this must have played as the British Empire pinked every corner of the globe. An entire culture, or perhaps a state of mind, had settled on the bareness of this landscape, he thought, and it wasn't a pretty sight.

From the cemetery, Rees drove Moncrieff to the very top of the Rock. It was much colder up here, the sun veiled by curtains of cloud, and he peered down at the tiny apron of streets and paved squares that stretched to the neat oblongs of the dockyard.

'Imagine we're Berbers, or Moors, or even Romans.' Rees had a private smile on his face. 'They'd all have stood here, shared this same view. Cavemen were probably here, too, and the Barbary apes have never left.'

'Meaning?'

'They all felt safe.'

Back in the car, they motored slowly down, negotiating a series of zigzags, until Rees stopped beside a gun emplacement.

'Ack-ack,' he said, getting out of the car again. 'They're shipping us the latest kit and not before time.'

Moncrieff followed him down the path and onto the emplacement. A couple of gunners in uniform snapped salutes but within seconds one of them was deep in conversation with Rees. It turned out he was a Wolves fan, football crazy, and couldn't wait for the final at the end of the month.

'Final?' They were back in the car.

'FA Cup, sir. The blokes follow it on the radio.'

'And they like being out here?'

'They love it. They all smell a war coming and they've decided that here is much safer than home. Most of them are city boys and they don't fancy getting a pasting from the *Luftwaffe*.'

'And you think they're right? About this place being so safe?'

Reece held his gaze for a moment, then slipped the key back into the ignition.

'Two more stops, sir. Then we'll meet the Colonel and you can make up your own mind.'

The first of the stops was another gun emplacement, bigger this time. Moncrieff circled the bulk of the six-inch naval gun, the twin barrels pointing towards some mythical target beyond the bay, and listened to the officer in charge tallying the details that seemed to matter: range, arcs and rates of fire. With a good crew, he said, he could lay down a barrage that would sink any vessel within ten miles.

'And down here?' Moncrieff was peering over the metal barrier that encircled the emplacement. The drop to the north-west side of the Rock felt near-vertical. 'What happens if the enemy get through and start climbing?'

The officer paused, exchanging looks with Rees.

'I think it's fair to say we'd have a tiny problem with close-order engagements,' Rees said smoothly. 'I gather it's a depression issue. Not being able to get at the buggers.'

Depression issue. Moncrieff tabled the phrase half an hour later. By now they'd driven to the entrance to the complex of tunnels that riddled the Rock's bony interior. At Rees's insistence, they'd walked a hundred yards into the tunnel under the pale glare of the lamps that receded into the far distance. The rock walls were moist, the air strangely warm, and when they paused before retracing their steps, Moncrieff could hear falling water.

Back in the Morris, Rees admitted he'd used the phrase on purpose.

'Technically, of course, depression issue means what it says. At close range, the bigger guns can't point vertically down so they'd be useless if it came to any kind of close-quarters engagement.'

'But that wasn't your drift. Am I right?'

'You are, sir. The blokes are able and willing. We can ask for no more. But do they really understand how badly it could go for us? Does anyone? That, I doubt.'

'Because?'

'Because there are some areas we simply couldn't deal with, especially if the enemy has done his homework. There are places to hide, places where we can't bring fire to bear. We have a term for it, always have had, and I'm guessing you'll know it too.'

'Dead ground?' Moncrieff was looking at the remains of an insect on the windscreen. 'Beyond reach?'

'Exactly. And you can bet the *Abwehr* boys know it, too.'

In every sense, Colonel Austin Montague turned out to be a large man: heavy-set, heavy-lidded eyes, heavy everything. He occupied a substantial office in the main garrison complex and struggled to his feet to offer a damp handshake and a glass of sherry from a cut-glass decanter on a nearby shelf. Looking round the office, Moncrieff noticed a riding crop half-wedged behind a bookcase. Too many mess dinners and not enough time in the saddle, he thought, accepting a glass of Amontillado.

As they settled in chairs in front of the Colonel's desk, it was obvious at once that Rees didn't much like his superior officer. Equally obvious was the fact that the Colonel either hadn't noticed or didn't care. When he demanded an account of their brief tour of the Rock, and Rees tallied the places where they'd stopped, he nodded, seeming to approve.

'Excellent,' he said. 'And you've shared our plans with our esteemed visitor?'

'No, sir. I thought I'd leave that to you.'

This invitation won emphatic approval from the Colonel, and after he'd checked Moncrieff's security clearance – a single question, a single nod in response to Moncrieff's answer – he spread his hands wide and outlined how busy the likes of Rees would be over the coming months and years.

The racecourse, alas, was already a goner. Work would shortly be starting on a proper paved runway, able to take the heaviest aircraft anticipated on the run south from GB. With it would come a comprehensive series of improvements in the dockyard: more emplaced ack-ack, counter-batteries able to hurl a shell more than a dozen miles, a new strategy to combat frogman incursions from the mainland, plus a number of other measures guaranteed to surprise any enemy silly enough to chance his arm.

Under the Rock, meanwhile, specialist teams of engineers, amply furnished with limitless quantities of explosives, would be creating mile after mile of new tunnels, with enough accommodation and supplies to keep up to sixteen thousand men – the entire garrison – tucked up safe and sound. In short, he said, the precious bloody Rock would be secured tighter than a curate's arsehole and God help any bloody German who thought otherwise.

Rees was studying his hands. Moncrieff took another sip of sherry. Had this terrifying braggart been at the bottle since breakfast? Did he truly believe a word of what he was appearing to say? But worse was to come.

'Shall I, young Martin?'

'Shall you what, sir?'

'The icing on the cake? Our little surprise should everything go tits-up?'

Rees didn't answer, not that it mattered.

'We'll be calling it the stay-behind cave,' the Colonel was looking at Moncrieff, 'and this is top secret. The thinking goes as follows. Should anything truly unthinkable happen then of course we have to make provision. So imagine a hidden entrance on the eastern cliffs. Concrete steps lead down to a carefully hidden room. Spring water hand-pumped from below. Enough food for a couple of years for a couple of men. Another entrance leads through a brand-new tunnel to an observation point on the other side of the Rock. No one has a clue that this place exists. Walk every other tunnel and there's absolutely no trace of it. When the concept was first explained to me I must say I had my doubts but now I regard it as a stroke of genius.' He reached for the decanter again. 'So what do you think, Moncrieff? Have we not been magnificently served?'

Moncrieff sat back a moment, marshalling his thoughts. Finally, he shifted his weight in the chair.

'But what is it *for*?' he asked. 'What do these men *do*?'

'Do, Moncrieff? Put him out of his misery, young Martin. Let him into the secret.'

'Of course, sir.' Rees turned to Moncrieff. 'They look. They observe. They make notes and report back.'

'On what?'

'On whatever's happening outside.'

'Reporting to whom?'

'To London, of course.' The Colonel was getting to his feet. 'Where else, for God's sake?'

Moncrieff said his goodbyes to Rees back at the airstrip, where the waiting de Havilland Rapide had been refuelled. Something had been snagging at the very back of his mind, something that required just a word of explanation.

He extended a hand and thanked Rees for his time and – more importantly – for his candour. Then he paused and enquired about a neat pile of framed prints stacked on a shelf in the Colonel's office, and on the presence of two cardboard boxes in the outer office.

Rees smiled. 'He's on the move, thank God.'

'You mean leaving?'

'Yes.'

'Aldershot? Portsmouth?'

'Cairo.' A thin smile. 'Lucky them.'

11

Annie Wrenne jerked into wakefulness, dawn at the tall window, a bitter wind stirring the curtains at the top where the warped frame wouldn't quite close. She lay still for a moment, listening. Even with two blankets, a pair of woollen socks and Ortega's borrowed greatcoat, she'd fought the cold for most of the night, her knees tucked into her chin, her body tightly knotted, trying to quieten the voices in her head. Peace on the streets of Madrid had brought few consolations, and lack of sleep had made her anxious and fretful.

Then it happened again. Voices out in the garden, one of them very angry. She lay still for a moment longer then slipped out from under the covers, wrapped herself in the greatcoat and ghosted across to the window. The room was on the third floor of *La Vieja Escuela* and from here she had a perfect view of the property's extensive garden. Every square metre had been cultivated during the war, plot after plot of winter vegetables and summer salads, and now she watched the pair of local toughs paid to mount a nightly guard over the property. They seemed to have cornered someone beneath the giant elm that hung over the main gates. A tiny body lay at their feet, one bare arm trying to shield his face from the heavy boots, the other hugging what looked like a cabbage and a handful of potatoes.

One of the watchmen launched another volley of oaths, while the other hauled the youth to his feet. He must have been thirteen at the most. He was begging them to leave him alone, told them to take the stuff he'd stolen, promised never to do it again, then came a scream as both men set about him, beating him around the head and face until he sagged between them and they threw him onto the street.

Shocked, Annie lingered a moment longer as one of the men briefly examined the potatoes before tossing them aside. Back in bed, she lay in the half-darkness, trying to make sense of what she'd just witnessed. Arriving from Alicante, Ortega had driven her to this big, handsome house in the city's rich northern suburbs. He'd told her that a Republican militia had liberated it in the war's opening weeks, expelling the family in residence and throwing the property open to an assortment of Madrid's homeless. Three years later, the surrender of the city to Franco's rebel army had brought the original owners back to the house. Ortega, it appeared, knew them well and assured Annie that her presence would be more than welcome. When she'd asked why, he'd simply shrugged and grunted something about her Spanish and her nursing experience and her good looks. None of these explanations made any sense but within a couple of days the body count from Alicante was in every newspaper and Annie was simply grateful to have been spared.

Her host had turned out to be a tallish aristocrat with a mane of greying hair who owed his wealth to a bank inherited from his father. He confessed he'd been pleasantly surprised by the state of *La Vieja Escuela* after nearly three years of occupation, and Annie had begun a cautious friendship with his wife, a younger woman called Francesca. The house, she explained, owed its name to the Republicans, who had a ready ear for a pun. The Old School had never opened its doors to a single pupil. The name simply referred to the way things had always been in the Spain the Republicans had vowed to destroy. To the rich, the pickings. To the poor, if they were very lucky, a cabbage and a handful of bruised potatoes.

Annie gazed across at the window, knowing she should go out to the street. The young thief, at best, would be badly injured. Francesca might be prepared to summon help, and Annie herself could certainly bandage his wounds. She nodded to herself, ashamed to be back in bed, and quickly dressed before unlocking her door.

The house was on three levels and the grander parts of it reminded her of the Villa Paz, the same attention to the blessings of scale and careful ornamentation, the same self-confidence celebrated in stone and mortar. On the ground floor she paused a moment, aware of the murmur of voices, the two watchmen talking in the big kitchen, then she let herself out into the chill of the grey dawn light.

A gravel drive led to the tall double gates. The watchmen had left them unlocked and she stepped into the broadness of the avenue outside. Anticipating a body on the pavement, she found nothing but a pool of blood next to the gutter. A closer look revealed more bloodstains, tiny drops of the deepest, freshest red leading in the direction of the city's centre. He must have had the energy and the good sense to run, she told herself.

She followed the trail down the flagstones that served as a pavement, the drops becoming more and more widely spaced, the boy running faster and faster, maybe frightened by something, maybe trying to conjure some story to explain his failed expedition, then – where the avenue intersected with one of the city's major roads – the spill of young blood abruptly came to an end. Had he been picked up by some passer-by? Had the return of peace pricked a conscience or two?

She knew the answer was probably no. She'd been back in this city for more than a week now, glad of the perch that Ortega had found for her but determined to get out among the *Madrileños* she remembered from the outbreak of war. Then, barely three years ago, it had been a time of public rejoicing and baking heat. Franco's rebel garrison had been routed at the Montana Barracks. Every public building was draped in socialist flags. The Anarchists had put a smile on the country's future in Barcelona, while here in the capital open trucks full of workers in blue boiler suits and scarlet kerchiefs round their necks were on their way to the front, men already drunk on victory, their fists in the air. This had been the moment of reckoning, of defiance chalked on every passing tram: *Abajo fascismo!* Down with Fascism! This had been the moment an entire city had glimpsed just what might be possible, strangers partying in the street, every driver's hand flat on the horn, part carnival, part madness.

Annie remembered sitting in a working-class bar in La Latino. The owner had once been a bullfighter, not very famous, but there were the heads of *toros* mounted on the walls, and copies of that morning's *El Socialista* piled on a corner of the bar, and working men bent over plates of greasy stew, discussing the season's prospects of Real Madrid. Later that same afternoon, she'd made her way to a popular local market in an even poorer part of the city where the prettier women inked a thin black seam down the backs of their legs in lieu of nylons, and where you could pick up anything you fancied for a song. Better still, the new Republican government had just ordered every pawnshop to hand back the people's pledges, and the streets had been full of scruffy crowds heading home, nursing their rescued treasures.

Then had come the Villa Paz, and Giles Roper, and the Pablo Iglesias, and everything that had followed, and now, back in Madrid, Annie had found herself in a very different city. Years of hunger and fear had hollowed face after face. Three years of shelling, bombardment and siege had brought down one building after another until major streets looked like the open mouths of the working poor. Naturally, the rebel artillery had been careful to spare the richer suburbs, but explore a little further, penetrate the maze of narrow cobbled streets across the river, and it was a very different story. Men in torn overalls and women younger than they looked in much-mended black shawls. Plaster falling from the brickwork, rotting window frames, rusty iron balconies shuttered against prying eyes. Fly-blown shops, the scuttling of fat black rats, plus a litter of empty sardine tins embellished with faint hints of Cyrillic script. Precious protein, she thought, probably years old, shipped in from Moscow.

That was bad enough, testament to fading dreams and the implacable return of an older Spain, but the real story as the Republic drew its final breaths was written on the Gran Via. Franco's troops had finally seized the city, marching unchallenged through empty streets, and everywhere you looked there were posters of the *Caudillo*, and the yoke and arrows of the Falange. Swastikas and Nazi banners flew alongside the Spanish national flag and deafening propaganda boomed from every loudspeaker. A city centre so lately open to everyone had suddenly become the property of elderly priests and stern-faced nuns and uniformed army officers and the hurrying and scuttling of businessmen. Wear a shirt on the street these days, and you *had* to wear a jacket. Why? Because the *Caudillo* insisted.

Annie shook her head, her gaze returning to that last drop of blood on the flagstones at her feet. In so many ways, she thought, the plight of this hapless youth had been the story of the civil war. So easy to get your hands on something valuable, something that might keep you and your family alive. So easy, and so painful, to lose it.

She got back to *La Vieja Escuela* to find Ortega in the kitchen. She hadn't seen him for nearly a week and the watchmen, who didn't know him at all, seemed awed by his *appearance*. One of them still had blood on his knuckles and when Ortega put down his mug of coffee and asked him why, he blamed an encounter with a couple of intruders, ex-militiamen up to no good. Minutes later, back in her own room, Annie told Ortega the real story. If he wanted to check, he need only step outside the gate.

'How old?' he grunted.

'A kid. Twelve? Thirteen? His only crime was to be hungry.'

Ortega nodded, said nothing. He was carrying a parcel wrapped in brown paper and secured with string. When Annie opened it, she found herself looking at a poorly framed print of a pen and ink engraving. A wild-looking man in a waistcoat was about to chop the head off a French cuirassier. More bodies lay at his feet. This, Annie knew at once, was the work of Goya. It came from a series of sketches he'd made during the guerrilla war against the invading French back at the start of the nineteenth century. She'd told Ortega about these prints in the car en route from Alicante and had marvelled that nothing seemed to have changed since.

'This is one of *Los desastres de la guerra*,' she said now. 'Where on earth did you get it?'

'I was at the Prado yesterday. The picture was lying around and when I explained about you and Goya they gave it to me. The job could be yours. They're expecting you this afternoon. The man's name is Juan Arteta. The museum's closed, of course, but if you wait outside the main entrance, he'll come and collect you.'

'What job?'

'I don't know. I told him you were very clever and I told him you spoke every language ever invented. I also explained how you'd survived Alicante.'

'But I didn't. I ran away.'

'That sounds like guilt.'

'You're right. It is. But that's my business. If I didn't say thank you, then now's the time.'

'For getting you out of there?'

'Of course. And for this so-called job.'

Ortega didn't seem to be listening. Instead, he'd retrieved the picture and was moving from wall to wall trying to gauge where it might best hang. Annie watched him for a moment. The last three years had taught her a great deal about human nature, about what it took to survive in a war as brutal as this one had been, but never had she met anyone quite like Ortega.

'Do you mind me asking you a question?' She offered him a handkerchief for the bubbling spittle running down his newly shaved chin.

'Go ahead. How about here?' He stood aside, one enormous hand holding the print flat against the wall.

'Perfect. It's about Murcia.'

'What about Murcia?'

'What were you really doing there? And how come you keep company like this?' she gestured round.

The question seemed to amuse him. He carried on looking for likely spots to hang the engraving, then told her he hadn't been lying.

'About what?'

'About watching. That was what I was there for. That's what they told me to do. Watch and listen and wait. I suppose one word is spy. That's not how the story started but after what happened ...' His spare hand touched his ruined face, '... I was grateful to be spared the madhouse.'

'*They* told you to do?'

'The rebels.'

'You were spying for Franco?'

'I was shooting people for Franco. That makes me a sniper. I was good at it. Still am.'

'And this was here? In Madrid?'

'It was. When the Republicans talk about the Fifth Column, they're talking about people like me, people who lurk, people who know how to disappear when it most matters. I was here to kill people. They gave me a list, and a photograph of the target, and made sure that face appeared in my sights. I chose churches for the firing position because the Republicans left them in ruins inside and because the rebels would never shell them. In the end, of course, I was wrong. Bombing isn't quite as accurate as it should be, even with the Germans in charge. Does that make me lucky? Was God on my side? I've no idea.'

'You're telling me you believe all that nonsense?'

'About God?'

'About Franco.'

'Christ, no. The rebels pay well. People on the right always do. The Republicans are babes in the wood, not a centimo to their names. In my soul I've always been one of the damned so I sleep like a baby.'

'But you've killed people.'

'I have.'

'Lots?'

'Enough to earn my keep.'

'As simple as that?'

'Probably simpler.'

'No conscience? No regrets?'

'None.' He studied her for a long moment. 'You sound angry,' he said at last.

'Disappointed.'

'Surprised?'

'Disappointed.'

'You think I should be a better human being?'

'I think you should have told me before.'

'And would it have made a difference?'

'To what?'

'To this,' Ortega gestured at the space between them. 'So far you trust me, and that doesn't happen very often. Am I right?'

Annie held his gaze. The touch on her shoulder among the madness on the dockside, she thought. The waiting limousine. The tavern he'd found on the road to Madrid where they'd stopped for goat stew and a flask of the roughest red wine and where he'd parried her every question with a shrug and what might have been a smile. Now, at last, she knew the worst. Or maybe not.

'There's more?' she asked. 'To this story of yours?'

'Of course,' he offered her the picture. 'There's always more.'

Those three words returned to haunt Annie and afterwards, years later, she realised why. She'd made mistakes all her life. One of them, in the shape of Giles Roper, had been unforgiveable, a tribute to an eagerness and a naivety she'd never suspected, but she liked to think that the ashes of that relationship had taught her a great deal. In most respects she'd become harder – harder to impress, harder to persuade – and yet here she was again, a newcomer in a very different Madrid, a victim not of circumstance but of her own blind faith.

Something had prompted her to minister to this man, to bathe his wounds back in the sunshine and warmth of Murcia. It had seemed the smallest gesture at the time, but she'd admired his fortitude, whatever else it masked, and now that she knew the truth about who he really was, or perhaps a little of the truth, nothing had changed. Sudden death had become the currency of the last three years and while killing in cold blood still mattered, there was something inside her that admired the clarity of the bargain he'd struck. Whoever paid best got Carlos Ortega's fullest attention until, perhaps, someone richer came along.

The latter thought stayed with her for the rest of the morning, until she left to walk the three miles to the Prado Museum. She was thinking of what might await her, and of Goya. What would he make of this city where he'd won the approval of the King and made his reputation? How would he cope when heads on the street were down, and even the shopkeepers had lost the energy to gossip, and few strangers would meet your eye? Would this morning's bloodbath beneath the window of her room prompt him to reach for his pen and pad? In the hands of this deaf genius would Madrid, the entire city, become just another *desastre de la guerra*?

In truth she didn't know, but the closer she got to the Prado, the more she recognised the first stirrings of excitement at the prospect of what might happen next. Working night and day at the Pablo Iglesias in Murcia, Madrid had been another world, hopelessly remote, but she remembered one evening last summer when she'd found herself talking to an English volunteer who'd just arrived from the capital. She'd had a long affair with a French journalist, a man of culture with a lively interest in Spanish art, and before he'd returned to his wife in Lyons he'd told her about the bomb damage the museum had suffered in the war's early months.

The prime casualty had evidently been a Goya canvas Annie knew well, the artist's account of the charge of the French

Imperial Guard during one of the many Spanish uprisings against the Napoleonic occupation. Mounted or otherwise, everyone has either a knife or a sabre. A maddened killer sits astride a horse. The busy foreground is littered with bodies while the faces of spectators recede down the Calle de Alcalá. Annie had walked this street in the months before the war, an act of homage to an artist she'd come to revere, and later she'd revisited the canvas. This was *Los desastres de la guerra* in full colour, she'd decided, the work of a genius determined to capture the essence of what the Spanish called *la sed de sangre*, or bloodlust.

Bloodlust.

She'd arrived at the steps leading up to the museum's main entrance. It was a grey day, still cold, and the few passers-by wore thin coats buttoned against the icy wind blasting down from the Sierra de Guadalajara. Try as she might, she couldn't rid herself of the image of the apprentice thief cowering under a torrent of violence in the thin light of dawn, and she was half hoping that Ortega might get round to administering a little rough justice of his own when she heard a cough behind her, and a muttered apology.

'Miss Wrenne?'

She turned round. He was tall, with a spare, weathered face and more than a hint of Scots in his accent. Good shoes, she thought, and a lovely pair of corduroy trousers, and a thick woollen scarf in a greenish plaid artfully knotted over his heavy tweed jacket.

'Señor Arteta?' Annie nodded towards the museum, trying to hide her confusion.

'I'm afraid not.'

'You're not from the Prado?'

'No. But we do have a post in mind that might intrigue you.'

'We?' she asked.

He studied her a moment and then eased his tall frame and nodded in the direction of the city centre.

'A coffee, perhaps? In view of this bloody weather? Might I tempt you?'

He took her to the lounge of a nearby hotel on the Calle de Moratín. By the time they'd arrived, she'd established that he was British, that he was a fellow admirer of the great Francisco Goya, and that – yes – he knew Carlos Ortega.

'A ruse, I'm afraid. My apologies.' He extended a bony hand. 'Tam Moncrieff. Something tells me you're tempted to leave but that might be a mistake on both our parts. Give me half an hour and let's see where that takes us.'

Annie nodded, said nothing, settled back into the plush purple velour of the armchair. There's always more, Ortega had promised her. Always.

Moncrieff was peering into the coffee pot. Annie said yes to cream, no to sugar and wanted to know more about Ortega.

'He's a friend?' she asked.

'More an associate, though given a man like that I'd rule nothing out. He thinks the world of you, by the way.'

'Should I be flattered?'

'Very much so. The man's a misanthrope. He has a very dark view of human nature. Under the circumstances, that might not come as a surprise. I understand you repaired bits of him a while back. Is that true?'

Annie nodded. 'You know what he did for a living? Here in Madrid? Then in Murcia?'

'I do, yes. I'm afraid I'm in the same game.'

'Shooting people?'

'Intelligence. MI5, to be precise. The Security Service.'

Annie reached for her cup, not knowing quite what to say, feeling the first hot stir of anger. The coffee was delicious, with an authentic bitterness that took her back to summer breakfasts with her mother in the depths of Normandy. She studied Moncrieff over the brim of the cup. His face was a mask but she sensed just a hint of real interest.

'So why me?' she said at last. 'Why all this subterfuge? All this theatre? Is a girl allowed to ask?'

'Of course. After the last couple of years it won't surprise you that we have a presence in this country.'

'On the contrary. I'm astonished.'

'May I ask why?'

'Because the Germans never bothered to hide their interest. They may have been backing the wrong side but at least they were in the fight. Britain sent volunteers, lots of volunteers, and some of them lent more than a hand, but when it came to help that might have made a difference, your government turned its back.' She paused, taken aback by her own vehemence. 'You want me to tell you how that felt out here?'

'Of course.'

'It felt terrible, worse than terrible. It felt like betrayal. The volunteers I've known were full of good intentions but good intentions count for nothing on the battlefield. What the Spanish wanted was something to fight with: weapons, guns, tanks, aircraft. Instead they got nothing but speeches and communiqués and reasons why no one could do anything that might help. Non-intervention left a very bad smell in this country, Mr Moncrieff, and it's still there.' She paused. 'If that sounds like a speech, then I'm sorry.'

'You said my government.'

'I did.'

'I suspect it's yours, as well.'

'Then you'd be wrong. Did I vote for it? No. Am I British through and through? Again, no. The best parts of me are French. And that's something I only twigged recently.'

'Because of what you've seen?'

'Of course. The French government wasn't much use either but that's something you learn to expect.'

'*Touché.*' Moncrieff permitted himself a smile. 'Your father sends his regards, by the way.'

'My father?' Annie was staring at him now, still flushed, still angry, but wrongfooted by this abrupt conversational swerve. 'You're telling me you've met him? Talked to him?'

'I have, yes. Two weeks ago. Does Chalfont St Peter ring any bells?'

'None. Except I understand he lives there.'

'You've never paid a visit?'

'Never. Is there a new woman in his life? Is my poor mother off the hook?'

'I'm afraid I don't know.'

'So why did you meet him? What was the point?'

'We call it positive vetting.'

'You were trying to recruit him? He's a diplomat already. Isn't it a bit late to ask his views on King and Country?'

'We're interested in you, not him.'

'I see,' Annie was trying to calm herself down. 'And what did he have to say?'

'I'm afraid it's a bit delicate.'

'You mean secret?'

'I mean delicate.'

'Then try me. I've just come out of a war, Mr Moncrieff, as you've probably gathered. I won't break if you drop me.'

'OK,' Moncrieff gazed at the remains of his coffee. 'He said you could be difficult.'

'Difficult?'

'Stubborn. Sometimes impossibly so. One of the words he used was unbiddable.'

'Then he's right for once. Does that make this conversation any easier? Somehow I doubt it.' She frowned. 'So what exactly do you have in mind? You owe me very little, Mr Moncrieff, but some kind of explanation might not go amiss.'

Moncrieff reached for the coffee pot and Annie submitted to a refill. Then he asked for her views on what might happen next.

'Here, you mean? In Spain?'

'In Europe as a whole.'

'There'll be a war, a proper war, everyone says so.'

'Because …?'

'Because we should have taken on the Germans and we didn't.'

'You're right.' An emphatic nod from Moncrieff. 'Peace is a comfort. Given Hitler's table manners, it's also an illusion. The man's a messy eater, and it shows. It'll be Poland next, and then we'll fight, and that's a proposition that fills me with gloom.'

'You're some kind of pacifist?'

'On the contrary. I'm an ex-bootneck. I know about fighting.'

'Bootneck?'

'Royal Marines.'

'So why the gloom?'

'Because we're unprepared. Because we've let our guard down. Because non-intervention, as you so rightly say, has rotted our soul.'

'Golly,' Annie reached for her coffee. 'You're telling me we agree?'

'I'm telling you the Germans are in the driving seat. I was in Berlin last year and I know that the Hitler-gang have absolutely no doubts that Europe is there for the taking. They have their own people by the throat and so far your average German is very happy. After Poland, it'll be the turn of Norway, and Denmark, and Belgium, and France, and very possibly us. And after that, because Hitler will have got his second wind, they'll turn up here.'

'By invitation?'

'Possibly, possibly not.'

'But why? This country is on its knees. Who needs millions more mouths to feed?'

'That's not the point. In my trade, we try to anticipate events. Imagine that Hitler hasn't quite managed to cross the Channel. Pretend our government have somehow managed to keep him at arm's length or maybe they've sued for peace. Either way, Hitler wants to lay hands on the empire, on what we own overseas, and it's not his style to ask nicely and hope we agree. Possession, Hitler thinks, is nine-tenths of the law. So where does he go next?'

The question hung between them. Annie had settled down by now and recognised the effort that this stranger was making. She'd even begun to warm to his turn of phrase. 'The Hitler-gang' she liked very much, and the thought of the *Führer* gobbling up country after country sounded horribly true.

'Madrid?' she queried. 'Jackboots in the Gran Via?'

'That's happening already. You may have noticed. The Germans are everywhere.'

'Further south? Andalus?'

'Keep going.'

'Cádiz?'

'Go left. Not Spain at all.'

'Ah ...' she'd got it at last. 'Gibraltar.'

It was a full week before Annie next laid eyes on Ortega. He'd dropped by *La Vieja Escuela* on some errand or other and Annie intercepted him before he left. They talked on the gravel drive where it curved around the beds of vegetables. He admitted at once that he'd lied about the job at the Prado but claimed it was in Annie's best interests.

'How come?'

'They pay shit money. You'd earn more as a street cleaner.'

'You think I'd want a job in the Prado to get rich?'

'I think you need to feed yourself. This place won't last forever. Sooner or later you'll have to move on.' He shrugged. 'You may be rich already. Who knows?'

'I'm not.'

'That's what I thought. So what did you make of our English friend?'

'He's a Scot. And in the end I liked him.'

'He made you a proposition?'

'He did. I think it was the language thing that impressed him. He said it was rare to meet someone foreign who spoke Spanish like a native.'

'And what did you say?'

'I told him he moved in the wrong circles. That made him laugh.'

'He offered you money?'

'He did. Quite a lot of money. He was polite enough to call it a retainer but that was to spare my blushes.'

'So what did you say?'

'I took a leaf out of your book. I told him to double it.'

'And?'

'He agreed.' Annie gestured back towards the house. 'I'm leaving next week, as soon as I find somewhere else. Francesca said she was sorry to see me go but that woman has perfect manners.'

Ortega nodded, said he was pleased.

'You have no right to be pleased. You lied to me. Again.' She paused. 'Where did you get that engraving, by the way? The Goya print that's hanging on my wall?'

'I bought it in one of the markets. The old woman couldn't wait to get rid of it.'

'Why?'

'She said it was gloomy. The war's over. We all need to move on.'

Annie nodded. As a proposition, it sounded more than sane.

'You'll let me have an address?' Ortega asked. 'Wherever you end up?'

'I might.'

'Leave it with Francesca.' He paused. 'Moncrieff was impressed, by the way. He told me anger was a very good sign.'

'Of?'

Ortega shook his head, his gaze drifting towards the vegetable plot. By now, Annie was oblivious of the facial damage that turned heads in the street. All that mattered was the corner of this strange, strange world Ortega had decided to make his own. He seemed to understand the tides of war, and exactly where they might take a man, and he'd made it his business to ride the bigger waves in whichever direction offered most promise. A watcher, she thought, stealing a word of his own. An observer entirely without scruples. A self-confessed mercenary who rarely left the shadows. An aficionado of violence and its many consequences. Much like Goya.

'Whatever they did to that kid you mentioned,' Ortega nodded at the line of tiny cabbages. 'I don't think it'll happen again.'

Book Three

12

Canaris had never liked the journey to the Berghof. The bumpy landings in the tight little airstrip outside Berchtesgaden. The endless zigzags on the road up the Obersalzberg. Then the looming, surrounding mountains and that change of gear for the final corner beyond which lay Hitler's pride and joy.

The *Abwehr*'s *Direktor* happened to know a little about the history of the place: that Hitler had bought it in 1933, that he'd determined to expand it in keeping with his stewardship of the Reich, that he'd spent months poring over plans and elevations and dramatic renditions of the many views, and that he'd plundered the torrent of royalties from the publication and republication of *Mein Kampf* to pay for it all.

Canaris' taste would never run to cembra pine panelling and heavy Teutonic antique furniture but that wasn't the point. The point was the setting of the *Führer*-house. It had been built and extended to feast on the view, on the peaks and valleys rolling away towards the Austrian border, on the constant changes in the light, on the sudden shafts of sunshine that speared through the veils of cloud. This was theatre in the raw, Wagnerian in scale, and it was a landscape like this, Canaris had long concluded, that had finally detached Hitler from reality. Shut your door on the world, get up early, plant yourself four square in front of a view like that, a view you now *owned*, tuck your hands behind your back, gaze out at the rising sun beyond the Untersberg, and literally anything could be possible.

The summons had come at the start of the week, Monday 21 August 1939. Canaris was to report to the Berghof by noon the following day. There he joined Raeder, Goering and Brauchitsch, the Reich's three commanders-in-chief, plus an assortment of other senior officers. Everyone had been instructed not to wear uniform in order to keep the conference as secret as possible, and Canaris watched a hush descend on the swirl of civilian suits as word spread of Hitler's impending arrival from his study on the second floor. There was coffee for those who wanted it, and plates of delicate pastries to sustain you through the hours before lunch, but Canaris suspected that these men anticipated that something momentous was about to happen and there were few takers. Foreign Minister Ribbentrop was rumoured to be ready to fly to Moscow, and Hitler, when he finally stepped into the room, barely acknowledged the forest of salutes.

The most senior commanders had been offered armchairs; everyone else stood, keeping their host at a respectful distance. Canaris was at the back of the room, leaning on a column. Like everyone else, he'd been forbidden to make notes, but he, too, sensed history in the making and he'd come equipped with a silver pencil and a small pad.

Hitler's gaze roamed over the watching faces before he launched into a brisk analysis of the international situation. The need to address what he termed 'the Polish situation' had arisen earlier than he'd anticipated. Fate, he said, had given him the confidence of the entire German people, a responsibility that weighed heavily on his shoulders, but he was determined to make the best use of this limitless power for the sake of the Reich and if that meant war against the Poles, then so be it.

The nearest of the seated generals stirred as the *Führer* paused to look beyond them, briefly savouring the view from the huge picture window, before returning to his sheaf of notes. 'Poland', Canaris scribbled. 'But when?'

The answer, it seemed, was very soon. Germany, Hitler insisted, faced the harshest possible choice. Either we strike now or face certain defeat later. Britain, for the time being, was in no mood for a war. France was still recovering from the last one. A pact with Russia, he announced, would be signed within the next two days, so thanks to his own foresight Poland was isolated, friendless, and ripe for total destruction.

Ninety minutes later, when the speech finally came to an end, Goering was the only one to speak. He'd arrived in an outlandish hunting garb – a theatrical swirl of green cloak over a pair of lederhosen – and as the senior officer present he assured Hitler that the *Luftwaffe* would do its duty. There came nods across the room and a murmur of assent before the conference broke up for a light lunch on the terrace while Hitler escorted Ribbentrop to his waiting car. The Reich's Foreign Minister, it appeared, had indeed been invited to Moscow.

Back on the terrace, the mood was sombre, conversation sparse, but Canaris could detect a feeling that this morning's performance hadn't shown Hitler at his best. At close quarters, the inspirational Leader who could bring tens of thousands to their feet at a Nuremberg rally had become a braggart and a bully. This was a man, thought Canaris, who seemed to relish the imminence of extreme violence, who seemed to be taking a wanton pleasure in anticipating the deaths of countless Poles, and after lunch when Hitler reappeared, his hunger for war was even more intense. He repeated the need for 'iron determination'. In the life and death struggle to come, he was adamant there'd be no room for pity, nor half-measures, nor anything short of total annihilation. A leader's duty, he insisted, was to urge his people, his *Volk*, to the most extreme lengths to achieve an end that history had willed, and one only had to spare a glance at worms like Chamberlain and Daladier to know that yet another victory was within the grasp of the Reich.

The meeting broke up. Senior commanders hurried to their respective cars while Hitler stood at the top of the stairs that led up from the road, glowering down. Canaris had time to snatch a word with a navy colleague who looked visibly shaken by what he'd just heard. 'There's no thread,' he muttered. 'No logic. Just a leap in the dark.'

Canaris took his scribbled notes back to Berlin. Every morning, he summoned senior *Abwehr* officers to a briefing, and back from the Berghof he used the notes to outline the shape of the days and weeks to come. The attack on Poland, he said, would probably begin within the week. The SS had cooked up a pantomime scripted for murdered inmates from various concentration camps to be dressed up as provocateurs in Polish uniforms. This, promised Hitler, would serve as the thinnest pretext for a declaration of war. Consulting his notes, Canaris quoted Hitler verbatim: 'Whether the world believes this or not, I don't give a shit,' he'd said. 'Why? Because the world believes only in success.'

This, promised Canaris, would be the overture to a bloodbath. Hitler was no longer interested in territory, in *Lebensraum*. What mattered from now on was the line he was drawing across Europe. East of that line, where Germany ran out, SS-Death's Head units advancing behind the front line would be ordered to murder at will any Polish citizen standing in the way of the German steamroller.

'Close your hearts to pity,' Canaris was reading from his notes, quoting Hitler. 'Act brutally. The stronger man is always right.

Eighty million people must obtain what is their due.' Canaris looked up, putting his notes to one side. 'And that, gentlemen ...' he murmured, '... signals the end of the Germany we once knew.'

Hitler sent his armies into Poland a week later, on Friday 1 September. Two days later, Britain declared war. Hans Zimmermann, who'd attended the briefing on Canaris' return from the Berghof, made it his business to be out and about in Berlin, testing the public mood.

In the morning, he rode in the Tiergarten; in the afternoon, casually dressed for yet another hot weekend, he strolled along Unter den Linden with a friend. Twice they stopped for a beer, both times at popular street cafés, but no matter how hard he listened for alarm or even anxiety at the dizzy passage of events, he found the calm of a Berlin Sunday afternoon unruffled. True, there were food cards and soap cards and at night it could be difficult stumbling around in the blackout, but what people were calling 'the Polish thing' seemed very far away, a foreign adventure of little consequence. The Poles were famously difficult and doubtless deserved whatever was coming to them, but in the meantime there was a full programme of weekend football matches, and if you fancied something a little heavier Goethe's *Iphigenie auf Tauris* was playing at the State Theatre.

That evening, Zimmermann took this news back to the Bendlerstrasse, reducing Canaris to something close to despair. Once again, he told Zimmermann, Hitler's gamble was paying off. He knew his people. He knew they cared for nothing as long as the sun shone, and the beer was cold, and the *Wehrmacht*'s armoured columns thundered ever-deeper east. Wars doubtless spilled blood but as long as most of it was Polish, no one was really bothered.

Zimmermann could only agree. Unlike Canaris, he had little faith in the notion of German decency but that wasn't really the point. Wear an *Abwehr* uniform these days and it was impossible to kid yourself that you were winning the other war, the war against the men in black, the war against the zealots in the Gestapo, the war against *Onkel Heine* and the Death's Head *Einsatzgruppen* he'd despatched to Poland. As ever, the Reich's Leader had a term for it. *Politische Bodenreinigung.* Political floor cleaning. At a stroke, Himmler had read his master's mind, seized his opportunity, and plunged into the enveloping darkness.

The following morning, Canaris sent Zimmermann into Poland on a fact-finding mission. Distracted by a proposal to organise support for Irish terrorists in their struggle against the English, Canaris still needed first-hand intelligence to confirm reports of SS atrocities in the city of Bromberg where the Polish military were allegedly exacting vengeance on the German minority, thus triggering similar incidents across newly occupied areas in Upper Silesia. Zimmermann had ridden east with an escort of heavily armed *Abwehr* regulars, quickly confirming that SS killing squads were shooting Poles in their hundreds without either warning or due trial.

In Bromberg, armed with the authority of Canaris, Zimmermann confronted SS leadership on the spot, demanding an explanation for the butchery. The brief interview took place in a commandeered school. The *Wehrmacht* front line had long moved on and the SS commander in charge confirmed that punishment killings had now taken on a new dimension.

'We may spare the small people,' he said, 'but the rest must all be killed, especially the intellectuals, the patriots, the functionaries, and of course the Jews. Taxing work but, alas, necessary. If that gives you a problem, Herr Zimmermann, I suggest you take it up with the *Führer.*' He shrugged. 'Orders, I'm afraid, are orders.'

Even Zimmermann, who had a high tolerance for excess of many kinds, was appalled by this exchange. Reporting back to Canaris in Berlin, he said the SS were out of control, a bunch of psychopaths who were changing the face of warfare without any regard for either compassion or international law. While this degree of brutality had been implicit in the notes Canaris had brought back from the Berghof, it was still a shock to see sadism on this scale masquerading as official policy.

Canaris could only agree, and a week later he put all his other work aside and journeyed east to join the *Führer*-train in a siding in Illnau, at the heart of the newly occupied Silesia. Hitler himself occupied a carriage at the head of the train and was busy in meeting after meeting but Canaris managed to corner *Generaloberst* Wilhelm Keitel, currently serving as Hitler's War Minister, alerting him to a programme of mass shootings linked to the extermination of whole swathes of Polish society. One day, he warned Keitel, the world would wake up to atrocities like these and it would be Keitel's *Wehrmacht* they'd hold responsible.

Keitel, as Canaris knew only too well, was Hitler's tame poodle, hand-picked to do his master's bidding. Policy in Poland, the general insisted, had already been decided. There was a clear line that separated his own front-line troops from whatever might be happening to Poles at the hands of the SS and the Gestapo. His own boys were fighting the war. Himmler was taking care of whatever followed.

'And that's it?' Canaris couldn't believe his ears.

'This is Poland,' Keitel muttered. 'We handle things differently here.'

Canaris carried the news back to Berlin, arriving late in the afternoon at Berlin's Stettin station. The long train journey west had given him the chance to brood on what he'd seen and heard and that evening he sought out Zimmermann, telling him that the situation in Poland was even worse than they'd thought. Zimmermann had been right. Himmler was off the leash, ever-eager to turn his master's ravings into murderous *Aktionen*, and what would happen next was all too clear. In the shape of the *Wehrmacht* and the *Luftwaffe* Hitler had created a strike force no other army in Europe could hope to resist. Stuka dive bombers had routed Polish defences, rewriting the laws of trench warfare. Heinkels and Dorniers had reduced Warsaw to ruins. Armoured columns had raced across Poland posting victory after victory at a speed unthinkable in the last war.

Thanks to the approach of winter, the campaign season was virtually over but by next spring Hitler could point his armies in any direction he chose. Thanks to the non-aggression pact Ribbentrop had signed in Moscow, the Soviets were now allies of the ever-Greater Reich. The logic of conquest therefore lay to the west. To live in Brussels, or Paris, or even London was to live under the shadow of the *Luftwaffe*. Fear of bombing was bad enough but after *Onkel Heine*'s zeal in the east there was now a darker future in store for the flabby democracies the thirties had left in their wake. Poland had unmasked a new Germany, a Reich schooled in the savage arts of indiscriminate slaughter, a leader determined to rid the earth of *Untermenschen*, a country with neither an ounce of compassion nor a soul.

'You agree, Zimmermann?'

'I do, yes.'

'So?'

'We tried to get rid of Hitler before. Last year. You probably remember.'

'And failed.'

'Indeed, and need I remind you why?'

'Because of that fool Chamberlain.' Canaris looked briefly pained. 'Appeasement. Munich. Peace in our time. And look where that took them. Even the British admit the error of their ways but they should have stood up to him, they should have called his bluff.'

'Exactly. And now?'

'Now is too late. Hitler is now beyond their reach and probably beyond ours, too. But *Onkel Heine*? Might that be a step in the right direction?'

Zimmermann raised an eyebrow, said nothing. Canaris knew him in these moods. He has something up his sleeve, he told himself. Something undisclosed.

'Well, Hans?' he enquired wearily. 'You'll light me a candle in this darkness?'

Zimmermann took his time. Then he announced he'd managed to re-establish contact with the British agent he'd met in Oberstdorf.

'Moncrieff?'

'Yes.'

'And?'

'He has access to money, quite a lot of money, Jewish money mainly, and most of it from London. Which might make all the difference if we're serious about *Onkel Heine*.'

13

The outbreak of war took Annie Wrenne by surprise, not because German designs on Poland were unexpected but because it was hard to imagine places she knew well – London, Paris, northern France – being so suddenly pitched into the front line. She thought about phoning her mother in Normandy. She wondered how busy London streets would react to the wail of air raid sirens. She even contemplated her father's life in leafy Chalfont St Peter. Would the *Luftwaffe* waste their bombs on the Home Counties? Could he cope with sharing a bunker with idiot neighbours who never stopped talking?

By now, in Madrid, she was living in four modest rooms on the top floor of lodgings in a street off the Calle de Alcalá. She'd lied to Ortega about doubling Moncrieff's offer but the monthly sum he'd tabled was more than adequate to keep her head above water in a city still battling to feed itself. The country's new masters had pledged to fill bellies and brighten lives but so far the evidence of any real change was thin. Annie had little affection for this abrupt return of the old Spain, despite the grace and kindness of her hosts at *La Vieja Escuela*, but the knowledge that she'd somehow qualified to become a spy had begun to gladden her. By taking Moncrieff's money, by saying yes to whatever he might have in mind, she'd at least won herself a role in whatever dramas might next unfold.

Have in mind? Moncrieff, she suspected, was close to being overwhelmed by the outbreak of war. She'd met him twice in the week after they'd agreed terms and on both occasions he'd seemed distracted by the chaos in what he called the hen coop back home. Hitler's fox was on the loose and the chickens in his own organisation, he'd told her, were totally headless. Quite how he was maintaining contact with MI5 headquarters was never clear, but he was terrifyingly frank about the nation's degree of unreadiness. Worse still, it seemed, was the spreading panic in Europe. Poland had fallen in mere weeks, sending a message to millions of the racially impure who already feared for their lives. Most of them were far too poor to flee, but those with money and connections were already beating on the doors of British embassies across Europe. How to tell the crooks, and knaves, and enemy agents from those with a genuine case for asylum?

Moncrieff had voiced the question the last time they'd met, hunched in the corner of an empty bar near the Calle de Alcalá, Annie's new address, and after some gentle probing he'd admitted that no one in real authority back home seemed to have a clue. At this point, Annie had feared the worst. Was she to join the army of bureaucrats sorting through endless paperwork, checking one document against thousands of others, hunting for signs of enemies at the gate? Was she to take a train home, patrol the nation's ramparts, haul up the drawbridge and prepare the boiling oil?

Happily, the answer was no. Moncrieff wanted her to stay here in Madrid. He told her there was every indication that Franco, now the unquestioned *Jefe* of everything, would be siding with the Germans and the Italians as the dominoes fell across Europe. They'd already fought a war together. Franco owed Berlin a debt of gratitude for the Condor Legion and for much else. Given his native caution, said Moncrieff, Franco would always be an awkward bedfellow, even among fellow Fascists, but London was determined if possible to keep the wretched man out of the war. A neutral Spain might quietly be offering Hitler all kinds of support, but the real nightmare would be a Greater Reich that extended all the way down to Gibraltar.

'And you think that might be possible?'

'Of course, unless we take steps to ensure it doesn't happen.'

'And that's where I come in? You want me to pop round to the German Embassy and tell them to watch their manners?'

Moncrieff, who looked exhausted, had the grace to smile. The German Embassy, he said, was certainly ripe for a spot of quiet infiltration. If she could trail her coat and nurture a relationship or two, that might well open all kinds of doors but in the first place he had something else in mind.

'Such as?'

'Such as our foreign scribblers.'

He wanted her to mix with Madrid's fast-shrinking community of foreign journalists, Americans especially. A lot of these people, he said, lived and partied at the Hotel Florida in the Gran Via. Most of them spoke rudimentary Spanish. They had a need for that special someone who could bring a little Spanish sunshine to their grey, grey lives and on that score he had no doubts that Annie could deliver.

'Deliver what, exactly?'

'We need to gauge the mood back where these people come from. We need to know whether the Americans might one day see this war as theirs. Despatches from abroad can shape that debate.'

'I'm telling them what to write?'

'You're giving them lots of background. You're offering them your own take on the civil war and you can do that because you were part of it. That will intrigue them. What were you doing here? How did all that happen? And when it comes to their own assignments I'm sure you'll be only too happy to pop along and help with the language. Most of them have a need for a talented translator. They also have an eye for a pretty girl. On both counts you'll be making your own weather.'

'You really think so?'

'I'm absolutely certain.'

'How come?'

'Because I trust Ortega. If he says you're up to the challenge, that's a judgement I'm prepared to buy. One word of caution. The best of the journalists are very good indeed, very low maintenance, but the rest tend to be needy. A listening ear and an iron liver will make you lots of friends. Write down the stuff that seems important.'

'And then what?'

'Take it to our embassy. You'll find it in one of those narrow little streets off the Castellana. I'm afraid it's seen better days but there's a helpful man called Bottomley who looks after our interests. Write it down. Christian Bottomley. He's fully briefed and will be expecting you. If anything's really urgent, make sure he knows. After encryption it can be in London within the hour but don't waste the coding people's time because they have no sense of humour. Everything else, everything routine, goes in the diplomatic bag. That'll be a day or two later. Bottomley,' he handed her a pen. 'With an "e" before the "y". If he does something especially wonderful for the cause, buy him a box of chocolates, Belgian if possible. One too many of those *truffes* with acacia honey and he gets very silly indeed.'

At this, Moncrieff had checked his watch, bade Annie to finish her glass of thin Rioja, struggled to his feet and walked her across the road to her new lodgings. He was taking the train back to Britain first thing tomorrow. With luck and a following wind, he said, he might be back in Madrid before the New Year, but if that proved impossible he wished her a very happy Christmas. In the meantime, good luck with everything and everybody, including Christian Bottomley.

'The *truffes*,' he reminded her. 'Don't forget.'

And so, as winter crept ever closer and breath on the streets began to cloud, Annie did his bidding. Moncrieff had been wrong, as it turned out, about foreign journalists abandoning Spain once the shooting had stopped. Word had spread that cities like Madrid and Lisbon were quickly becoming nests of spies, a neutral space where rival camps could size up each other and plot lots of mischief, and when she paid her first visit to the big bar at the Hotel Florida it was the work of minutes to catch an eye or two, start a conversation, and let these strangers into a world she'd decided to largely invent. By late in the evening, she'd yet to buy a drink. She had an impressive list of names already memorised and three firm offers of supper over the coming days.

Most of these men, as Moncrieff had anticipated, were American. Some had served their newspapers throughout the war, with breaks to catch their breath in Paris or Toulouse, and she knew at once by their reticence that there was little she could bring to their tables. One or two of them even spoke passable Spanish, and one in particular, the second time she turned up at the bar, turned out to be an admirer of Goya.

His name was Whittaker. He was a thin man, tall, and Annie judged him to be in his forties. Unlike a louder set that drank around a table in the corner, he was shy, bookish, and slightly melancholy, nursing a beer that appeared to last him most of the evening. The first time they had a proper conversation he confessed that he'd fallen a little in love with Spain and feared for what would doubtless happen next. Genuinely intrigued, Annie wanted more and he studied her carefully for a moment or two before offering a prediction.

'Franco had a mission from the start,' he said. 'He's here to put the French Revolution into reverse. That might turn out to be a mighty accomplishment in certain books but in mine, poor Spain deserves better.'

Poor Spain. This wasn't a judgement shared by other journalists, especially the newer arrivals. They were infuriated by the *Madrileño* talent for courtesy and delay, for extending every conversation far longer than it deserved, and some of them were openly contemptuous about a city that could barely manage to organise a decent barter economy. Annie played along with most of this nonsense, occasionally adding a *sotto voce* warning about the perils of German efficiency, but the younger of these men were strangers to irony, their opinions already set in concrete, and no matter how much she drank she was ruthless in deciding who might – in Moncrieff's happy phrase – be of some service to the cause, and who were more interested in bedding her.

The cause? This was a word she bore in mind when she compiled her regular reports for Moncrieff, delivered as requested to the British Embassy. She'd yet to set eyes on Bottomley but he definitely existed because mention of his name had raised an eyebrow and a smile when she left her first envelope at the embassy's reception, but she was glad to be spared a conversation because these reports of hers owed more to diligence, alcohol and a light dusting of invention than any particle of genuine intelligence that might win a war. This realisation, oddly enough, caused her no embarrassment whatsoever. The world of spies, she'd decided already, was second cousin to the world of journalism: full of fake drama, cheap emotion and inflated expense claims.

Whittaker, though, was different. They'd become friends by now, and Annie had been glad to set aside any agenda on her part except the comforts of a decent conversation. What also helped was Whittaker's candour about important relationships in his life. He confessed he'd never properly figured women, probably never would. He'd married early, divorced within months, and was indifferent to most of the carnal pleasures. After Giles Roper, Annie was wary about her own judgement when it came to men but the harder she listened to Whittaker, the more she took him at his word. He was a man, she'd decided, for whom solitude held a quiet delight.

By now it was early December, and he chose an evening that turned out to be his birthday to invite her back to his lodgings for a light supper of whatever he could find. He lived in a suite of draughty barn-like rooms up five flights of wooden stairs in a street within walking distance of the big telecoms building where reporters filed their copy.

Annie arrived with a bottle of French Côtes du Rhone she'd acquired from Ortega, whom she still saw regularly. Whittaker, clad in a rather fetching apron he'd stolen from the Hotel Florida, offered her a glass of sherry and retreated to a stove in the corner, apologising for the mess. Annie shed her coat and gazed around her. The only table was dominated by a huge typewriter surrounded by sheets of carbon paper, most of them used and reused. Ancient copies of newspapers from every corner of Europe were scattered on the bare wooden floorboards, and there were piles of books beneath the curtainless window. A single

torn poster for pre-war summers in San Sebastian brightened
the peeling flakes of paint on the biggest wall, and one of the
two sagging armchairs was occupied by a bony cat. Given the
circumstances, she decided, any Hollywood set designer would
have come up with exactly this.

Whittaker served a stew of withered-looking vegetables,
undistinguished in every respect but enlivened by generous
splashes of brandy. Annie nibbled at a frost-blackened potato
while they talked at length about the latter stages of Goya's
life when his deafness had walled him off from real life. It was
Whittaker's view that the paintings that came from this period
were far superior to the artful daubs that had so delighted the
royal court and with this Annie could only agree. They also
compared notes on which of the *Pinturas negras* they liked the
most. Whittaker chose Goya's treatment of two men fighting
against a backdrop of looming clouds and mountains, telling
her that fifteen minutes in front of the original would change
anyone's life, not necessarily for the better, and it was at this
point that Annie realised he must have some kind of special
access to the Prado Museum.

'It's true,' Whittaker was wrestling with an underboiled disc
of parsnip. 'I got a bunch of stories from them in the early days
and they've been generous ever since.'

'You were here when the Germans bombed the place?'

'I went round that night. Direct hit on the *Second of May*
canvas. There were guys on their hands and knees for days
afterwards, collecting every last fragment. One day, I guess,
they may be able to restore the piece but no one's holding their
breath.'

Annie nodded. Goya's take on the charge of Napoleon's
Imperial Guard, she thought, remembering the painted faces
in the Calle de Alcalá, bewitched by the carnage.

'And that's when the museum people started moving everything else out?' she asked.

'Sure. I watched them do it, even lent a hand some nights. Everything crated, wrapped in blankets, wedged in the back of a bunch of trucks. They went to Figueras first, then France, then Geneva. Some of the better stuff has been returned, now the German bombers are busy elsewhere. This isn't a story that plays well in Des Moines but keeping track of national treasures was never going to be easy and I'm still trying to sell my editor a follow-up. The Spanish are canny. The Soviets took all of their gold and now they're outta funds. Some of those pictures are worth a fortune. Best get them all back before the world blows up.'

Before the world blows up. That night Annie drank far too much, making inroads into Whittaker's stash of yet more brandy, and happily accepted his offer of a bunch of cushions on the floor and a couple of blankets against the worst of the cold. Within weeks, they were celebrating Christmas together – her place this time – with Whittaker offering choice morsels from his collection of unpublished scuttlebutt by way of a present. Which of Madrid's new masters were helping themselves to priceless art from the Prado. How one of the younger American scribblers had fallen in love with a hooker who was servicing the German Embassy. How plans were taking shape for Franco's huge mausoleum out in the mountains north of the city. Each of these titbits she passed on to Moncrieff, payment for the monthly envelope of fifty peseta notes she was still collecting from the embassy.

From Moncrieff himself she heard absolutely nothing. When she tried to account for this silence, a whisper of conscience which was increasingly rare, she imagined him drowning or even dead beneath a breaking wave of enemy aliens, and in one of her regular conversations with Ortega she wondered whether her unforeseen relationship with HM Treasury might last forever, a constant trickle of funds from the nation's war chest.

Then, quite suddenly, spring arrived, the cherry trees beside the river frothy with blossom, Madrid at last waking up to blue skies and more than a hint of warmth in the morning sun. By now, Annie had said no to four proposals of marriage, and offered detailed advice to a scribe from Chicago who suspected his pretty young wife was up to no good. She'd also hooked a junior German diplomat called Friedrich who used his perfect Spanish to tell her she had wonderful ankles, and that she reminded him of the first woman he'd ever properly loved. *Properly* sounded slightly ominous in this declaration and it was barely days before Annie's hopes of unlimited intelligence windfalls gave way to her realisation that any frankness on his part relied on her agreeing to a number of conditions, beginning with an evening of what he delicately termed 'physical intimacy'. With regret, the next time she met him, she took care to cover her ankles before announcing that their brief relationship, such as it had been, was *kaput*.

So far, so nearly good. Thanks to Moncrieff's continuing largesse, she still had money in her purse, and occasional evenings with Whittaker were as delightful as ever. In the unmistakable shape of Ortega, she also kept her thumb on a very different Madrid, exclusively Spanish, and when the more callow scribblers at the Hotel Florida told her about the blessings of law and order that Franco had brought to this once lawless city, she was able to offer a private prayer of thanks that – so far – she'd been spared the attentions of the secret police. The Germans, Ortega told her, had shared their expertise with their new allies, and the torture routines now regularly applied in police stations across the city had surprised even him.

Then, one evening in early April, came a knock at Annie's door. Visitors were largely discouraged and therefore rare, and it was only after the fifth knock, when she heard her name called in an accent she couldn't quite place, that she finally opened the door. He was small but personable, an imp of a man. He offered her a slightly awkward handshake, which felt totally out of place, and told her his name was Werner Nehmann. He said he'd got her name from the guys at the Hotel Florida, and if she could spare the time he'd be glad of a little advice.

'And the address?'

'That came from somewhere else.'

'Care to tell me where?'

'I can't. Because he'd probably kill me.'

'He?'

'A friend of yours.' He scowled and gestured briefly at his own face. 'He says he knows you well. And he says he'll kill me if I ever pass this address on.'

'You're dead twice, then. Not a cheerful outlook. Might this be Carlos?'

'You're right. It is.'

'So what's his second name?'

'Ortega.' A winning smile. 'And he says the kids in the street still call him *El Diablo*.'

After a moment's hesitation, Annie let him in. Given the name, she suspected this stranger was German. He spoke comedy French, mangling the accents, but it was serviceable enough.

'Are you a journalist?'

'Yes. Sometimes.'

'And when you're not a journalist?'

'I run errands, do favours, mainly for friends back home.'

'Home?'

'The mighty Reich. Berlin.'

Annie nodded, invited him to sit down. At last this mystery visit was beginning to make sense. Ortega knew Annie's eagerness to make contacts among Madrid's ever-growing community of Germans. Maybe that explained the knock on her door.

'So how can I help you?' she asked.

Nehmann was looking round. He wore a tiny silver ring in the lobe of his left ear, an act of some defiance in Franco's stern new regime, and the square of scarlet knotted loosely at his throat was a throwback to kindlier, more interesting days when the Republic was still intact.

'Carlos told me to look for a picture,' he nodded up at the Goya etching. 'That's got to be it.'

'You haven't answered the question.'

Nehmann looked briefly reproachful, as if this hurry of hers was somehow out of place, and then mentioned another name, Whittaker this time. He'd met the American only recently, at the Florida, and they'd ended up chatting about the return of the Prado's holdings from Geneva.

'You want to write the story, too?'

'I want to lay hands on a painting.'

'Something in particular?'

'Yes. It's a Rubens but Whittaker thinks it's not his best work. Happily I have a friend in Berlin who disagrees.'

'It has a name, this painting?'

'*Nude Woman.*'

'That could be one of hundreds. What's happening on the canvas?'

'A naked woman is lying in bed. There's lots of her. The bed is curtained but the curtains are drawn back. She has one arm raised, the right arm I think, and there's a guy's face peeping round.'

'He's carrying slippers, this guy?'

'Yes.'

'And there's another pair on the floor beside the bed?'

'Yes.'

'I know the painting. I didn't realise it was in the Prado.'

Nehmann shrugged. That, he said, was what he'd been told. His friend had seen the picture in Geneva nearly a year ago. He was silly about women and he was even sillier about Rubens, and he was absolutely determined the painting should be his.

'So why don't you go to the Prado and ask?'

'It needs to come from someone who knows more about art than I do.'

'Whittaker?'

'He says he's too busy. Then he mentioned you. So ...' that smile again, '... here I am.'

Annie considered the proposition for a moment.

'Any Rubens will cost a fortune,' she pointed out.

'Money won't be a problem. Neither will a commission, or maybe we should call it a fee.'

'For doing what?'

'For talking to the people at the Prado, for agreeing a price, for making arrangements. Whittaker says most of the museum's pictures were brought back from Geneva by train in September. The Rubens should be among them.' He paused, looking round at the scraps of furniture Annie had managed to put together, the single armchair with the poorly repaired leg, the battered table, the threadbare carpet cratered with cigarette burns. 'Ten per cent? What do you think?'

He got up without waiting for an answer, thanked Annie for her time, and then gave her an address where he was staying. It was a hotel she'd never heard of, out near *La Vieja Escuela*. He'd crossed the room and opened the door to the stairs before he paused and looked back. 'I should be there for at least a month. Ten's an insult. These could be happier days. Let's say fifteen.'

'Fifteen?'

'Per cent.'

Annie brooded for the rest of the day. She couldn't be certain but she thought the current value of an original Rubens, measured in US dollars, would be – at the very least – in six figures. Fifteen per cent of six figures was at least $15,000. For a week's work? Was this little imp serious? In truth, she had no idea but the longer she thought about the proposition, the more she suspected she had nothing to lose. Still haunted by her act of desertion on the dockside at Alicante, what she hadn't done to help those poor bloody women, she'd been scouring her conscience for some way of making good. The Quakers back in Murcia were always running out of funds and if they were still there, still trying to make ends meet, then a windfall like this would be more than welcome.

That evening she found Whittaker at the bar in the Florida. He remembered his conversation with Werner Nehmann and confirmed that the painting, once Europe had settled down, might fetch a great deal of money. When Annie reproached him for judging the painting second-rate, he shot her a rare grin.

'She looked like I remember my wife,' he said. 'Never marry an older woman.'

Ortega, when Annie tracked him down a couple of days later, agreed he'd also met Nehmann.

'That little man has friends,' he said, 'in very high places. For Moncrieff's sake you might work on him a little harder.'

'You know this?'

'I do.'

'How?'

Ortega touched his ruined nose, a gesture that told her to mind her own business, and changed the subject.

'Have you heard the rumours?' he asked.

'About?'

'The Germans. The snow's melting. Hitler's on the march any day now. He's a child at heart and he gets bored far too easily.'

It was 8 April 1940. Next morning, German troops crossed the Norwegian border and quickly occupied Oslo, Bergen, Trondheim and Narvik. Annie ran Ortega to earth at a bodega he'd adopted just off the Gran Via. He was sitting in the fall of spring sunshine beneath a window, nursing a glass of red wine, watching Annie as she stepped in through the door.

'So how did you know?' she demanded. 'About Norway?'

'Werner Nehmann told me.' He signalled the barman to bring them the rest of the bottle. 'That little man knows everything.'

14

Hans Zimmermann was quick to recognise the real meaning of his Leader's lightning descent on Norway.

'This is the hors d'oeuvre,' he told Canaris. 'Hitler's a glutton. He has the appetite of twenty men and absolutely no table manners. This is not the year to be French, or Danish, or Belgian, or even English.'

Canaris could only agree. Unlike most of his *Abwehr* officers, he had access to *Fall Gelb*, the *Führer's* comprehensive plan to unleash a torrent of violence once the new campaign season got properly under way, and he knew what was in store for countries desperate to put a halt to German expansion. The howl of Stuka dive bombers was about to become the soundtrack underscoring months of busy conquest.

The first divisions pounced on 10 May 1940. Within ten days, Denmark had fallen, Belgium was fighting for its life and German armoured columns had speared through France to pause for breath on the Channel coast. Hundreds of thousands of British troops were trudging back towards Dunkirk, while Parisian bookshelves were suddenly making space for Franco-German dictionaries. A week later, arriving at dawn for a brief tour of the new jewel in the Reich's crown, even Hitler appeared to be surprised at the speed and completeness of his latest victory. Peering at the distant Eiffel Tower from the terrace at the Trocadero, he shook his head, offered the briefest of salutes and was driven back to Le Bourget airfield, never to return. Only the British, to Hitler's bewilderment, refused to bend the knee.

Canaris, both impressed and appalled by this extraordinary feat of German arms, called an unofficial meeting of the *Abwehr*'s inner circle, just a handful of men he'd literally trusted with his life. Months earlier, before Christmas, two developments had shaken his faith in the future of the country he loved. The first was the litter of atrocities the SS and the Gestapo had left across Poland; pleas for *Onkel Heine* to rein in his killing squads had fallen on deaf ears. The second was the alarmed reluctance of senior *Wehrmacht* commanders to restore a little sanity, even compassion, to the Greater Reich. Their business, they insisted, lay strictly on the battlefield. Anything else was mere rumour.

Not good enough. Back at the end of last year, at considerable personal risk, Canaris and his fellow conspirators had once again plotted to kill Hitler but the military support they so desperately needed was finally denied. Everyone, in discreet conversations across Berlin, agreed that Hitler was reckless, ungovernable, and could – when it suited him – play the madman. But as long as his gambles paid off – in *Lebensraum*, in treasure, in jobs – no one wanted anyone else's hand on the national tiller.

And so high summer found Hitler bestriding the entire Continent. From the North Cape above the Arctic Circle to the shores of the Mediterranean, cowed shoppers were paying in German currency, obeying strict curfew rules, adjusting their clocks to Berlin time, and debating the ethics of betraying their Jewish neighbours. By and large, to no one's surprise, it was said that the *Führer* was satisfied with the current turn of events. The cream of European produce was flooding into the *Heimat* and

Germans were only too happy to feast on Danish pork, Belgian chocolates and French wine.

True, there were one or two wrinkles in the spread of Nazi conquests to tidy up, chiefly the need to bring the British to the negotiating table, and it was at this point, 23 July 1940, that Canaris found himself once again despatched to Spain, along with an assortment of senior *Wehrmacht* commanders, all of them in civilian dress and carrying false passports. This, as Zimmermann was the first to point out, was a different kind of invasion, discreet, unreported, but no less momentous. The only word on the lips of the German delegation? Gibraltar.

By now, Franco was occupying the Royal Palace of El Pardo, a grand residence designed, fittingly enough, for a series of absolute monarchs. According to reports from the German Embassy, Franco lived here in heavily guarded isolation, a state of mind one senior diplomat had likened to an oriental despot. The *Caudillo* held cabinet meetings, demanded deference from a carefully screened assortment of visitors, and frequently ventured out to hunt game in the wooded hills of the surrounding estate.

Canaris, in nearby Madrid, had already been in touch with the *Abwehr*'s K-Organisation, the agency's local presence in Spain. The K-Org had feelers deeply embedded in the new state apparatus and quickly arranged for a top-level meeting to address what Berlin might need for a projected operation on Spanish soil. Canaris and his half-dozen senior officers, each of whom would be key to this operation, were invited to a conference room at military headquarters in the city's centre.

General Vigon was a courteous, slightly academic figure who'd masterminded Franco's war in the north and had now been appointed Chief of the Spanish General Staff. Canaris knew him only by reputation but a briefing from K-Org, to his relief, recommended a brisk presentation of what exactly Berlin might have in mind.

'We're here because of Gibraltar, General. We need to gather as much intelligence as we can in the little time we have at our disposal. I anticipate pulling all our thoughts together before the end of the month and naturally you and your staff would be part of that exercise.'

The other Spanish presence at the table was a younger Lieutenant-Colonel whose name Canaris recognised from a K-Org analysis of the headquarters section dealing with military intelligence. Now the two Spanish officers exchanged glances.

'You have an operation in mind?' Vigon's gaze had returned to Canaris. 'Against Gibraltar?'

'Yes.'

'When, exactly?'

'Within months. If that proves practical.'

'And you really think you can *surprise* the British? Given the task at hand? The geography of the place? The statement it makes? If we Spanish wanted another word for *inexpugnable*, it might be Gibraltar.'

'*Inexpugnable?*' This from Rudolf Witzig, a paratrooper officer with no Spanish.

'Impregnable,' Canaris murmured, his eyes still fixed on Vigon. 'Our job is to test that supposition. That's why we're here. Of course the battlefield odds favour the British but there may be ways of shortening those odds. As for the appetite for such an operation, here in Spain ...' Canaris sat back, '... need I go on?'

Vigon conceded the point with the faintest smile. Only last week, after quiet prompting from Canaris, Hitler had awarded Franco the Grand Cross of Gold of the Order of the German Eagle, the highest decoration the Reich could bestow on a foreigner. This was a bauble that had delighted the *Caudillo* and that same day, at the first anniversary Civil War Victory parade here in Madrid, Franco had beamed at the carefully orchestrated crowds roaring for *Gibraltar español*. This demand for the return of precious Spanish soil had prompted the abrupt departure of the new British Ambassador and his wife from the reviewing VIP stand, and now the capital was awash with rumours that the Spanish army might soon be marching south, a prospect that filled many with glee, and a few – better briefed – with foreboding.

'Only one road leads to that lump of Rock, Herr *Admiral*. It's overlooked from a million ledges. The British have had ample time to prepare themselves. Your armies may have chased them out of France but their navy can still give anyone a hiding.' A brief pause for another whispered conference with the Lt-Colonel before returning to Canaris. 'This would be a joint operation? You and us?'

'It couldn't be done without you.'

'With respect, Herr *Admiral*, that wasn't my question. I'm asking whether you envisage us working together at the tactical level. Artillery, for instance. Softening up the British before any main assault.'

'That would be a decision for others.'

'That I accept but this whole enterprise is fraught with difficulty. Getting the guns down there, laying in supplies of munitions, all of this takes time. The gauge of French railways is different from ours. More delay. More fuss. More people. More *visibility*. Every loyal Spaniard might have Gibraltar etched on his heart but, as ever, we military folk must deal in facts, not fairy tales.'

'You have maps of the British defence systems?' Canaris asked.

'Of course.'

'Compiled from direct observation?'

'Partly.'

'You have agents in place?'

Vigon glanced at the Lieutenant-Colonel. A nod told him to field the question.

'The British have a labour force they depend on,' the intelligence officer murmured. 'They come in daily from the mainland. Do they need the money? Of course they do. But they're Spanish first and foremost. They have eyes. They watch, they listen, they remember.'

'And afterwards they talk to you.'

'They do. Especially now. The British are building themselves a proper airstrip. They're tunnelling, too, opening up new areas under the Rock. They're using lots of dynamite. You can hear the explosions from the mainland.'

'So they're digging in?'

'Of course. And so would you under their circumstances. Many of the British see no point in keeping this war going but, alas, they're not in Downing Street. Churchill thinks otherwise, Herr *Admiral*, but I'm sure you know about all that already.'

Canaris nodded. This young man was right, he thought. More dynamite to hollow out the Rock. More Spitfires to hollow out the *Luftwaffe*. More everything to make life impossibly tough for the marauding Hun.

'So you think any operation against Gibraltar is doomed?' Canaris queried. 'You think there's no point continuing this conversation?'

The Lieutenant-Colonel, about to answer, was restrained by his superior.

'We think we can help you with the military details,' Vigon was smiling. 'Any real decision about attacking Gibraltar belongs elsewhere.'

*

The meeting with Franco, evidently foreseen, took place three hours later. Canaris, alone this time, was driven out to his palace among the wooded slopes of the El Pardo estate and conducted upstairs to a study on the first floor where he found Franco sitting beside an ornate writing desk. From somewhere, the *Caudillo* had managed to lay his hands on a colour photograph of the Grand Cross of Gold. The award would, in due course, be awarded personally but in the meantime the photograph had been framed alongside signed photographs of Hitler and Mussolini. In a gesture towards the intimacy of their previous meeting, Franco – unusually – was alone.

Canaris offered greetings and congratulations from the Chancellery in Berlin. The *Führer*, he said, was delighted that the new regime was in rude health and had matured sufficiently to warrant a second Victory Parade. The *Caudillo*, a little plumper than Canaris remembered, was visibly pleased, but then his dark, moist, *Gallego* eyes were suddenly clouded.

'*General* Vigon ...' he nodded towards the phone, '... has spoken of your plans for Gibraltar. In principle, you'll know already that we have every expectation of mounting an attack of our own to drive the British into the sea but now may not be the time. The British still have the biggest navy in the world and for all their *politesse* and diplomatic games they are never slow to use it. If we move on Gibraltar, I fear they will retaliate in the Canary Isles. Could we fend them off? Even with German support? The answer, I suspect, is no. My task ...' he gestured vaguely at the view from the window, '... is to somehow tend to my flock. I must feed them, clothe them, keep them together in body and spirit. A responsibility like this can weigh heavy, *Admiral*, as I'm sure you appreciate.' He paused. 'Be frank with me. Is there a reason the British won't come to the negotiating table?'

'Churchill,' Canaris grunted.

'And is there no way of getting rid of him? Or making him change his mind?'

'I fear not,' Canaris fought the temptation to smile. 'Men with absolute power have no incentive to share it.'

Franco nodded, said nothing. Then Canaris bent forward slightly, a gesture – he hoped – of renewed intimacy.

'A burden shared is a burden halved,' he said.

'Meaning?'

'I'm sure there are ways our two great nations can get their heads together and agree a sharing of the spoils of war. There's a debt still owing for all the help we gave you against the Republicans. I understand you still need oil, foodstuffs, arms, ammunition. In return, you have much to offer in the way of raw materials such as wolfram and copper. Your Atlantic ports, and perhaps the Canaries, might be open to our shipping. None of this is in my gift to negotiate, of course, but I have the ear of those who matter in Berlin and I'm confident we can all arrive at ...' he shrugged, '... some kind of arrangement. Might that ease the burden just a little?'

Canaris was certain that there was nothing in this little speech that had taken Franco remotely by surprise but it was part of his *Gallego* nature to effect a sudden blush of gratitude. Both hands reached out and Canaris gripped them, flabby and slightly damp.

'Three houses in Algeciras have been placed at your disposal, Herr *Admiral*. Two of them have uninterrupted views of the Rock, and a selection of powerful telescopes. The other you may use as a residence. We have made arrangements for you to travel round the bay to similar vantage points in La Línea. You may wish to conduct further expeditions into the Campo to check possible artillery emplacements. All that access comes from the bottom of our Spanish hearts. All we request in response is an understanding of the price we've paid so far for peace of a kind, and ways in which we may meet our future obligations.' A longish pause, and then that same moistness around the eyes again. 'I sense we speak the same language, *Admiral*, in your case literally. Might I be right?'

Canaris nodded.

'*Absolutamente*,' he murmured.

Canaris and his party flew to Algeciras at dawn the following morning. Once the sun was up, the cabin of the *Tante-Ju* was warm and Canaris took one of the seats beside a window, gazing down at the bareness of the yellows and browns as Spain slowly unfurled beneath. Algeciras was ringed by mountains, and the pilot, aware of Canaris' interest in Gibraltar, banked gently to the left.

The mountains rose and then suddenly fell away to reveal the long sweep of Algeciras Bay, guarded in the east by the dirty white tooth of limestone that was Gibraltar. The Ju-52 carried no markings but the pilot kept carefully out of range of British ack-ack gunners on the Rock, dropping a wing over the scatter of rooftops that was La Línea and offering a slow flypast to the north of Gibraltar. Seen from this altitude, work on the new airstrip made perfect sense, bulldozers scouring the dark earth, driving the broad line of the new runway, yet to be hardened with concrete, ever closer to the waters of the bay. Visible, too, was a gaping hole at the seat of the Rock with its newly excavated innards neatly readied for disposal.

With Gibraltar suddenly gone, Canaris craned his neck to watch the last of the anchored British warships disappear beneath the port wing. Vigon had been right, he thought. Generations of British troops had defended this little Spanish appendix and it would take a great deal of *Wehrmacht* effort to winkle them out.

Two cars met them at the airstrip in Algeciras. It was hot by now, and with every window open the cars dropped down through the narrow streets to the town itself, a nest of bright façades softened by bougainvillea and morning glory. Here, the street was choked with carts hauled by high-stepping donkeys and barefoot kids begging for small change at the classier cafés, and the moment they rounded the corner there came a stink of fish from the boxes lying open on the quayside. This was a tableau, Canaris thought, perfectly scored for the clouds of seagulls quarrelling over discarded viscera while nut-brown fishermen attended to their nets.

But this was local colour, a postcard Algeciras liked to send to the rest of the world, while the real centre of attention was Gibraltar. The Rock dominated every view from the city, a looming grey presence beyond the blue shimmer of the bay, and Canaris spent the early afternoon examining the long profile of the British colony through a powerful telescope at the waterfront house assigned by Vigon. The Zeiss optics were perfect for this kind of work and he scanned the waterfront yard by yard through a forest of moored warships, trying to understand the geography of the place.

On the other side of the Rock, he knew the limestone cliff face fell near-vertically towards the water but on the western flank overlooking the bay the topography was kinder, the fall terraced and terraced again until the Rock shook itself into an apron of usable land that had become a tangle of rooftops. Canaris had never been to Gibraltar, but he imagined that it would be here that you'd find the real fingerprints of the British: the shops, dwellings, offices, cafés, barracks, repair workshops, dry docks and every other facility that would keep the precious Mediterranean gateway to the empire intact and open. Reduce this maze to rubble, storm what was left of the garrison, effect an abrupt change of ownership, and Hitler's dreams of an empire of his own would take a giant step forward.

Except, as Vigon had been kind enough to point out, it would never be that simple. Or even, as Canaris had begun to suspect, desirable. Hitler was already too rampant, and too powerful. He'd laid a steaming pile of trophies at Germany's door, campaign kills fresh from the battlefield, whole countries trussed and bound. He'd become the victim of his own success, a dictator full of rage and madness, determined to wreak a terrible vengeance on any enemies, real or imagined, that crossed his path. Feeding that appetite, making it more possible for more of God's earth to march in lockstep to the thunder of Nazi boots, was no longer the work of a civilised man. There had to be a better way, and Canaris sensed that journey might start here in Algeciras.

Canaris knew a little about this place: how it owed its patchy fortune to various forms of contraband, how the smells and spices of nearby Africa had brightened the offerings in the seafront cafés, and how a floating population of spies, smugglers, arms dealers and a certain breed of journalist congregated nightly at the Reina Christina Hotel.

It was late afternoon by the time Canaris made his way to the hotel. He'd agreed a rendezvous with one of the local *Abwehr* K-Org agents and he spent the best part of an hour listening to the officer's thoughts on the outcome of any serious bid to mount an assault on Gibraltar. The word he used at least twice was 'mad'. Mad, in the first place, even to contemplate juggling the logistics involved. And mad, more importantly, to ignore the crushing weight of the limestone Rock.

'This country regards itself as a fortress,' he muttered. 'The Pyrenees to the north, water on the other three sides. That makes them feel safe. That gives them comfort. Gibraltar is simply Spain writ small. The perfect fortress, Herr *Direktor*, and a come-on to any army silly enough to ignore the laws of nature.'

With this, the agent made his excuses and departed for another appointment, leaving Canaris to settle in an armchair beside the window, absorbed in his thoughts, half-aware of the play of shadows thrown on the encircling lawn by the hotel's palm trees. The sun was beginning to set, away to the west, and the long shape of the Rock had acquired a strange colour.

'I'd suggest pink, *Admiral*,' Scots accent. 'Rather appropriate, *nicht war?*'

Canaris frowned for a moment, then put his glass carefully on the table beside his chair and looked up.

'Tam Moncrieff?' He got to his feet and extended a hand. 'Should I have expected this pleasure?'

Much to the surprise of the rest of the German *Abwehr* party, by now assembled in a loose knot at the bar, the two men had dinner together. It was Canaris' idea and Canaris' choice of table, set discreetly beside a half-curtained window at the far end of the main restaurant. Both men under-ordered, keener on conversation than food, a poached halibut with two delicate florets of broccoli for Canaris, a brochette of lightly grilled langoustine on a bed of steamed rice for Moncrieff. Canaris insisted this surprise treat was *un regalito* from the Bendlerstrasse, perhaps some modest compensation for Moncrieff's abuse at the hands of the Gestapo two years earlier back in Berlin, but both men knew that no present, big or small, would ever wash the taste of *Onkel Heine* from Moncrieff's lips.

'I understand why you loathe the man,' Moncrieff had bought a very expensive bottle of Chablis, and promised another the moment they finished the first. 'But hating's not enough, is it?'

Canaris, still examining the bottle, ignored Moncrieff's question. First Schultz, and then Zimmermann had spoken highly of this Scots warrior who seemed to carry his wounds so lightly. Nimble, Zimmermann had said, but brave when it matters. If we ever end up in London, you should summon him to the colours.

An *Abwehr* presence in London? Canaris regarded that possibility as vanishingly unlikely. More to the point, he viewed Britain as civilisation's last best hope. He was tempted to share this thought with Moncrieff but a long life in all kinds of company had kept his lips sealed when it came to thoughts that truly mattered, and his challenge just now was to deal with the existential threat to his own organisation embodied by *Onkel Heine*.

'History has a way of dealing with men like Himmler,' Canaris said carefully. 'Spill too much blood, start killing the wrong people, and after a while the consequences can be overwhelming.'

'But that makes you a patient man,' Moncrieff reached for his wine glass. 'Doesn't history need a shove from time to time?'

A shove. It was a schoolboy thought on Moncrieff's part, carefully planted to tempt the German into an indiscretion or two, and Canaris approved.

'You think I should shoot him? Find somewhere dark to take him by surprise? Wait for him to appear on the staircase of some walk-up apartment block? Wait for him to press the time switch on the wall? Wait for a glint or two of light on those glasses of his? Is that the way this pretty little story goes?'

'You're telling me the thought has never occurred?'

'I'm telling you the man has a private army numbered in thousands, tens of thousands. And I'm telling you there's no way anyone will ever get to him. Not yet. Not until the whole contraption blows itself up.'

'Contraption?'

'Us. The Reich. The men in black. The men in grey. The women. The kids. The Hitler Youth. Us. Everyone. Ask Heckmair. He knows best of all.'

'I did.'

'You did what?'

'Ask Heckmair. I met Zimmermann in Oberstdorf. You'll be aware of that. Heckmair's a hero of anyone who knows anything about mountains. I happen to love mountains, have done all my life, and Zimmermann knew where he lived. We knocked on the door before we left Oberstdorf. Zimmermann did the introductions. We talked for perhaps ten minutes, out in the cold, the last of the daylight, but that was more than I ever expected. The man, and the three others he climbed with, achieved the impossible. Then Robert Ley came along, and Goebbels, and finally Hitler, and after that it wasn't Heckmair's story at all. It belonged to the Reich, to Hitler, to *Onkel Heine*, to the whole sorry gang, and Heckmair found himself on a hotel balcony in Nuremberg, Hitler's newest trophy, staring at men and women, *German* men and women, reduced to screaming infants at the very sight of someone who'd spent nearly three days on the north face of the Eiger, climbed the beast, and emerged alive. Why was that? Because Goebbels had put him on the cover of countless national magazines. None of those infants in the street truly understood what he and those men had done. Hitler certainly didn't. And Heckmair came away from all that madness a much wiser man. Not because of the Eiger, for which he had much respect, but because of Nuremberg and Hitler, for whom he had none. He told me it was disturbing, that was the word he used, *disturbing*, but he was being polite. Do I detect a smile, Herr *Direktor*? Or even a nod of agreement?'

Moncrieff wasn't in the business of delivering long speeches but on this occasion his respect for the mountains, and for the man across the table, amply justified the indulgence. In any event, he knew Canaris was impressed. He also suspected that the *Abwehr*'s boss had taken a drink or two before they'd met, and after another half-hour of conversation Canaris judged it wise to stage a tactical retreat before his own tongue gave him away and so he laid a brief hand on Moncrieff's arm, murmured a word of thanks for a truly wonderful bottle of wine, expressed his own admiration for Aryan prowess on Alpine peaks, got to his feet and left.

Moncrieff watched him crossing the restaurant. The knot of *Abwehr* agents occupied a table near the door but Canaris barely spared them a glance. Once he'd gone, heads at the table returned to Moncrieff. With the dribble of remaining wine, he raised his glass in a toast.

'*Prosit*,' he mouthed. '*Und Weidmannsheil.*'

Cheers. And good hunting.

15

That same evening, Annie Wrenne was alone in her lodgings after another sweltering day. At last she'd managed to find a French newspaper. It came from a kiosk on the Gran Via. It was nearly two weeks old, the print already beginning to fade, but it confirmed everything that she'd picked up from the reporters at the Hotel Florida.

That the French fleet anchored at Mers-el-Kébir had refused to surrender to a British task force. That the Royal Navy had broken off negotiations in mid-afternoon and that Churchill, no less, had ordered Force H to open fire. Under the bombardment that followed, a French battleship, *Bretagne*, had exploded and sunk within minutes. After thirty answering salvos, according to the newspaper, the French had ceased fire but the British had continued to pound the French fleet, killing thirteen hundred *matelots* and wreaking havoc – in a picturesque phrase – on more capital ships. Even worse, the British had returned to Mers-el-Kébir five days later to finish the job, killing yet more French sailors. It was, according to *La Dépêche de Toulouse*, *l'atrocité la plus sale*. The vilest atrocity.

Annie sat back, the paper abandoned. Mers-el-Kébir was a key French naval port in North Africa. According to Whittaker, whose sources and judgement she trusted, the British had been determined to keep the French fleet out of the hands of the Germans after the armistice. A French admiral, Darlan, had pledged that this would never happen, but diplomatic assurances were never enough for Churchill and he demanded that the French sail under Royal Navy escort to a British port. This the French had refused to do.

Thirteen hundred dead. Countless more wounded. Not by the Germans, or the Italians, both declared enemies, but by a British prime minister who refused to accept the word of his so-called ally. This, as Whittaker had readily agreed, was an act of the utmost ruthlessness, barbaric in its cynicism and violence. Even Whittaker, who was no stranger to war's limitless appetite for slaughter, had appeared a little shaken, though a later aside after a couple of glasses of wine suggested otherwise. Churchill's sending a message, he'd murmured. And the Germans are probably impressed.

Were they? Could they ever be? Annie had no idea but this was the first time she'd truly understood what was at stake in this hideous new war. She was half-British, half-French. She knew young men in Dieppe and along the coast who might well have joined the French navy. If that was possible, and it most certainly was, then how many of them might have been serving on the *Bretagne*, or the *Provence*, or the *Dunkerque*, once-proud battleships now blown apart? Imagining faces she knew drifting among the wreckage off the North African coast was hard to bear. According to the account in *La Dépêche*, the British had closed the range as soon as the French had stopped firing, turning a naval battle into an act of carnage. All that mattered to Churchill was sending as many French ships to the bottom as possible, regardless of the consequences. How could British officers, British sailors, fire on their comrades-in-arms?

And what did that say about the country that was currently paying her bills?

She brooded savagely on these and other questions for the rest of the day. Regardless of the news from Mers-el-Kébir, it was still a matter of some pride that she'd lately passed on a fragment of gossip from Ortega to Moncrieff in London. Ortega had heard that *Admiral* Canaris, the head of a German spy organisation called the *Abwehr*, was due in Madrid for talks with Franco. After that, he was heading south to Algeciras to take a close look at the Rock of Gibraltar. This, said Ortega, might raise an eyebrow or two in London and for the first time Annie had insisted at the British Embassy that her message be encrypted and marked Urgent. She'd had no personal response from Moncrieff but a scribbled note from Bottomley suggested her stock at MI5 might have soared.

After a while, her bewilderment and disgust over the events at Mers-el-Kébir turned to something much closer to rage. She needed to make a gesture, to raise her voice, to establish – yet again – that she wasn't entirely at the mercy of circumstance. To date, she'd done nothing about Werner Nehmann, and the Rubens canvas he was so keen on acquiring. Indeed, she didn't even know if the little German was still in Madrid. But the thought of running *Nude Woman* to ground raised her spirits.

Before civil war broke over Spain, she'd spent one of the best years of her life in this city. She'd prowled gallery after gallery, getting to know a country she'd begun to love. Not through its history or thanks to conversations with strangers, but by a minute observation of successive Spanish canvases. Brushwork, vision, each artist's palette of colours, their special point of view, these were the clues she gathered, the dots she tried to join. Quickly, they'd taken her to a single looming presence, Francisco Goya, but that was another story and for the time being she was happy to concentrate on the buxom figure sprawled on the bed, her slippers abandoned on the floor.

She started in a bookshop she knew off the Plaza Mayor. She'd been here often and she was on first-name terms with the owner, a small hunchbacked presence who lurked in the shadows behind the scavenged planking that served as a counter. Like Annie, he half lived in the era of Velásquez, and Goya, happy to turn his back on the many rigours of life under the new *Caudillo*, and he stood beside her while she sketched the principal elements of the Rubens Nehmann had described. It was the slippers that put a smile on his face, together with the winged angel that watched over the woman while she slept.

'*Sí, sí ...*' he disappeared into the back of the shop where he kept his precious art books. A while later he returned. He knew exactly where he ought to have found the volume he was after, a collection of Rubens' nude women, but for some reason it had gone. No matter. He had a friend who had a copy of his own and he knew Annie would be welcome to borrow it. Come back tomorrow. All will be well.

Annie returned the next day and picked the book up. Whittaker had lent her a spare radio and last night, on a Toulouse station she trusted, she'd listened to a first-hand account of the attack on the French fleet. The speaker, a young-sounding *matelot* with a Midi accent, had been injured during the latter stages of the bombardment and was still recovering from his wounds.

Most of the fleet, he'd said, knew about the presence of the Royal Navy, hull-down on the horizon, but had no idea of the on-going negotiations nor of what to expect next. The first British salvos had therefore come as a complete surprise, and he'd assumed there must have been some kind of mistake before a huge explosion aboard the *Bretagne* sent her to the bottom. Aboard a destroyer, with its puny guns, he and his mates were completely outranged and after the battleships had taken a beating it was simply a question of time before a British shell came their way.

With no means to defend themselves, the crew had crouched behind whatever cover they could find until a killer salvo straddled the destroyer, wiping out the bridge and tearing a huge hole in the foredeck. The skipper had beached the destroyer on a shoal and ordered the crew to abandon ship. More British shells found the crew waist deep in water and the luckless speaker had suffered shrapnel damage to his upper chest. Mercifully, he'd survived semi-intact but breathing still hurt, as did the memory of those terrible hours. These guys were supposed to be our friends, he muttered at the radio programme's end. God help their enemies.

Indeed. Annie took the Rubens book to the Prado. Ortega had used his mysterious authority yet again and secured her an appointment with Juan Arteta, the name he'd mentioned before. The museum was still closed to visitors but the promised rendezvous with Arteta got her into the building. Arteta himself turned out to be younger than she'd somehow imagined. Like everyone else in Madrid, he needed to eat more but her fluency in Spanish drew a nod of approval and a volley of questions. How long had she been in Spain? How come she spoke like a *Madrileña*? Annie told him briefly about her early pre-war days in the city, and what had happened since, and then produced the book.

Arteta studied the plate of the roused woman for a moment and then led Annie into the depths of the museum. Annie knew these galleries well but many of the walls were bare, still awaiting paintings returned from Geneva to be minutely inspected, assessed for possible damage, and – if necessary – repaired. Rubens, she remembered, had half a gallery to himself, and this is where Arteta took her.

He gestured around him. Every wall was occupied by a range of Rubens' work, just the way she remembered it. The highlights, she thought, gazing round. *St George and the Dragon*, an intensely dramatic rendering of the ever-popular legend. *The Rape of Ganymede*, a picture Annie remembered tracing to a story recounted in Ovid's *Metamorphoses*. And *Saturn Devouring his Son*, a graphic glimpse of the darkness in the Flemish soul, a picture commissioned by King Philip IV of Spain. But no roused woman, no abandoned slippers, and no guardian angel.

'It doesn't belong to you?'

'It does. I checked after I talked to Ortega. It's still in Geneva.'

'So why hasn't it come back?'

'It seems there's an issue with provenance. It definitely comes from Rubens' studio, but an expert here detects other hands at work. Maybe Peter Paul added the finishing touches. Maybe not. But we have to be sure.'

Annie nodded. All of that sounded eminently sane and when Arteta enquired about the reason for her interest she told him about the possibility of a foreign bid. The prospect of money changing hands at once brightened the conversation. The Prado, like every other corner of post-war Spain, was acutely short of funds.

'He's seen the canvas? This person?'

'I'm afraid I've no idea.'

'But he's definitely interested?'

'So I understand.'

'And he has money?'

'Again, I can only assume so.'

'I see.' Arteta nodded and Annie sensed at once his disappointment. These days, access to any kind of windfall – financial or otherwise – was the shortest cut to advancement, and the least she could do was to seek some kind of clarification.

'I'll get you some answers,' she promised. 'All I know for sure is the buyer's interest. I'm sure it'll be a question of negotiation, but I'm told he's prepared to pay in gold or in US dollars.'

'And you have a nationality?' Arteta was smiling again. 'For this person?'

'German,' Annie's gaze had returned to the St George canvas. 'And I gather he's from Berlin.'

Finding Werner Nehmann proved tougher than Annie had anticipated. She still had the address of the hotel he'd given her but once she found it the woman who ran the place said he'd moved on.

'Any idea where?'

'He mentioned a cheap hotel down near the German Embassy. El Barcelo? Pension Antonio? You might try there. You know this little guy?'

'Not really. What was he like?'

'That's a question you should ask my daughter. She's crazy about him. Her husband? My son-in-law? Not so much. He has magic, this man. It's in his smile. He can warm an entire room. In winter I might get him back, but if you find him, tell him he still owes me.'

'For what?'

'Just owes me. That's all you need to say.'

Annie went to the German Embassy, still carrying the book she'd borrowed. Yes, they knew of a Werner Nehmann, but, no, they'd never heard of the two cheap hotels Annie had carefully noted, and enquiries among the staff, all of them *Madrileños*, drew a blank.

Before she left the embassy, Annie found a woman who'd spent a little time with Nehmann when he was pursuing a story about deposits of wolfram and copper ore in the Basque country around Pamplona. The woman was Spanish and very striking. She had a natural arrogance married to a superb body, not a line out of place, and without much effort Annie could imagine her in one of the bars that offered traditional flamenco during the early months of the siege.

Nehmann, she said, had taken her out to the cheapest café he could find. There was nothing on the chalked menu board she could possibly eat but he'd held her attention for nearly two hours, prompting a rap on her knuckles when she returned to the embassy, and she'd been reflecting on their conversation ever since.

'Where did it lead?'

'Very good question. I knew where he wanted it to lead, and I told him no from the start, but men like him only hear what they want to hear. He's not German at all, by the way. He comes from Georgia, some town way up in the Caucasus. It was a tortuous story, and I think I followed most of it, but in the end he gave up on being Georgian and decided that German offered a better fit. He lives on his wits. He made me laugh. Had we stayed another hour or so I might even have changed my mind.' She smiled. 'Take care, my child. He told me no man can resist a Spanish woman.'

'I'm French.'

'Really?' Her surprise was genuine. 'Then take even greater care. Why? Because the love of his life still lives in Paris. He told me he still mourns for her but never explained why.'

In the end, utterly in keeping with the way knots seemed to untangle themselves in this battered city, finding Nehmann was simplicity itself. After leaving the German Embassy and criss-crossing the neighbourhood looking for any trace of the two hotels, Annie gave up and walked back to the Gran Via, hoping to find Whittaker settled in his adopted corner of the Hotel Florida bar with his barely touched beer. Unusually for this time of the early evening, the bar was half empty except for a diminutive figure perched on one of the leather stools. Werner Nehmann.

Annie touched him lightly on the shoulder. His hand at once covered hers, and the moment he turned round to face her she knew he'd been expecting someone else.

'I'm sorry,' she said. 'Am I intruding?'

'Not at all. You mind if we speak in English? I did my best last time, but my French isn't what it was. Listen,' he checked his watch, 'you look hungry. I have the perfect answer.' He nodded at the paper bag she was still carrying. 'What's in there?'

'This.' She slipped the book from the bag and leafed through until she found the roused woman. 'Is that the picture your friend wants to buy?'

'It is, yes. That's exactly it.'

His head lifted from the book. He wore a grin Annie had last seen on the face of a street urchin in the slums across the river.

'This makes you happy?' she asked.

'Very. I do magic,' he nodded down at the woman in the bed. 'And so do you.'

He took her to a tiny street corner café maybe half an hour away. There was a chalked blackboard propped against the scruffy bar and Annie sensed at once that this was the place he'd taken the woman from the embassy. Most of the offers on the blackboard had been crossed out, leaving would-be diners with a choice between tripe and a sausage Annie had never heard of.

They settled at one of the handful of vacant tables while he gestured in the direction of the woman behind the bar. She appeared moments later with a flask of cloudy wine and two glass tumblers.

'Red OK?' Nehmann poured without waiting for an answer.

Annie sat back, waiting for this little flurry of business to subside. Then she leaned forward, faux-intimate.

'So tell me about those mountains,' she murmured.

'Mountains?'

'The Caucasus. What you got up to as a kid. Why being Georgian was never enough. What was so special about Paris.'

He was staring at her, a surprise and a wonderment so unguarded that it made her heart sing.

'How do you know about the Caucasus? Who told you any of that?'

'Are you denying it?'

'Not at all. It's true. It's all true. You're looking at the best thing ever to crawl out of those fucking mountains but that's not the point. It can't have been Whittaker because I never tell men any of this stuff.'

'Why on earth not?'

'Waste of time. Men never listen. My Georgia was full of stories but only women have the patience and the wit to tune in. Whittaker's a nice guy and he's done well to get you on board. Is it the older statesman? All that experience? All that fucking *wisdom*? And is he good when it matters?'

'Good?'

'In bed. Between the sheets. Over the back of the sofa. Wherever feels best.'

'You're crazy.'

'I hope so. Was her name Luisa, incidentally? And does she still work at the German Embassy?'

'No comment.'

'Then I'm right. No magic, this time, just the expression on your face. That woman was a huge disappointment, by the way.'

'Because she said no?'

'She did. Unforgiveable. Beyond rational explanation. Would you like me to tell you about my little home in the mountains? Playing the fool with the kids at school? Getting on the wrong side of the fucking priest? Making up all the responses when it came to confirmation? Would you like to know how hard my dad tried to turn me into a butcher? How he made me swear an oath that I'd never fool around with women? How far would a question like that take us?'

Annie did her best to mask a smile. A proposition this shameless, this naked, untethered by any of the usual conversational nonsense, was deeply unusual. Giles Roper had laboured up the foothills of a relationship and it had been all too easy to take her with him, but this was something very different. It had a playfulness, or perhaps an honesty, that she rather liked. This man, she told herself, had the knack of not taking himself remotely seriously. He was light on his feet. He seemed to float above the surface of things. He might, in a different world, have been a butterfly with decidedly carnal tastes.

'The Rubens,' she opened the book again. 'It may not be all it seems.'

'Fuck the Rubens. Let's talk about you.'

'You're telling me your client, this friend of yours, doesn't want it?'

'Of course he wants it, and between us we can make that happen. Does he have money? He has lots and lots of money. Does he have taste? Absolutely none. But he has an ego the size of Berlin and a body to match and he throws amazing parties. One day you may even meet him.'

'So what do I tell my new friends at the Prado?'

'Tell them he'll pay whatever they want. Tell them to name a price. Where is it, by the way?' He tapped the book. 'This masterpiece?'

'Geneva.'

'Then get them to send it back. We need it here, and if we're talking money it needs to be soon, really soon. My friend has no patience and no manners. We need to know exactly where the fucking thing is, how much they want for it, exactly when it's leaving, and exactly when my friend can expect to pick it up.'

'He'll be here in person?'

'He'll fly in with the money or the gold, whichever suits, and leave the same day. He's German. That's the way these people work. Even sitting down, the man's a handful. Now then ...' he reached for the flask of wine, '... let's talk about you.'

To her surprise, Annie stayed the whole evening. She'd weathered the storm, Nehmann's opening bombardment, and she liked to think that something about her had genuinely caught his interest. When she tried to do justice to the passion that her early years in Spain had aroused he nodded, said he understood. She, like him, had been a solitary, content in her own company, soaking up the language, zigzagging from endless conversations with endless strangers, sustained all the time by her determination to coax an extra dimension to her understanding of this extraordinary country by getting to know the artists who had caught the essence of what they saw, and heard, and smelled, and put all that on raw canvas.

At this, Nehmann had nodded again, curious not to know how this party trick of hers had worked, but why.

'Party trick?'

'Kidding yourself into being Spanish.'

'Is that what I was doing?'

'Of course. You're talking to an expert. I used to be Georgian, now I'm not. That's not willpower, that's years of practice. The real question is why.'

'And the answer?'

'Me? You're talking to me?'

'Yes.'

'I was bored. Being Georgian hadn't worked for me. Guys I knew back home couldn't get too much of the mountains. Settle them somewhere flat, show them a city, trams, cafés, the whole schtick, and they were seriously troubled. Me? I went to Paris first, caught sight of myself in a mirror, knew I'd been here all my life.'

'And the woman? Care to tell me about her?'

'This is Luisa's big mouth again, yeah?'

'Yes.'

'The woman in Paris was French, ten years older. She took me apart, stole the bits that mattered, and kicked me out. That had never happened before, ever, and I took it personally. We had less than three months together and I can account for every last fucking second. After that there was no going back to the mountains and no going back to the old me. That turned out to be a blessing. Not in Paris, but Berlin. The Germans are way more reckless than anyone believes and that was something I could handle. New name, new language, Berlin accent but none of that Berliner gloom. I learned party tricks of my own, largely to get my name in front of the right people. The right people loved me. When it came to words on paper I'd make those words dance and I still do. I'm their performing scribe. I have absolutely no regard for the truth and that's something else they love. To lie like an angel is the Nazi wet dream. If that sounds coarse I apologise, but that doesn't mean it isn't true. To survive in Berlin these days, you have to have a lively sense of what people want to believe. The rest of it, the truth, doesn't matter in the slightest. If you're relying on the old rules, the old Germany, you're already on the way to the graveyard.'

Annie was happy to settle for another flask, and a third after that. There was no way this little imp of a man was going to get into her knickers but in any event he'd given up trying and what remained was a conversation rich in candour and the sane acceptance that the rest of the world was crazy. As the café began to fill with the late evening crowd, they were still comparing notes, still musing on the blessings of the solitary life, unmoored to any of the usual bourgeois blessings. No husband, no wife, no kids, no real sense of permanence, just a shared acknowledgement that you ducked the wilder punches and relied on your wits to survive. It was at this point that Nehmann beckoned her closer and tabled the name again.

'This Giles Roper …'

'I told you just now. He went to Murcia, then a place by the sea called Benicàssim. I thought we had a relationship. In fact I thought we were in bloody *love*. But then I took him by surprise, found him with another woman, same lies, same nonsense, same routine. I saw them together. I watched. It was over.'

'Really?'

'Really. If you want the truth, I'd never been so angry in my life.'

'With him?'

'Of course. But mainly me. How come I'd ever believed a word he'd said? How come I was so naïve about the stuff he wrote, the promises he made? How come I'd ever let him so *close*?'

'So what happened?'

'I took a leaf out of your book. I became someone else. Spain helped, but then Spain has never let me down.'

'And that was it? This Roper fuckwit? You dropped him in the trash bin where he belongs?'

Annie held his gaze, then nodded. He knows, she realised. He's taken a good look at me, and cocked a listening ear, and connected all the dots. Magic, she thought grimly. But what the hell.

'Not quite,' she admitted. 'Three months later I had a miscarriage.'

'And?'

'I was at work. I was always at work. It was a huge building. There were kids running around everywhere, screaming the place down. There wasn't a closet with a door. It was a little baby girl. I flushed it away with a bucket of dirty water.'

'*Finito?*'

'Alas, yes.'

Nehmann gazed at her for a long moment.

'You've told this story to anyone else?'

'No.'

'Then don't.' He took her hands, the briefest, lightest touch, almost weightless. 'Life's a bitch,' he murmured. 'Whatever you say, say nothing.'

16

Canaris was up at dawn. He'd booked himself a room at the Reina Christina Hotel, rather than stay in the allotted house down near the waterfront, and now he was alone in a perch at the very top of the hotel with a perfect view across the bay towards Gibraltar. He'd brought the camera from Berlin, a Leica IIIb with a 135mm lens and a wooden tripod to keep the camera steady.

With Gibraltar silhouetted against the rising sun, he shot a complete roll of black and white film, thirty-six exposures, the Rock framed at maximum magnification in a variety of lights as the sun spilled onto the dockyard. He knew already that one of the hotel bedrooms on the top floor had been turned into a photographic darkroom, and he returned to his room for the map of Gibraltar he'd marked up the night before.

Canaris knew the technicians in the darkroom offered an enlargement service that would blow up designated areas on the negative. All the areas that interested Canaris were of obvious military significance and, once he'd given each a number, he took his roll of film and his map and knocked on the door of the darkroom. When the taciturn Spaniard who worked the night shift appeared, Canaris explained exactly what he wanted and folded a fifty peseta note into the man's hand. Canaris was confident that copies of these images, plus probably a photograph of the map, would find its way to a number of clients, all of whom paid well. The *Abwehr* have been here. And look what they're up to.

His work done, Canaris enjoyed a plate of scrambled eggs with a curl or two of bacon before rejoining his team. He offered no explanation for his overnight stay, neither were any of the accompanying officers bold or foolish enough to enquire about his unannounced absence. *Abwehr* people, it was agreed, played by a different set of rules. Best to assume that nothing in their world ever happened by accident.

By mid-morning, the Canaris team had arrived in La Línea, immediately opposite the promontory that was Gibraltar. The *Abwehr* had a heavy presence along this strip of coastline, including four agents quartered in a building towards the rear of the town where the road began to climb towards the mountains and the backcountry known as the Campo. The building had a flat roof and powerful binoculars had already been mounted on a tripod by the time Canaris climbed the stairs with one of the local *Abwehr* agents and clambered out into the blinding sunshine.

Looking south, the Rock was head-on, and the jut of grubby limestone felt close enough to touch.

'The border's still open for local labour?' Canaris was studying a straggle of figures making their way across the construction site that would soon be the new airstrip.

'Has to be. The place couldn't function without them.'

'And you talk to some of these men?'

'Of course, Herr *Direktor*. The best of the files are downstairs. The local working Spanish were Republican to a man during the civil war. The Moors took the place during the early weeks and then moved on. The Spanish still don't like us but most of them like the English even less.'

'Because?' Canaris was still intent on the view.

'The officers over there treat them like Arabs. Or maybe Indians. The Spanish can be sensitive. They had an empire of their own not so long ago and it doesn't take much to upset them.'

Canaris stepped back, making way for the rest of his party. He nodded at the Rock, at the binoculars, a gesture openly freighted with something close to resignation. Take a look for yourselves. And see what you think.

Back downstairs, Canaris asked to see the interview records. An office had already been readied, the manila files in a neat pile beside a pad and a fan of newly sharpened pencils. Canaris counted the files. There were seven in all. He opened the top one and flicked quickly through the contents before looking up.

'You have a typewriter?'

'Of course, Herr *Direktor.*'

'The same machine that typed these reports?'

'Yes.'

The typewriter had been parked on a wooden cabinet under a framed picture of Hitler at full throttle, probably snapped at Nuremberg. The machine was a new-looking Groma in a rather fetching shade of pale green.

'Paper?'

'In the drawer, sir.' The *Abwehr* officer was looking slightly bemused, raising an eyebrow as he left the office.

For the next two hours, while the rest of his party prowled the waterfront with their binoculars and their busy pencils, Canaris went through every file. There was little here that he didn't know already: how the British were visibly preparing for the possibility of some kind of attack, how the resident Gibraltarians had recently been evacuated, clearing the decks and making space for a reinforced garrison, how French aircraft had retaliated for the attacks at Mers-el-Kébir, swooping low over the dockyard and machine-gunning anything that moved, and how security checks had tightened on the morning flood of Spanish labour. In the view of one interviewee, the British were looking, above all, for explosive devices, fearing acts of sabotage. This, he said, had to be a joke because the Rock was full of dynamite for the blasting operations to create new tunnels, and everyone knew where this stuff – including the detonators – was stored.

By mid-morning, Canaris was done. He'd put one file aside and when the same *Abwehr* officer reappeared with a mug of thin coffee, he took another look at the name.

'Mañuel Garrido?'

'An electrician, sir.'

'I know that, I've just read the file. Can you get him in? Can I meet him? This evening, maybe? After he's back from work?'

Canaris' party spent the rest of the day journeying into the bony foothills of the Sierra Carbonera. It was here that *Wehrmacht* planners would have to emplace heavy artillery for the bombardment that would precede any assault on the Rock itself. An *Abwehr* specialist had already scouted promising locations, and the German visitors bumped and lurched up a succession of rocky paths to assess the merits of each.

Canaris had taken care to include a specialist from the Jüterbog School of Artillery. His name was Major Langkau and he'd radiated self-importance from the start of the expedition but now he obviously sensed that his moment had come. Sweating in the midday heat, he climbed rocky bluff after rocky bluff with his binoculars and his compass and his field-grey notebook, looking for dead ground where his guns would be invisible from counter-batteries on the Rock. Finally, he boiled his list of prospects down to just six sites he considered suitable for the coming operation.

'Enough, Herr *Major*?'

'Just. The challenge will be munitions and resupply. Guns are hungry, especially in a situation as tight as this. We have to haul all this stuff the length of Spain. It won't be simple.'

Canaris nodded, shrugged, mopped his forehead with a handkerchief. Nothing seemed to surprise him.

Back at the *Abwehr* house in La Línea, Canaris waited for his interviewee while the rest of the party returned to Algeciras. They'd been comparing notes all afternoon, each specialist keen to address each perceived problem as it arose, everyone determined to bring a little of the *Blitzkrieg* sparkle to what everyone accepted was a major challenge. The *Wehrmacht*'s pathways into Belgium and France had been littered with obstacles that everyone had judged impregnable. The fortress at Eben-Emael, sunk deep on the Belgian–Dutch border, had been just one of them, yet it had been the work of mere hours for glider-borne troops to capture it intact.

This discussion had taken place around the bonnet of one of the two *Abwehr* cars, high on the sierra, safe from listening ears. Memories of Eben-Emael, still barely months old, had stirred a ripple of approval. Heads nodded. If a monster like that could topple over then surely the same fate awaited the British. Heads had nodded but it was Canaris, as ever, who'd added a cautionary word.

'Those troops had surprise on their side,' he grunted. 'No one saw them coming. Let's not kid ourselves, gentlemen. By the time we arrive with our heavy guns, half the world will be watching.'

*

The interviewee arrived a little earlier than Canaris had expected. Mañuel Garrido was a big man, still wearing his working clothes. The *Abwehr* had arranged for him to be intercepted on the border and brought straight to the house.

'Please,' Canaris gestured at the empty chair. 'Sit.'

Garrido settled heavily in front of the desk. He looked far from comfortable.

'So what have I done?'

Canaris offered him a cigarette, apologised for getting in the way of his supper. He'd been through the transcript of Garrido's interview and he simply wanted to check a detail or two.

'Like?'

'Like the tunnelling. This is restricted work. You have to be British to get inside the Rock. So how come they let you in?'

Garrido took a long drag on the cigarette, visibly relaxing. He'd been working on various buildings in the Admiralty estate, he explained, mainly maintenance stuff. This had gone on for months and they were pleased with what he'd done. Then the English engineers installing the power feeds in the tunnels had been knocked about by some illness and so they'd come to him.

'And what did you think?'

'Think? I just did it.'

'But the project. The tunnels. The *speed* of the operation. What were your impressions? What did you *think*?'

Garrido was beginning to understand. Canaris could see it in his eyes.

'I'm not paid to think.'

'You might be now.'

'You're serious?'

'About the tunnels, yes.' Canaris tapped the file. 'You don't spell anything out but there's just a hint that the

British were getting one or two things wrong. Might that be the case?'

'You want me to tell you it was a shit show? That everything was behind schedule? That the ventilation shafts were in the wrong place? Is that what you're after?'

Canaris smiled. He needed to take his time here. And he needed above all to leave no hostages to fortune.

'I want you to trust me,' his hand settled on the file. 'I don't want to know about any shit show. I'm not interested that things are going badly underground. On the contrary, I'm glad you're telling me how well they're doing. Not just in the tunnels but everywhere else over there. The British, as we'd all expect, are building themselves a fortress to be proud of. You've been part of that. You're watching it happen. You don't have to do another interview, nothing like that. All you have to do is nod, and leave it to me.'

Garrido held his gaze. Surprise had turned into something else. Calculation.

'And the money?'

'A thousand pesetas. To be paid on the last day of the year. If any word of this conversation goes any further, I'll have you shot.' Canaris sat back and smiled. 'Might we have a deal?'

The following day, late afternoon, Canaris convened a conference in Algeciras to gather impressions and come to some kind of agreed recommendation before he and his team returned to Berlin. They'd come to Spain to take a close look at Gibraltar and they agreed they didn't like what they'd seen. The steepness of the Rock and the volatile winds ruled out gliders and parachute drops. The main approach from La Línea was evidently mined and every square metre of the killing zone in front of the Rock itself would be plotted on dozens of fire plans. Admittedly there would be areas of dead ground, immune from defensive fire, but first you had to get there. Artillery and munitions shipping south would be at the mercy of a poorly maintained railway system and atrocious roads. Resupply, if the initial assault faltered, would be a nightmare. Success might – just – be possible but a high casualty rate was guaranteed.

Did the *Wehrmacht* High Command really want to entertain a bloodbath like this? Back in Berlin, Canaris took the question to Hitler's uniformed War Minister. Keitel had just been promoted to *Generalfeldmarschall*, a pat on the snout, said some, for being the *Führer*'s favourite lapdog. By now, the attack on Gibraltar had acquired a formal codename, Operation *Felix*, and having studied the report Canaris had brought back from Algeciras, Hitler had drafted what he termed 'the great solution'. The *Führer*-plan was lying on Keitel's desk, and the *Generalfeldmarschall* busied himself with a phone call while Canaris did his best to absorb it.

The prelude to Operation *Felix*, in Hitler's view, demanded a carefully negotiated prior agreement with General Franco allowing German troops and air assets to take the lead in the assault on Gibraltar. The campaign itself would open with an attack by massed *Luftwaffe* groups operating from Bordeaux, supported by Stuka dive bombers flying from Spanish airfields, plus bombardment from emplaced German artillery on the mainland opposite the Rock. All elements of the British fleet in the dockyard, and at anchor in the bay, would be destroyed, while specially trained mountain troops would finally spearhead an assault on key British positions.

Canaris looked up. Keitel was still on the phone. The weight of assumption that lay behind this fantasy of Hitler's came as no surprise to Canaris. While continental Europe was settling mutely into submission to Berlin, the British were still at war. Fighter pilots from Goering's *Luftwaffe* were tussling with the RAF over the Channel and barely a day passed without another fat pile of downed Hurricanes and Spitfires delivered to Hitler's desk. Canaris was in a position to know that most of these kill claims were wildly inflated, owing more to Goering's ballooning ego than any objective account of the on-going battle, and he suspected that Hitler was far too suspicious to take any of this nonsense at face value.

The reality was far more sombre. Operation *Seelöwe* called for the invasion of the British Isles. The barges were readied in French and Belgian Channel ports, and there were plenty of eager, battle-hardened troops to parade the swastika banners in London after the inevitable victory, but without command of the air, and of the Channel itself, no invasion fleet would ever sail. Hence, Canaris thought, Hitler's bid to attack the underbelly of Britain's fabled empire, exactly where it would hurt most. Seize Gibraltar, and Hitler could close the door to the Mediterranean whenever he chose.

Keitel, at last, had finished. He nodded at the single sheet of paper on Canaris' lap.

'Well?'

'It's an outline, a list of wishes, nothing more.'

'But you think it'll work?' Keitel risked a rare smile. 'Because, my dear Canaris, it has to.'

In the days that followed, Hitler's 'solution' was handed to *Wehrmacht* staff officers who thickened it with Motorised Infantry Divisions, flank protection for the transit south, Engineer and Smoke units, mine-clearance assets, plus twenty-six battalions of medium and heavy artillery, thus turning a gleam in the eye into a set of operational orders. Limestone terrain in the Jura Mountains was assessed to be similar to Gibraltar's rocky slopes, and advance contingents of the Army Mountain Corps were despatched to prepare for further intensive training. On 24 August, Canaris arrived at the Bendlerstrasse to learn that Hitler had just given the operational plan his approval. Franco, meanwhile, was facing concerted opposition at home to the prospect of German boots on Spanish soil. Both the clergy and his own generals believed that, once invited, the Germans would never leave.

Franco, as ever, was playing a waiting game but had drawn up a lengthy shopping list of weapons, food and fuel to keep his regime safe from predators. Franco's position, as Canaris understood only too well, was pivotal. Without his agreement, barring a military invasion, nothing could happen. And so Canaris lifted his telephone, ordered Hans Zimmermann to his office and told him to close the door.

Zimmermann had just returned from a lengthy visit to Paris where everything, he was glad to report, was perfectly in order in every respect but one. The *Abwehr* had again taken charge of what Canaris had delicately termed 'the transfer of national assets'. This was Reich-speak for the wholesale looting of conquered cities. The houses of wealthy Jews, many of them abandoned, were being systematically looted, the contents trucked to sidings in Saint-Denis from where trains departed three times weekly for the *Heimat*.

'And?' Canaris wanted to know more.

'The SS want a stake in the business. They've made friends with a French gangster called Henri Chamberlin and I'm afraid to say it's working. They've even given him a uniform, and a nice car, and premises of his own, everything fancy, expensive, just the way he likes it, and now they're using him and his criminal friends to move onto our territory. I'm afraid it's the same story. *Onkel Heine* can't keep his hands out of our pockets.'

Zimmermann, clearly irritated, changed the subject.

'So tell me about Gibraltar,' he said.

'It's a disaster,' Canaris grunted. 'With luck it'll never happen but we'll make of it what we can.'

'Meaning?'

'There may be opportunities.'

Later that same morning, Canaris paid Ribbentrop a visit. By now, word of Hitler's interest in Gibraltar had spread to the Foreign Ministry and Ribbentrop was predictably eager to climb on board whatever operation he might have in mind. He knew Canaris had been in Spain and he demanded his thoughts on what might be possible.

'A full-scale assault, you think?'

'Entirely feasible,' Canaris conceded.

'But obvious difficulties?'

'Of course. But when did that ever change our plans?'

Ribbentrop was a stranger to irony and therefore hopeless with the reefs that lay beneath most conversations. All that mattered was the thunder of the guns and the glory afterwards.

'No problems, then?' he asked.

'Just one. You know Franco. You understand how hard it can be to deal with a man like that. He loves us, he truly does, but he's still frightened of the British. He thinks they may refuse to surrender. He worries that the Royal Navy may turn up and make life hard for him.'

'Then he needs time with the *Führer*.'

'My thoughts entirely,' Canaris gestured round. 'Here?'

'I don't think so. I have in mind a meeting with Pétain. It has to happen soon and our Vichy President being French, it has to happen in France. The *Führer* has much to discuss, much to settle. We could extend that visit, perhaps by a day or so, head south in the train. Leave it to me, Herr *Direktor*,' he scribbled himself a note. 'I'll see what I can do.'

The wheels of diplomacy ground slowly on. Franco would soon be appointing his brother-in-law, Ramón Suñer, to be the regime's new Foreign Minister, but by the time Ribbentrop summoned him to Berlin for talks about Operation *Felix*, Franco's position had hardened. By now it was mid-September, and the Battle of Britain had clearly been won by the RAF. Suñer knew nothing of this but Hitler was on the verge of cancelling his plans for a full-scale invasion, a decision creating a glorious vacuum that Ribbentrop knew exactly how to fill.

Suñer, who loathed Ribbentrop, tabled Franco's latest terms that might ease the progress of Operation *Felix*. A German request for a naval base on the Canary Islands he refused to entertain. Instead, Suñer presented a long list of territorial demands. Franco wanted Gibraltar, to be taken by a joint German/Spanish assault, plus he demanded French Morocco and Oran in return for safe passage through Spain. This, as Hitler would know only too well, was getting a Spanish empire on the cheap, largely at the expense of the French whom the *Führer* was keen not to upset, and so Ribbentrop demurred. On the accompanying plea for arms, foodstuffs and fuel, he thought there might be some movement, and he was about to declare the meeting at an end when Suñer tabled once last thought.

'The *Caudillo*,' he said, 'would be very happy to meet the *Führer* to discuss these issues face to face.'

'He has somewhere in mind?'

'Hendaye,' Suñer got to his feet and extended a hand. 'On the French border.'

*

The news arrived in the Bendlerstrasse an hour later, not from Ribbentrop's Foreign Ministry, but from SS headquarters in Prinz-Albrecht-Strasse. *Reichsführer-SS* Heinrich Himmler was pleased to announce that he would be personally in charge of the security operations surrounding the *Führer*'s forthcoming visit to Spain. Dates remained to be confirmed but it was the *Reichsführer*'s intention to arrive in Madrid several days ahead of the meeting of the Heads of State in order to co-ordinate protection plans with the local police and anti-terrorist authorities.

The typed message had arrived on Canaris' desk from one of the secretaries in his outer office. He studied it a moment before reaching for the phone. *Onkel Heine*, like Ribbentrop, couldn't resist the lure of another call to arms. These people, he thought, are insatiable.

Zimmermann answered on the first ring. Canaris rarely smiled.

'A moment?' he asked.

Zimmermann was at the door within seconds. Canaris asked him to close it.

'*Onkel Heine*'s going to Spain,' he nodded at the message on his desk. 'With luck, Hans, it may be the death of him.'

17

Agnès. Annie roused herself from a night's fitful sleep. Late summer was at the open window, the smell of drains and last night's cooking from the rooms below, and the murmur of early morning traffic carried on the warmth of the gusting wind. Agnès, she thought again. I used to be Agnès. Agnès to my mother. Agnès to my teachers. Agnès to my friends in class. She'd always liked the sound and the taste of the name in her mouth. It was soft, like your favourite *chocolat*, with that chewy syllable at the end. Agnès. So how did she ever become Annie? And did that even matter?

She'd put the question to Werner Nehmann only days ago. She was seeing far too much of him, she knew that, but they'd established a rapport, a mutual understanding, that she cherished. While it was true that he might be making up most of the confidences he laid at her door, she didn't really care. He was *sympa*, and nimble, and inventive, and his impatience with cumbersome ideas like truth and falsehood made her laugh, and after a day of disbelief, and then irritation, she'd even forgiven him the Rubens.

She'd come home to it nearly a month ago, unlocking her front door to find an oblong package, carefully wrapped and taped, leaning against the wall of her living room. There was no indication what might be inside. It never occurred to her that it might contain a canvas, least of all the Rubens she'd so gamely tried to track down, but minutes later there it was, the framed picture of a naked woman in her fancy bed, her arm raised, her plump wrists girdled with bracelets, her head turned with a hint of impatience at the sight of the offered slippers.

It had to be Nehmann. She found him within the hour, in his suite at the Hotel Florida where he now lived. How he'd found the money for this kind of indulgence he'd never explained, but the moment she pressed him on her surprise discovery, she began to understand. Certainly he'd been grateful for the information she'd brought back from the Prado. It was good to know that the Rubens would so soon be on the move. The museum had hired a car and a driver to bring it back to Spain. From Switzerland they'd be travelling through France at night, with dimmed lights, to deter any interference from the Vichy police, but once they'd crossed the border all would be well.

Except it wasn't.

'So what happened?'

'We ambushed the car. Foothills of the Pyrenees. The driver had taken a back road. Big mistake.'

'You were following the car?'

'We were.'

'We?'

'Me and a friend.'

'And?'

'We pulled him over, helped ourselves, drove away. I left a hundred US dollars on the dashboard and told him to blame the bandits in the mountains. He did OK, more than OK. You like the painting? You approve?'

'Of the painting, yes. But why me? Why leave it with me?'

'Because you're safest. No one will ever look. My client will be flying in any day now. Happily, he's already paid half the fee.'

'Which is?'

'Half a million US. Wasn't that what the Prado wanted?'

'Yes. But you're telling me now they'll never get the picture.'

'That's true. But the client is still paying. You think there's a problem?'

Annie hadn't bothered with an answer. She insisted he accompany her back to her little suite of rooms. En route, she disappeared into a goods store she knew and emerged with a hammer, a screwdriver, a saw, a ball of string and two dozen nails wrapped in a twist of newsprint. Back in her living room, she locked and bolted the door before repacking the Rubens and tying down all the rough edges.

'So what next?' Nehmann seemed impressed by the painting.

'You find somewhere safe to hide it.' She gestured at the tools.

'Here?'

'Of course.'

It took him a while to lift a floorboard in Annie's bedroom and confirm that there was no room on top of the joists for the Rubens. A brief survey of the wonky structure that served as a wardrobe ruled out another solution. Finally, Annie suggested the bed. For whatever reason, it didn't really belong in the bareness of her handful of rooms. It was too well made, too solid, too comfortable. She'd loved it from the start but now it occurred to her that it might have another use.

She joined Nehmann in the bedroom. The plump mattress lay on top of a solid rectangle of wood, no springs. The wood hinged open to reveal a storage space for bedding which Annie had never used. Empty, it might do very nicely. And so it proved. Together, she and Nehmann wrestled the mattress onto the floor, fetched the Rubens and laid it carefully in the empty space. It was a near-perfect fit, and once the mattress and the bedding were back in place there was no indication that she might be sleeping on half a million dollars' worth of fine art.

'You've turned me into a thief,' she said.

'Only if you take your fee.'

'How much?'

'We agreed fifteen per cent. I make that seventy-five thousand.'

'Open a bank account. I'll get you details for a money transfer. Her name's Wilson. First name Francesca. This will mean nothing to you but she's a Quaker, and a good woman, and kept me sane when I needed it most. Agreed?'

Nehmann didn't answer. Instead, he was looking at the bed.

'Shall we?' he said. 'Just the once?'

Annie knew the question had been coming and was rather glad he'd asked.

'Call me Agnès,' she said. 'Just the once.'

Guilt tracked Annie through the city for perhaps a couple of days. She made a conscious effort to avoid going anywhere near the Prado and devoted most of her time to trying to find Francesca Wilson. Thanks to contacts she'd remembered in Murcia, she finally managed to lay hands on a telephone number in Paris. Making international calls from street boxes in Madrid was the shortest cut to madness and so she insisted on dialling the number from Nehmann's hotel suite. When Wilson answered, she knew at once who was calling.

'Annie,' she said. 'Annie Wrenne.'

'How do you know?'

'No one speaks Spanish like you, my dear, and that's a compliment.'

Annie explained very briefly that she'd come into a windfall. She offered no details but insisted the money be put to whatever use Mrs Wilson judged most suitable. When she asked whether there was still work to be done, her question sparked a dry laugh.

'It's never-ending, Annie,' she said. 'And in my judgement it always will be. War takes no prisoners when it comes to kids. How much are we talking about?'

'My windfall? Seventy-five thousand American dollars.'

'*How* much?'

Annie repeated the figure. Maybe a bit more.

'You're serious?'

'I'm afraid I am.'

'Golly.'

The conversation came to an end. Annie admired the woman's sangfroid, no stagey gasps, no enquiries about where the money might have come from, but she supposed that little could surprise this tireless Quaker after her surreal years at the Pablo Iglesias.

Nehmann, sprawled on the bed, had been monitoring the conversation.

'Agnès?' he shifted his weight and made room for her.

'It's Annie,' she gazed down at him. 'And the answer's no.'

Three weeks later, a coolish morning towards the end of September, Moncrieff reappeared in her life. He'd made contact through Ortega and invited Annie to lunch at a restaurant off the beaten track that was a favourite of Ortega's.

'We'll call and pick you up,' Moncrieff said.

The walk to the restaurant, for Annie, parted the curtains on a city she barely recognised. Back in May, the bread ration of 500 grammes per person every second day had been slashed in half. Over the summer, meat of any description had become scarce and even eggs were hard to come by. Now, the back streets were full of beggars. Whores lingered at street corners, casting listless glances at the occasional passer-by, while kids with swollen bellies scavenged for potato peelings from bins brimming with uncollected rubbish. Even Moncrieff looked shocked.

'These are the fruits of victory?' he queried.

Annie wondered whether she should apologise. Lately she'd kept herself to the city centre where there was at least a hint of normal life, but the thought of the Rubens under her bed felt somehow shaming. Giving her comission away to a good cause was one thing. Laying hands on that kind of money in the first place quite another.

The restaurant, mercifully, was full. The waiter in charge appeared to know Ortega well. The two men embraced, something that didn't happen to Ortega very often, and heads turned at the sight of Ortega's ruined face as the waiter led them through a curtained door to a small private room lined with a gallery of fading black and white photographs from the bullring.

'You asked for privacy, *señor*?' the waiter gestured at the single table laid for three. 'Our pleasure.'

Ortega studied the menu while Moncrieff thanked them both for the tip about Canaris, and his recent visit to Algeciras.

Moncrieff turned to Ortega, who wanted to know whether the package had arrived.

'It has, and it certainly looks the part. I don't know how many owners, but I'm assured it's in perfect working order.'

'I'll need to try it out,' Ortega said at once.

'Very wise.'

'Sights?' Ortega was frowning now.

'PE four-power scope with adjustments for elevation and windage. It's got a focus ring as well, which means you can adjust for focal length and magnification. Perfect optics. The scope is the one thing that looks brand new.'

'Ammunition?'

'Two boxes of hollow-nose. Exactly as you ordered.'

Annie, who was translating for Moncrieff's benefit, was bewildered. Her Spanish had so far coped with every occasion, but this conversation had wandered deep into the tallest grass. Focus rings? Elevation? Windage? Hollow-nose?

She was looking at Moncrieff. No more translation until he explained what might be going on. It was at this point that the waiter reappeared. He gave Ortega a folded slip of paper and whispered something in his ear. Ortega read the message, nodded and stood up. Something had happened. Apologies, but he had to attend to it.

Annie watched him leave before turning back to Moncrieff. Nothing surprised her any more, least of all Ortega.

'Well?'

Moncrieff took his time. He told her that Ortega had recommended the knuckle of pork, and that the dumplings were said to be good. A bottle of the house red might also add to the gaiety of nations.

Annie ignored him.

'Elevation,' she repeated. 'Hollow-nose. I suspect I'm getting the drift here but I'd appreciate a few more clues. Is there a problem? Don't you trust me? In which case why do I keep picking up all those envelopes from the embassy?'

Moncrieff looked briefly hurt. Of course he trusted her. She'd been diligent, and watchful, and the intel about Canaris and Algeciras had been absolutely key.

'Key to what?'

'Key to a situation we're trying to develop.'

'We?'

'Us. My greedy pals in MI5. Everyone loves the taste of victory, digging traps for the opposition, laying bait, playing to their worst instincts, watching them make fools of themselves. The taste of victory alas is nothing but a memory. Life in London, thanks to the *Luftwaffe*, promises to become unbearable. They've started bombing. They've already got the hang of it over Warsaw and Rotterdam and winter promises to be seriously rough. And so we need a little light relief.'

'The gaiety of nations?'

'Exactly.'

'And elevation? Hollow-nose?'

Moncrieff nodded, then sat back and gazed at the line of photographs, his long, bony fingers toying with his fork.

'You know about our friend Ortega?'

'I know he's a sniper. I know he's killed people. Is that your question?'

'Yes. As it happens, he's very good. In fact he was the best, and that comes from people I trust.'

'And now? You think he's still good?'

'I don't know. He says he is, in fact he insists he is, but I simply don't know. He says his good eye, the right one, the one that matters, is unaffected, but we only have his word.'

'You need to check?'

'Of course,' Moncrieff finally abandoned the fork, and gestured Annie a little closer. 'Once we've eaten, I'm taking you to the General Hospital. That's the big one down in Atocha, and that's where they sort of patched Ortega up. I've made contact with the surgeon who looked after him and we're expected at three o'clock. He has Ortega's permission to discuss the case and hand over any records they might have kept.'

'You need translation?'

'I'm afraid so. The surgeon speaks no English.'

'So why do you need the records?'

'Because we may be trusting the man to deliver ...' he shrugged, '... let's call it a service.'

'You want him to kill someone?'

'We do.'

'Who?'

'I'm afraid I can't tell you.'

'Franco?'

'Christ, no.' A bark of laughter. 'Even the Brits aren't that silly. Franco will have his uses. Our target won't.'

Annie nodded, trying to digest this latest development.

'And you'd be paying Carlos? For this service? Assuming he can still shoot straight?'

'Of course. Anyone who deals with Ortega knows the price of the man. He never comes cheap. As it happens we're sugaring the offer with a couple of months at a hospital back in Kent. They specialise in restoring the looks of badly burned pilots and they may be able to do something for Ortega in the way of cosmetic surgery. That's why we need his hospital notes.'

Annie nodded, said she understood. The fact that Franco wasn't the intended target came as a relief but as soon as she tried to come up with a substitute, she knew it was pointless. Evil, and the bullet it deserved, was the currency of war. Goya again, she thought.

'This must cost a fortune,' she said, 'if it happens.'

'You're right. I'm glad to say that we've raised the money and even agreed a figure.'

'You had a whip-round? Back at the ranch?'

'We had conversations. There are pockets of wealth in London you wouldn't believe, but what we need to do now is put Ortega to the test. The surgeon should be able to help but there's nothing like the real thing.'

'You want him to shoot someone else first? Prove he's still got the nerve?'

'I want him to go somewhere nice and quiet with his special rifle, and his focus rings and his hollow-nose bullets, and some targets of our choice. I want him four hundred yards away from those targets, and I want him to fire at least seven rounds, and I want someone I trust to make a note of the results.'

Annie ducked her head, studied her hands.

'And might that be me?' she murmured, knowing already the answer.

The hospital, like the city it served, was over-full, under-staffed, visibly decrepit and in a state of enveloping chaos. With Moncrieff in tow, Annie hunted for someone in authority to direct them to Ortega's surgeon. His name was Felipe De Almeida and she finally ran him to ground in a cluttered first-floor office at the very back of the hospital. Like everyone else in the hospital, staff and patients alike, he was thin to the point of emaciation. There were hints of dried blood on his shabby surgical scrubs, tiny islets of dark brown, and Annie noticed a delicate gold cross on the thin chain around his neck. He gestured Annie into the only chair and, unprompted, produced a battered manila envelope. Time was evidently short.

'Here—' He shook the contents of the envelope onto the desk and Annie found herself staring at two photographs. The bigger of the black and white prints showed Ortega's hospital face against the whiteness of a pillow. There were darkly bloodied swellings everywhere, especially around the eyes and nose. His left cheek was latticed with sutures and his scalp was swathed in a bandage. It was just possible to draw a line that would sensibly connect this image with the Ortega she'd got to know, the seated beggar she'd first met in the cathedral plaza in Murcia, but the real surprise was the other shot.

Judging from the embossed stamp in one corner, it must have come from his passport, and it showed an Ortega she'd never met, a young stranger, darkly handsome, wonderful eyes. He had a full head of black, thick-looking hair and there was more than a hint of mischief in his smile. This was someone, she thought, you'd very definitely tempt into a conversation. He'd have a lot to say for himself, all of it worth listening to, and the longer she gazed at the face, the more she sensed the loss that Ortega himself must have felt.

'May I?' It was Moncrieff. He, too, she thought, was fascinated by what can happen in a single heartbeat. Intact one moment, broken the next. 'Remarkable,' he muttered. 'Most of us would have given up.'

Annie could only nod. She was going through the notes now. They were sparse, a busy hand scribbling in haste, lots of figures, lots of medical jargon in impenetrable Spanish, plus a diagram or two, with a final paragraph on the last page that appeared to serve as a kind of *adieu*. *Señor Ortega*, the surgeon had written, *has survived substantial trauma. None of his injuries were immediately life-threatening but further cosmetic repair is beyond the resources of this or any other hospital in the city. To everyone's surprise, he made us laugh and for that small gift, at a difficult time, we thank him.*

Annie looked up, aware that the surgeon had been watching her closely.

'You liked him?' Annie enquired.

'We did. And the women loved him. It was good to hear him on the phone. He's well?'

'He is.'

'And busy?'

'That, too.' Annie permitted herself a brief smile. 'We hope.'

The surgeon made them a gift of the photographs and the notes, and they left the hospital shortly afterwards. Moncrieff, it turned out, had a series of meetings he had to attend in Lisbon and was due on a train that left the Atocha station within the hour. Ortega, he said, had made arrangements to put his sniper skills to the test the following morning, which happened to be a Saturday. He had access to a car and would pick Annie up around nine.

'We're going far?'

'I've no idea. It's certainly somewhere remote.' He paused. 'We have to be very sure that he can handle this.'

'You mean I have to be very sure.'

'Yes.'

'Then what is it he has to handle?'

Moncrieff wouldn't answer the question. Instead, unusually, he kissed her lightly on the cheek, checked his watch, and said he had to run for his train. Moments later, he'd disappeared.

Annie spent the evening alone in her perch off the Calle de Alcalá. She emptied the hospital envelope and once again laid the two photographs side by side. The longer she let the twin images imprint themselves, the more she realised that they told a bigger, wider story, not about this one individual, poor Carlos Ortega, the lone sniper flushed out of his lair by a German bomb, but about Madrid, the city itself.

When she'd first arrived, like Ortega's passport photograph, it had been full of promise. Now, years later, it was a grotesque shadow of its former self, an assortment of ruined buildings, feral dogs, starving kids and hospitals bursting with unfinished business. She opened a bottle of cheap wine and poured herself a generous glass, testing the parallel, but then – over the second glass – she was honest enough to recognise that this fancy of hers didn't quite work.

Ortega, as the surgeon had pointed out, had immense spirit. This was a man able to fend off any disaster, cope with a degree of physical mutilation that would have felled most men. Would Madrid pull through in similar style? Did it have the reserves, the sheer fortitude to rise from the ashes of first the rebel siege, and now the Franco dictatorship? She took both the question and the rest of the bottle to bed and did neither full justice.

Next morning, rising late, she stepped into Ortega's borrowed car after a hasty cold-water wash, a tussle with yesterday's clothes, and little else. Ortega, whose many talents extended to an almost telepathic awareness of other people's needs, drove her at once to a nearby café he knew she sometimes frequented. Before he locked the car, he removed a long bag secured with ties from the back seat and propped it carefully against their table in the café.

'Is that what I think it is?'

'Yes. It's Soviet-issue, probably been through a thousand hands. You need something to eat.'

As ever, there was no menu, simply a choice of churros or churros. Annie settled cheerfully for a plate of the little fingers of fried dough, dipped in sugar and dusted with cinnamon. This morning's were especially good, hot and fluffy on the inside, and by the time they were on the road again she'd readied herself for the conversation she was determined they should have.

'We met your surgeon yesterday,' she said lightly. 'But, then, you know that.'

'Nice guy. Cared too much for his own good.'

'You say.'

'I know. I spent more than a month looking at that man and you know what I thought by the end? That he needed help more than I did.'

'Maybe that's why he wears a cross.'

'Sure. And let's hope his *amigo* up there is listening.'

'Do you have an *amigo* up there?' Annie asked lightly.

'No. I have me down here and that's more than plenty.'

More than plenty. She carried the thought for the next mile or so as they drove out of the suburbs. Then she asked him who he was going to kill next.

'You've talked to your Scots friend?'

'You know I have.'

'And what did he say?'

'He wouldn't tell me.'

'Very wise. For the time being, nothing happens until you make your report.'

'You think you'll pass?'

'I know I will.'

'Then give me a name.'

'I can't.'

'Why not?'

'Because I don't know either.' He slowed, and then pulled in beside a stall heaped with pumpkins. 'Yet.'

More than an hour later they were out in the mountains beyond El Escorial, the huge sixteenth-century royal palace that Annie had visited before the civil war. The road climbed and dipped, narrowed and then climbed again until Ortega slowed to take a turning on the right. The track beyond was roughly gravelled but the recent rains had turned the ground on either side to mud. The mud carried the imprint of heavy tyres and in the far distance, against the tree-clad green of the encircling mountains, Annie could see a tiny square of what looked like hutments.

'What's this?' she asked. 'Where are we?'

The valley, said Ortega, had been chosen as the site for Franco's monument to the dead of the civil war. It was here that he wanted to build an enormous mausoleum that would proclaim the sacrifices the nation had made for a cleaner, more God-fearing Spain. Ortega had seen a handful of advance sketches for what Franco had in mind and he gestured at the enormous outcrop of rock that dominated the site.

'He's going to put a cross on top. It won't be subtle and it won't be pretty but you'll see it from twenty kilometres on a good day and I gather that's the point. The tallest cross in Europe, maybe the world. If you're the *Caudillo*, you have to think big. People in this country are right. We've got the wretched man for good and when he dies my guess is he'll end up here.'

'And after that?'

'After that, we may become Spaniards again. People, not subjects.'

Annie nodded, staring out at the mountains, trying to imagine the wildness of this landscape accommodating whatever else Franco had in mind. Not just a cross but a cathedral of some sort, and worshippers, and tourists, all of them paying their respects to an episode of history that a future Spain would probably prefer to forget.

'And is there anyone here?' she gestured at the long bag on the back seat. 'Anyone who might be a problem?'

'It's Saturday,' Ortega laughed. 'Nobody works at the weekend in Spain.'

He parked the car at the very edge of the treeline where the pines crowded onto an area that had already been levelled. Next, he opened the boot and took out a wooden tripod, spreading the legs and setting it up against a background of the trees.

'Those pumpkins?' Ortega was checking to make sure the tripod was level. 'There are chalks in a bag. Put faces on them all. Any colour. Any expression.'

Annie did his bidding. There were seven pumpkins in all. The biggest of them were the size of the human head and she felt a shiver of anticipation she didn't quite understand as she drew cartoon eyes and a smiley mouth in green chalk on the first.

Ortega took the pumpkin and held it at arm's length.

'This guy's happy?'

'He's oblivious. He hasn't a clue what's going to happen next. Isn't that the way most people die?'

Ortega appreciated the quickness of her wit. Still chuckling, he drove the base of the pumpkin onto the long metal shaft he'd secured to the top plate of the tripod, and then spread the legs a little wider to carry the weight.

Annie had already fetched the long bag from the back seat and now she watched Ortega extracting the rifle. He was right. The wooden stock, lightly polished, carried a lifetime's scars, doubtless from countless engagements. The telescopic sights were already attached and Ortega returned to the boot to collect a pair of binoculars and a box of what he called shells. He gave the box to Annie, and finally extracted an old groundsheet before nodding towards the far edge of the recently levelled space.

'Four hundred metres,' he grunted. 'You count.'

They set off, the rifle slung over Ortega's shoulder. Annie was counting their footsteps and she'd got halfway there before it occurred to her that Ortega's box of shells was far heavier than she'd anticipated. Opening the top, she glimpsed the tight square of copper-coloured bullets, their points neatly trimmed, and tried to imagine the damage they'd do over four hundred metres.

'Hollow-points?' she queried. 'What does that mean?'

'They expand on impact. Maximum damage. That way not much survives.'

Annie nodded, still counting her paces. Nearly there, she thought, suddenly wanting this little game at an end.

Annie stopped. 'Four hundred,' she muttered.

Ortega nodded, gave her the rifle and carefully spread the groundsheet on the wet earth. From here, the tripod and the pumpkin were a dot in the distance, hard to spot against the green fall of the trees. Ortega released the magazine from the rifle and carefully filled it with bullets from the box. Then he knelt on the groundsheet before lying full length, the carrying strap of the rifle looped around his left shoulder, and then tightened it until the rifle was rock-steady, anchored by his left elbow dug into the groundsheet.

Happy with the balance, he relaxed and put the rifle to one side before wetting a finger and holding it up.

'Light breeze,' he muttered. 'Left to right. Maybe five miles an hour.'

He frowned for a moment, as if dredging some long-ago computation from the depths of his memory, and then his fingers found a knob on the telescopic sight and he made a tiny adjustment.

Down on his belly once more, the rifle tight to his shoulder again, his ruined cheek nuzzling the wooden stock, he sighted on the pumpkin and made another adjustment, this time to the focus ring.

For a long second, nothing happened. Then he told her to pick up the binoculars.

'The pumpkin,' he said. 'Tell me when you're ready.'

The binoculars, like the shells, were heavy. Annie sighted on the pumpkin, amazed by the size and clarity of the image over a distance like this, but knew she'd never be able to hold the binos steady. And so she knelt quickly and made herself comfortable in the space beside him, flat on her belly, supporting the binos on both elbows. Perfect.

'You OK?' This from Ortega.

'I'm fine. Never better.'

'Good.'

By this, she assumed he was ready. She had no idea how loud the shot might be but all her concentration was on the cartoon smile that filled the lens. This was for Moncrieff, she told herself. This was the moment when she might, at last, properly earn the money they were paying her.

Still nothing.

The image in her lens was beginning to waver, and she shifted her weight slightly until it stabilised again. Then came the faintest inhalation of breath from the body beside her, followed by a deafening crack as he pulled the trigger. At the same time, as if by magic, the smile in her lens exploded, leaving nothing but a fine orange mist of pulped flesh, drifting slowly away on the faintest whisper of wind.

'Christ,' she said, fighting the sudden taste of vomit in the back of her throat.

18

On Tuesday 17 September 1940, Hitler finally took the decision to postpone Operation *Seelöwe*. The invasion of the British Isles had been in the balance for a while. Regardless of Goering's bluster, reports from front-line bases in France and Belgium confirmed that *Luftwaffe* fighter squadrons were bleeding heavily. The RAF had acquired control of the skies over the Channel and now they were turning their attention to the invasion fleets tied up in French ports. To date, more than 10 per cent of the transports and barges had been destroyed, and German ack-ack crews had learned to dread the constant wail of sirens that announced yet another raid.

The following day, with Berlin basking in autumn sunshine, Canaris was driven from *Abwehr* headquarters to a restaurant in Augsburger Strasse. Horcher's had long been a favourite with the tribal chiefs of the Nazi Party. They loved the impeccable service from waiters who'd been attending on these tables since anyone could remember, they felt at home in largely uniformed company among the wood-panelled walls and sprays of fresh flowers on every carefully laid table, and most of all they were very happy to gorge on game and fish, delivered daily from the Black Forest. There was no provision for any of these midday treats on Third Reich ration cards.

All you needed for a plate of pressed partridge were the right connections.

Joachim von Ribbentrop had the right connections, or so he believed. Indeed, as he never tired of telling a smallish circle of friends and colleagues, his personal journey to the very top of the all-conquering Reich was the living proof that limitless opportunities awaited any man with the guts and the good sense to seize them. This was the champagne salesman who'd dined at some of the grandest tables in London and Paris, the diplomat who'd conjured an agreement with the Soviets that had left the rest of Europe dumbstruck, the *Führer*'s trusted envoy as the summer's victories fattened the German waistband and yet more adventures beckoned.

'Spain, Canaris. We need to talk, you and I. I've rarely seen the *Führer* so *engaged*. We need to make the most of that passion.'

We? Really?

Ribbentrop had reserved one of the small private dining rooms at the restaurant. He didn't bother to get to his feet when the waiter showed Canaris in. Neither, at first, did he even lift his head to acknowledge the *Abwehr* Chief's presence. Bent over a copy of that morning's *Völkischer Beobachter*, he was wearing the black uniform of a *Gruppenführer-SS*, a political gesture so boorish and so obvious that Canaris was obliged to mask a smile. Ribbentrop was already Hitler's Foreign Minister. The fancy dress was exclusively for the benefit of the man who headed the intelligence agency *Reichsführer-SS* Himmler had sworn to destroy.

Ribbentrop wanted to know about the bombs.

'Bombs?' Canaris enquired mildly.

'The *Reichsführer-SS* sent me a file yesterday. Some of it, to be frank, is alarming but his people have excellent penetration in Spain, way beyond Madrid, and I have no reason to believe the intelligence lacks credibility. Spain is a mess. On the *Führer*'s behalf, and on ours, we should be very, very careful.'

'Bombs?' Canaris repeated. Ribbentrop had words to spare on any occasion. Plant a thought in his fat head, thought Canaris, and you'd still be listening hours later.

'Anarchists, obviously,' Ribbentrop had returned briefly to his paper. 'Riff-raff washed up from that bloody war of theirs. The *Reichsführer-SS* has a clear concern for the *Führer*'s safety. Gibraltar is a prize worth having but are we really prepared to risk the *Führer*'s life?'

'That serious, you think?'

'I have no idea, which is rather the point.' He finally folded the newspaper and put it carefully to one side. 'Last time anyone counted, my dear Canaris, you'd managed to put thousands of men in *Abwehr* uniform. That, may I say, deserves a round of applause. The *Sicherheitsdienst* can muster barely a fraction of a force that size. And yet news of this threat to the *Führer*'s life comes from the Prinz-Albrecht-Strasse, not that palace of yours on the Bendlerstrasse. Resources on the one hand,' he tapped the tablecloth, 'and results on the other. There's not an ounce of fat on the SD, Herr *Direktor*. They move fast, a great deal faster than we've grown used to, and they move with purpose. Their reports are models of their kind, compulsory reading, and this is just the latest example. I fancy it's been a while since we enjoyed a service of this quality, a failing that hasn't gone unremarked.'

Canaris didn't respond. Instead he picked up the menu. He guessed that Ribbentrop would start with *Kartoffelpuffer*, potato cakes, with fermented herring in a cream sauce. After that, because it was Goering's favourite dish, he'd wolf a helping of Viennese chicken.

'But is it *true*?' he said at last. 'About the bombs?'

'The *Reichsführer-SS* appears to believe it, and I have to say that's good enough for me. As you doubtless know, we now have a date for the meeting with Franco. The *Führer* is already booked to confer with Pétain at Vichy. Happily, I've been able to extend the southward leg of that journey to Hendaye, on the Spanish border. I hope to be there myself, other commitments permitting, and we'll all be in the train, of course, which makes things a good deal simpler. The date, Herr Canaris, will be 23 October. Currently we anticipate three or four hours, with a break for lunch.' He paused, at last looking Canaris in the eye. 'I gather you've had words with the *Führer* about the *Generalissimo.*'

'Of course, it's my job. You're right about Spain. It's barely functioning at all, which means there are traps we should avoid.'

'Like?'

'Like expecting too much from four hours of conversation. Franco's a *Gallego*. After four hours he's barely warmed up.'

'You think the *Führer* lacks stamina?' Ribbentrop looked astonished.

'I think the *Führer* can sometimes lack patience. Franco plays the long game, that's why he's become *Caudillo*, and he very rarely raises his voice, which is unusual these days. That you might mistake for weakness but it's nothing of the kind. Put the two men together, and it might be worth marking the *Führer*'s card.'

'The *Führer* will get what he wants, what he needs. Of that I have no doubt. Franco will be presented with a choice, not in terms quite that crude but a choice nonetheless.'

'Between?'

'Supporting our plans for Gibraltar or ...' He shrugged, '... not.'

'And if he chooses the latter? Or *appears* to say no?'

'Then we get our heads together and decide where best to apply a little extra pressure. God knows, the *Führer* may decide to play the fairy godmother, lots of food, lots of fuel, lots of money. I've listened to the Spanish, remember. They want every day to be Christmas and in a way who can blame them? The country's wrecked. Mending it shouldn't fall to us, not given all our other plans, but it might offer an opportunity or two.'

Canaris offered a bleak smile, then changed the subject. He'd heard that the *Reichsführer-SS* was planning a visit to Madrid ahead of the meeting at Hendaye.

'Of course. He's already in touch with their security people, and he's explained our concerns. They're promising a round-up of the obvious suspects, but he needs to look them in the eye, make certain that none of those big Spanish stones have been left unturned. To be frank, it's also a diplomatic opportunity. The *Reichsführer-SS* has a certain presence. He fights his corner back here in Berlin and the Spanish respect that. Nowadays, they too live in a police state. That has its advantages, as we all know, but I sense they'll be grateful for any further advice.'

'He'll be staying long?'

'We've yet to decide, he and I. Personally, and he knows this, I favour maximum visibility. He needs to show himself to the Spanish people. He needs to be seen, to be admired. These are tools in my bag, not his. The *Reichsführer*'s a warrior, not a diplomat, but so far I've been heartened at his preparedness to take the challenge on.'

'Challenge?'

'Spain. Shaking a hand or two. Admiring the sights. Maybe even a speech. The Condor Legion did a fine job but most Spaniards have never seen a German because we've been invisible. The *Reichsführer* can help change that. Perhaps we need to bring Spain's new allies down to earth. We're mortal, after all.'

Ribbentrop leaned back, pleased with himself, and Canaris realised the comment was offered as a joke. No longer supergods, Franco's fellow Fascists might benefit from closer inspection.

'So what do you have in mind for the *Reichsführer*?' Canaris asked. 'Apart from meetings about bombs?'

'We're still at the planning stage but I'm estimating a couple of days. He'll be in Madrid, obviously, and they already have a *corrida* in mind, a taste of the real Spain, the people's Spain, though the *Reichsführer* is surprisingly ambivalent about violence as far as animals are concerned.'

Canaris nodded. He, too, had picked up rumours that Himmler was toying with a meatless diet, a decision that would doubtless play well with his vegetarian *Führer*.

'Anything outside Madrid?'

'Not so far, though I've made it plain that we rule nothing out. By this time next year, we may well have a regular presence in Spain. Whatever happens, I suspect next month will mark a turning point.' He paused, reaching for the dainty silver bell that would summon the waiter. 'You've been on travels of your own, Canaris. Gibraltar? What did you make of it?'

'I sent you a copy of my report.'

'I know. I read it. But what did you *really* think?'

Canaris, who'd spent a long and busy life avoiding far subtler traps than this, repeated the obvious military problems.

'The British have geography on their side,' he concluded, 'which makes them remarkably lucky. First the Channel. Then the Rock. When God made the world Churchill must have been whispering in his ear.'

'You think Gibraltar's impossible?'

'I think it's difficult.'

'That's what they said about Eben-Emael. And France as a whole. They were wrong then, Canaris, and they'll be wrong again. Conquest, I'm beginning to suspect, is a state of mind. Want anything badly enough, and it will happen.'

'Indeed, but conquest can also become a habit. Necessity may be the mother of invention but so is novelty. Never take anything for granted. Look at everything through fresh eyes.'

Ribbentrop, a frown on his face, was losing the thread. Canaris had seeded the conversation with meaningless homilies and the Foreign Minister was trying to work out whether the wretched *Abwehr* was taking him for a fool. Novelty? Fresh eyes? The mother of invention?

It was at this point that the waiter appeared. He hovered for a moment at Ribbentrop's elbow, his pad readied for the order.

Ribbentrop ignored the waiter. His eyes hadn't left Canaris' face.

'We'll have the Viennese chicken,' he said. 'Both I and my colleague.'

Zimmermann was with Canaris by mid-afternoon, summoned from a conference at *Wehrmacht* headquarters. Canaris' office door was shut, all phone calls diverted until further notice.

'It was a game, Zimmermann. Not once did the wretched man enquire about our own findings. Instead, he spent a great deal of money putting us in our place. *Onkel Heine* is the new face of our glorious Reich, and Ribbentrop very much wants to be his puppeteer. He wants to breathe life into *Onkel Heine* and bask in whatever glory comes his way thereafter. Whether an alliance like that will ever work I have no idea. On the whole I doubt it because *Onkel Heine* is not without talent but that's hardly the point. Ribbentrop came with a stick to beat me. It appears he's trying to put himself in charge of arrangements for

Onkel Heine's forthcoming state visit and this is what he has in mind. You have a pen?'

Canaris tallied the highlights of the *Reichsführer*'s forthcoming expedition: the date, the meetings with Spanish security chiefs in Madrid, the bullfight, plus the possibility of some out-of-town excursion. Zimmermann, he knew, had sources inside Prinz-Albrecht-Strasse and he pressed him to make the most discreet of enquiries in terms of further information.

Zimmermann briefly studied the list. Unspoken was the absolute need to keep the head of the *Abwehr* at arm's length from whatever might happen next. Nonetheless, as he rose to leave the office and make his calls, Zimmermann mentioned Tam Moncrieff.

'And?'

'He left a message in Stockholm last night. We put the Matador to the test two days ago. Four hundred yards. A succession of targets.'

Canaris nodded, said nothing. The Matador was the codename they'd adopted for Carlos Ortega, a doff of the *Abwehr*'s cap to a real-life bullfighter of the same name.

'You want the message?'

'I do.'

'It was simply yes. Yes, the test has happened. Yes, the Matador has passed. And, yes, Moncrieff's funds have been well invested. On all three counts ...' a rare smile from Zimmermann, '... a success.'

19

Annie was late getting back that night. With Whittaker, a little against her better judgement, she'd gone to a night club in the *barrio de Salamanca*, a honeypot for the city's slowly diminishing community of expats. It was here that the journalists, and spies, and merchants, and arms dealers booked their tables and settled down for an evening of drinking and gossip. You needed serious money to be allowed past the door, but the laughter was contagious and there was a promise of entertainment later.

It was mid-week, and the Spanish businessmen at the neighbouring table had just returned from the Chamartín stadium where they'd watched Real Madrid give rivals Barcelona a thorough beating. Whittaker, whose enthusiasm for football had taken Annie by surprise, got himself involved in a lively exchange about the talents of a great Spanish defender called Jacinto Quincoces, who'd taken the wheel of a Red Cross ambulance during the civil war. Annie happened to know that the national heart-throb had driven for the rebel side, and her spirits were further dampened when the entertainment arrived on the night club's tiny stage in the shape of Celia Gámez, a singer famous throughout the city. With a fervent tango-style backing, she entertained a full house with her special take on La Pasionaria's now-legendary cry. Instead of *No pasarán*, she sang, *Ya hemos pasado*, sparking wild applause. *They shall not pass* had become *We have already passed*, a bitter truth that, for Annie, soured the evening.

The walk back to her lodgings passed in near-silence. Whittaker, she knew, had enjoyed himself mightily and the last thing he needed was a dreary lecture on the rights and wrongs of life in Franco's newly disinfected *España*. At the entrance to her lodgings, he wished her goodnight and gave her arm a tiny squeeze. Relax a little, he was trying to tell her. Everything moves on. All the time.

She let herself into the building and climbed the stairs to the top floor. By early October, the nights were getting cold again and she toured the ill-fitting windows one by one, still in her coat, doing her best to minimise the draughts. The last of the windows, in her bedroom, overlooked the street and she caught sight of two black vans parked against the kerbstone. Had they been there just minutes before? As she'd arrived? She didn't know, couldn't remember, but as she lingered for a moment, watching the cats suddenly scatter on the other side of the street and disappear into the darkness, she became aware of the doors of both vans opening.

Moments later, the street was full of bodies, men clad in black, some carrying weapons and heavy-looking bags. She counted seven of them vanishing below her window. Then came the splintering of wood and the first thud-thud of heavy boots on the stairs, the noise louder and louder until there were voices on the nearby landing and a volley of blows on her door. She stepped back into the bareness of her living room as the door burst open.

The first of the men had a handgun levelled at her chest. He hadn't quite mastered her name.

'Wrenny?' he shouted.

He took her roughly by the arm, pulled her to one side, gestured for the rest of the men to get to work.

'What is this? What's going on?' Annie had recovered a little.

The lead man with the gun pushed her against the wall. He hadn't shaved for a while and his breath stank.

'The picture,' he said.

'What picture? And who are you?'

'Police. So where is it?'

'Show me.'

'Show you what?'

'ID. Papers.' She put her hand out, rock-steady.

'You think you have rights here?' He was laughing in her face. 'You think thieves can answer back?'

Annie held his gaze, wondering how much he'd had to drink, then – quite suddenly – she was looking at an official pass she recognised as the real thing. *Guardia Civil. Subteniente* Morales. Photograph. Everything.

Already three of the men were prising up the floorboards, tossing them aside, while the rest of the party were watching her and the *subteniente* with some interest. Her role here, she suspected, was to give these men what they wanted, a raw display of female hysteria, but she was determined to keep her nerve. Things would doubtless get worse, a great deal worse, but all she could hear, all she was aware of, was Nehmann's voice. *Whatever you say, say nothing*, he'd told her. Wise counsel.

'OK,' she nodded. 'You're police. You've proved it. Just tell me what you want, why you're here, then maybe I can help you.'

The offer took the officer by surprise. She could see it in his face.

'You lie,' he said softly. 'They were wrong.'

'Wrong how?'

'They told me you were English.'

'I am English. Mainly. A bit. And it's Wrenne. Not Wrenny.'

'So how come your Spanish is so good?'

'Because I've been here a while.'

'Excellent.' A hint of a smile. 'Because you'll be here a great while longer. You know where they speak real Spanish in this country? In prison.' He nodded heavily, just to reinforce the point, then half turned to his men. 'Everywhere,' he grunted. 'Look everywhere.'

At this, Annie's blood iced. There were only four rooms. Already she could hear them tearing the kitchen apart. What few items of crockery she possessed, a handful of cups and saucers and unmatched plates, she'd never be able to use again.

'Well?' The *subteniente* was watching her carefully. 'You want us to stop?'

'I want you to go away. I want you to believe me. I know nothing of any picture. I have no idea why you're here. My name is Annie Wrenne, I have a passport, I have rights, I know nothing of any picture, and I want you to leave me alone. Is that asking too much?'

The *subteniente* shook his head, then wiped his mouth with the back of his hand, and pushed her towards the bedroom.

'In there,' he said. 'It has to be in there.'

'What has to be?'

'This.'

Annie suddenly found herself looking at the torn scrap of paper he was flattening against the palm of his hand. It must have come out of a book, she thought. Maybe even the same edition she'd acquired from the hunchback near the Plaza Mayor. The same woman. The same lazy nakedness as she roused herself from the bed.

'What's that?' Annie was squinting hard.

'It's the picture. Rubens? You know Rubens?'

'I do, yes.'

'It's him. Rubens.' He rubbed a dirty thumb and forefinger together. 'Much money.'

'And that's who you're looking for? This Rubens?'

The *subteniente* was losing patience, and once again Annie got the feeling that she was straying way off the script these men must have written for themselves. Then she became aware of another figure in black stepping out of the kitchen, shaking his head.

'Nothing, *Jefe*,' he muttered. 'You're right, it has to be the bedroom.'

Annie's mouth was dry. She tried to swallow but couldn't, thought of asking for a glass of water, but didn't. The least she owed herself, and perhaps Nehmann as well, was just a little dignity as these wild men tore the bed apart and the rest of her life dissolved in front of her eyes. Might there be some advantage in a late confession? In sparing these animals any further effort?

One of them had lifted her pillow to his face, burying himself in her smell, in the thimbleful of perfume she had left, and the exchange of grins the gesture aroused from the other men in the bedroom told her that her breezy self-possession was about to crack, that the discovery of Rubens' *Nude Woman* might well turn this episode into something very dark indeed.

'Well?'

That question again, this time from another of the men in black. He was standing beside the bed, looking at the *subteniente*. He wanted orders. He wanted a nod of the officer's head. He wanted permission to turn Annie's life in Spain totally upside down, like a brimming sack of treasured memories, probably forever. Goya, she thought miserably. *Un Desastre de la guerra.*

The *subteniente* grunted an OK and the man in black tore the bedding off before feeling beneath the mattress.

'*Nada.*' Nothing.

The officer gestured at the mattress. Get rid of it. Then he bent low, examining the seam between the flat wooden base and the side of the bed. His fingers found the metal clasp and he glanced up at her the way a magician might extend the tension ahead of his favourite trick. Just take a look at what comes next. Just watch what I can do.

Annie smiled gamely back. Go ahead, she thought. Help yourself.

And with a tiny flick of his forefinger, he did exactly that. The clasp sprung back and two pairs of hands lifted the hinged base until it was nearly vertical. There was a stir of movement. Heads craned for a better look. Then Annie herself stepped forward, knowing all was lost, and peered down.

The space beneath the mattress was empty.

They took her to what she assumed was a police station. No one in the leading van said a word. Most silent of all was the *subteniente*, who didn't bother to hide his disappointment. For her part, Annie concentrated on staying in role, on playing the part of the outraged Englishwoman with the perfect Spanish accent. Twice she enquired about compensation for the damage these men had done, for replacement crockery and maybe even a word or two of apology, but she knew she was talking to an empty theatre, that the lights were up, and the stalls were empty, and the Rubens was unaccountably gone. The expression on the officer's face stayed with her: first bewilderment, then something closer to rage. Thank God for Nehmann, she thought. However he'd done it, whatever magic he'd conjured, it had to be him.

At the police station, she was handcuffed, photographed and fingerprinted. She'd had the presence of mind to leave her lodgings with her passport and her other papers and these, too, were photographed before being put carefully to one side, along with her watch. Escorted to a biggish room already peopled with a number of other prisoners, she sat alone in one corner beneath the intermittent glare of a light that was about to expire. Under most circumstances, the constant flicker would have driven her insane but sheer relief was more consoling than anything else she could imagine, and she was just happy to have avoided the moment of truth. *Whatever you say, say nothing*, she thought, tasting the sweetness of the phrase again and again.

Annie knew a little about police stations, largely thanks to Whittaker. *Flagelación* was the softening-up that all suspects, regardless of their guilt or otherwise, could expect before anything else happened. Something similar was common in France, and one of her schoolfriends, barely seventeen, had been given the treatment after emptying his bladder on the base of a lamppost.

For nearly an hour in the waiting room nobody stirred, then a door opened somewhere in the bowels of the building and she heard a muttered oath or two before two uniformed jailers appeared, hauling a figure between them. It was hard to judge the man's age because his face was a mask of blood. More blood pinked the soiled grey of his torn shirt and when he tried to whisper something to one of the jailers a line of bubbles appeared between his swollen lips. The jailers surveyed the room, and then lowered their charge into the empty seat beside Annie. The man slumped sideways, his head on her lap, while the jailers rubbed their hands on their trousers and left.

Annie gazed down at the ruined face, thinking suddenly of Ortega, and wondered absently whether she might be next for a spot of *flagelación*. Oddly enough, the prospect didn't frighten her and she wondered why. Was it because she knew she had nothing to answer for? That she occupied the moral high ground? That she'd denied them the pleasures they'd been anticipating? Or was it simply that Franco's Spain, for once, had been kind to her, and that good fortune could take her to another country that the likes of Celia Gámez could never soil. To all these questions she had no answer, but she tended the face on her lap, tried a whispered question or two, and finally concluded that the poor soul had sensibly gone to sleep.

They came for her in the middle of the night. Without her watch it was impossible to be exact and looking up at the uniformed warder, she did her best to get her possessions back but try as she might she could get no response from the warder. Expecting the treatment, she found herself being led into the chilly darkness outside where a waiting van already had its engine running. She was the only passenger. A policeman sat beside her, two more were in the front. No one said a word throughout the journey, which was short. When the driver slowed to make a turn off the empty main road, she glimpsed high walls topped with barbed wire, and a couple of unmuzzled dogs barely restrained by the uniformed guards at the gate.

'Prison?'

'*Sí.*'

More uniforms helped her out of the van and escorted her through an entry cut into an enormous pair of doors. There was no interview, no pressure of any kind. The same escort accompanied her up four flights of stairs and along a corridor of what she judged to be cell doors. Towards the end, one of the two officers produced a set of keys. The cell was narrow, the concrete floor unevenly ribbed. There was a single barred window, high up on the facing wall, and when she turned to ask for water the cell door was already slamming shut. The inside of the door was metal with no handles, only locks, a single peephole and a hatch for the delivery of food. She asked again for water, a shout this time, but all she could hear was the faintest hint of departing boots.

She turned again, angry now. Everything in the cell was welded to the floor, the bed, the tiny square table, even the chair, and the thought that these people might be worried about theft briefly cheered her up. In the corner of the cell was a water closet that reeked of unflushed shit, the cracked bowl leaking a dribble of moisture onto the floor, and when she tried the single tap on the hand basin nothing happened. All that was left was the bed. The springs within the metal frame were broken and when she tried to lay full length she felt bare ends of wire cutting into her flesh. For warmth, she had a single blanket, and in the end she used it to cover the springs, lying on her side and pulling her legs up into her chest. The blanket stank of cheap tobacco and as a hint of dawn appeared at the window she tried to trick her body into sleep by remembering the brand of cigarette. By the time she'd got it – *Hebras* – it was full daylight and the chill of the cell had seeped deep into her bones.

She stayed in the cell for two nights and nearly three days, according to the careful record she kept by using a tiny length of wire from the mattress to scratch marks on the wall. Unseen hands delivered food twice daily, a thin gruel enlivened by a spoonful of *garbanzos*, but she was grateful for the sweetened coffee, and said so.

Talking to the hands, which she judged to be male and always belonging to the same owner, became a kind of game. She had absolutely no idea where this episode in her life might take her, and whether it would ever end, but she was very happy to babble away in her perfect Spanish, taking care to keep the one-way conversation as light and inconsequential as possible. There was a hint of madness in these non-exchanges but her spirits soared on the last occasion the hands appeared.

She'd been treating the hands to a fullish account of an episode in her youth when, at seventeen, she'd taken up with a fisherman called Marcel in Dieppe. He was an older man, with a wonderful presence, and a smile to match and a boat of his own he'd inherited from his father. He'd taken her to sea as often as she could make it, and they'd brightened the intervals between hauling the nets in all kinds of inventive ways. Thinking back to those days had been a real tonic given her current circumstances and she was approaching the point in her story when she might have to share a confidence or two when – for the first time – she was looking at a single erect thumb. What this gesture meant was never clear. At the time, it seemed to register approval, a tale well told. Later, looking back, she suspected it might have been a kind of farewell: *adieu et bonne chance*. But whatever the truth, only one more Arctic night lay between her and freedom.

The following morning, with an oblong of blue sky high on the outside wall beside her bed, she heard footsteps approaching along the corridor outside. Then, unusually, came the scrape of a key, first in one lock and then the other, before the door swung open to reveal a uniformed warder standing aside to admit a tallish, middle-aged figure in a rather nice suit. He stood in the cell for a moment, looking down at her, then pulled a face at the sight of the brimming closet. Annie swung her legs off the bed and perched on the edge of the metal frame. His shoes were nice, too, highly polished brogues with a hint of red socks. Absurdly, she wondered whether she owed this man an apology for the state of the place but he spared her the effort.

'I'm from the embassy,' he murmured. 'My name's Christian Bottomley, and you'll be glad to know I'm here to take you away.'

20

Five days later, on 14 October 1940, Tam Moncrieff took a telephone call at his London desk. The call came from Stockholm. Birger Dahlerus was a Swedish businessman who'd done his heroic best to broker talks between London and Berlin in the summer of 1939 before Hitler invaded Poland and plunged the entire continent into war. Moncrieff, who'd performed a number of duties on the margins of this little peace dance, knew and liked Dahlerus, and was grateful that he was still prepared to act as a go-between. Now, the Swede told him to return at once to Madrid.

'May I ask why?'

'Hans Zimmermann, whom I think you know. He says he has news.'

'And that's it?'

'I'm afraid so. This will mean more to you than me, Tam, but I guess it's best to keep it simple.'

Moncrieff agreed. That very morning, he'd read a report from an agent in Antwerp that *Luftwaffe* Chief Hermann Goering was touring German air bases along the Channel coast, testing the morale of bomber crews ahead of an imminent intensification of the raids on London. A glance from the window at smoke still drifting along the river from the still-burning docks in the

East End told him that Dornier and Heinkel squadrons needed little encouragement, but he knew that Dahlerus was a good friend of Goering, and enquired about the *Reichsmarschall*'s health.

'He's in good form, my friend. I didn't realise you knew him.'

'1938,' Moncrieff sat back at his desk. 'Nuremberg. We spent an entire night emptying two bottles of Spanish brandy. Goering is built on different lines from the rest of us. Having two livers must have helped him no end. Mine has never been the same since.'

Dahlerus chuckled. Alone among the Third Reich chieftains, he told Moncrieff, Hermann Goering understood the difference between insanity and real life. He was also, he added in an aside, a man who knew how to enjoy himself. With Hermann, you'd always be sure that the right kind of party came first.

'Madrid,' he repeated. 'Book yourself into the Palace Hotel and await developments.'

At noon, a passenger was quietly bumped from the Pan American flying boat that served Lisbon from Poole Harbour, which was otherwise fully booked. Moncrieff – the late arrival – landed in Lisbon at dusk but managed to get the night train to Madrid. It pulled into the Atocha station as dawn was breaking and Moncrieff walked the mile and a half to the Palace Hotel. Collecting his key at the hotel's reception desk, he asked for any messages that might have been left.

The overnight receptionist was about to end her shift. At the mention of his name, she checked, and then eyed him curiously before shaking her head.

'Nothing,' she said.

'Wonderful flowers,' Moncrieff had noticed an explosion of white blooms in a beautiful cut-glass vase. 'Roses in October? Remarkable.'

The receptionist agreed. The flowers had been a gift from a guest. Business at the hotel, she said, was picking up. Thank God for the Germans.

Moncrieff took the stairs to the first floor. Room 117 lay towards the end of the corridor. He had the key readied but, to his surprise, the door was unlocked. It opened to the slightest pressure from his fingertips and the moment he stepped inside he could hear the fall of water into a bath. He hesitated a moment, rechecking the room's number, and then closed the door. On the low table beside the crescent of sofa stood a vase of white roses identical to the blooms he'd noticed in reception.

Wary now, he put his suitcase down. On trips like this he always carried a small Italian automatic, a Beretta M1934 semi-automatic, and he drew the gun before approaching the bedroom. The bath was clearly occupied, not only the splash of water but a male voice humming the 'Pilgrims' Chorus' from *Tannhäuser*.

The bedroom, to Moncrieff's relief, was empty but the bed had clearly been slept in and there were various items of underwear scattered across the carpet. A plain black suit had been carefully hung in the spacious closet and an empty wine bottle and two glasses had been abandoned on the occasional table beneath the window. Mystified, Moncrieff returned to the lounge. The bathroom door was an inch or so ajar, and the 'Pilgrims' Chorus' was in the rudest health. Moncrieff had watched a performance years ago in Bayreuth and he paused a moment, still more bemused. Then, very slowly, the Beretta rock-steady, he opened the door. The bathroom was thick with steam but as it thinned in the draught from the door he recognised the recumbent figure in the bath, water lapping at his chest, one toe poised over the hot tap. The head barely moved, just a nod of what might have been welcome and a forefinger raised to his lips.

Zimmermann.

Moncrieff stepped into the room, closed the door behind him. He was about to ask what the hell was going on but the forefinger was doing the talking, urgent movements side to side. Say nothing. Give nothing away. Then Zimmermann moved his weight and the water lapped over the side of the bath as he stood up. Both forefingers this time, spooling in the same direction before Zimmermann nodded upwards towards the ceiling, rolling his eyes.

Microphones, Moncrieff thought. He nodded, smiled, tucked the gun away. Obvious, really.

Zimmermann, too, looked pleased, gesturing for Moncrieff to toss him a towel. He mopped his face and hair and then raised his wet arm to his lips and gave it a long kiss.

'Pieter and Sebastian send their love,' he murmured. 'And those naughty young things from the Casbah, too. We've missed you, *Liebling*, much to tell, much to confess.'

'Confess?'

'Last night, alas.' Zimmermann gestured towards the bedroom. 'In this city, appetite is everything. A Rhineland boy from the embassy. I think you'll approve, at least I hope you will. His name's Otto, something else we have in common, and he's *very* eager.'

Moncrieff could do nothing but nod and grunt his rough approval, and as he backed out of the bathroom Zimmermann was kissing his arm again and promising all kinds of restitution.

They left the hotel less than thirty minutes later, Zimmermann having schooled Moncrieff in this pantomime performance for the sake of the hidden microphones. Walking in the bright autumn sunshine, followed at a discreet distance by a lone tail, Moncrieff quizzed the rising *Abwehr* star on how, exactly, he'd helped himself to Moncrieff's room. The answer, it turned out, was a happy marriage of money and circumstances gifted to him on his arrival.

He'd booked a room in the name of Constanz. The room was on the first floor, like Moncrieff's, but when he arrived he'd noticed comings and goings in Room 117. These were all men and Zimmermann knew enough about the new field of electronic surveillance to recognise what they were up to. Microphones, he thought. Plural. And all of them doubtless linked to a recording system.

Enquiries at reception had revealed that Room 117 had been assigned to Moncrieff, who by now was not expected for at least twenty-four hours, so Zimmermann had made it his business to press for a transfer. Tam Moncrieff, he told the receptionist, was a very good friend of his. They'd agreed to share a room together and the hotel would be doing the pair of them a very big favour if it cancelled his own booking and allowed him to move down the corridor to join his special friend.

The receptionist had been dubious at first, confused rather than suspicious, but a $20 note had resolved the problem. Given the heavy presence of yet more surveillance, Zimmermann now announced that they were pledged to each other for at least a day or two, or as long, certainly, as interest in their activities continued.

'So who are these people?' Moncrieff nodded back towards the road where their shadow appeared to be enjoying a cigarette.

'Gestapo, almost certainly. Probably flown in from Berlin.'

'And the microphones?'

'Same outfit. *Onkel Heine*'s building a case. All we can do is look besotted.' He gave Moncrieff a playful peck on his cheek. 'Play the game, Tam. Isn't that what they teach you back home?'

Moncrieff, acutely uncomfortable, was watching a pair of passing nuns turn their heads away. One of them was crossing herself.

'In MI6,' he muttered, 'they'd call this tradecraft. Go to the right schools and you've been in training most of your life.'

Zimmermann's laughter was unforced, and Moncrieff realised there was a very different side to this forbidding *Abwehr* spy. He appeared to relish the part that necessity had scripted for the slightly uptight Scot.

'You mentioned the manse back home last time we met,' Zimmermann said. 'I had to look the word up but if it helps you have my sympathies. The blood runs hotter in a climate like this.'

'I'll take your word for it,' Moncrieff was still watching their assigned escort. 'The last time I got propositioned I broke the bloody man's neck, but you know that already. Tell me what brought you down here. Make me feel normal again.'

Another smile from Zimmermann, and a gloved hand feeling for his. Moncrieff shook him off. Lovers' tiff, he thought bleakly, certain their Gestapo friend would be making a mental note.

'I'm serious, Hans. Tell me about *Onkel Heine*'s little adventure while no one's bloody listening.'

Zimmermann nodded, slipping an arm through Moncrieff's as they continued their walk. The *Reichsführer-SS*, he said, would be appearing in Madrid on 20 October, which was less than a week away. There were plans for him to enjoy a ride down the Gran Via before attending a succession of meetings with various Spanish heads of security. In the late afternoon, he would be guest of honour at Las Ventas, the city's showcase bullring, where Manolete was the *corrida*'s star attraction. The following day, there were plans to take him to Toledo, the old Imperial capital of Spain, which had by now become a shrine to the triumph of Franco's rebel armies.

'Toledo?' Moncrieff queried.

'You don't know what happened?' Zimmermann could scarcely believe it.

'Tell me.'

'This was the first year of the war. The Republicans had chased the rebels into the Alcázar at Toledo. That's the huge fortress that dominates the place. Franco was advancing on Madrid but took the time to make a little detour and raise the siege. The rebels walked free and the Moors were off the leash for days. Total carnage, just the way Franco liked it, and a warning for all the other Republican cities foolish enough to resist.'

Moncrieff could do nothing but nod. Try as he might to sustain the romance, he badly wanted Zimmermann to keep his distance.

'So what do you think?' he said. 'About Ortega?'

'We delivered the rifle he wanted and the man passed all our tests. Seven targets, four hundred metres, every single one destroyed.'

'This is from Annie Wrenne?'

'Yes. She's moved out of the place she's been renting and just now she's living with Ortega. I've no idea why.'

'So where's best? For *Onkel Heine*?'

'We have a choice. Ortega could hit him on the Gran Via. He'll need a place to hole up to take the shot and there's no guarantee of an open car. Las Ventas is out of the question. I've been there. Sunday's matador is Manolete. He draws huge crowds. *Onkel* will be with the VIPs. The range across the bullring is fine but where do you hide a rifle?' He shook his head. 'It wouldn't work, and more to the point a wise man wouldn't even try.'

'You think Ortega's wise?'

'Very. Why? Because he's a survivor. He calculates the odds. He wants to be very rich and he wants to be alive to enjoy it. Who can question a logic like that?'

Moncrieff could only agree. His own protracted negotiations with Ortega had been near-ruinous. Jewish monies had given him a war chest of nearly ten thousand pounds, a sum unimaginable for a working man. Ortega wouldn't settle for a penny less than fifteen, with a thousand as a down payment against expenses and the rest payable as soon as the *Reichsführer-SS* was pronounced dead. This had driven Moncrieff back into the arms of his benefactors and even now he was far from certain that the full sum would ever be guaranteed.

'Toledo, then,' Moncrieff dug his hands deeper into his pockets. 'Has to be.'

Annie knew all about Toledo, and the Alcázar, and the Moors running rampant through hospital wards heaped with Republican wounded after the raising of the siege. As Franco had intended, word had spread quickly to Madrid, where waiting defenders of the nation's capital could expect the same treatment. But the atrocities at Toledo, in ways Franco had never anticipated, had stiffened resistance, and by the time she left Madrid, the civil war had dug itself in around the edges of the university. This, Annie remembered only too well. What she knew nothing about was *Onkel Heine*.

'Tell me again,' she said to Ortega.

'*Onkel Heine* is Heinrich Himmler. Heinrich Himmler is a very bad man indeed. Hitler's told him to frighten the Jews and he's obliged by killing them in their thousands. It's started in Poland but it won't end there. He's also upset Germans, powerful Germans, who still belong to the human race.

Himmler makes a choirboy of Franco. Lots of people want him dead.'

'And you?'

'My job is to make that happen.'

'When?'

'Next Monday.'

'Where?'

'Toledo.' Ortega explained the reason for Himmler's visit. A couple of hours at the most, he said. But ample time to get the job done.

The job. Annie had been living in Ortega's new apartment for a couple of weeks, invited to occupy his spare bedroom after her release from prison. On that occasion she'd pressed him about the Rubens picture, demanding to know who might have spared her a lifetime behind bars, but he'd pleaded ignorance. He'd heard rumours about the painting being intercepted en route back from Geneva, and he knew that Nehmann had a rich client in Berlin who never bothered with the obvious questions, but aside from that he simply shrugged.

'You think it was Nehmann who took it?'

'I've no idea. Does it matter?'

'Of course it does. Just now my life has ceased to be my own. One day that may happen to you. Be warned, eh?'

Annie held his gaze, knowing that this feeling of helplessness was all too real. Life and liberty had suddenly become intensely precious, and moving body and soul into Ortega's world now added an element of the surreal. Surreal because she'd never enjoyed surroundings like these. Surreal because money – Ortega's money – seemed suddenly limitless. And surreal because she woke up to views from her bedroom window a world away from the draughty squalor of her previous lodgings. No one in this *quartier*, she told herself, would appear after midnight and tear up the floorboards. No one in the fashionable restaurants where Ortega seemed so at home would dream of hauling her off for a taste of *flagelación* in some poorly lit police station. And no one would produce a grubby corner of some art book and accuse her of stuffing an Old Master under her bed.

But that, she knew, was merely a truce in the on-going war. Why? Because of the job.

That night, she pressed Ortega for what he wanted from her. What role was she to play? Why did he even need her in the first place? To these questions, and many others, he had no ready answers. They were drinking an excellent Rioja from crystal glasses that came with the apartment and in the end, when she refused to give up, he admitted the time had arrived to be straight with her.

'The British are paying for this,' he said softly.

'The wine? The apartment?'

'Both. And much else.'

'This is Moncrieff?'

'Of course it's Moncrieff. He's been paying you for months. It all comes from the same source. Different scale maybe, but the same paymaster.'

'So why does he want this person dead?'

'Because Himmler frightens the Jews, and disgusts some of the Gentiles. These people have deep pockets. They want him gone.'

'And will that cure the problem?'

'I've no idea. I just pull the trigger.'

'At Toledo.'

'At Toledo.'

'And will it be dangerous?'

'For Himmler, yes. For us? As long as we take the right precautions? I think not.' He offered her the remains of the bottle. 'Remember I had half a church on my head. Nothing can ever be as bad again.'

They departed for Toledo the following day. Ortega, who called the expedition a recce, had acquired a rattletrap Ford Roadster with dented bodywork and a wheezy engine that faltered on the steeper hills out of the city.

'So where's Moncrieff?'

'I have no idea. God's truth.'

'But why isn't he with us?'

'Because he needs to stay at arm's length. Moncrieff is playing God in this little adventure and you know who he's trusted to look after his best interests?'

Annie nodded, largely because the answer was so obvious.

'Me,' she said. 'Because I can pass as a Spaniard. Because I have no obvious connections anywhere else. Because, God help me, I'm *clean.*'

'It's more than that.'

'How?'

'A face like mine is hard to forget. I can do the looking, the planning, the plotting. It's getting colder. I can wrap myself up, make myself invisible. But we'll also need to talk to people face to face.'

'About what?'

'About hiring somewhere. Probably a whole house. Cash in the hand and no questions. Someone has to make that arrangement.'

'And that's my job?'

'Yes. The rifle's in the trunk. Once we've found somewhere, we'll offload it. If we get this right, one bullet should do it. Then we're gone.'

'The noise? The gun going off?'

'A car backfiring. Happens all the time.'

'As simple as that?'

'Probably simpler.'

Annie raised an eyebrow. The image that wouldn't leave her was the moment the first pumpkin had exploded in the Valle de los Caidos. Annie could remember the knobbly dampness of the turf through the groundsheet, the smell of autumn in the mountain air, and above all the presence of Ortega beside her, absolutely motionless, concentrating only on that final delicate pressure on the trigger. She'd watched the cartoon face blown away in the shiver of wind from the nearby peaks. Himmler might be evil, but did any man deserve that?

They were in Toledo by noon, after three stops to let the water in the radiator cool down. Annie had never been here before but was immediately impressed. The heart of the old town was surrounded on three sides by the green waters of the river surging through a gorge. Ancient stone fortifications latticed the slopes and beyond the main road she counted terrace after terrace of houses that climbed up towards the Alcázar.

They stayed two nights in a grand hotel in the shadows of the fortress walls, and while Ortega, huddled in layers of scarf, scouted for angles, and viewpoints, and all the other impedimenta that went with the business of killing someone, Annie wandered the more deserted alleys, pursued by sudden unexpected glimpses of that same looming presence. The Alcázar was more a gesture, she thought, than a building. In some lights, with a decent coat of paint, it might look like the holiday destination of your dreams. In others, especially as night fell, it acquired a more sinister air, the four corner towers silhouetted against the dying light, a row of cypress trees doing nothing to soften the message it sent.

This was a building, she concluded, that spoke of raw power and the simplicities of a country of which she was beginning to despair. The brief flirtation with liberty had come and gone. Once again Spain was in thrall to the murmurings of the priesthood and the merciless extortions of businessmen and the aristocracy. Annie was still a little woolly about the menace of Heinrich Himmler but where better to settle one of history's more recent debts?

Ortega had no time for these fancy musings. Himmler, he reminded her, was money. The English were prepared to pay a great deal for his body on the mortician's slab, and Ortega refused to trouble himself with anything but the smallest print of putting him there.

On the second day, he led her around the four sides of the Alcázar, coming to a halt on the elevation that looked out across the river gorge. He told her he'd had word from Berlin that a balcony ran the length of this side of the building, protected by a brick crenellation. A door midway along provided access to the open air, and from here special guests could command the best of the Alcázar's many views. Ortega had no means of confirming the view but knew it must look out over the river gorge and the mountains beyond.

Himmler, he'd been assured, would be here around midday. The sun would be high, the river itself deep in shadow. There was provision in the *Reichsführer-SS*'s schedule for a moment of lingering enjoyment, doubtless listening to some local historian conjuring long-ago enemies advancing on Toledo over the mountains, after which Himmler would probably nod and offer a word of appreciation about the view, and then step back indoors to attend a modest banquet to be held in his honour.

'Except that won't happen,' Annie pointed out. 'Because he'll be dead.'

Dead. The word – so simple, so final – chilled her. It seemed, at once, the simplest proposition and yet the grossest outcome, but the more she thought about it, the more certain she became that her options were fast running out. There was no one she could turn to, no one she could trust with a story this unlikely. That a one-eyed sniper and his tame nurse would settle briefly on the face of history, attend to a nasty boil, and depart.

That night, they dined from a trolley in their hotel suite. Ortega hid in the bathroom while the waiter laid out the filet mignon and the glistening fan of accompanying vegetables before reappearing to swallow a glass of Château Lafite. The occasional lamp threw a soft light onto his ruined face but for the first time Annie detected a real tension around his one good eye. He seemed nervous, ill at ease. She lifted the biggest of the two steaks onto a plate, knowing how much he adored rare prime beef, but he barely touched any of it, mumbling an excuse about the beginnings of a head cold and disappearing into one of the two bedrooms. A little later, she tiptoed in, and perched on the edge of the bed. He was flat on his back, the sheet and blankets heaped around the pitted flesh of his chin, and when she took his proffered hand he turned to look up at her.

'It has to work,' he muttered.

'Why?'

For a long moment he said nothing, just stared up at her, and for a moment she was reminded of the bloodied suspect she'd tried to comfort at the police station only days ago. How much did she really know about this man? And was he really as invulnerable as he tried to make out? Then Ortega tried to smile, never an easy exercise.

'Why?' he repeated. 'Good question.'

21

Zimmermann, as promised, was already at the restaurant but what Moncrieff hadn't expected was the other figure sitting beside him. Moncrieff had never had the pleasure of meeting him in person before but the face – available in dozens of shots in his MI5 file – was unmistakable.

Smuggler. Arms dealer. Banker. Mainstay of countless shadowy international networks. Friend of the powerful. And now a very rich man. A colleague of Moncrieff's in St James's Place had recently described him as Mallorca's most successful export. Another colleague in the same conversation had been blunter. 'Lovely manners,' he'd grunted. 'But never trust the smile.'

The surprise guest was smiling now as he rose from the table and shook Moncrieff's hand. Zimmermann made the introductions.

'A good friend of mine,' was all he said. 'Juan March.'

After the light, dry touch of March's handshake, Moncrieff settled at the table. He knew that this was a familiar face at countless German consular outposts across Europe and the wider world. He knew that this slim, balding, beautifully suited figure had devoted many years and much guile to building an enormous personal fortune. A recent addition to the Juan March empire had been a bespoke palace in Palma, centrepiece of his sprawling web of commercial interests. He'd installed his immediate family in marbled luxury on the first floor upwards while the space at street level had sensibly been turned into yet another business. Money, as this man knew only too well, has a habit of breeding yet more wealth. Welcome to the Banca March.

Moncrieff had half expected lunch to offer new clues to events playing out over the coming days but he quickly realised that Zimmermann was interested only in a social occasion. He looked relaxed, even playful. The restaurant, within easy walking distance of the German Embassy, was full and judging by the uniforms, and the laughter, and the raised voices, many of these diners were Zimmermann's countrymen. Some of them, according to their rank insignia, came from the upper echelons of the considerable SS presence in Madrid, and when Zimmermann made a joke about the comforts of the Palace Hotel, and his hand lingered on Moncrieff's arm, he knew he was back in the world of pantomime. The *Abwehr*'s rising star is parading his latest conquest, Moncrieff thought. His brief dalliance with the world of British intelligence had called for many disguises but this was a role Moncrieff would never want to play again.

They were all happy to accept the *maître d*'s word that the roasted haunch of wild venison, running with juices and thickly cut, would be a decision they'd never regret. The vegetables were in the rudest health, freshly picked and perfectly steamed. Juan March insisted on contributing two bottles of a fine Rioja from a vineyard he appeared to own. And by the time the waiter returned with a bottle of brandy after the dessert course, the conversation had turned to Heinrich Himmler.

March, inevitably, counted him as a good friend. They'd met, he said, on a number of occasions, all of them in Berlin. In his view, the SS *Jefe* was much misunderstood. Some of the wilder stories about runic SS initiation rites and the mad pursuit of eugenics were doubtless inventions spread by the poor man's many enemies, but in March's opinion it took a rare talent to secure a place at Hitler's elbow, build an empire on the current scale of the SS and defend your little craft against all boarders.

'The man is shy,' he murmured. 'He has few of the conversational gifts we Spanish take for granted. Home is what matters, whether it be the *Heimat* or that *gemütlich* little chalet he's building for his pudding of a wife. To get him on an aircraft and bring him here is a tribute to our sainted *Caudillo*. To prove we matter, we need look no further than Sunday. Speaking personally, I hope Herr Himmler falls for Manolete's charms, and if that doesn't work then I'm sure that Toledo will take him in its arms.'

Zimmermann caught Moncrieff's eye, and for the first time there was a hint of something chillier in the briefness of his smile. Unfinished business, Moncrieff thought. *Onkel Heine* in the sights of a master sniper who never missed.

'And security?' Moncrieff enquired. 'Keeping this visitor of yours in one piece?'

March shrugged. As far as he was concerned, the battle over Heinrich Himmler had already been won. The man had no taste for foreign travel. To get him here at all, even for three days, was a powerful nod to the coming importance of Spain in what he called the New Order. Franco had earned himself a place at the top table in distinguished Fascist company and Himmler's arrival on the Gran Via was the living proof that times were changing.

'*España arriba!*' he raised his glass in a toast, a twinkle in his dark eyes, watching Zimmermann whispering something in Moncrieff's ear. 'Am I making sense, Hans?' March asked. 'And have you arrested everyone with darkness in their souls?'

Zimmermann was much amused. Security, he said, was a local affair, though it was Himmler's style to insist on checking the smallest print. To that end, he understood that Gestapo and SS units would be shortly despatched to throw a wide cordon around the Toledo Alcázar. Together with hundreds of Spanish police they'd be under orders to detain and body-search anyone attracting the faintest hint of suspicion ahead of Himmler's visit. The fortress, he said, was the jewel in Franco's crown. That was the moment he could truly show off, not just to Hitler's fearsome SS *Jefe* but the entire world, an opportunity he had no intention of missing.

'Impressive, Hans.' March was offering a selection of huge cigars. 'Thank God we peasants have a proper government at last.'

This comment, as Moncrieff realised only too well, was intended for a wider audience, and as March raised his glass in a second toast, a neighbouring table of Germans, most of them in senior rank SS uniforms, got to their feet.

'*España arriba!*' they chorused, much to Zimmermann's amusement.

Half an hour later, out in the street, Moncrieff took him aside for a private word. With a final wave of his cigar, having settled the bill, Juan March had just departed in the back of a gleaming Hispano-Suiza.

'It's true about Toledo? The cordon? The body searches?'

'I'm afraid it is. We're dealing with the SS. They have a view of human nature that was never pretty, and I'm afraid they rarely take risks.'

'And does Ortega know any of this?'

'No,' Zimmermann checked his watch. 'Not yet.'

*

Annie was looking for somewhere, in Ortega's phrase, to finish the business. Ortega had spent the hours before dawn prowling the warren of streets between the Alcázar and the river, noting the houses that offered a good view of the crenellated balcony lit by newly installed arc lamps in the surrounding gardens. These were the dead hours in any Spanish township, large or small, just a scamper of cats to keep him company, and he'd moved silently from street to street, gauging distances, angles, fields of fire. He needed the privacy of an entire house to get the job done properly, but in times like this he knew that few challenges would resist a handful of large denomination notes, preferably American dollars.

Dawn finally stole across the mountains in the east, shades of grey pinked with the promise of another glorious day, and the street beside the Alcázar was full of long shadows by the time he returned to the hotel. Annie was still asleep, the single sheet tucked around her chin, but she stirred as he opened the door and padded softly across to the bed.

'Here—' He gave her a notebook, and then opened the wooden shutters on the nearby window.

'What's this?'

'Addresses I checked this morning. We're news people. We're making a movie. Himmler's coming to town and we need shots. We also need somewhere to live. Four nights. Start at a hundred dollars. Can you do an American accent? In Spanish?'

'I can try.'

'Do your best. What matters is the view. Remember the balcony? The fancy brickwork? Look for the door among the windows. That's where he should appear.'

'How many addresses?' Annie was rubbing her eyes.

'Nineteen. Life starts early in places like this. You want me to order you coffee? Something to eat?' He gazed down at her, then dug in his pocket and produced a thick roll of bank notes. 'Take the lot,' he grunted. 'But don't come back without the key to somebody's door.'

And so Annie found herself out in the early sunshine, criss-crossing the warren of streets that had long served as a kind of moat protecting the Alcázar from intruders climbing up from the river. From time to time, she paused to consult Ortega's scribbled notes before recognising a particular door or entry. These houses were old, often in poor repair, and only a handful carried numbers or names. In their absence, Ortega had written of a particular feature, an earthenware pot brimful of rosemary and sage, a crudely fashioned wooden cross hanging from a nail on a door, a faded warning to beggars that they were not welcome. In every case, once she took a step back or walked to the end of the street to look up at the sheer walls of Toledo's fortress, she knew that Ortega's judgement was faultless. The line of crenellated brickwork, and even the door offering access to the balcony behind, were clearly visible.

Yet no one seemed to be at home. She knocked at door after door in this *barrio* of the dead, waiting patiently in the autumn sunshine, awaiting footsteps that never came. Finally, in mid-afternoon, she managed to rouse a response. It was a woman, younger than she'd expected. She was nursing a tiny baby and Annie could hear a male voice from the depths of the house. Who's there? What's going on?

Annie did her best to explain. She was a translator for an American newsreel crew. They needed a base to cover Monday's big event. Happily, the woman knew exactly what she was talking about.

'This is the German person?'
'It is.'

'And you want to bring a camera here?'

'We do.'

'To film what?'

Annie explained about Himmler making an appearance, enjoying the view from the fortress, then stepping back inside for a spot of lunch. She did her best to weave this little vignette into their wider coverage of his visit but as she did so she became aware of how wildly implausible this pitch of hers must sound. Not that it appeared to matter.

'You pay?'

'Of course.'

'How much?'

'One hundred dollars,' Annie smiled. 'US.'

'For one shot?' Astonished, she gestured behind her. 'In here?'

Annie shook her head. They'd need to be staying in the house while they got themselves ready. It would save on a hotel. Maybe a hundred and fifty dollars?

'How many of you?' The woman was frowning now.

'Two.'

'No problem. We have three bedrooms.'

'And you?'

'We live here. You want meals? You want to eat? Two hundred.'

'But we'd need the whole house.'

'Why? Come in. Have a look. I show you the view. I show you everything. A hundred and seventy-five dollars?'

With some reluctance, Annie stepped into the house. There was a heavy smell of nappies and she could hear something bubbling on a stove. A face swam out of the semi-darkness. This must be the woman's husband, she thought. He'd heard the bargaining on the front doorstep, and doubtless everything else, and he wasn't settling for a cent under two hundred dollars. The woman swore at him and disappeared with the baby. The man, heavy-set, in singlet and work trousers, was gesturing towards the stairs.

'Please. The view. I show you the view.'

Annie tried to protest, attempted an excuse or two, said she was allergic to babies. Anything, she thought. Anything to bring this comic opera to an end. Killing people should be simpler than this.

They'd got to the top of the second flight of stairs. The man half kicked a door open with one bare foot, and then stepped aside in the way a conjurer might invite applause.

'You go,' he nodded past the door. 'You look.'

Annie did his bidding. The window was small, the access awkward, and at once she shook her head.

'Why not?' The man was staring at a view of the eastern face of the Alcázar.

Annie mumbled something about the bed getting in the way, and the sagging armchair, and seconds later the man was hauling the bed backwards, clearing a space, showing her – insisting – that everything was possible.

Annie shook her head. The floor was all wrong, too crooked, too bumpy, too everything. They had a tripod. The camera had to be level.

'But you sleep here, too. Perfect. We cook. You eat. A hundred and ninety.'

For a long moment, they just stared at each other. Mercifully, the man wanted to show her something else from the window, a little portion of the view she might not have seen properly, an added detail that would make this film of theirs world famous. He beckoned her towards the window, insisting she take a look, leaving the bedroom door wide open.

Annie gulped, muttered a final apology, and then fled. Hopeless, she thought, emerging into the sunshine on the street, hearing the furious patter of bare feet on the stairs behind her. Never again.

Wrong. She found a café and consoled herself with a cup of thin brown liquid that might have been coffee. She wanted to go back to the hotel. She wanted to explain to Ortega that this whole adventure was misconceived and ridiculous and would probably spell the end of both of them. She wanted to be away from Toledo, away from Madrid, away from the spell that this savage country seemed to have cast on her. No more Giles Roper. No more weeks of exhausting chaos in the Pablo Iglesias. No more moments of blind helplessness on the quayside at Alicante before Carlos Ortega, himself maimed, hauled her back onstage for the war's final act.

After that, of course, had come Tam Moncrieff, Whittaker and Werner Nehmann, and long nights sleeping on top of an Old Master before she'd been hauled away, but the most recent exchange – barely an hour ago – had told her something else. That nothing in Spain could ever be taken for granted. That war of a different kind had settled on life after life, not just here but probably across Europe, and that what she'd foolishly mistaken for normal no longer existed.

And so she left the coffee untouched, consulted the last two pages of Ortega's notebook, left a five-peseta coin on the greasy table, and headed – once again – for the street. She had just two possibilities left when she finally found the answer to Ortega's dreams.

He was old, maybe in his sixties. He had the smooth, untroubled features of a priest. He was wearing a blue smock that might have belonged to a fisherman. The smock was daubed here and there with paint and his long fingers played among the scabs of yellow and green while he listened patiently to a slightly shortened version of her plea for help.

She was in luck, he said. Tomorrow morning, early, he was catching the train to Granada. The journey would take all day and at the end of it lay his ancient mother who'd taken a fall and broken her leg. The doctor had done his best but what she needed now was rest and someone to look after her. That someone was her ever-loyal son. He'd spent all day, he said, wondering how to secure his precious house once he was away and here, a blessing from the Almighty, was the answer. A hundred dollars would be more than welcome and if she and her friend wanted to stay until Christmas, no one would be happier.

At this, he led her upstairs. The house smelled of lemons with hints of lavender. Even in the fading light, the crudely framed canvases that seemed to hang everywhere were truly accomplished, most of them featuring views of the Alcázar. When Annie enquired whether they were his work, he simply nodded, and when they finally made it to the top floor the view took her breath away. The face of that same building was bathed in the soft yellow glow of the new arc lights. It looked like a stage set, quietly theatrical, the presence of the fortress softened by wisps of cloud in the darkening sky. She could see the brick crenellations, the row of windows catching the throw of the arc lights, and – most important of all – that single door through which the German person, as she now called him, would step to his doom.

'It's what you need?' a voice asked.

Annie nodded. She'd been unaware of his presence at her elbow.

'It's perfect,' she said. 'Better than perfect.'

'Good.' Pale fingers in the half-darkness as the man crossed himself.

Annie lingered, still staring out at the view, knowing that patience and a kind of belief had brought her this moment.

'You have a spare key?' she murmured.

'Of course. I'll fetch it.'

'Here. Wait a moment.' Annie dug in her purse, then examined the roll of notes in the spill of light from the Alcázar. 'Five hundred dollars,' she counted them out and pressed them into the whiteness of his hand. 'Tell me where to leave the key once we're done.'

Done. Annie hurried back to the hotel. Expecting Ortega, she found their suite empty. The key she'd been given, heavy with a hint of rust, had already become a trophy. She laid it carefully on the table beside Ortega's bed, together with a page torn from his notebook. *Calle de Santiago*, she wrote. *Red door with the house name on a white tile. Vista maravillosa.*

Wonderful view.

Ortega returned past midnight. When she asked him where he'd been, he wouldn't tell her. A friend, he said. Someone from Madrid. He seemed more relaxed now, less nervous, less fretful. When she asked about the friend, he dismissed the question with a shake of his head. Tomorrow, he said, they'd have to be up early again to smuggle the rifle into the house she'd found. Why? Because from noon onwards Security police, SS and Gestapo would be flooding the city. Anyone out of place, anyone raising the faintest whiff of suspicion, would be detained and searched.

'You know this for certain?'

'I do, yes.'

'From this friend of yours?'

'Yes.'

'But there isn't a problem. I can lay in food. You'll have the rifle. We can lock the door on the world. We can wait until Monday.'

'No,' he shook his head.

'Why not?'

'Because the shells are still in Madrid, as I already told you.' He drew a thick finger across his throat. 'No shells, no hit.'

22

Moncrieff had been invited to drinks at the British Embassy. The invitation, in the first place, came from Christian Bottomley, whom he knew already, and to whom he owed a personal thank you for acting as Annie Wrenne's point of contact at the embassy.

'She had a spot of bother with the *Guardia*,' murmured Bottomley. 'As I expect you've gathered.'

Moncrieff raised an eyebrow. All he knew was that Annie had left her lodgings and moved in with Ortega. In view of the coming operation in Toledo, about which Bottomley knew nothing, that made perfect sense.

'The *Guardia*?'

Bottomley filled in the details. A Rubens canvas had been stolen from a car en route from Geneva. *Guardia* enquiries at the Prado had unearthed Annie's interest on behalf of some unnamed client, and they'd traced her to the lodgings off the Calle de Alcalá. The suspect, a *Guardia subteniente* told Bottomley, had denied everything. There was no evidence worth the name and she was now available for collection from the city's biggest prison.

'So how was she?'

'Understandably shaken. And perhaps a little vague. She told me she had to move out of her apartment.'

'You discussed the picture?'

'We did. She admitted going to the Prado and asking about the canvas but denied everything else. The goons from the *Guardia* arrived and terrified the life out of her. Ortega may prove a godsend. I don't know what there is between them but from what I've seen, he's a remarkable man.'

Moncrieff nodded. He, too, had occasionally wondered whether Annie had developed a *tendresse* for Ortega but had never given it serious thought.

'And this mystery client?' he asked. 'Who wanted to buy the canvas?'

'She said she doesn't know. I got the impression she might have been running an errand for someone but she denied that, too.'

'Ortega, maybe?'

'I suppose that's possible. When it comes to keeping secrets, she certainly has a mind of her own.' Bottomley paused. He had a delicacy of conversational touch that Moncrieff was beginning to admire. 'You've been happy with her performance to date?'

'Very. I gave her a watching brief, foreign journalists mainly, and she kept her ear to the ground. I've been in London most of the time, as you know, but thanks to our Annie I felt I had my finger on the pulse here. She gave us a steer on the Canaris deputation. The one that went to Algeciras.'

'And I understand you joined the party.'

'I did,' Moncrieff shot him a look. 'How did you know?'

'We have sources in the German Embassy. Madrid has superb acoustics. If you keep your ears open, there are few secrets in this city.'

Nicely put, Moncrieff thought. They were talking in Bottomley's hutch of an office. Here were two desks crammed in beneath the shadow of a huge filing cabinet. A family photo propped on the filing cabinet featured a plain-looking girl in plaits on a pony, and one of the newly fashionable quotation calendars hung from a nail on the wall. October's entry featured a series of homilies about the perils of mute submission. 'There is no such thing as an inevitable war,' it warned. 'If war comes, it will be from the failure of human wisdom.'

'It amused me, too,' Bottomley had followed Moncrieff's eyeline. 'Though I doubt very much that we were ever wise.'

Glancing at his watch, he announced that the Ambassador would be ready to receive them in a couple of minutes. He was sure that Moncrieff was au fait with the ups and downs of Sir Samuel Hoare's political career but now was maybe the time to add a dab or two of colour in the interests of a companionable hour or so.

'He can be a dry old stick,' Bottomley murmured, 'but he's a terrier with a bone when it comes to Franco. He can't abide the man. He tried conversation first, and that definitely didn't work because Franco never stops talking. Churchill sent Sir Samuel here to keep Spain out of the war and I'm sure that's exactly what he'll try and do but nothing is easy in this country. All we can really do is carry on fighting because the Royal Navy, believe it or not, still frightens our *Franquito*. Keep the battleships at sea and the *Caudillo* will mind his manners. Otherwise, I suspect the Spaniards will all start learning German.'

Moncrieff nodded. Hoare was a Chamberlain man, loyal as ever to the ex-Prime Minister. After a brief career with MI6 in revolutionary Russia, he'd headed a series of ministries between the wars and still wanted to be Viceroy of India, but the stain of appeasement had followed him to the end of the thirties, and one of Churchill's first actions in Downing Street was to despatch him to Madrid. His friends were few and Moncrieff knew his many enemies called him 'Slippery Sam'.

'Anything else?'

'Captain Hillgarth, our esteemed naval attaché. He's Churchill's eyes and ears in the building. He's here to keep us honest and, like Sam, he knows a thing or two about intelligence.'

Moncrieff nodded. Zimmermann, he thought. Wilhelm Canaris, Juan March and now a late appearance by the canny British Ambassador and his bulldog minder. Intersecting circles, powerful interests from rival sides of the battlefield, the constant swirl of rumour and counter-rumour, and soon – perhaps – the suck of an especially vicious eddy that might capsize MI5's little boat. Was it really possible that his carefully shielded plot to remove Himmler had gone unremarked upon? Or was the notion of a proper secret, properly guarded, just another casualty of this insane war?

The answer, it seemed, was no. Drinks with the Ambassador turned out to be delightful, a breezy exchange of opinions and gossip among like-minded courtiers, a soufflé rather than a pudding. It took place in a rather dowdy drawing room which seemed to serve all manner of social purposes. The framed photograph of the King had seen far too much sun, as had the vase of flowers. Damp had penetrated one corner where the wall met the ceiling, and the wallpaper, in a tired Regency stripe, was beginning to bubble.

None of this neglect appeared to trouble the Ambassador. Hoare was short and slightly built. Moncrieff understood he'd been something of an athlete in his youth and it showed in the leanness of his face and the speed of his conversational responses. He let nothing poorly phrased or sloppy pass muster in this company, no matter how convivial, and when it came to Himmler's impending visit he pressed Moncrieff for the view from the battlements of MI5.

'We suspect another play for his master's attention,' Moncrieff said. 'All eyes in Berlin are on Gibraltar but you don't need me to tell you that. The place to be seen over the next few days before the great men meet is here in Spain. Himmler isn't much of a traveller but ambition has coaxed him out of his kennel.'

Hoare nodded. Moncrieff detected a twinkle in his eye which might have been rare, and Bottomley was definitely impressed.

'And Canaris?' Hoare enquired. 'Our wily *Admiral*?'

'Canaris has loyalties of his own. One is to the *Abwehr*, which has become his life's work. Just now, Himmler appears to have the Bendlerstrasse by the throat so nothing is easy for the *Admiral*.'

'And his other loyalty?'

'To Germany. The old Germany. The Germany that never fell in love with the gangsters at court. He hates them, he truly does. Berlin just now disgusts him.'

'Fighting talk, Moncrieff,' Hoare stirred in his armchair, his thin fingers plucking at his perfectly pressed trousers. 'You can evidence that? You have a source?'

'I have, yes.' Moncrieff was thinking of Zimmermann, who'd recently used the very same phrase.

'Care to share it with us?'

'Alas, no.'

Hoare held his gaze for a moment, testing his resolve, then seized the conversational wheel and turned their exchange in a new direction.

'And next week at Hendaye? Care to hazard a guess at the outcome?'

'Franco will do what he does best,' Moncrieff murmured.

'Which is?'

'Play for time. State his terms, then re-state them, and in case Hitler hasn't caught the drift, lay them all out a third time. This will drive Hitler crazy. It isn't the way he does business and the man has no patience.'

'You know Franco? You've met him? Talked to him? Or should I say *listened* to him?'

'Never.'

'Remarkable, Moncrieff, and that's a compliment.'

'For what?'

'For getting the essence of the bloody man. I've come a very long way to try and muster a relationship of some sort, but he just retires to the shadows and talks whatever nonsense comes into his head.'

'Canaris thinks otherwise. I gather the key word is *Gallego*.'

'You've talked to Canaris? Compared notes?'

'I've listened to him.'

'And this happens often?'

'Only when necessary.'

'Care to elaborate?'

'I'm afraid not.'

The Ambassador held his glance for a long moment, and then shrugged.

'So Franco and Hitler shake hands ...' Hoare was back at Hendaye, '... and exchange the usual claptrap compliments, and Hitler thumps the table while Franco takes absolutely no notice. Is that what we should anticipate?'

'More or less.'

'Hardly a meeting of minds, Moncrieff, or is that too harsh?'

'Not at all. You've obviously met Franco yourself. The prospects are never rosy ...' Moncrieff smiled, '... at any level.'

'You're right. The bloody man's impossible. I used to listen to Chamberlain talking about his meetings with Hitler. None of them were pretty but if you poked the man in the right spot at least you got a reaction. With Franco, there's a real danger of falling asleep. That's not diplomacy, Moncrieff, that's bedtime.' Hoare turned to Bottomley and gestured at the sherry decanter. 'Another, perhaps? Before we start slandering someone else?'

Moncrieff left the embassy an hour later. Bottomley walked him out of the building and onto the street, plainly delighted by the brief soirée.

'You made a mark,' he nodded back towards the lit windows beyond the iron gate. 'His Slipperiness doesn't suffer fools and that story of yours about drinking Spanish brandy all night with Goering actually made him laugh. That doesn't happen often, believe me.'

Moncrieff smiled at the compliment. His Slipperiness, he thought. Nice.

'One thing I never mentioned,' he gestured Bottomley closer. 'It's about Toledo.'

'And?'

'I hear there's to be a big security presence. Local *Guardia*, SS, Gestapo, a small army on the streets. It makes perfect sense, of course, but with those contacts of yours in the German Embassy...' He shrugged, leaving the sentence unfinished.

Bottomley was frowning. Then he shook his head.

'News to me,' he said. 'Why do you ask?'

23

On Saturday 19 October 1940, *Reichsführer-SS* Heinrich Himmler left Berlin's Lehrter station for his overnight journey to Madrid. Himmler was travelling with a small coterie of security specialists and occupied a tightly guarded personal carriage in the middle of the special train. An *Abwehr* agent on the platform watched the train leave in a cloud of steam before placing a phone call to the *Direktor*'s office at the Bendlerstrasse.

'He's gone,' the agent grunted.

Canaris thanked him for the news. He'd spent the previous night on a camp bed beside his cluttered desk, his normal routine when events began to gather speed.

Himmler arrived at Madrid's Chamartín station the following morning. Just days earlier, Ramón Suñer had been appointed Spain's Foreign Minister. He stepped forward from a knot of top Spanish officials from the Falange and threw a Hitler salute as Himmler clambered carefully down the steps to the platform.

From Chamartín, a limousine with an escort of motorcycle riders sped the guest of honour to the city centre. The last few days, workers had decorated the route with Nazi flags and huge swastika banners, and among a thinnish crowd on the Gran Via were Carlos Ortega, muffled in a grey scarf, and Annie Wrenne.

They occupied one corner of the intersection between the Gran Via and the Calle de Hortaleza, and it was Annie who was using the binoculars as the convoy swept towards them.

'Cap. Glasses. Uniform,' she murmured. 'The man looks like an owl.'

The cars and the escorts disappeared towards the Royal Palace. The watching crowds began to thin out and Annie sensed a little disappointment as the Gran Via reverted to an early Sunday afternoon. The city's premier bullring was a forty-minute stroll away and en route Ortega had selected a taverna in the *barrio de Salamanca* for a snack. The taverna was dark after the bright autumn sunshine outside, and he led Annie to the table furthest from the bar before signalling for a flask of red wine.

Annie still had the binoculars. They lay in her lap and she stared down at them as Ortega dug around in the bag he always carried. She was thinking yet again about the figure in the back of the limousine, about the way he stared out at the sea of faces at the kerbside, about the clumsy lift of his pale hand as excited *Madrileñas* blew him kisses. This was a setting conjured for royalty or movie stars. It spoke of mass adulation, of a frenzied abandonment of the normal Spanish detachment. And yet there was nothing to be seen beyond the thick plate glass but a middle-aged man you'd never, in real life, spare a second glance.

Was the glass bullet-proof? And if so, what other precautions did this man take to preserve his sorry life? Here in Madrid? At home in Berlin? And very soon, God help us all, in Toledo? The word 'owl' had been more exact than she'd somehow intended. The man looked blank. His eyes were too big for his face. He had no substance, no apparent acknowledgement that he might even exist. He was built, in short, in two dimensions. Owl, she thought again. A creature of the night.

'Here—' Ortega pushed a twist of handkerchief towards her across the tabletop. She picked it up. It felt heavier than she'd expected.

She put the binoculars on the table and unwrapped the handkerchief in her lap. It was a bullet of the kind she'd seen out in the Valley of the Fallen, the day Ortega had attended to the pumpkins.

'Just the one?' She looked up.

'That's all we need, all we can risk. In Toledo, they're searching everyone already. The rifle's fine. The view's perfect. The moment we get greedy is the moment this whole thing becomes a death trap. These people take their time, especially the Gestapo. They sweat the truth out of you. One bullet.' He nodded down towards her lap. 'That's all it will take.'

Annie was staring at the copper jacket, at the sawn-off tip, listening to Ortega's dark warnings about what might happen if they risked the whole box of bullets. And then she nodded because she'd seen the living evidence of what happened behind closed doors. In police stations. In torture chambers. Maybe even in the privacy of her own flat had the *subteniente*'s men laid hands on the Rubens. The bloodied face on her lap, she thought. And the poor man's breath bubbling pink between his swollen lips.

'You're right,' she said. 'And I expect I have to hide it.'

Ortega indicated the closet with a nod of his head. He was still at the table, minutes later, when she returned.

'Done.' She patted her belly, then reached for her glass. 'Here's to the Owl.'

Crowds were queuing at the entrances to the bullring by the time they got to Las Ventas. Annie was surprised by the sheer scale of the place, three storeys of red brickwork with a grand entrance that sucked in wave after wave of *aficionistas*. Many wore badges or printed vests, tributes to this afternoon's prime attraction. The young Manolete had won a huge following in *corridas* across Spain, and Ortega, it turned out, loved bullfighting. It was real life in perfect focus, he told her as they jostled for a place in the queue. It was black and white, you or the bull, victory or death, life laid bare.

The bullring, he said, gave you nowhere to hide. You could smell trickery or fake courage the moment a man refused to look his fate in the eye. Manolete, said Ortega, knew all this, understood it, turned guts and calculation into an art form. Above all, he'd perfected the skill of standing still, his legs absolutely motionless while his scarlet cape built successive passes into one long flirtation with *la suerte de la Muerte*.

The kill, thought Annie, one hand straying down towards her belly.

Ortega bought tickets for one of the front rows facing the VIP area across the compacted sand of the ring itself. Himmler, he told Annie, was this afternoon's guest of honour and their seats would let them study him in detail. They queued in the thin warmth of the late autumn sun and joined the crowds shuffling upwards. Already, tier after tier of the bullring was full, and when the Foreign Minister arrived with Himmler in tow there was a ripple of applause as people rose to acknowledge their presence.

'We clap?' She glanced at Ortega.

'We clap,' he confirmed.

And so Annie got to her feet, joining her neighbour as they made the *Reichsführer-SS* welcome. Himmler appeared delighted with his reception. Suddenly animated, he acknowledged the crowd with a Hitler salute from his uniformed arm, and as

Annie's neighbour resumed his seat he muttered something about the distinguished visitor's respect for Manolete.

'Only the best for our German friends,' he grunted. Indeed, Annie thought.

Manolete appeared in person shortly afterwards for the first of his afternoon's kills. He was a slender figure in the tightness of his blue costume and he moved, thought Annie, like a ballerina, perfect posture, perfect balance. He also understood the popular draw of anticipation, of watching the bull's every move as the picadors circled on their horses, their sharp pikes stabbing at the compacted muscle on the beast's shoulders. Manolete's trying to get inside the bull's head, Annie concluded, as blood began to stream down the animal's flanks, and it turned this way and that, trying to burst out of this cage of pain.

Then came the moment when the stage suddenly belonged to no one but man and beast, Manolete and the bull, the young matador standing stock-still. He'd swapped his scarlet cape for the smaller *muleta*, weaving shadow patterns on the sand as he taunted the animal, beckoning it closer, and then closer still. This was the last and final part of the bullfight and Manolete's every pass drew a sigh from the crowd, then ripples of applause at the fineness of the young matador's judgement, up on his toes as the bull thundered past and then turned for more humiliation.

Already sickened by what she guessed was coming next, Annie raised the binoculars and abandoned the action to settle on the fleshy features of the *Reichsführer-SS*. Somehow she expected excitement but Himmler was looking pensive, his gloved hand raised to his mouth, and when Suñer bent closer from the adjacent seat, pointing out some technical detail, the tiny nod of acknowledgement told Annie that he wasn't listening at all, that stories of his distaste for real violence were probably true, and that he found this festival of carefully choreographed murder hard to take.

Hard to take? Annie glanced back at the middle of the ring where, with each pass, Manolete was stepping closer and closer to the now exhausted animal until at last he drew his sword, looked the bull in the eyes, gestured it a step or two closer still, and then danced nimbly aside as it made one final maddened lurch before Manolete plunged the blade deep between the shoulder blades and into the animal's heart. The crowd were already on their feet, the tiers of seating around the bullring white with waving handkerchiefs. The bull looked briefly confused, shook its massive head, then its front legs buckled and it collapsed sideways at Manolete's feet.

Himmler again. He was looking at something in his lap. He was blowing his nose. He was checking his watch. Anything to be spared the sight of two horses being hitched to the corpse of the dead bull before it was dragged away to the specialist butchers already sharpening their knives.

'He cares,' Annie muttered, her gaze returning to Himmler. Only the Spanish, she thought, could turn violence this intimate into an afternoon's entertainment.

It was Moncrieff who drove them to Toledo that night. Ortega found him parked five streets away from Las Ventas. Manolete had despatched five more luckless fighting bulls and Himmler had been assigned the task of presenting him with both ears of the last bull in recognition of his matchless skill and courage. The *Reichsführer-SS* did it with as much grace as he could muster, carefully wiping his hands once the presentation was over. Manolete was hoisted on the shoulders of his supporters and acknowledged the roar of the crowd before files of spectators got to their feet and shuffled towards the nearest exit.

'Your first *corrida*?' The question came from Moncrieff, at the wheel. He was eyeing Annie in the rear-view mirror.

'Yes.'

'And?'

'Ghastly. Truly horrible.'

Ortega chuckled. There was another matador, it turned out, who was almost as famous as Manolete and he, too, was called Ortega. His speciality, said Carlos, was getting in death's way and then leading it past in an arc, with a single swirl of the *muleta*. More to the point, he was also a man of words.

'Words how?'

Ortega was sitting beside Moncrieff. He twisted round, looking at Annie.

'You're serious? You want to hear his poem?' Without waiting for an answer, he launched into the single verse:

Bullfight critics ranked in rows
Crowd the enormous Plaza full
But he's the only one who knows
And he's the man who fights the bull.

Annie nodded. She thought she understood. 'And you're the bullfighter?' she muttered. 'Tomorrow?'

It was dark when they reached Toledo. Moncrieff was driving a car he'd borrowed with help from Bottomley at the embassy and the engine laboured as he urged it up the steepness of the slope towards the Alcázar. Ortega gave him directions to the Calle de Santiago. So far, they'd yet to see any sign of the rumoured security.

'Here?' Moncrieff was staring at the front door of the house they'd rented.

It was Annie who confirmed the address. Ortega was already out of the car, standing on the wet cobblestones, his face turned upwards to the thin rain that had been falling for nearly an hour. Annie had no intention of getting wet. Ortega had the key. He could open the door.

'So how do you feel?' This from Moncrieff.

'Terrible.'

'Terrible why?'

'Because I don't want to do it.'

'Then don't. Give the bullet to Ortega. Your job is done.'

'Too easy.'

'*Easy?*'

'Easy.' She nodded through the pebbled windscreen at the figure in the rain. 'That man's been through more than any of us can possibly imagine. Everyone, he says, has his price and you've obviously met his. The least I can do, *must* do, is to be there for him. That's how it began and ...' she shrugged, '... it'll end however it ends.'

Moncrieff held her gaze. He said he understood. He admired the gesture she was making but he had to tell her it was unnecessary. He'd already given Ortega a thousand pounds sterling. Killing Himmler would earn him another fourteen thousand. That's what he wanted. That's the deal he'd made with himself. Fourteen thousand pounds would feed most Spanish families for the rest of their lives.

'We might get it wrong.'

'We?'

'Me and Carlos. I'm sorry.' She turned her head away. 'Long day. Too much blood. Next week in Madrid? You're telling me you'll be around?'

Without waiting, she wrestled with the door handle of the car and then made it out into the street. Ortega had already found the key, and she hung on his arm as he made for the house. *Vista maravillosa*. Once seen, never forgotten. As Moncrieff drove slowly away, she barely had the strength to lift an arm in farewell.

In the small hours of the night, under cover of darkness, Ortega prowled the neighbourhood, returning with the good news that he'd found a local well that had evidently run dry. He'd tossed in a handful of stones, one after another, and not once had he heard any evidence of water. Tomorrow, the job done, he'd put the rifle back in its carry-bag and drop it into the well. After that, he said, they were free to leave.

'So how do we get back to Madrid?'

'Moncrieff. He'll pick us up.'

'And Himmler? My owl?'

'Moncrieff still thinks midday.'

Midday. High noon. Annie slept badly, fragments of dreams ghosting to and fro, faces from the Villa Paz, a child she'd watched die of typhoid at the Pablo Iglesias, and then – from nowhere – her mother's front door opening to a very old man she barely recognised as her father. She sat him down and made him tea. She couldn't find the milk, nor were there any of his favourite biscuits. She was eight years old. She was late for school. The nun who kept the register would be even angrier than usual. Then, very suddenly, came a heavy weight on her chest and a soft rumbling she mistook for the beginnings of an earthquake.

She awoke. A faint spill of light from the arc lights around the Alcázar revealed something soft, something fluffy, something alive just inches away. It was a cat. The moment she moved, it extended a lazy paw and touched her gently on the cheek. The Villa Paz again, she thought. The thin feral tabby that Giles had so nearly befriended. Except that this was a proper cat, a domestic cat, knew its manners, welcomed affection, wanted a chat.

Chat. She spoke to it in French and it purred a little more loudly at the murmur of her voice. Hungry, she thought, and probably thirsty, too. She lay back, her fingertips tickling the hollows of the animal's face, aware of the house moving around her, tiny creaks and groans as the night wind rose and died away, and finally she moved the deadweight of the cat sideways and slipped out of bed. Earlier she'd noticed a jar of candles and a box of matches on the chest of drawers with a note telling her to help herself. She struck a match, and the lit candle revealed the cat pawing the rough nap of the blanket before sniffing the pillow where she'd laid her head. The cat was black with a single white blaze on half its pretty face.

'*Chat*,' she called softly. '*Viens.*'

She made for the door, holding the candle at an angle to avoid the hot wax. The cat was following her, a soft furriness around her bare ankles, and as she descended carefully step by step she became aware of her own shadow guttering among the hung pictures on the staircase. She stopped, took a closer look, admiring the way their host had used his oils to capture the sheer presence of the Alcázar. It rose above the scruffy tumble of tiled rooftops, impregnable, four-square, each of the corner towers stoutly rendered. Live with a view like this, she thought, and the harsh, unsparing Spanish light, briefly softened at dusk and dawn, would last you a lifetime.

Towards the bottom of the staircase, yet another interpretation, winter this time, the battlements crusted with snow. She paused again, telling the cat to wait, to be patient while she took a final look at the canvas. Did it really snow? Here in Castile? Or had their host eyed his tube of white and conjured the smallest lie for the benefit of his occasional guests? She put the question to the cat, who was becoming ever more vocal. Food, Annie thought. But where?

The kitchen, she knew, was on the ground floor. She followed the cat down another flight of stairs, pausing to peek inside the room at the bottom. This was the owner's studio, a biggish space, largely empty except for an ancient table laden with brushes, and tubes of oil paint, and a corked bottle of linseed oil.

In the corner, mounted on an easel, was a canvas he'd yet to complete, not the Alcázar this time but a very different study, far more intimate, with a ghostly presence, semi-human, seeming to appear through a swirl of greys and whites. She looked at it from every angle, trying to tease out some story, some narrative, but the longer she gazed at it, the more she realised that it was deliberately keeping her at arm's length. It wasn't meant to be interpreted, to be understood. *Au contraire*, it bade you keep your distance, pay your respects, and then move on.

Very wise, she told the cat. In the tiny kitchen she found an unsteady pile of sardine cans, all of them Russian in origin. In a drawer, among the carefully organised assortment of cutlery, was a tin opener. With no danger of disturbing Ortega, she thought of putting the kitchen light on but there was something about the candle that conferred a welcome sense of peace. Her early days at the Villa Paz had been candlelit before the madness had engulfed her and now she was grateful for its company.

The tin opener was sharper than she'd expected. She pushed it through the thin metal and began to saw away, following the rim of the tin. The weight of her hand expelled a little of the oil inside, no more than a smear, but the cat had scented the fish and was winding itself around her ankles again, mewing softly. She gazed down at it for a second, losing her concentration, and the opener slipped, cutting deep into the fleshy part of her thumb on the other hand. It drew blood at once, quite a lot of blood, and she found a cloth beneath the sink to stop the bleeding. The wound bound with the cloth, she finally prised the top off the tin and shook the nest of tiny fish onto a plate. As she did so, her thumb started to bleed again and as she laid the sardines in front of the cat, drops of the richest scarlet appeared on the whiteness of the plate.

The cloth bound tighter, Annie leaned against the sink, watching the cat wolf the fish. Once the last particle had gone, it began to lick the rest of the plate, pinked where the blood had mixed with the oil, and Annie at last remembered the bullet, still inside her. By now the cat was washing itself, a study in neatness, extracting the last traces of sardine oil from the fur around its busy mouth, and Annie turned away, shielding herself from the animal as her good hand tracked down her belly, and her fingers slowly worked the bullet free. She wiped it clean on the bloodied cloth and then stood it upright on the counter beside the sink. Should she tell the cat about it? Should she share what this war had in store for Spain's distinguished visitor? She shook her head, watching the little head turn towards the door, then hearing the soft patter of paws on wood as the animal made its way back upstairs.

Annie woke for the second time in broad daylight to the faintest scent of sardine oil. The cat was curled beside her now, occupying most of the pillow, and she studied it for a long moment, wanting the image to last forever. When she unwound the cloth from her injured hand she found the wound had closed during the night. From next door came the scrape of furniture being moved, and then a squeal of unoiled hinges as someone wrestled to open the window. Ortega, she thought, making his final preparations.

As soon as she was dressed, she went next door and gave him the bullet. He'd cleared the space around the window and was making adjustments to the telescopic sight. An assortment of tiny feathers lay on the windowsill beside his binoculars and when she asked why he said he'd used a handful to test the wind.

'Right to left,' he nodded towards the Alcázar. 'Nothing much to worry about.'

Annie nodded, watching him examine the bullet with his good eye and then work it carefully into the breech of the rifle. When he asked whether she'd minded smuggling it in, she shook her head.

'I forgot all about it. Sometimes it pays not to have a memory.'

'You're serious?'

'I'm afraid I am. I have a new friend. She kept me up most of the night.'

She told him about the cat, and the sardines, and showed him the wound at the base of her thumb. He spared it a brief glance, told her she needed a nurse, and returned to the rifle.

'But I am a nurse,' she frowned. 'Aren't I?' Talking to thin air, she left.

The morning passed. When she checked the room upstairs again, everything seemed prepared. Ortega would be shooting from within the room, the rifle steadied on top of a chest of drawers. The angle of fire was upwards, towards the balcony on the Alcázar, and the rifle would be invisible from outside the house. He wanted her to understand exactly what he was up to, how the shot would work, and so he showed her where to stand, how to spread her legs for maximum comfort, how to use the rifle's strap to tighten the butt against her shoulder, and then lined up the shot so she could check it. Peering through the telescopic sight, she was startled by how close it seemed to take her. Everything was in perfect focus, the access door to the balcony, even a course of bricks on the crenellation.

'You can't miss,' she muttered.

Ortega grunted something she didn't catch, and then reclaimed the rifle.

'An hour to go.' He tapped his watch, then nodded at the open door. The cat was awake again, sitting outside on the bare boards, eyeing them both. 'You know about black cats?'

'Tell me they're bad luck.' Annie tried to coax a smile, failed completely.

'Get rid of it, yeah?' He turned away.

Annie carried the cat downstairs, opened the front door, tried to shoo it out. The cat wasn't interested, and so she carried it into the kitchen and shut the door. The tension in Ortega, she thought, was all too predictable, and so she resisted the temptation to rejoin him. Better to leave him alone and make whatever peace he could with what had to follow.

Had to follow? She stepped once again into the artist's studio, and stood before the unfinished canvas, debating exactly how she'd complete the work. A little more detail on the ghost-like figure? Absolutely not. Something to brighten the greyness of the greys and the whiteness of the whites? Some tiny daub of colour to offer just a hint of relief? Again, no. Goya had taught her many things, and the lesson she treasured most of all was the artist's absolute right to reach for his pens or his brushes and compose his own truth. *Los desastres de la guerra* and the *Pinturas negras*, she knew, could be deeply uncomfortable viewing, but that, as Ortega had just confirmed, was the whole point of the exercise. Goya had immortalised a hundred deaths. One more, she tried to tell herself, would hardly matter.

She was back upstairs a couple of minutes before noon. Ortega, at the window, confirmed distant sirens and the growl of some kind of convoy. The Alcázar, as ever, was yielding no clues, its windows shuttered, the balcony behind the crenellation empty. Annie stood beside Ortega, trying to visualise what must be happening inside as Himmler made his entrance. Did the Spanish offer a welcoming handshake or the brutal upward jerk of the Hitler salute? Were armies of women preparing the lunchtime banquet? Opening bottles of wine? Attending to creases in the tablecloth? And how exactly might you best whet the *Reichsführer-SS*'s appetite? Was he really a vegetarian, as Hitler was rumoured to be? Or had he got over the bull's ears at the *corrida*, still warm from the kill?

'He's here.' Ortega was suddenly behind the chest of drawers, telling her to keep out of the way, making a final adjustment to the sling of the rifle before getting himself into the firing position.

He was right. Annie had the binoculars now. She could still see the line of crenellations, and once she'd adjusted the focus she realised the access door had opened. For a moment, nothing happened. Then a shortish figure she recognised as Suñer appeared, peering over the brickwork before glancing over his shoulder and gesturing for someone to join him. That someone, Annie told herself, had to be Himmler and she was right. He stepped into the milky sunshine. He was wearing a black uniform, and he had a peaked cap tucked beneath one arm. The contrast with yesterday afternoon couldn't have been more marked. There were no crowds, no violence, not a trace of blood. Just a view across the river gorge that probably went on and on forever.

The Owl, she thought again. He looked relaxed, content. Maybe he was hungry. Maybe he was anticipating a decent lunch. Suñer made a gesture out towards the view and then murmured something in his ear that made Himmler laugh.

'Get out of the fucking way,' Ortega growled.

Suñer did nothing of the sort. If anything, the shot became more impossible, one body shielding the other, then Suñer suddenly stepped backwards, roaring with laughter, nodding back at the open door, leaving his guest totally exposed, and Annie looked away and closed her eyes, aware once again of that tell-tale intake of the lightest breath as Ortega steadied himself. The instant before he finally took the shot, Annie was glad the cat wasn't here. The noise, she thought. That terrifying explosion, so loud, so unexpected.

Nothing. Just a click.

'*Puta*,' this from Ortega. No second bullet. No second chance.

Annie was back with the binoculars. Himmler was still on the balcony, still happy, still enthralled by the view. Annie stared at him, thinking it must be an illusion, a trick of the light. Then she lowered the binoculars and went to the window, before Ortega pushed her roughly aside. He had the bullet between his fingers, and with another oath he hurled it out of the window.

'*Hijo de puta*,' he snarled. Son of a bitch.

It was barely minutes before the figure appeared in the street outside. He was tall, also uniformed, green this time, and he briefly checked the name of the house before striding across the cobblestones and rapping on the door. Ortega, still trying to decide whether or not to get rid of the rifle, took no notice. The rapping again, louder, then a tremor through the whole house as he launched a boot at the door lock.

Ortega and Annie exchanged glances, then Ortega dropped the rifle out of the window before leading the way downstairs.

The door was beginning to give, the woodwork splintering around the frame. Ortega barked another oath, telling the intruder to stop. Moments later, he opened the door and stepped back.

'You,' he muttered.

Annie was looking at this man. She had absolutely no idea what was going on but she sensed at once that everything – once again – was out of her hands.

'And you are …?' She did her best to summon a smile.

'*Oberst* Hans Zimmermann,' he gestured at a car parked across the road. '*Komm.*'

Annie was looking at Ortega. Ortega shook his head, then shrugged, a gesture – concluded Annie later – of studied resignation. Zimmermann pulled the door shut, tested it once, then looked at Ortega.

'The rifle?'

'I dropped it out of the window.'

'Then get it.'

Zimmermann watched him making his way round to the back of the property, then walked Annie across the road towards the car. Annie had seen the figure behind the wheel already but couldn't be sure until he turned round to open the rear door, and it was then that she knew she'd been right.

Tam Moncrieff.

Book Four

24

The news from Toledo reached Canaris at his Berlin office in the Bendlerstrasse nearly twenty hours later. It came fully encrypted from a non-embassy source and the key sentence read *Matador aborted. More follows.* The sign-off, 'Erasmus', was *Abwehr* code for Zimmermann. Canaris, beset by a number of other crises, scanned it quickly and ordered a discreet priority check on its provenance. After some effort, one of his senior aides traced it to the Banca March in Palma. Canaris, ever-courteous, said he was grateful for the information and watched the aide depart.

The following day, shortly after three o'clock in the afternoon, Adolf Hitler met General Franco on the railway platform at Hendaye station. The old medieval Basque town virtually straddles the Franco-Spanish border, which suited both dictators, but the *Caudillo*'s train was late, which didn't please the *Führer* at all.

In the middle of a small knot of senior advisers, he'd begun to fidget, never a good sign. He checked and rechecked his watch, then clasped his hands behind his back. He stared down the broadness of the railway tracks that led south into Spain as if German will alone could summon the wretched train, and when it finally appeared, the ancient engine wreathed in steam, Franco was profuse in his apologies. The train, he explained gamely, was like the rest of Spain. It had broken down.

Suddenly affable, Hitler shared an exchange of salutes and shepherded the little Spaniard towards the *Führer*-carriage on his own train where the talks were to take place.

That same afternoon found Annie Wrenne back in Madrid. Moncrieff was late. He'd made contact through Ortega, telling her they needed to meet. Your choice of venue. Your choice of time. Annie had settled for a remote corner of the Campo beneath Madrid's university, a stone's throw from the river. Two days after returning from Toledo, she was still angry.

The weather in Madrid had suddenly turned. Autumn had dissolved overnight and she'd woken in Ortega's apartment to grey skies and a keen wind off the Sierra de Guadarrama that tasted already of winter. Choosing the Campo to meet Moncrieff had been deliberate. The savage claw marks of the civil war were still visible all over the city but the truly lasting scars were embedded here, beside the turbid waters of the Manzanares River: the crumbling zigzag trenches where Franco's rebel army had dug in for a two-year halt, the shell and mortar holes stubbornly resisting any kind of regrowth, and the long lines of once-white tape that danced in the wind and told you where was safe to walk. There were minefields as far as the eye could see, still uncleared, and even in the city centre you got used to the distant percussive thump of yet another explosion. Who cleared up the mess after the civil war briefly returned to claim yet another victim was never entirely clear but a sense of stoic resignation had settled on every passing face and Annie understood why.

Before she'd volunteered as a nurse, she'd once accompanied a foreign journalist to a safeish perch up in the university's Faculty of Medicine. The guy had been French. He spoke little Spanish but *Libération* was demanding a feature on *Madrileño* Republicans doing their best to defend the city against Franco's brutal onslaught. Annie had been happy to oblige and to her slight surprise the interview had taught her a great deal about the marriage of fervour, outrage and the rawest military skills that had – so far – kept the city safe.

One of the interviewees was determined to become a sniper. In retrospect this was more than ironic but at the time Annie had immediately warmed to the man. He was young, unschooled, barely twenty at a guess, but he'd had a playful sense of the absurd and – like Goya and maybe Ortega – a taste for the darker side of life. Towards the end of the interview, he'd gestured out of the glassless window at the invisible enemy.

'First you spot that turban the Moors all wear,' he'd circled his own head. 'Then, if you're lucky, you get the entire face. The man's obviously crazy, or maybe he believes his precious Allah will look after him, and you know what? He's right. Why? Because I take the shot and I fucking miss.' He'd pulled a face. 'Again.'

'Why on earth here?'

Annie jumped. Scots accent, she thought. Moncrieff, has to be, and she was right. She looked up, pulling her new coat around her.

'Why on earth not?' she said.

Moncrieff was staring down at the bench. The armrest at one end was twisted and bent out of shape and the whole structure moved uneasily under Annie's weight.

'The Republicans were up there. Have I got that right?' Moncrieff gestured towards the looming jigsaw of university buildings.

'Right, Mr M.'

'And Franco's lot?'

'Some made it into the university. The rest were down here freezing their bottoms off like everyone else.'

'Really?' Moncrieff was eyeing the damage to the bench. 'Probably mortar blast. Could have been either side. Where on earth did you get that coat?'

Annie had sensed the question was coming, but still didn't have a proper excuse.

'Ortega,' she muttered. 'He gave it to me yesterday. He said he owed me a present.'

'It looks like mink.'

'It's fox, or that's what he told me.'

'Would mink be embarrassing?'

'Fox is embarrassing. Look.' She opened the coat and showed him the label inside. 'That's a Paris house. *Haut de gamme*. Top of the range. Even my mother wouldn't give it house room. Not at a time like this.'

'And you?'

'I'm ashamed.'

'But warm, I suspect.'

'Indeed, Mr M ...' She nodded down at the pitted iron slats beside her. 'An explanation, if you don't mind, and then we might be friends again.'

Moncrieff turned up the collar of his greatcoat against the wind and sat down. His big hands, ungloved, were red from the biting wind. For a long moment, neither of them stirred. Moncrieff was staring at the river, his face a mask.

'Ortega sends his apologies,' he muttered at last. 'He says he's sorry, whatever that means.'

'About?'

'Toledo. You. Whatever else.'

'I don't understand.'

'Neither did I.'

'Until ...?'

Annie waited for an answer. A dog had appeared nearby, rooting among the tangled weeds beyond the white tape, and she wondered whether its body weight was enough to trigger a landmine. Moncrieff, she thought, would know and the fact that he'd barely noticed told her all was probably well.

Probably.

'You're not going to like this,' he said at last.

'Try me.'

'Ortega's been working for me, for us.'

'For the British?'

'Indeed. We had a deal, as I suspect you know. We were paying him a great deal of money, Jewish money, to get rid of Himmler, to send the whole wretched SS machine a message, to tell the world that evil carries a price. The bulk of that money, that fee, was payable on completion. The rest, the deposit if you like, wasn't.'

Completion. Annie was looking at the pumpkin again, out in the wilds of nowhere, and the cartoon smile so suddenly pulped. Ortega was a generous man, as well as an unerring shot, and with Himmler dead a million fur coats would doubtless have been hers.

'But he's still alive,' she said tonelessly. 'Because it didn't bloody work.'

'You mean Himmler?'

'Of course. So why? Just tell me why.'

'Because your friend got a better offer. That may sound unduly crude but it happens to be true.'

'Someone bought him off?'

'Indeed.'

'So he wouldn't kill Himmler?'

'Couldn't kill Himmler. The bullet was doctored. The detonator would never work.'

'And Ortega knew that?'

'He did, yes.'

'So this was some kind of pantomime? A pretend assassination? All the risks we took? Me carrying the bloody thing?' She gestured down at her lap.

'I'm afraid so.'

Annie turned her face away from the wind, shook her head, trying to fight a rising tide of rage. Lied to, fooled, ignored. The charge sheet went on and on.

'So how come he was bought off?' she managed at last. 'And who was this someone?'

'Zimmermann.'

'And you knew about this? You were part of it?'

'Christ, no. It happens that I like the man, respect him, but there it ends. We're at war with these people, Annie. You may have noticed.'

'No quarter either side?'

'Absolutely none.'

'So why did he do it? Zimmermann? Why did he buy Carlos off?'

Moncrieff wouldn't answer. Annie put the question again but he simply shook his head and turned away. Annie stared at him a moment longer, and then pulled him closer. It was an abrupt gesture, wholly instinctive, anger sharpened by a determination to get to the truth.

'Carlos told me about the *Abwehr* and the SS,' she said quietly. 'I got the impression they were never the best of friends. He told me that there was another war out there, the men in green, he said, against the men in black. Carlos thinks in pictures. It's one of the reasons I used to trust him. He's a child at heart. Lots of spirit, lots of heart, oodles of courage. A happy combination, I always thought, until Toledo.'

'He was probably protecting you.'

'By lying?'

'By rationing the truth.'

'Same thing, Mr M. But tell me about Zimmermann. He's in the green team, the *Abwehr*, am I right?'

'Yes.'

'So why spare Himmler? When he's got everything else so right? The house we found? The firing position? The view of the Alcázar? The time? The place? The opportunity? Nothing makes sense here, Mr M, unless you're telling me different.'

Moncrieff was watching the dog again. Then he shrugged.

'I wish I could,' he said at last. 'But Zimmermann is playing by different rules. He called off the hit on Himmler because he thinks the SS had wised up. How, I don't know, not yet, but to protect the *Abwehr* he had to put Ortega back in his box, and that – at least – was simple.'

'Surprise me.'

'Money. Always money. Zimmermann matched the fee we were paying and then doubled it. All Ortega had to do was agree.'

'Not to kill Himmler?'

'Of course. Money for nothing. The perfect deal.'

'And where did this money come from?'

'A Spanish banker called Juan March. He and Zimmermann are close, which suits them both. March has money to spare, lots of money. Some of it has just gone to Ortega.'

Annie nodded. In this tangle of motives and opportunities, of loyalties and betrayals, it made a kind of sense.

'And now?'

'Now it's our turn to apply a little pressure, earn our corn, think of King and Country. Zimmermann's left himself exposed, and so has his boss, Canaris. I'm guessing that doesn't happen very often, but in circumstances like this opportunity's a fine thing.'

'Opportunity to do what?'

Moncrieff studied her a moment, and then offered a brief, mirthless laugh.

'You're not going to like this at all,' he said again. 'I'd apologise in advance but you're worth a great deal more than that.'

'So?' She was still holding Moncrieff's gaze, still waiting for an answer.

'Your journalist friend, Whittaker.'

'What about him?'

'You need to invite him to dinner. I'll arrange a place and a time. I'll be in the same restaurant. With Zimmermann.'

'And?'

'You were the sole witness when Ortega pulled the trigger. You were there. You were a witness, the only witness. You know the whole story, as Zimmermann understands only too well.' He paused. 'Zimmermann's met Whittaker. He knows he's an American journalist.'

'Really?' Annie was staring at Moncrieff. 'And you want me to tell *Whittaker* what happened? The whole story? Ortega? Toledo? Himmler?'

'God, no.' Moncrieff at last smiled. 'But I want Zimmermann to believe that under certain circumstances that might well happen.'

25

A week later, 2 November 1940, *Admiral* Canaris paid a visit to General Franz Halder, the *Führer*'s appointed Commander for the coming offensive against Gibraltar. Halder was a veteran of the Polish campaign with a deserved reputation for doing his master's bidding while carefully sieving diktats from the Reich Chancellery, flushing away the louder bits and turning bombast into a set of operational orders that merited – at the very least – debate among the regime's military elders.

Halder worked from OKW headquarters at Zossen, south of Berlin, and Canaris was gratified to find an enormous map of the Iberian Peninsula hanging on his office wall. The access points of the two railways into Spain, one at Hendaye in the west, and the other at Portbou on the Mediterranean coast, were flagged with small swastikas, and red lines tracked south towards the hanging tail of Gibraltar.

Canaris waited for Halder to complete his morning's paperwork before pushing the documents to one side. His briskness and sense of unfailing purpose went down well, Canaris knew, in the corridors of the Chancellery and in the vast space of the *Führer*'s office.

'Well, Herr *Direktor*? You've managed to make any sense of the bloody man?'

The bloody man was Franco but what Halder really meant was the recent meeting at Hendaye.

'A disaster, Herr *General*, entirely foreseeable. The immovable force? The iron will? Our Leader's used to rapt attention and a signature on the dotted line. At Hendaye, he got neither.'

'And you think any of this nonsense matters? Or not?'

'It matters to our *Führer* and it should matter to us because Spain remains a neutral country. She has a mind of her own, essentially Franco's, and unless we choose to invade and bring any conversations to an end, we have to make some accommodation to his views. Invasion, I suspect, would be a step too far. The Spanish can be difficult, especially when they're starving.'

'And the British?' Halder enquired. 'According to your sources? They understand our interest in that wretched Rock? They appreciate the logic of conquest?'

'Only too well. They've been doing it for centuries. Are they worried? I suspect the answer is no. The British are stoic. They're also ruthless. They understand power at sea and their navy is the living proof. France, incidentally, is also impressed.'

'By the Royal Navy?'

'By the British. Most of Europe and all of Germany can't fathom why Churchill won't agree a peace. Franco is different. He's a *Gallego*. He's used to standing up for himself and he has no illusions about what Churchill is prepared to do to safeguard his own interests. The French should have listened harder at Mers-el-Kébir. That man's a warrior. He'll spill anyone's blood to get his way and Franco doesn't want that blood to be Spanish. So ...' Canaris shrugged and then gestured up at the map, '... it might serve our best interests to give Franco a decent hearing.'

'Hitler called him Jesuit swine,' Halder pointed out.

'So I heard.'

'Fair, you think?'

'Only if you worship other gods.'

Halder nodded. Already, it was obvious to Canaris that the direction of this meeting wasn't at all to the general's taste. Identify your target. Make your plans. Agree a start date. Everything else, in a favourite *Wehrmacht* phrase, was conversation.

'So you have doubts, Herr *Direktor*? Be honest.'

'Doubts? No. Am I alive to certain difficulties? Yes.'

'Explain.'

'Let's suppose that Franco invites us in. Let's pretend we get passage rights all the way through Spain. There are different railway gauges on either side of the frontier. That means long delays for trans-shipment. The tracks themselves are falling apart, as is the rolling stock. The roads are in an even worse state, and if you use the line south from Hendaye, every train will be targeted from the sea.'

'You make this thing sound crazy. Should we send the Hitler Youth and ask them to walk to Gibraltar?'

'That's not my point. My point is visibility. Every successful attack needs just a hint of surprise. Spain is crawling with spies. Some of them work for the English. Word will get to London weeks before a single *Wehrmacht* grenadier makes it down to Gibraltar.'

'And should that alarm us?' A casual nod at the mountain of completed paperwork. 'Given a carefully prepared plan?'

'That's for you to decide, Herr *General*.' Another smile from Canaris, glacial this time. 'I'm simply a bystander, well-briefed, well-intentioned.'

'Looking in? Drawing your own conclusions?'

'Exactly.'

*

Despite the ongoing plunge in temperatures, Annie had decided against wearing her new fox fur to the meal with Whittaker. The American journalist, whom she hadn't seen for at least a couple of weeks, had been delighted by her suggestion of a meal together. Moncrieff had stipulated a highly recommended restaurant off the Plaza Mayor and the moment Annie mentioned the name, Whittaker raised an eyebrow.

'It'll cost you a fortune,' he said at once. 'We'll eat on the paper.'

His new employer was the *Miami Herald* and on the strength of what Annie assumed was a sizeable promotion – bigger salary, lavish allowances – she'd decided after all to don the fox fur.

Whittaker loved it, hadn't the least qualm about any statement it might make.

'Beautiful woman? Swank coat? You're telling me there's a problem here?'

Annie dropped a playful curtsey. The restaurant was nearly full when they arrived. Moncrieff and Zimmermann were already installed at a table in the far corner, their heads bent over the menu, and Annie asked the waiter to move their own table a little to the left for a better view. Whittaker, as always, was alert to every nuance when it came to promising developments.

'The two guys in the corner?' He'd barely settled in his chair. 'These are friends of yours?'

'Sort of.'

'Then you'll know already, I guess. The taller one with the swept-back hair? He's *Abwehr*, class operator, close to Canaris, answers to the name Zimmermann.'

'And the other one?'

'British intelligence. Supposed to be a gentle soul but that's to fool the enemy. Probably eats babies for breakfast. You like songbirds?'

'I love songbirds.'

'I meant on the plate. They net them up in France during the migration and send them packed in ice. You have to buy them in threes here, along with the potato mash. Your friends have taken care of half a dozen between them. Highly recommended if you don't mind the little bones.'

Whittaker laughed his knowing laugh and Annie remembered again what a delight he could be. A waiter arrived with a bottle of Chablis and they gossiped for a while: which of Whittaker's fellow scribes had done well from the civil war, how many had peeled off in the run-up to the current conflict, finding themselves in Berlin or Brussels or Paris as the map of Europe turned remorselessly *Wehrmacht* field-grey. One reporter Annie knew well had apparently smuggled his German girlfriend aboard the last evacuation train from Berlin on the outbreak of war, only to be intercepted on the Swiss border and hauled away. His girlfriend's father was pressing charges of kidnapping and the *Milwaukee Times* may have lost their star correspondent until the war came to some kind of end.

'And when might that be?' Annie enquired.

'Depends.'

'On what?'

'You guys, the Brits. From where I'm sitting Hitler can't figure what makes Churchill tick. Anyone half sane would have seen the light by now, given up gracefully, learned a little German, gotten himself a taste for *Blutwurst* and that fine Bavarian lager, but the way I'm hearing it London might not exist by Christmas.'

Annie was toying with her glass, eyeing the table across the room. Whittaker was right, she thought. London under the blitz was Madrid under siege but probably far worse. Rubble everywhere. The gritty taste of brick dust in the back of your throat. The sour sweetness of ruptured sewers.

'And you guys?' she asked.

'Us Yanks? We bide our time, try and figure out which way the wind's blowing. The polite phrase is non-intervention but I guess that's been used before.'

'And Roosevelt?'

'The guy's half in already but he lives in a democracy, which can be awkward. Most Americans left Europe for good reason. They never much liked it, and they definitely don't want to go back, Churchill or no Churchill. I guess that leaves us still watching, still waiting.'

'You sound like Franco.'

'That's because we're wise. Bravery comes much later.'

Annie nodded, her gaze drifting back to Zimmermann and Moncrieff, chuckling together over some morsel on the German's plate. Make sure he's looking at you, Moncrieff had said. And don't forget the place is full of mirrors.

'And Gibraltar?' Annie said lightly. 'Any views on our mighty Rock?'

Whittaker drained the last of the bottle into Annie's glass, signalled for another, and then settled back.

'No question Hitler wants it, needs it. Kick the Brits into the sea and he shuts the door to the Med and pockets the key. Lovely thought, except that this is Spain and nothing ever goes to plan. Hitler can't quite figure that. Seizing Gibraltar would be a master stroke yet Franco hasn't read the script. That meeting on the train in Hendaye should have given Hitler all the clues yet somehow it didn't. Result? He gnaws the carpet and shouts a lot. No news there, alas, but then nobody in Miami gives a damn. The Mediterranean? Some kind of fancy cocktail? Gibraltar? One of those heavy cakes the Brits love so much? We're Americans, Annie. Nothing much matters unless you can eat or drink it.'

Annie smiled. She'd been watching Zimmermann. At last he'd edged his seat away from the table, carefully folding his napkin, and then half turned in Annie's direction. Now, she thought.

She leaned across the table, reached for Whittaker's hand.

'Kiss me?' she said.

The American stopped in mid-sentence. Astonishment first, then delight.

'You're serious?'

'Always.'

'Now?'

'Now.'

Annie cupped his thin face and drew him in, kissing him on the lips, aware of the man's awkwardness. She lingered a little, drawing the moment out, tracing the line of a single cheekbone with a wettened fingertip, and then settled back in her seat. That Zimmermann had watched the whole performance was incontestable. He even offered a tiny nod of approval, or perhaps amusement.

There, she thought. Done.

Two days later, a member of a nascent Resistance network operating near France's eastern border with Switzerland reported the arrival of another troop train from Munich. According to their shoulder flashes, these men belonged to an elite regiment of mountain assault specialists, and further sightings pursued them to an area of the Jura Mountains reportedly similar to the topography of Gibraltar. Another agent, who happened to be a shepherd in the high pastureland, watched these same troops from a distance. Like an earlier contingent, they appeared to be rehearsing pin-point artillery strikes on a variety of targets, followed by carefully sequenced infantry assaults against a strongly entrenched enemy over a narrow strip of land with very little natural cover.

These observations, co-ordinated and cross-checked, were delivered to the network's head in a suburb of Besançon. In the light of what happened at Mers-el-Kébir just a handful of months earlier, there was fierce debate over whether the British deserved intelligence of this quality, but in the end a report was despatched to London.

Moncrieff, still in Madrid, received a decrypted copy from Christian Bottomley at the British Embassy. Having read it, Bottomley took him in to see the Ambassador.

Sir Samuel Hoare, berating someone on the telephone, waved Moncrieff into the empty seat in front of his desk. Another copy of the decrypt lay at the Ambassador's elbow.

'Well?' Hoare had finished on the phone. 'Any surprises there?'

'None at all, sir. The Germans love rehearsing.'

'So should we be in the least bit anxious?'

'I think not.'

'You're sure?'

'As sure as I can be, sir.'

'How come?'

'With respect, sir, I think we may have found a chink in their armour. Early days, I'm afraid, but we live in hope.'

Three days later, still early November, Canaris bowed to a series of terse messages from *General* Halder and despatched a trusted *Abwehr* operative to Algeciras. *Kapitan* Hans-Erich Voss's task was to scout once again for sites in the hills behind La Línea from which heavy artillery could lob shells at identified targets on and around Gibraltar. For two long days, Voss was driven from site to site by a local *Abwehr* agent, making careful notes, taking photographs, scaling hill after hill to check the ever-looming Rock. By the evening of the second day, his list complete, he typed a full report for *General* Halder at OKW headquarters and retired to the bar of the Reina Christina Hotel for a well-earned drink.

In the meantime, two other Berlin-based *Abwehr* specialists had arrived in Algeciras to address equally vital elements in Halder's masterplan. One of them was *Hauptmann* Hermann Menzell, a jovial soul from Bremerhaven. He already knew the local *Abwehr* K-Org Chief and together they journeyed to La Línea to probe for weak spots in the Rock's defences. Binoculars and a high-powered telescope offered a clue or two but the best intelligence, as ever, came from face-to-face interviews with Spanish labourers employed by the British in Gibraltar.

One of them, an older man, a bricklayer, described some of the intermittent bombing raids on the Rock and the anchorage conducted by the Vichy French in the wake of Mers-el-Kébir. The French, he said, were mere beginners. Most of their bombs fell in the sea and on some occasions they were gone before the air raid sirens had stopped. But the British, he said, were in some respects even worse. Many of the ack-ack guns had a habit of jamming and the ones that still worked were poorly aimed. Menzell, keeping notes, wrote the word 'Stuka', added a question mark, and exchanged smiles with the K-Org Chief.

The other *Abwehr* arrival was *Oberst* Erwin Lahausen, head of Canaris' precious sabotage team at the Bendlerstrasse. After an exhaustive survey of the frontier between Spanish and British soil, he decided to recommend that elite troops from the Brandenburg Regiment be tasked with removing the heavy iron fence separating Gibraltar from the mainland, before digging in to keep the access road open for the main assault. With the operation under way, he wrote to Halder, the *Abwehr*'s own sabotage troops would be more than happy to destroy the Rock's fuel supplies, airfield runway, power station, gas works and the colony's plant for distilling seawater. A copy of these recommendations landed on Canaris' desk two days later. 'Agreed,' he scribbled in what one of his secretaries dubbed *eine müde Hand.*

A tired hand.

26

Annie had been back in her old room at *La Vieja Escuela* for over a week when she awoke to a sharp knock at her door. It was Ortega, whom she hadn't seen since leaving his new apartment in the aftermath of Toledo. He told her there were a couple of *Guardia* downstairs. She should get dressed and join them.

'Why?'

'They say it's routine. A matter of identification. I'll be with you. Don't worry.'

Don't worry? Annie cast around for her clothes. It was still dark outside and the room was freezing and when she checked through the window she recognised the shape of the unmarked *Guardia* van parked on the gravel. She'd ridden to prison in a van like this, she thought. Dear God, help me.

It got worse. Downstairs in the kitchen she found herself face to face with the same *subteniente* who'd torn her lodgings apart. He spared her the curtest nod, tapped his watch and escorted her out of the house. Ortega followed and when the *subteniente* told him his presence was unnecessary, Ortega bent over him and whispered something in his ear. A threat? A name of someone powerful? Some precious scrap of information? Annie had no idea but it was definitely a comfort to feel Ortega's bulk beside her in the back of the van.

They drove at speed through the empty streets until the driver slowed at the oncoming bulk of a sizeable building.

'Hospital,' Ortega grunted.

They parked, and Annie and Ortega followed the *subteniente* into the building. He'd clearly made this journey before, first down a long central corridor past empty noticeboards and fading stick figures probably crayoned by sick children. Then left, then right, then a clatter of footsteps down a staircase that took them deep into the hospital's basement. The door that mattered was at the very end of yet another corridor and the moment the *subteniente* hauled it open Annie knew exactly what to expect. The gust of freezing air, spiked with disinfectant, told her that this was a mortuary.

'What's going on?' She was looking at Ortega.

He shook his big head, said he didn't know. Ortega rarely looked troubled but now was different.

The *subteniente* had summoned an attendant from a glass-walled office beyond a bank of fridges. He muttered something Annie didn't catch and she watched as the man nodded, consulted a list on the wall, and stepped across to a particular fridge door. Inside, three of the four racks were empty but a shrouded body occupied the one at the bottom. The attendant pulled it out and waited for the *subteniente*'s nod before exposing the face. As ever, the *Guardia* badly needed a shave and his breath stank, but that was hardly the point. He's enjoying this, Annie told herself. He's drawing the moment out, making the most of it. He wants to frighten me, disgust me, break me.

'This is someone you think I might know?' Annie enquired.

'Yes.'

'How come?'

The *subteniente* wouldn't answer. Instead, with a casual flick of the wrist, he drew the shroud back and revealed the face. Annie stared down at it, feeling the warmth of Ortega's hand closing on hers.

Whittaker.

She shut her eyes. She was appalled. His face was intact, no visible injuries, but death had stilled the quiet urgency of the man, stealing the person she'd known and – in a way – loved.

'What happened?' she heard herself mutter.

'You recognise him?'

'I do, yes. His name's Forrest Whittaker. He's an American journalist. He works for the *Miami Herald*.' She paused, her gaze returning to the pale white face. No glasses. 'So what happened?'

'He was killed.'

'How?'

'An accident on the street. Someone ran him over so maybe he should have stayed on the pavement.'

'Who?' This from Ortega. 'Who ran him over?'

The *subteniente* turned to Ortega and shrugged. He had no idea. *Madrileños* still drove like monkeys. A million suspects, maybe more.

'Witnesses?' Ortega asked.

'None.'

'So when did it happen?'

'Yesterday.'

'Time?'

'Why the questions? I have no idea.'

'Where?'

'La Calle de Atocha.'

'That's a long road,' Ortega had stepped very close. 'You want to tell me more?'

The *subteniente* shook his head, refused to answer. His work here was plainly done. He gestured for the attendant to take care

347

of the body and waited for the soft thud of the closing fridge door before accompanying the attendant back to his office.

Annie was clinging to Ortega, too shocked to talk. Moments passed, and then the *subteniente* was back with them. He had two items in his hand. One was a small white envelope, the other a pair of glasses that Annie recognised as Whittaker's. Both lenses were cracked and one of the metal arms was parting company with the frame.

'Why me?' Annie was looking at the *subteniente*. 'Why give me these?'

'Read it.' The *subteniente* gave her the envelope.

Every instinct told Annie to resist this invitation but events, once again, had got the better of her. She opened the envelope, recognising Whittaker's careful script. The letter was brief, a single paragraph. He thanked her for the meal, for her company, and for the kiss. The latter, he wrote, had come as the most delicious of surprises and if he'd been a little unnerved he hoped she'd understand. Another evening, maybe? Somewhere a little less public?

Annie read the note a second time, determined to deny the *subteniente* the pleasure he was so obviously anticipating. What began as a smile turned quickly into a leer. An outsider, he seemed to be implying. With no business to be here in Spain.

'I keep these?' Annie took the glasses.

'Your choice.' The attendant had reappeared with a form attached to a clipboard. 'Your signature on the bottom.'

The form attested to Whittaker's formal identification. Señora Wrenne's name was accompanied by her passport number. She had, she realised, become part of a legal process.

'You'll be investigating what happened?' Annie nodded towards the fridge door.

'Of course.' The leer again. 'But now we go.'

The journey back to *La Vieja Escuela* passed in total silence. Only when Annie and Ortega were standing in the half-light of dawn outside the big old house, the *Guardia* van departed, did Ortega finally stir.

'They're sending us a message,' he grunted.

'Who? Who's sending us a message?'

'The Germans. Zimmermann.'

Annie shook her head and then closed her eyes. She was still holding the glasses and the envelope.

'Me, Carlos,' she muttered. 'They're sending me a message.'

The following day, Tuesday 12 November 1940, Hitler called a post-lunch meeting of his senior officers in Berlin and confirmed his intention to attack Gibraltar with or without the support of *Generalissimo* Franco. The announcement stirred a ripple of approval at the prospect of the Reich shrugging off the embrace of the filthy Jesuit, and there followed an eager if brief review of progress in the drawing-up of operational plans.

Halder did his best to present the passage of a sizeable German task force the entire length of Spain as a routine military exercise, but when challenged by a fellow general he had to admit that Franco's support would lend the entire operation at least a modicum of respectability in the eyes of the world. At this, Hitler – barely listening – merely shrugged. The eyes of the world had ceased to interest him.

That same afternoon, Annie was driven from *La Vieja Escuela* to the British Embassy. As instructed, she had a bag of belongings, including a change of clothes, and she wore the fox fur against an Arctic wind whistling through the city from the north. Christian Bottomley was waiting in the embassy's modest reception area, fielded Annie's bag, and took her immediately to the Ambassador's office. Sir Samuel Hoare was perched behind his desk, deep in conversation with Tam Moncrieff. Moncrieff did the introductions and Annie submitted to a dry handshake.

'Wonderful coat,' Hoare was reputed to have an eye for life's blessings.

'It keeps me warm,' Annie told him, wanting the subject to drop.

Hoare took the hint, waving Annie into the waiting chair. He wanted, he said, to clear the air, to step back and take perhaps a wider view of what, exactly, was going on. This drew a nod from Moncrieff.

'In the first place,' Hoare continued, 'our commiserations over the death of the American. I understand you two were close.'

'Socially, yes. In spirit, definitely.'

'And?'

'And nothing. If you're asking whether we ever slept together, the answer is no. Anything else, I suspect, is nobody's business but my own.'

Anger, and a growing weariness at the passage of events, had prompted this little outburst but to Annie's surprise Hoare appeared to take the rebuke in good heart. Judging by the hint of a smile and the way his fingers stopped drumming on the desk top she suspected he may even have approved. A girl with heart. A woman with a little self-respect.

'We understand you speak Spanish.'

'I do.'

'Fluently?'

'Try me.'

'That won't be necessary, my dear. I know these are difficult times but we still take people at their word.'

'The right people?'

'Of course. The other sort don't get past the front door.' A bleak smile. 'Now then, a word about my own role. The PM sent me here with one instruction only: to keep Spain out of the war. That means keeping bloody Franco on his toes. To date, if I may say so, we've done rather well but things are about to get tricky.' He paused, shot Moncrieff an appraising glance, and then returned to Annie. 'This conversation goes no further. Are we agreed on that?'

'Of course.'

'I'm very glad to hear it, my dear. Moncrieff?'

Moncrieff stirred in the sagging armchair. Word from Berlin, he said, indicated that Hitler was about to issue another of his *Führer* Directives. For the record, this would be number eighteen in the series and would formally launch the bid to capture and occupy Gibraltar.

'They're calling it Operation *Felix*,' he continued. 'Hitler appears to have come to the conclusion that he doesn't need the support of his good friend the *Caudillo*, so it's happy time on the Wilhelmstrasse. They can do exactly what they want, whenever they want, to whomever they want. This was once a fairy tale, of course, but after the last six months it's become a state of mind. The triumph of the will, *ja*?'

'Move on, dear chap,' Hoare wasn't amused. 'No history lessons. Our guest awaits her instructions.'

'Of course, sir.' Moncrieff turned back to Annie. 'We need you to pen a full account of exactly what's happened over the past few weeks, one draft in Spanish, the other in English. It should cover all your dealings with Ortega, and with me. Ortega's sniper rifle came from Zimmermann, as did the box of dum-dum shells, and you can take that as fact. I suspect the involvement of Canaris himself further up the line but that's something I've yet to prove. Should you so wish, all of this should appear in your report. Why? Because it's our business, and thus yours, to link the attempt on Himmler's life to Canaris and the *Abwehr*.'

'But that's what got Whittaker killed.'

'You may be right.'

'So who next?' A thin smile. 'Me?'

After an exchange of glances came a long silence. Both men looked less than comfortable.

'Well?' The question came once again from Annie and was directed at Moncrieff. At length, after another check on the little figure behind the desk, he cleared his throat. He doesn't want to answer me, Annie thought. He has no interest in hit-and-run accidents, in a body sprawled at the kerbside, in the contents of a mortuary fridge. All that matters is his bloody report.

'You need to trust us, Annie.' Moncrieff was frowning now. 'Believe me, words on paper will make a big difference. Once you've typed the thing up the Ambassador and I will read the draft, and maybe suggest an amendment or two before it's signed, witnessed, duplicated, and the copies popped into Christian's safe. The top copy, encoded, will go to London. The rest are for us to use as we think fit.'

'We?'

Moncrieff held her gaze, saying nothing. Then Hoare smothered a cough and lowered his voice a conversational tone or two.

'We, in this context, means the three of us in this room, my dear. Moncrieff, may I say, has come up with a proposal that has the twin merits of being both practical and rather clever. The plan involves the pair of you flying south to Algeciras. It's been my pleasure to arrange for the services of an English flight crew and a suitable aircraft. It's a de Havilland Rapide and happens to be the very same beast that flew Franco out of the Canary Islands back in '36 when this whole imbroglio started.

Keeping the wretched man out of this bloody war of ours is my one and only concern as I think I've explained already. Your written statement, if it turns out the way we all expect, will offer Moncrieff the leverage he needs to apply a little pressure where it matters most, but I hardly need add that your own safety, especially after what happened to poor Mr Whittaker, has become something of an issue. We'll therefore be suggesting, in fact insisting, that you stay here in the embassy until you fly south. If I tell you that the good *Admiral* is also in Algeciras, perhaps the implications might become clearer.'

'The good *Admiral*?'

'Canaris.' This from Moncrieff. 'He's been there several days.'

'And will you be talking to him?'

Hoare raised an eyebrow. Then came a shrug from Moncrieff and the spread of his big hands in what Annie took as a gesture of apology. No comment.

Annie looked away. She could hear the squeak of unoiled wheels as Whittaker's tray was withdrawn from the mortuary fridge. She could see, once again, the bony outlines of his very dead face.

'One question,' she was looking at Hoare. 'Just one.'

'Which is?'

'Who makes sure the *Guardia* find whoever killed him?'

'Him?'

'Whittaker. My friend.'

'Ahhh …' At last, a proper smile from Hoare. 'Enquiries are already under way. The *Guardia* may be less than efficient, but we understand your pal Ortega has the matter well in hand.'

27

After word from what he termed 'sources' in the Reina Christina Hotel, Moncrieff and Annie flew south two days later. Canaris, it appeared, was still occupying an *Abwehr* safe house on the waterfront at Algeciras and had indicated his preparedness to meet Moncrieff.

Somewhat to her alarm, Moncrieff had insisted that Annie carry a gun, a small Beretta she could keep in the pocket of her fox fur. At the height of Madrid's modest rush hour, amid the busy scurry of nearby traffic, Moncrieff led her into the embassy's tiny walled courtyard and taught her how to load and aim the weapon. At twenty metres he promised her a definite kill, and by the time they stepped back inside the building she'd put a full magazine of bullets within respectable distance of the paper target's bull, not once but twice. This performance had won her a round of applause from the Ambassador, who predicted a new career as a commando if she ever made it back to the UK.

Annie was pleased, not by the circle of hits around the bull, but by the knowledge that she'd been allowed to take her fate into her own hands. Moncrieff would be there for her, he'd made that crystal clear, but she, too, would be having a say in whatever might happen next.

The flight south was a delight. The Rapide was roomy and warm, and the tall, slightly scruffy figure at the controls turned out to be the same pilot who'd flown Franco out of the Canaries at the start of the civil war. Once he'd steadied the aircraft after take-off, he assigned control to his colleague and joined Moncrieff and Annie back in the cabin, only too happy to feed Moncrieff's curiosity about the *Caudillo*.

'He was very guarded back then. Nerves? I don't think so. In battle, I'm told he was brave as a lion, despite his size, and that kind of courage takes a man a very long way, but I get the impression he also picked up bad habits that never left him.'

'Like?'

'It seems he was careless about human body parts. It started with ears but didn't end there. If you were up against the Moors you'd do well to die outright rather than survive a day or two, and Franco was happy to indulge their little ways. He had rivals for the leadership, of course, in the early days. Some of these guys died. Some of them couldn't keep up. We also noticed the man got by on very little sleep, never trusted a pillow, so maybe that's another clue.'

By midday, they were cresting the mountains that circled Algeciras Bay, and for Annie's benefit Moncrieff asked the pilot to give her a glimpse of Gibraltar before turning west and heading for the airstrip. Annie, glued to her window, gazed down as the bare brown mountains disappeared and she was left with the towering grey slab of rock that hung from the very belly of Spain. The peak was scarfed with thin veils of cloud, an almost feminine touch, but there was no mistaking the message that this brutal appendage sent. The story writes itself, she thought. The vertiginous drop to the ocean and the airfield to the north, slightly gentler gradients folding down to the dockyard and the bay in the west. In short, she concluded, the perfect *alcázar*, a fortress *sans pareil*.

They bumped to a halt on the airstrip outside Algeciras. An *Abwehr* car had appeared from nowhere, quite unexpected, and a face Moncrieff recognised from his previous visit was holding open the rear passenger door. Moncrieff had no intention of accepting the lift but the *Abwehr* agent, in civilian dress, handed him a note. Moncrieff scanned it quickly, then offered it to Annie.

'This is from …?'

'Canaris.'

Annie nodded. There was a tidiness to the *Admiral*'s signature that she recognised from her father's rare letters. Careful men, she thought, who kept their inner thoughts to themselves.

'So what is it?' She nodded at the letter.

'It's a *laissez-passer*. If we accept the lift, we accept Canaris' word that we shall be in safe hands. If we don't …' he gestured briefly back at the aircraft, '… we may as well go home.'

'Clever.'

'Very.'

Moncrieff had already briefed Annie about the Reina Christina Hotel. A nest of spies, he'd told her. A carnival of loose talk and double-dealing but an excellent bar and reliable eats, especially when it came to fish. To Annie, this sounded more like a parlour game than a hotel, but she suspected that the Florida in Madrid was little different, another of the extravagant cuttings that root and bloom in times of war.

Moncrieff had booked adjacent rooms, telling her to keep the door locked and bolted. He'd be meeting Canaris at dusk at a selected spot in the hotel grounds, and before he left to take a nap he crossed to the window and showed her exactly where.

The bench lay in a shallow arbour, overhung with what looked like bougainvillea, and Annie studied it for a moment before putting the question that felt all too obvious.

'High hopes?' she asked.

'Of what?'

'Of getting your way with him?'

'Maybe. Maybe not. He's artful. In Scotland we'd call him canny, which would be a compliment. He's also decent to the core, though no less German than the next man, which is where this comes in ...'

Annie recognised the typed version of the statement she'd first drafted in longhand, reading it slowly to Hoare and Moncrieff in the privacy of the Ambassador's office. They'd made a couple of suggestions, stiffening a sentence here, suggesting a cut or two elsewhere, revisions that Annie was very happy to accept, but now she was curious to know what Canaris himself would make of it.

'He'll be expecting something like this?'

'Without question. In our situation, he'd be doing something very similar. He knows we have leverage. He knows this statement would be a death sentence in SS hands. That makes this evening very difficult for him but never underestimate the man. Survival at his level becomes an art form, believe me.'

'So why did Zimmermann buy Ortega off? Why spare the man's life?'

'That I don't know, not for sure. We have to suppose that the plan leaked but Canaris is too proud and too wary ever to tell me.'

Annie nodded. Werner Nehmann again, she thought. Whatever you say, say nothing.

*

Annie, sprawled fully clothed on the bed, was awoken hours later by the softest knock on the door. She retrieved the Beretta from her coat, wondering who it was.

'Me,' Moncrieff's voice.

She opened the door. The sight of the little automatic put a smile on his face.

'You'll need this,' he said.

Annie found herself looking at a camera, bulky, big lens. The light was fading fast, exactly the way Canaris wanted. Moncrieff quickly explained the controls and asked her to do her best. A shot of the two of them on the same bench, he murmured, would sit very nicely alongside her typed statement.

'Consorting with the enemy?'

'Sealing his fate.'

'But I thought you wanted to keep him onside?'

'I do. But a couple of photos might help.'

With Moncrieff gone, Annie pulled an armchair across the room, doused the lights and settled by the window. Long minutes passed. With dusk came the soft glow of lamps strung from the trees but the bench in the arbour was no more than a shadow in the gathering darkness. A stir of movement may, or may not, have been Moncrieff. The ghostly approach of another figure was probably Canaris but Annie had no way of knowing.

She raised the camera, took a couple of shots, then put it aside again, doing her best to conjure some sense, some story from the black hole where the two men were talking. She knew they'd met before, in this very hotel, because Moncrieff had told her so. She knew there'd been a meeting of minds, a sense of mutual respect, maybe even the beginnings of a friendship. Was that what Moncrieff was trying to develop? Down there on the bench? Might the implacable logic of this war make space for just a little sanity? One combatant accepting the word of another in the interests of a better, kinder world? In her heart she knew the answer was probably no, and in the end – still perched beside the window – she gave up even looking.

She heard him first, a key in his door, footsteps into his room, the murmur of his voice, presumably on the telephone, after which came a knock at that same door and the briefest conversation before silence fell again. Minutes later, a knock on her own door and an invitation from Moncrieff to join him for a drink.

'Now?'

'Now.'

'Does a girl have time for a wash?'

'I'm afraid not.'

In Moncrieff's room, Annie found herself looking at a little tableau carefully arranged on the low occasional table by the hotel's room service: a dish of canapés alongside a decent bottle of Rioja and three glasses.

'We're expecting company?'

'Canaris. Any moment now.'

He was at the door minutes later, smaller than she'd expected, rumpled grey suit, carefully knotted tie in the shade of red they used on the hanging Nazi banners back in Madrid. He extended a hand at once to Annie and said he was pleased to meet her. To impress a Scot like Moncrieff, he said, wasn't easy, and his congratulations were implicit in the sudden smile. His Spanish was fluent and carried underlying hints of South America.

Moncrieff waved them into the room's two armchairs and poured the wine. When Annie enquired about his Spanish, Canaris looked briefly surprised and then admitted he'd first picked the language up in Chile.

'You were working there?'

'I was interned there, jailed, along with my shipmates. We'd sunk a number of your warships and paid the price afterwards. The Royal Navy never gives up, not then and not now, and you know why?'

Annie shook her head, said she hadn't a clue.

'Churchill. This was the last war. He was in charge of your Admiralty. Find the enemy and give him a beating. We, alas, were the enemy.'

'So you spent the rest of the war in Chile?'

'I escaped. Partly boredom, though the food was awful, too.'

'The Andes,' Moncrieff said softly. 'In winter. Can you imagine that? On foot most of the time?'

Canaris shrugged. Life in the mountains, he said, couldn't have been simpler. Peasant bread when he could buy it and ice-cold water from the mountain streams, and the rising sun every morning to give him direction. He was young. He had no time for captivity. And the realisation that you could – *should* – be the master of your own destiny had stayed with him ever since.

Annie didn't know quite what to say. Extraordinary, she thought. First to live an experience like that, and then to distil its essence.

'And Spain? Tam says you love the country.'

'Moncrieff's right. The Spanish aren't European at all, not the way one imagines, and that's entirely to their benefit. They've picked up the best of two religions, two ways of life, and kept their dignity. Just now that's all they have but for some it's enough.' He reached for his glass. 'Another lesson we might usefully learn.'

Annie nodded, glad this man would never get to see her fox fur.

'And what about the other Spanish?' she queried. 'The ones who might want a little more?'

'They have patience. They wait for better days.' He was studying Annie over the rim of his glass. 'Moncrieff tells me you like Goya.'

'Love would be closer.'

'I'm not surprised. The *Pinturas negras*? That kinship with our worst fears? Might that not offer a clue or two?'

'To what?'

'The Spanish,' he raised the glass in a toast, 'and people like us who have the wit to appreciate them.'

The smile lingered for a moment on the fullness of his lips, then he put the glass aside and got to his feet. Moments later, with a farewell nod to Moncrieff, he'd gone.

Annie listened to the departing tread of his footsteps, and then the metallic rattle as he opened the lift doors at the end of the corridor.

'He wanted to look you over,' Moncrieff murmured. 'See what was on offer.'

'Offer? I'm some kind of *puta*? Some kind of whore?'

'*Au contraire*, you're all that stands between him and the SS. A word from you and the men in black will be all over the *Abwehr*, and the first to the gallows will be Canaris. So he needs to know you're serious, along with that statement of yours. In Whitehall they'd call it bottom.'

'I'm flattered.'

'Don't be. You were fine. In fact, you were perfect. What did you make of him?'

Annie held his gaze, still trying to tease her role into sharper focus. The news that her statement was somehow key to putting pressure onto this man was still daunting but she was glad to have put a face to what Moncrieff had recently described as 'a legend'.

'I thought he had a sadness about him,' she said at last. 'He reminded me of a favourite uncle who's just fallen out of love with his wife. His marriage is all over the place and he can't work out why.'

'Or what next, perhaps. Very astute.'

Moncrieff refilled her glass. The marriage, he said, was to Germany, the old Germany, the Germany that had won his heart all those years ago when he'd walked across South America to prove it. Now, to his bewilderment and growing despair, the love affair was over. The gangsters were in charge the length of the Wilhelmstrasse and there was very little he, or anybody else, could do about it.

'He's tried?'

Moncrieff nodded, then put a finger to his lips before nodding at the ceiling. Microphones, Annie thought. Listening ears.

'You want to tell me about the bench?' she whispered. 'What happened down there?'

Moncrieff shook his head. From a briefcase, he extracted a pad and a pen and scribbled a longish note. Zimmermann, he wrote, had picked up indications that the SS were building a detailed case against Canaris, alleging that he'd laid plans for an attempted *coup d'état* before the move into the Sudetenland.

Annie reached for the pen. 'True?' she scribbled.

Moncrieff nodded, then gestured at the rest of his note. A successful hit against Himmler, ruthlessly investigated, would have sealed Canaris' fate. Thus Zimmermann's despatch of a single hollow-point bullet to the armourer in Berlin to make it safe.

'So it wouldn't work?' Annie didn't bother with the pen.

Moncrieff nodded.

'And Ortega knew that?'

Another nod before Moncrieff reclaimed the pen. Money from Juan March, he wrote, had doubled the British fee, and

Ortega hadn't hesitated in agreeing the deal before they all set off for Toledo.

'And you knew this?'

'No.'

'Should I believe you?'

'Yes.'

Moncrieff held her gaze and then returned to the pad. This time, a single word. Pantomime.

A little later, Moncrieff ordered food. Annie, he said, would be spending the night in his room. She was very welcome to the big double bed and he'd be equally happy in the armchair. In the morning they'd be returning to the aircraft which had been guarded overnight but in the meantime, doubtless to her relief, they'd forget about this bloody war.

Annie gave a loud 'Amen' to that. She wanted to know more about this spare, bony man with a very obvious back problem. She wanted to know what had taken him into the Royal Marines and – far more importantly – to his current post. Mention of the Marines drew a smile from Moncrieff. He'd grown up in the Cairngorms, loved the mountains, loved the austere physicality of mountain living. Joining the Marines, accepting the obvious challenges, had been – in a way – an extension of his glorious adolescence.

'Hard?'

'Very. But that was the point. They make you find out about yourself and that knowledge never leaves you.'

'And now? MI5?'

At first, Moncrieff simply smiled.

'They recruit you,' he said at length. 'I'd left the Corps and if you want the truth I barely noticed it happening. King and Country? Take your partners for the opening waltz? You do the Marine thing. You just say yes and hope it all works out OK.'

'And did it? Has it?'

'Sometimes yes, sometimes no.'

'Tell me about no.'

'You really want all this?'

'I do,' Annie reached for the bottle, topped him up, and then proposed what might have been a toast.

'For tomorrow,' she murmured, 'we may die.'

Another smile, wider this time, before Moncrieff took a long sip of the wine. Her faux toast appeared to have concentrated his thoughts. He looked contemplative, then briefly troubled. Two years ago, he told her, he'd been in Germany. Hitler was in his pomp and Moncrieff's mission had taken him to Nuremberg for what proved to have been the last of the Nazi rallies. What he'd seen and heard there had shaken him to the core, and a bad error of judgement had put him at the mercy of the Gestapo.

'In Nuremberg?'

'In Berlin. I'd taken the train back. They arrested me, asked a question or two.'

'We're talking torture?'

'Inevitably. The Hungarians are best at it. I've hated basements ever since.'

'Horrible.' Annie was watching him very carefully. 'So who came to your rescue? How come you're still in one piece?'

For a long moment, Annie thought she'd gone too far. Then Moncrieff gave her a cautionary glance and shrugged. What the hell, he seemed to be saying.

'Her name was Bella. Short for Isobel. She had a desk in our embassy in Berlin. She worked the diplomatic scene for HMG and reported back. Everyone said she was bloody good at it and I'm sure she was.'

HMG, Annie thought. His Majesty's bloody Government.

'You got involved with her?'

'Yes.'

'Seriously? You meant it?'

'Yes.'

'And her?'

'I thought so.' He paused. 'She was beautiful. Tall, fit. She loved rowing, another thing she was good at. I'd rowed, too, at university and she found me a space in her crew. Those days couldn't have been sweeter.'

'Until the Gestapo came along?'

'Yes.'

'And then what?'

'They threw me out, gave me twenty-four hours to leave the country. That was part of the deal. Once I'd left I was never to darken their door again. I've been back, of course, but under assumed names, different passports.'

'And Bella?'

'She wanted us to head south, somewhere warm, Seville, make a new life.'

'And you?'

'I was on the next plane home.'

Annie nodded. More, she thought. There's more.

'So what happened?' she asked after a while.

'She defected. Joined the opposition.'

'The *Germans*?'

'The Russians. She got on a plane and flew to Moscow under an assumed name. It turned out she'd been an agent all along. No one could believe it, least of all me.'

Annie nodded. What you always see, she thought, is the very tip of the iceberg. The rest, the important bits, are always invisible, beyond reach.

The silence between them felt companionable and she, unprompted, told him about meeting Giles Roper on the operating table at the Villa Paz, and about everything else that had followed. At Benicàssim, she said, she'd met the real Giles Roper, his back to the window of the little schoolroom, unaware of her presence, and it was at this point she'd realised what a fool she'd been.

'To fall in love?'

'To believe him.'

'You blamed yourself?'

'I did. I should have been wiser, cannier. He helped himself. He took everything. I felt worse than betrayed. I felt empty.'

Moncrieff nodded, said he understood, and Annie sat back in the chair, her eyes on the ceiling, wondering what the hidden listeners would make of the last half-hour. The thought of transcribers committing it all to paper in the hope of sieving some nugget of useful intelligence filled her with a kind of savage glee. What really matters, she told herself, is of no interest to a single living soul.

Wrong.

Moncrieff was finishing the dregs of the bottle. His affair with Bella, he murmured, had died because there was something bigger in her life. She had a cause, a belief, and he – MI5 master spy – should have noticed. Had he done so, the course of both their lives might have been very different but he had no one to blame but himself. I was blind, he said. Which meant I'd never deserve her.

'And Giles Roper?' Annie enquired. 'My beloved warrior?'

'He sounds different.'

'Different how?'

'No cause, not even Spain, just himself, his own needs, his own ego. Does that sound unduly harsh?'

'Not at all,' Annie stifled a yawn. 'And that's something else I should have noticed.'

*

The night passed without incident. Waking at dawn, Annie stretched and rose from the sheets, rubbing her eyes. Moncrieff was exactly where she'd last seen him when the lights went out, upright in the armchair, a gun in his lap. Within the hour, in the back of a summoned taxi, they were en route to the airfield.

Yesterday's pilot was circling the aircraft in the early light, checking for possible damage. He and his co-pilot had spent the night on board with armed guards posted around the big biplane. Now he fired up the twin engines, let them clear their throats, and then throttled back before wheeling onto the end of the runway. Moments later the bumps and judders vanished as the Rapide lifted off, the pilot hauling the aircraft into a steep turn as soon as altitude allowed. Expecting the climb to take them over the mountains and north to Madrid, Annie found herself once again over the blue waters of the bay. She peered out at the familiar shape of the Rock growing bigger by the second. The pilot had ceased to climb and now appeared to be making preparations for a landing.

Moncrieff was in the seat across the aisle, deep in a book. As the aircraft steadied on the final approach, she touched him lightly on the arm.

'What's going on?'

Moncrieff glanced out of the window, as if surprised, then offered what might have been an apology.

'We needed somewhere safe to put you,' he said. 'And I thought Gibraltar might be perfect. Think bastion. Think fortress.'

'Think *alcázar*?'

'Precisely. A young man called Rees will be taking care of you. First name Martin. He's Intelligence Corps, our eyes and ears on the Rock. Have a good look round, Annie. Keep notes.

If he needs your translation skills, or any other help, I'm sure you'll oblige.'

A savage bump and a slight lurch to the left told Annie they'd landed. She gazed out of the window at the blur of bulldozers and other heavy plant.

'Do I have a choice here?' she asked, turning back to Moncrieff.

'A choice?' The bleakest smile. 'I'm afraid not.'

28

It took Ortega a while to come up with a name. He had the make of the car, the spot where it happened, and one passer-by's memory of the driver wearing a red beret. Days tracking down trusted underworld contacts, plus generous helpings of Juan March's money, finally yielded a name – Marco Fernandez – and an address. The guy's a piece of shit, said one contact who'd made a fortune from kidnapping daughters of the rich. He's working for the Germans now so why don't you do us all a favour?

And so Ortega, under a cloudless November sky, made his way to an address in Las Delicias. He knocked twice, and then again, his semi-automatic readied inside his brand-new leather jacket. A final volley of knocks at last brought a middle-aged figure to the door. No scarlet cap, just the usual taken-aback revulsion at the sight of Ortega's ruined face.

'Señor Fernandez?' Ortega grunted.

'*Sí.*'

Ortega drew the gun and shot him in the eye. *Finito*, he thought, as Fernandez collapsed backwards into the gloom of the house.

*

On 26 November 1940, Canaris returned to Berlin to brief *General* Halder on his conversations with *General* Vigon and other Spanish luminaries in Algeciras and Madrid. When Halder enquired about Franco, Canaris told him that the *Generalissimo* had yet to make a decision on Spain joining the war on the Axis side.

Two days later, as if Franco had been privy to this conversation, the *Caudillo* himself paid the German Ambassador in Madrid a personal visit. He'd decided, he said, to intensify co-operation with Berlin and thus hasten Spain's entry into active hostilities.

The news quickly spread, not least to the British Embassy where Sir Samuel Hoare, already in a foul mood, brusquely informed Bottomley that they were looking at a disaster. Bottomley, feeling himself somehow personally to blame, could only mutter about the *Caudillo*'s ever-changing mind. Dealing with Franco had become the cross they all had to bear.

That same afternoon, at the *Caudillo*'s prompting, Berlin despatched a liaison officer to, in Halder's delicate phrase, 'iron out any differences between the two armies'. This news made Hoare even grumpier. 'Moncrieff?' he muttered. 'Doesn't he have this wretched situation under control?'

Evidently not. And the wretched situation got measurably worse when, at the beginning of December, Hitler informed *General* Halder that Franco had finally agreed to allow Operation *Felix* to take place at the beginning of February 1941. Twenty to thirty munition trains were to be despatched the length of Spain, with heavy artillery destined for the hills behind La Línea. Advance commando units under *General* Halder's direct orders had already been sent to Cádiz to deal with logistics and supply issues, and conversations were under way between the Spanish air force and Halder's liaison officer to ease the transfer of *Luftwaffe* Stuka squadrons to mainland airfields less than an hour's flight time from Gibraltar.

At the British Embassy, alerted by intelligence reports from Cádiz, Hoare was starting to weigh up his options. Should Franco be lured into Hitler's arms, his mission, and his entire career, would lie in ruins.

On 5 December, Hitler led a final briefing on Operation *Felix*. The attack on Gibraltar was to be led by *Feldmarschall* von Reichenau. The Spanish border was to be crossed on 10 January 1941 and the attack itself was to start on 4 or 5 February after Gibraltar had been subject to the tender attentions of the *Luftwaffe*. If the Blitzkrieg strikes on the fortresses protecting Belgium and France were any guide, then Gibraltar – despite its fabled natural strengths – would be ripe for the taking.

Hitler certainly thought so. He'd already ordered a scale model of the Rock to be meticulously prepared, and now he convened a meeting of seven top generals to inspect it in detail, to match the geography and known strong points to every element in *General* Halder's masterplan, and thus identify possible traps that might cost the needless spilling of German blood. To Halder's intense relief, his plan passed muster and each of the generals present agreed that Operation *Felix* was in rude health. Hitler, to whom none of this came as a surprise, ordered the drafting of *Führer* Directive number nineteen, officially authorising Operation *Felix* to proceed.

That same day, 7 December 1940, Lieutenant Martin Rees accompanied Annie Wrenne to the railway station in Algeciras. As they both knew, this was in direct contravention of Moncrieff's explicit orders – stay on the Rock – but Annie sensed that her three encrypted reports on the dire state of Gibraltar's defences hadn't commanded the attention they deserved. Rees, whom she'd grown to trust as well as like, had agreed.

The tunnellers digging beneath the Rock were behind schedule. Artillery emplaced on the Rock's north near-vertical face couldn't depress enough to deal with a determined infantry thrust across the airfield and the approaches to the Rock beyond. And, even more importantly, Annie had detected an almost schoolboy enthusiasm for a wild scheme to take the battle to the enemy.

Dubbed Operation *Monkey*, the sparsely detailed plan called for a sizeable force to dress up as Moorish brigands, ship across the bay, make what was hoped to be an unopposed landing and then march through scrub and bush to spike the enemy's guns. Annie, who knew very little about *Wehrmacht* prowess on the battlefield, gave Operation *Monkey* full marks for imagination but it took Rees to bring her down to earth.

'They'll eat us alive,' he'd said. 'We'd never get off the beach. Every army has so far underestimated the Krauts and that's a mistake you only make once. We were lucky getting so many men off the beaches at Dunkirk, but the truth is they kicked us out of France without breaking sweat. That was one disaster. This will be another.'

Disaster. Annie sat in a packed compartment in the dusty sunlight as the train rattled north through the bony hills of Andalusia. Rees had managed to alert the Madrid Embassy to her imminent arrival and she'd prepared a full report, counter-signed by the young Intelligence Corps lieutenant, tallying the Rock's many points of weakness. Thanks to Rees, she could imagine only too well the carnage that would follow a successful German attack. In Rees's colourful phrase, there came a moment in any assault on a defended fortress when the defences themselves would start to favour the enemy, and the whole bloody shebang would fall flat on its bony arse. Dead ground, indeed.

'And at that point, excuse my French, we're all royally fucked.'

Annie could only nod in agreement. Two days ago, Rees had taken her to what the Rock's high command were calling the Stay Behind Cave. In essence, this offered two men the space, water and supplies to sit tight for a year or two if the Rock fell and other tenants took charge. Hidden deep within the limestone, the cave had covert access to observation points on both the eastern and western flanks of the Rock, offering the Stay Behinds the modest consolation of reporting back on German shipping and troop movements. Once Rees had explained the concept, and shown her the provision for power and desalination facilities, she'd asked him to leave her alone for a while and not return for – say – half an hour.

'I leave the lights on?'

'No.'

He'd nodded, said he thought he understood, and for the next thirty minutes or so Annie stood motionless in the inky darkness, listening to the occasional movement as the surrounding limestone sought some accommodation with the far-away tunnelling. This, she knew, was an experience, a sensation, that would stay with her forever, the sheer weight of history above her head, beneath her, all round. What should have been a feeling of security was anything but.

She felt smothered, suffocated by the generations who'd made their brief home on this lump of rock, who'd serviced the ships heading east, who'd guarded the key lifeline of empire. She thought of men like Rees, eager, gifted, articulate, who must have shared her sense of claustrophobia, and she thought as well of the lofty masters of empire, men like Sir Samuel Hoare, unyielding in their commitment to spilling someone else's blood in the hunt for someone else's treasure. When needs must, she thought grimly, nothing was allowed to menace British imperial power. Hence Mers-el-Kébir. By the time Rees returned and switched on the lights, she'd begun to understand what had persuaded Moncrieff's Bella to defect to Moscow.

The train arrived late at Madrid's Atocha station. Exhausted, Annie allowed the press of passengers to carry her towards the station's concourse. In truth, she had no idea what to expect next. The only thing that mattered was somehow getting herself to the embassy in one piece. Then came the lightest pressure on her arm.

'Tall guys? Two of them? Berlin haircuts? Good suits?'

It was Ortega. Christ, Annie thought, it's Alicante all over again. She looked up at him, managed a smile, said hello.

'Walk,' he growled. 'And hold my hand.'

Annie did his bidding. The crowd thinned as they left the station and a glance over her shoulder confirmed that Ortega was right. Two men, both suited, long strides, feigning indifference. Outside the station, the city was freezing, the sky cloudless under a full moon.

'I have a car,' Ortega muttered. 'They'll expect that. When it starts, do exactly as I say.'

Starts? Dear God.

Annie half closed her eyes, regretting the loss of her fox fur. She'd left it with Rees as a present for his wife when he returned to the UK. Now she was shaking with cold, an icy dread stealing deep into her bones.

They turned a corner. The car, Ortega told her, was a hundred metres away where the street ended in a T-junction. Parked sideways as they approached, Ortega told her to take cover behind the bonnet. The engine, he assured her, would stop any bullets.

'And you?'

'I'll take care of things.'

The car was close now, and Annie thought she detected a quickening in the footsteps behind her. At four in the morning there wasn't a soul around and Annie swallowed hard to ease a dryness in her throat. Was she frightened? Very. Did she regret surrendering her little gun to Moncrieff? Yes. Had she – once again – run out of options? Again, yes.

Metres away from the car, Annie heard the barked command from behind.

'Stop.' The briefest pause. 'Please.'

Please? In *English*? Annie was tempted to laugh but already Ortega had pushed her towards the shelter of the car's bonnet and turned to face the two men. She had time to register the lift of his arm and a tiny gleam of moonlight on the barrel of his gun before he fired. One of the men grunted, raised a gun of his own, then fell to Ortega's second bullet. By now, Annie was crouched behind the bonnet of the car. The other German was staring at his fallen comrade, which she knew was a big mistake. Ortega took three steps closer, the gun still levelled, and shot him in the head.

'We go.' He'd joined her beside the car.

Annie was still staring at the bodies on the road. Something bothered her. The accent? The use of the word 'Please'? She didn't know but either way it hardly mattered because Ortega had gunned the engine and they were on the move.

The embassy was barely minutes away and there were lights on as they braked to a halt outside. Moncrieff emerged from the shadows and opened the passenger door.

'You're OK?'

'I'm fine, thanks to Carlos.'

Moncrieff nodded, visibly confused.

'And the other two men we sent?' he queried.

Two hours earlier, *Admiral* Canaris had arrived in Madrid. Despatched by Hitler from Berlin, he'd been urged to get Franco's formal written consent to the passage of German troops through Spain. No one at the British Embassy had the first idea how these talks may have ended, but only Hoare – oddly enough – was looking on the bright side.

'That bloody man can't make a decision to save his life,' he said. 'I just hope Herr Hitler knows the Spanish for "disappointment".'

They were sitting in Hoare's office, the Ambassador behind his desk, Bottomley in attendance, Moncrieff and Annie in their separate armchairs. The post-mortem on the two hired bodyguards had been despatched in short order. The two men, it was agreed, should have identified themselves to Annie on the train. Ortega, with his own set of orders from the embassy, was entirely within his rights to identify them as a threat and act accordingly. There would doubtless be talk of compensation but that was for another day. What mattered now, grunted Hoare, was bloody Franco.

'Moncrieff?'

'You're right, sir. He'll procrastinate.'

'And what about Canaris?'

'I imagine Hitler will tell him to have another go.'

'Try harder?'

'Exactly.'

'And where will that take us?'

'Hopefully to the same result. I may be wrong. Canaris may already have Franco's permission in his pocket but somehow I doubt it.'

'But how can you be sure?'

'I can't, sir, but with respect I suggest we wait and see.'

Hoare hated an exchange like this. Annie could see it in his face. What mattered with ambassadorial conversations was a swift arrival at a joint conclusion entirely to Sir Samuel's liking. Hiding in the shadows, withholding key information, was very definitely not Hoare's style.

His gaze had settled on Annie's typed report from Gibraltar. He flicked through the pages, greeting the odd sentence with a grunt, then carefully collated the half-dozen sheets and put them to one side.

'Another disaster in the making,' he looked up. 'Or am I wrong?'

'Not at all, sir.' This from Moncrieff, who'd just finished reading his own copy. 'I suspect we owe Miss Wrenne a vote of thanks.'

'Goes without saying, Moncrieff. Shame about the hired hands, but there it is. All's fair in love and war, on that at least we might all agree.'

Annie ducked her head. The froideur of these men, the deep chill in their collective soul, had shocked her and now she wanted to know that blood hadn't been spilled in vain.

'So what next?' she murmured. 'Is a girl allowed to ask?'

'My question entirely.' Hoare was frowning. 'Moncrieff?'

That same morning, as predicted, Canaris reported back to Berlin that Franco was once again undecided about taking the plunge into war. Spain, he'd told Canaris, was desperate for food and fuel. At an absolute minimum, she needed one million tons of supplies. Any assault on Gibraltar would send the Royal Navy to the Canary Isles with the loss of precious Spanish soil. The RAF, meanwhile, remained undefeated and were mounting nightly bombing raids against German targets while Mussolini was getting himself into deep trouble in the Balkans. In short, as the guardian of his people's best interests, Franco had no option but to deny permission for German troops to enter Spain.

The cable from Canaris was received with incredulity in Berlin. Shocked and angered, Hitler ordered *General* Keitel to have Franco pressed for a different decision. Only days ago, the wily *Gallego* had announced for the Axis side. What on earth had led him yet again to change his mind?

Keitel's cable arrived in Madrid in the early afternoon. Canaris was already in the embassy and read it at once. An aide telephoned the Royal Palace and requested an urgent audience with the *Caudillo*. Franco said yes. This evening. Half past seven. Canaris was observed to check his watch and then smile. Four hours grace. More than enough.

Earlier, in anticipation of this development, he'd agreed to meet with Moncrieff. The meeting had to be covert, deniable and unmonitored. Further, Canaris expected Moncrieff's solemn promise, man to man, that no record of what might take place was to be passed on. Ever.

Moncrieff, expecting nothing less, agreed. Half past four. On Annie's bench in the Campo beside the Manzanares River.

Canaris was already there when Moncrieff arrived, his small figure perched uncomfortably on the serviceable end of the half-ruined seat. He looked, thought Moncrieff, suddenly old. His face was pale and drawn in the fading daylight, and he'd developed a habit of fiddling with his watch.

'Ten minutes, Moncrieff,' he barely looked up. 'Not a second more.'

Moncrieff nodded, said nothing. He understood how events had diminished a man he'd come to deeply respect, and he simply wanted to bring this whole sorry business to an end by conjuring a result they could both live with.

'Berlin?' he murmured at last. 'Your masters?'

'Berlin wants the impossible. They want Franco's name on the dotted line. It won't happen.'

'Shouldn't happen?'

'Not in any rational world.' Canaris shrank a little deeper into the gather of his greatcoat, staring bleakly at the ruins of the rebel trenches. 'But it's not about logic any more, Moncrieff. It's about face.'

'And?'

Canaris shook his head, deeply uncomfortable with the direction this conversation was beginning to take. Then he shrugged.

'Franco has a shopping list,' he said softly, 'as you doubtless know. It includes food, fuel, munitions, and territories the French still hold in North Africa. Some of these items we can help with, some we can't. Most days Franco doesn't accept the word "compromise", which is a tactic we've already perfected in Berlin, but in this instance it doesn't begin to resolve our problem.'

'So?'

Canaris seemed to physically flinch at the question and Moncrieff resisted the temptation to pat him on the knee. Calm down. Take a very deep breath. Relax.

'We talked in Algeciras,' Canaris was staring at the river now. 'We met in the garden and you mentioned adding something to that list of Franco's. Something, you said, that would be a test of our good faith.' He spared Moncrieff a sideways glance. 'You remember?'

'I do.'

'Well then ...' he bit his lip, ran a bony hand through his thinning hair, '... that something is heavy artillery. To be precise, ten 380mm cannon. I've planted the seed already. Franco's generals love a big gun and this is the biggest. Just one of those shells could wipe out any of the emplacements on the north face of the Rock.'

'And?'

'Franco sees the logic. It's on his list. He says they're vital. He insists he must have all ten. It's the peasant mentality, Moncrieff. Blood, and soil, and very big guns.' A sudden bark of mirthless laughter. 'God help us all.'

'And you have these guns?'

'Indeed, my friend, of course we have these guns, but I'm sure you can guess the problem here. Most of them are on battleships. A handful are in coastal batteries. Nothing on earth will ever get them to Spain.'

'Does Franco understand that?'

'I doubt it.'

'Why?'

'Because I haven't told him. It's your test of faith, Moncrieff. He asks, he insists, and this evening I shall bring him the answer from Berlin. The big guns will never arrive, I shall tell him, not because they can't but because the *Führer* has said no.'

'But isn't that a risk? From your point of view?'

'Of course it is. So why do I take it? Why do I give this little man more sticks to beat us with? Because no sane man wants us Germans anywhere near your precious Rock and that includes me.'

Moncrieff nodded. A lone duck had appeared on the turbulence of the river, paddling hard against the current, and both men watched it for a while before Canaris got to his feet.

'The Spanish are on their knees,' he muttered. 'The last thing they need just now is a helping of someone else's war.' He checked his watch and turned briefly back to Moncrieff. 'We agree?'

Moncrieff peered up at him. In a different setting, he thought, we could be friends for life.

'That statement I showed you in Algeciras? The one from the girl?' Moncrieff patted his greatcoat. 'It's safe with me. You have my word on that.'

Moncrieff returned to the embassy. When he met the Ambassador in the narrow corridor outside the shared lavatory, he said he'd enjoyed a bracing walk in the Retiro and taken a little stale bread to feed the birds. Hoare stared up at him in disbelief. Like Canaris, Moncrieff thought, he's making heavy weather of the crisis over Operation *Felix*. Embassy staff were resigned to outbursts of unconstrained temper, of brusque, waspish hand-scribbled notes criticising this performance or that. Even Lady Hoare, normally so placid, had this morning been heard to reprimand her husband. Poor manners and a sharp tongue, she'd warned him, make few friends.

But the mood at the embassy continued to darken and it was two full days later that Christian Bottomley knocked softly on the Ambassador's door and was summoned in. Hoare, a visibly shrunken figure behind the big desk, was staring up at the fading photograph of King George VI.

'What is it?' He didn't spare Bottomley a glance.

'Just a word in your ear, Sir Samuel. That source of mine in the German Embassy?'

Hoare stiffened, abandoned the King, looked up at Bottomley. 'News?' he queried.

'Indeed, sir. I've yet to confirm the details but I suspect a bottle or two of Krug might be in order.'

'You're serious, Bottomley?'

'I believe so, sir.'

'How many bottles, do you think?'

Bottomley hesitated, already wondering whether he'd gone too far. The inner team at the embassy numbered just eleven.

'Half-a-dozen, sir, minimum.'

'Care to tell me why?'

'Of course, sir. As soon as I have confirmation.'

'Of what, pray?'

For Bottomley, this was a question too far. He held Hoare's gaze for a moment or two and then fled. Hoare searched at once for Moncrieff. His secretary found him in the empty office he was temporarily sharing with Annie Wrenne and led them both back to the ambassadorial presence.

'You've heard, Moncrieff?'

'Heard what, sir?'

'Young Bottomley? It has to be the bloody Germans, bloody *Felix*, that bugger Franco.'

Moncrieff frowned, then shook his head.

'I've heard nothing, sir.'

The silence and the gathering anger on Hoare's face spoke volumes. Expecting a volley of insults, Moncrieff glanced round and found Bottomley at the still-open door.

'It's over, Sir Samuel.' Bottomley waved the sheet of paper in his hand. 'Hitler has ordered the immediate termination of all preparations for *Felix*.'

'You mean it's dead? Gone? Disappeared from the face of the earth?' Hoare's gaze returned to Moncrieff. 'You've been expecting this?'

Moncrieff glanced at Annie and then nodded.

'Yes,' he said.

A cloudless early winter afternoon had settled over Madrid. The icy wind lifted the remaining leaves in the embassy's tiny courtyard but the entire staff had obeyed Sir Samuel Hoare's order to attend what he termed a rather special celebration. He'd been preserving a brand-new Union Jack against the rumoured announcement from Buckingham Palace that the Queen was once again pregnant, but in the absence of any such news he'd decided to toast a more pressing victory. There was a murmur of approval from the gathering in front of him. Some of them, including the Ambassador himself, had been drinking for the last hour or so in the privacy of his office, and to Annie it rather showed.

Hoare offered a rambling toast to German duplicity and British pluck before ordering the new flag to be raised. Bottomley did the honours, hauling on the lanyard as heads tipped back and glasses were drained. The Ambassador, rocking back on his heels, ordered more champagne and after a ripple of applause and three cheers for the King, Annie found herself talking to Lady Hoare. She was gazing at her cherished Sam, and Annie was glad to sense that he'd been forgiven.

'You must pardon my husband,' she turned to Annie, beckoning her closer. 'He's a more emotional man than I suspect many of us realise. He gets this way when we go and watch a decent conjurer. He loves those magic shows as much as anyone but he gets really upset when he can't explain the key trick.'

AFTERWARDS

Five days later, as the year came to an end, Hitler met with Mussolini and told him that Operation *Felix* had been abandoned in the face of other demands on the Reich's armies. The news was received with quiet satisfaction at the British Embassy and the Ambassador was gratified by a personal letter from Winston Churchill commending his efforts in keeping Franco out of the war. 'The Rock,' the PM added, 'happily remains in British hands, as history and fate demand.'

On Christmas Day, the reinforced garrison at Gibraltar settled down to a full Yuletide dinner: turkey, stuffing, bread sauce, roast potatoes, a variety of vegetables and a generous allowance of locally brewed beer. The after-dinner entertainment featured a Royal Navy lieutenant who turned out to be a genius with a pack of cards. Dozens of squaddies and matelots accepted his challenge to guess the secret of this trick or that, and he returned to his ship a richer man.

Back in London, Annie was still working for Moncrieff at the MI5 offices in St James's Street. She'd moved into a rented flat in Bloomsbury, cycling to work every morning on a borrowed bicycle. On the night of 10 May, a huge *Luftwaffe* raid brought yet more devastation to the East End docks and set the House of Commons on fire. Among other areas affected was Bloomsbury and Annie spent the night helping firemen dig an entire family out of the rubble of their house. Three had been killed instantly, and the rest were critically injured. Annie, calling on all her nursing skills, saved the lives of two of them.

Days later, thanks to the efforts of grateful relatives and neighbours, her story appeared in the morning edition of the *News Chronicle*, along with a rather fetching photograph. MI5 frowned on any publicity for its employees, but Moncrieff clipped out the story and pinned it to a noticeboard on the building's first floor. Much to her surprise, for days afterwards Annie was steered into discreet corners and quietly congratulated for what she'd done. Moncrieff, on the other hand, was much blunter. 'Bloody good effort,' he told her. 'You were never shy when it came to action.'

Six weeks later, Hitler tore up the non-aggression Pact with Moscow and invaded the Soviet Union. The start of Operation *Barbarossa* came as no surprise to MI5 but nevertheless sparked much celebration. In the shape of the Russians, the British now had the unlikeliest allies in the battle against Hitler and were no longer fighting alone. Senior officers circulated with bottles of champagne from the cellars of the nearby Ritz Hotel, and Moncrieff and Annie found themselves in the office of Guy Liddell, Head of 'B' Section and Moncrieff's boss.

There was much speculation about the rapid progress of the lead German armoured thrusts into Soviet territory and a book was opened on the likelihood of Leningrad and Moscow falling before Christmas. The last toast of the evening, deeply ironic, was to the Reds for saving Churchill's bacon. Only Moncrieff refused to raise his glass. What bacon remained, he murmured to Annie, had been saved by Canaris. Which made him a very brave man.

That same evening, *Reichsmarschall* Hermann Goering staged an impromptu party at his hunting lodge Carinhall, north-east of Berlin. All the Reich's tribal chiefs attended, eager for their share of the publicity Goering attracted, and more than a hundred guests sat down to brimming platters of venison and wild boar from the surrounding forests. One of the guests was Josef Goebbels, the genius behind countless Reich propaganda coups and a favourite of Hitler. With the party beginning to break up, dawn found him admiring a lavishly framed canvas on an easel beside the sweep of a wooden staircase.

'It's a Rubens, Herr *Minister*. Perhaps one of his best.'

Goebbels nodded, still gazing at the painting. The naked woman roused from sleep. The servant in the shadows with the slippers. A guardian angel carefully placed in case anything went wrong.

Goebbels nodded to himself and finally turned round.

'Werner Nehmann,' he murmured with a smile. 'Is nowhere in this Reich of ours ever safe from you?'

Three days later, still June, Annie returned home to find a bulky envelope waiting on the doormat. Inside were a number of other envelopes all addressed to her with a covering note from the *News Chronicle*. The note offered apologies for the delay in forwarding the enclosed items and asked that she deal with them personally.

Annie sorted through the envelopes. There were seven letters in all and six of them commended her efforts during the big raid back in May. One correspondent turned out to be a woman whose life she'd saved, and she put the letter carefully to one side for an early reply.

There remained a single envelope. It carried a smudged postmark she couldn't read properly, a long word beginning with 'A', but what drew her attention was the handwritten address. She knew this person, the way he blurred his 'g's and his 'p's, the way he raced to the end of every word. Giles Roper.

She opened the envelope. He said he hoped this letter of his made it through. He said he'd read the report in the *Chronicle* and been amazingly proud of her. He said he'd joined the Royal Marines and had been suffering as a consequence ever since, not because he didn't deserve it but because the training was so bloody tough. If ever there might be the possibility of a meeting, and perhaps a glass or two, he'd be more than happy to be in the chair. Yours, Giles.

Mine? Annie rocked back. She could hear his voice, picture his face, see him bent over his writing pad in the hot Murcia sunshine, and she felt a stirring deep inside her, fiercely carnal. Ashamed, she blamed it at once on period pains. A difficult time of the month, she told herself, kneeling in front of the empty fireplace and taking a match to the discarded letter in the grate.

She watched the single sheet of paper curl and blacken before bursting into flame. Spain, she thought. She still dreamed constantly of those days under siege in Madrid, of the Villa Paz, of the Pablo Iglesias, of Moncrieff and Ortega and Algeciras and everything else that had followed, convinced in the vaguest way that she must return to Spain one day to collect something she'd left behind. She always thought she knew what that something might be but after a while, watching a final shy blossom of flame, she realised it was probably too complicated to explain.

AUTHOR NOTE

The *Abwehr* was disbanded in February 1944, its apparatus and responsibilities folded into the *Ausland-SD*, part of Heinrich Himmler's SS empire. Five months later, *Admiral* Wilhelm Canaris was arrested on suspicion of plotting against the Nazi regime. Investigations dragged on until 9 April 1945 when Canaris, judged guilty, was led naked to the gallows at Flossenbürg concentration camp, and hanged from a butcher's meat hook. According to a prisoner in an adjacent cell, Canaris tapped out a farewell message on the eve of his execution. He denied the accusation of being a traitor and insisted that he had always acted in the best interests of both his country, and his countrymen.

In the aftermath of Germany's surrender in May 1945, *Reichsführer-SS* Heinrich Himmler was arrested at a Soviet checkpoint in Bremervorde. Two days later, still claiming to be *Feldwebel* Heinrich Hitzinger, he was delivered to British custody at the 31st Civilian Investigation Camp near Lüneburg. When a doctor attempted to examine him, he bit into a hidden potassium cyanide pill. Despite attempts to flush the poison from his system, he was dead within fifteen minutes. Shortly afterwards, his body was buried in an unmarked grave. Its exact location remains unknown.

ABOUT THE AUTHOR

GRAHAM HURLEY is a documentary-maker and a novelist. For the last two decades he's written full-time, penning nearly fifty books. Two made the shortlist for the Theakston's Old Peculiar Crime Novel of the Year, while *Finisterre* – the first in the Spoils of War collection – was shortlisted for the Wilbur Smith Adventure Writing Award. Graham lives in East Devon with his lovely wife, Lin.

Follow Graham at www.grahamhurley.co.uk.